The Olive Tree

LUCINDA RILEY

MACMILLAN

First published 2016 by Macmillan
an imprint of Pan Macmillan
20 New Wharf Road, London N1 9RR
Associated companies throughout the world
www.panmacmillan.com

ISBN 978-1-5098-2476-2

1 3 5 7 9 8 6 4 2

A CIP catalogue record for this book is available from the British Library.

Typeset by Ellipsis Digital Limited, Glasgow
Printed and bound by CPI Group (UK) Ltd, Croydon, CR0 4YY

Visit www.panmacmillan.com to read more about all our books
and to buy them. You will also find features, author interviews and
news of any author events, and you can sign up for e-newsletters
so that you're always first to hear about our new releases.

For the 'real' Alexander

Follow a shadow, it still flies you;
Seem to fly it, it will pursue.

Ben Jonson

Alex

'Pandora', Cyprus

19th July 2016

The house comes into view as I steer the car around the perilous potholes – still not filled in from ten years ago, and growing ever deeper. I bump along a little further, then pull to a halt and stare at Pandora, thinking that it's really not that pretty, unlike the glossy shots of holiday homes you see on upmarket property websites. Rather, at least from the back, it is solid, sensible and almost austere, just as I've always imagined its former inhabitant to have been. Built from pale local stone, and square as the Lego houses I constructed as a boy, it rises up out of the arid chalky land surrounding it, which is covered for as far as the eye can see with tender, burgeoning vines. I try to reconcile its reality with the virtual snapshot in my mind – taken and stored ten summers ago – and decide that memory has served me well.

After parking the car, I skirt round the sturdy walls to the front of the house and onto the terrace, which is what lifts Pandora out of the ordinary and into a spectacular league of its own. Crossing the terrace, I head for the balustraded wall at its edge, set just at the point before the terrain begins to tumble gently downwards: a landscape filled with yet more vines, the odd whitewashed homestead and clusters of olive trees. Far in the distance, there is a line of shimmering aquamarine separating land and sky.

I notice the sun is performing a masterclass as it sets, its yellow rays seeping into the blue and turning it to umber. Which is an interesting point, actually, as I always thought that yellow and blue made green. I look to my right, at the garden below the terrace. The pretty borders my mother had so carefully planted ten years ago have not been maintained and, starved of attention and water, have been subsumed by the arid earth and supplanted by ugly, spiky weeds – genus unknown.

But there, in the centre of the garden, with one end of the hammock my mother used to lie in still attached – its strings like old and fraying spaghetti – stands the olive tree. 'Old', I nicknamed it back then, due to being told by the various adults around me that it *was*. If anything, whilst all around it has died and fermented, it seems to have grown in stature and majesty, perhaps stealing the life force from its collapsing botanical neighbours, determined over the centuries to survive.

It is quite beautiful, a metaphoric triumph over adversity, with every millimetre of its gnarled trunk proudly displaying its struggle.

I wonder now why humans hate the map of their life that appears on their own bodies, when a tree like this, or a faded painting, or a near-derelict uninhabited building is lauded for its antiquity.

Thinking of such, I turn towards the house, and am relieved to see that at least from the outside Pandora seems to have survived its recent neglect. At the main entrance, I take the iron key from my pocket and open the door. As I walk through the shadowy rooms, shrouded from the light by the closed shutters, I realise that my emotions are numb, and perhaps it's for the best. I don't dare to begin to feel, because here – perhaps more than anywhere – holds the essence of *her* . . .

Half an hour later, I've opened the shutters downstairs and removed the sheets from the furniture in the drawing room. As I stand in a mist of dust motes catching the light from the setting sun, I remember thinking how everything seemed so old in here the first time I saw it. And I wonder, as I look at the sagging chairs and the threadbare sofa, if like the olive tree, beyond a certain point old was simply old and didn't visibly age further, like grey-haired grand-parents to a young child.

Of course, the one thing in this room that has changed beyond all recognition is me. We humans complete the vast majority of our physical and mental evolution during our first few years on planet Earth – baby to full-grown adult within the blink of an eye. After that, outwardly at least, we spend the rest of our lives looking more or less the same, simply becoming saggier and less attractive versions of our younger selves, as genes and gravity do their worst.

As for the emotional and intellectual side of things . . . well, I have to believe there are some bonuses to make up for the slow decline of our outer packaging. And being back here at Pandora shows me clearly that there are. As I walk back into the hall, I chuckle at the 'Alex' I used to be.

And cringe at my former self – thirteen years old and, in retrospect, a self-absorbed right royal pain in the backside.

I open the door to the 'Broom Cupboard' – my affectionate term for the room I inhabited during that long, hot summer ten years ago. Reaching for the light, I realise I was not underestimating its miniature size and if anything, the space seems to have shrunk further. All six foot one of me now steps inside and I wonder if I closed the door and lay down, whether my feet would need to hang out of the tiny window, rather like Alice in her Wonderland.

I look up at the shelves on either side of this claustrophobic corridor, and see that the books I painstakingly arranged into alphabetical order are still there. Instinctively, I pull one down – Rudyard Kipling's *Rewards and Fairies* – and leaf through it to find the famous poem the book contains. Reading through the lines of 'If' – the words of wisdom written from a father to a son – I find tears welling in my eyes for the adolescent boy I was then: so desperate to find a father. And then, having found him, realising I had one already.

As I return Rudyard to his place on the shelf, I spot a small hardback book beside it. I realise it's the diary my mother gave me for Christmas a few months before I came to Pandora for the first time. Every day for seven months, I wrote in it assiduously and, knowing me back then, pompously. Like all teenagers, I believed my ideas and feelings were unique and ground-breaking; thoughts never had by another human being before me.

I shake my head sadly, and sigh like an old man at my naivety. I left the diary behind when we went home to England after that long summer at Pandora. And here it is, ten years on, sitting once more in the palms of my now far larger hands. A memoir of the last few months of myself as a child, before life dragged me into adulthood.

Taking the diary with me, I leave the room and go upstairs. As I wander along the dim, airless corridor, unsure in exactly which bedroom I want to plant myself during my stay here, I take a deep breath and head towards *her* room. With all the courage I possess, I open the door. Perhaps it is my imagination – after ten years of absence, I guess it must be – but I'm convinced my senses are assailed by the smell of that perfume she once wore . . .

Closing the door again firmly, not yet able to deal with the Pandora's Box of memories that would fly out of any of these bedrooms, I retreat back downstairs. I see night has fallen, and it's pitch-black outside. I check my watch, add two hours for the time difference and realise it's almost nine in the evening here – my empty stomach is growling for food.

I unpack the car and stow the supplies I picked up from the shop in the local village in the pantry, then take some bread, feta cheese and a very warm beer out onto the terrace. Sitting there in the silence, with only the odd sleepy cicada to interrupt its purity, I sip the beer, wondering if it was really a good idea to arrive two days earlier than the others. Navel-gazing is something I have a double first in, after all – to the point where someone has recently offered me a job doing it professionally. This thought, at least, makes me chuckle.

To take my mind off the situation, I open my diary and read the inscription on the first page.

'*Darling Alex, Happy Christmas! Try and keep this regularly. It might be interesting to read when you're older.*

All my love, M xxx'

'Well, Mum, let's hope you're right.' I smile wanly as I skip through the pages of self-important prose and arrive at the beginning of July. And by the light of the one dim bulb that hangs above me in the pergola, I begin to read.

July 2006

Arrivals

ALEX'S DIARY

10th July 2006

My face is perfectly round. I'm sure you could draw it with a compass, and only very rarely, the edges of the circle and my face wouldn't combine. I hate it.

I also have, inside the circle, a pair of apple cheeks. When I was younger, adults used to pull at them, take my flesh between their fingers and squeeze it. They forgot that my cheeks were not like apples. Apples are inanimate. They are hard, they don't feel pain. If they're bruised, it's only on the surface.

I do have nice eyes, mind you. They change colour. My mother says that when I'm alive inside, energised, they are a vivid green. When I'm feeling stressed, they become the colour of the North Sea. Personally, I think they're grey rather a lot, but they are quite large and shaped like peach-stones, and my eyebrows, darker than my hair – which is girly-blonde and straight as straw – frame them well.

I'm currently staring into the mirror. Tears prick my eyes

because when I'm not looking at my face, in my imagination, I can be anyone I choose. The light here in the tiny on-board toilet is harsh, shining like a halo above my head. Mirrors on planes are the worst: they make you look like a two-thousand-year-old dead person who's been freshly dug up.

Beneath my T-shirt I can see the flesh rising above my shorts. I take a handful and mould it into a passable impression of the Gobi Desert. I create dunes, with small pouches between them, from which could sprout the odd palm tree around the oasis.

I then wash my hands thoroughly.

I actually like my hands, because they don't seem to have joined the march towards Blob Land, which is where the rest of my body has currently decided to live. My mother says it's puppy fat, that the hormonal button labelled 'shoot sideways' worked at first press. Sadly, at the same time, the 'shoot upwards' button malfunctioned. And it doesn't seem to have been fixed since.

Besides, how many fat puppies have I ever seen? Most of them are sleek from the exhaustion of excitement.

Maybe I need some excitement.

The good news is this: flying gives you a feeling of weightlessness, even if you *are* fat. And there are lots of people on this plane far fatter than me, because I've looked. If I'm the Gobi, my current seat neighbour is the Sahara, all on his own. His forearms hog the armrest, skin and muscle and fat spreading like a mutating virus into my personal space. It really irritates me, that. I keep my flesh to myself, in my designated space, even if I end up with a bad muscle spasm in the process.

For some reason, whenever I'm on a plane I think about

dying. To be fair, I think about dying wherever I am. Perhaps being dead is a bit like the weightlessness you feel here, now, inside this metal tube. My little sister asked if she was dead the last time we flew, because someone had told her Grandpa was up on a cloud. She thought she was joining him when we passed one.

Why do adults tell kids such ridiculous stories? It only leads to trouble. For myself, I never believed any of them.

My own mother gave up trying them on me years ago.

She loves me, my mother, even if I've morphed into Mr Blob in the past few months. And she promises that one day, I will have to crouch down to see my face in water-splashed mirrors such as this. I come from a family of tall men, apparently. Not that this comforts me. I've read about genes skipping generations and knowing my luck, I shall be the first fat dwarf in hundreds of years of Beaumont males.

Besides, she forgets she's ignoring the opposing DNA which helped create me . . .

It's a conversation I am determined to have during this holiday. I don't care how many times she tries to wimp out of it and conveniently changes the subject. A gooseberry bush for a father is no longer satisfactory.

I need to know.

Everyone says I'm like her. But then, they would, wouldn't they? They can hardly liken me to an unidentified sperm cell.

Actually, the fact I don't know who my father is might also add to any delusions of grandeur I already harbour. Which is very unhealthy, especially for a child like me, if I am still a child. Or have ever been, which personally I doubt.

At this very moment, as my body hurtles across central Europe, my father could be anyone I choose to imagine;

whoever suits me at the time. For example: we may be about to crash, and the captain has only one spare parachute. I could introduce myself to him as his son and he would have to save *me*, surely?

On second thoughts, perhaps it's better if I don't know. My stem cells might originate from somewhere in the Orient and then I would have to learn Mandarin to communicate with my father, which is a mega-hard language to master.

Sometimes, I wish Mum looked more like other mothers. I mean, she's not Kate Moss or anything, because she's quite old. But it's embarrassing when my classmates and my teachers and any man that comes into our house looks at *her* in *that* way. Everyone loves her, because she is kind, and funny, and cooks and dances at the same time. And sometimes, my bit of her doesn't seem large enough and I wish I didn't have to share her the way I do.

Because I love her best.

She was unmarried when she gave birth to me. A hundred years ago, I would have been born in a poorhouse and we'd probably both have expired of TB a few months later. We'd have been buried in a pauper's grave, our skeletons lying together for eternity.

I often wonder if she is embarrassed by the living reminder of her immorality, which is me. Is that why she's sending me away to school?

I mouth *immorality* in the mirror. I like words. I collect them, like my classmates collect football cards or girls, depending on their maturity levels. I like bringing them out, slotting them into a sentence to express the thought I'm having as accurately as I can. Perhaps one day, I might like to play with them professionally. Let's face it, I'm never going to play for Manchester United, given my current physique.

Someone is banging on the door. I've lost track of time, as usual. I check my watch and realise I've been in here for over twenty minutes. I will now have to face a queue of angry passengers desperate to pee.

I glance in the mirror one more time – a last look at Mr Blob. Then I avert my eyes, take a deep breath and step outside as Brad Pitt.

α

One

'We're lost. I'll have to pull over.'

'Christ, Mum! It's pitch-black and we're hanging off the side of a mountain! There *is* nowhere to pull over.'

'Just stop panicking, darling. I'll find somewhere safe.'

'Safe? Hah! I'd have brought my crampons and ice pick if I'd known.'

'There's a lay-by up there.' Helena steered the unfamiliar rental car jerkily round the hairpin bend and brought it to a halt. She glanced at her son, his fingers covering his eyes, and put a hand on his knee. 'You can look now.' Then she peered through the window, down into the steep valley far below, and saw the firefly lights of the coast twinkling beneath them. 'It's so beautiful,' she breathed.

'No, Mum, it is not "beautiful". "Beautiful" is when we're no longer lost in the hinterland of a foreign country, a few yards away from hurtling two thousand feet down a valley to our certain deaths. Haven't they heard of crash barriers here?'

Helena ignored him and fumbled above her head for the interior light switch. 'Pass me that map, darling.'

Alex did so, and Helena studied it. 'It's upside down, Mum,' he observed.

'Okay, okay.' She turned the map round. 'Immy still asleep?'

Alex turned to look at his five-year-old sister, spread-eagled across the back seat with Lamby, her cuddly sheep, tucked safely under her arm. 'Yup. Good thing too. This journey might scar her for life. We'll never get her on Oblivion at Alton Towers if she sees where we are now.'

'Right, I know what I've done. We need to go back down the hill—'

'Mountain,' corrected Alex.

'– turn left at the sign for Kathikas and follow that road up. Here.' Helena handed the map to Alex and put the gear-stick into what she thought was reverse. They lurched forward.

'*MUM!* Christ!'

'Sorry.' Helena executed an inelegant three-point turn and steered the car back onto the main road.

'Thought you knew where this place was,' Alex muttered.

'Darling, I was only a couple of years older than you the last time I came here. For your information, that's almost twenty-four years ago. But I'm sure I'll recognise it when we reach the village.'

'If we ever do.'

'Oh, stop being such a misery! Have you got no sense of adventure?' Helena was relieved when she saw a turning signposted to Kathikas. She took it. 'It'll be worth it when we get there, you'll see.'

'It's not even near a beach. And I hate olives. *And* the Chandlers. Rupert's an arseho—'

'Alex, enough! If you can't say anything positive, then just shut up and let me drive.'

Alex lapsed into a grumpy silence as Helena encouraged the Citroën up the steep incline, thinking what a shame it was that the plane had been delayed, landing them in Paphos just after the sun had set. By the time they'd cleared immigration and found their hire car, it had been dark. She'd been relishing the thought of making this journey up into the mountains, revisiting her vivid childhood memory and seeing it anew through the eyes of her own offspring.

But life often failed to live up to expectations, she thought, especially when it came to seminal memories. And she was aware that the summer she'd spent here at her godfather's house when she was fifteen was sprinkled with historical fairy dust.

And however ridiculous, she needed Pandora to be as perfect as she remembered. Logically, she knew it couldn't possibly be, that seeing it again might be akin to meeting a first love after twenty-four years: captured in the mind's eye, glowing with the strength and beauty of youth, but in reality, greying and slowly disintegrating.

And she knew *that* was another possibility too . . .

Would he still be here?

Helena's hands tightened on the steering wheel, and she pushed the thought firmly away.

The house, named Pandora, which had felt like a mansion back then, was bound to be smaller than she remembered. The antique furniture, shipped from England by Angus, her godfather, whilst he reigned supreme over the remnants of the British Army still stationed in Cyprus, had seemed exquisite, elegant, untouchable. The powder-blue damask sofas in the darkened drawing room – its shutters habitually closed to keep out the fading glare of the sun – the Georgian desk in the study where Angus sat every morning, slitting his letters open with a slim miniature sword, and the vast mahogany dining table whose smooth surface resembled a skating rink . . . all stood sentinel-like in her memory.

Pandora had been empty now for three years, since Angus had been forced back to England due to ill health. Complaining bitterly that the medical care in Cyprus was every bit as good, if not better than the National Health Service at home, even he had grudgingly admitted that the lack of a pair of reliable legs, and constant trips to a hospital forty-five minutes away did not make living up in a mountainside village particularly convenient.

He'd finally given up his fight to stay in his beloved Pandora, and had died six months ago of pneumonia and misery. An already fragile body which had spent the vast majority of its seventy-eight years in sub-tropical climes had always been unlikely to adjust to the unremitting damp greyness of a Scottish suburb.

He'd left everything to Helena, his goddaughter – including Pandora.

She had wept when she'd heard the news; tears tinged with guilt that she hadn't acted on all those recent plans she'd made to visit him more often in his care home.

The clanging of her mobile phone from the depths of her handbag broke into her thoughts.

'Get that, will you, darling?' she said to Alex. 'It's probably Dad to see if we've arrived.'

Alex made the usual unsuccessful forage into his mother's bag, fishing the mobile out a few moments after it had stopped ringing. He checked the call register. 'It *was* Dad. Want me to call him back?'

'No. We'll do it when we get there.'

'*If* we get there.'

'Of course we will. I'm beginning to recognise this. We're no more than ten minutes away now.'

'Was Hari's Tavern here when you were?' enquired Alex as they passed a glowing neon palm tree in front of a garish restaurant, filled with slot machines and white plastic chairs.

'No, but this is a new link road with lots of potential passing trade. There was little more than a rough track up to the village in my day.'

'That place had Sky TV. Can we go one night?' he asked hopefully.

'Perhaps.' Helena's vision of balmy evenings spent on Pandora's wonderful terrace overlooking the olive groves, drinking the locally produced wine and feasting on figs picked straight from the branch, had not included television or neon palm trees.

'Mum, just how basic is this house we're heading for? I mean, does it have electricity?'

'Of course it does, silly.' Helena prayed it had been switched on by the local woman who held the keys. 'Look, we're turning into the village now. Only a few more minutes and we'll be there.'

''S'pose I could cycle back down to that bar,' muttered Alex, 'if I could get a bike.'

'I cycled up to the village from the house almost every day.'

'Was it a penny-farthing?'

'Oh, very funny! It was a proper, old-fashioned upright bicycle with three gears and a basket on the front.' Helena smiled as she remembered it. 'I used to collect the bread from the bakery.'

'Like the bike the witch rides in *The Wizard of Oz* as she cycles past Dorothy's window?'

'Exactly. Now, shush, I need to concentrate. We've come in from the other end of the street because of the new road, and I need to get my bearings.'

Ahead of her, Helena could see the lights of the village. She slowed down as the road began to narrow and the chalky gravel crunched under the tyres. Buildings began to appear, fashioned from creamy Cyprus stone, finally forming a continuous wall on either side of them.

'Look, there's the church, just up ahead.' Helena indicated the building that had been the heartbeat of the small community of Kathikas. As they passed, she saw some youths hanging around a bench in the courtyard outside, their attention focused on the two dark-eyed young girls lolling idly on it. 'This is the centre of the village.'

'A veritable hotspot, obviously.'

'Apparently, a couple of very good tavernas have opened up here in the past few years. And look, there's the shop. They've extended it into the next house. They sell absolutely everything you could ever want.'

'I'll pop in to collect the latest *All American Rejects* CD, shall I?'

'Oh Alex!' Helena's patience snapped. 'I know you don't

want to be here, but for goodness' sake, you haven't even seen Pandora yet. At least give it a chance, for me, if not for yourself!'

'Okay. Sorry, Mum, sorry.'

'The village used to be very picturesque and from what I can see, it doesn't seem to have changed that much,' Helena said with relief. 'But we can explore tomorrow.'

'We're going out of the village now, Mum,' commented Alex nervously.

'Yes. You can't see it now, but on either side of you there are acres of grapevines. The pharaohs once used to ship wine from here to Egypt because it was so good. We turn here, I'm sure we do. Hold on tight. This road is pretty bouncy.'

As the rough gravel track wound down and through the vines, Helena changed down to first gear and switched the headlights to full beam to negotiate the treacherous potholes.

'You biked up here every day?' said Alex in surprise. 'Wow! I'm amazed you didn't end up in the grapes.'

'I did sometimes, but you get to know where the worst patches are.' Helena was strangely comforted by the fact that the potholes were just as bad as she remembered them. She'd been dreading tarmac.

'Are we nearly there, Mummy?' A sleepy voice came from the back seat. 'It's very bumpy.'

'Yes, we are, darling. A few more seconds, literally.'

Yes, we are . . .

A mixture of excitement and trepidation coursed through her as they turned down a narrower track and the dark, solid silhouette of Pandora came into view. She drove the car through the rusting wrought-iron gates, eternally open all those years ago, and by now almost certainly incapable of movement.

She brought the car to a halt and switched off the engine.

'We're here.'

There was no response from her two children. Glancing round, she saw Immy had fallen asleep again. Alex sat next to her, staring straight ahead.

'We'll leave Immy to sleep while we find the key,' Helena suggested as she opened the door and a blast of warm night air assaulted her. Climbing out, she stood and breathed in the half-remembered potent smell of olive, grape and dust – a world away from tarmac roads and neon palm trees. Smell really *was* the most powerful of all the senses, she thought. It evoked a particular moment, an atmosphere, with pinpoint accuracy.

She refrained from asking Alex what he thought of the house, because there was nothing *to* think yet and she couldn't bear a negative response. They were standing in the deep blackness at the back of Pandora, its shuttered windows closed and locked up like a garrison.

'It's awfully dark, Mum.'

'I'll put the headlights back on. Angelina said she'd leave the back door open.' Helena reached inside the car and switched on the beam. Then she walked across the gravel to the door, Alex following closely behind her. The brass handle turned easily and she pushed the door open to fumble for a light switch. Finding it, she held her breath as she pressed it. The back hall was suddenly awash with light.

'Thank goodness,' she mumbled, opening another door and flicking a switch. 'This is the kitchen.'

'Yes, I can see that.' Alex ambled through the large, airless room, which contained a sink unit, an ancient oven, a large wooden table and a Welsh dresser that filled an entire wall. 'It's pretty basic.'

'Angus rarely came in here. His housekeeper did all the domestic stuff. I don't think he cooked a meal in his entire life. This was very much a workstation, not the comfort zone that kitchens are these days.'

'Where did he eat, then?'

'Outside on the terrace, of course. Everyone does here.' Helena turned on the tap. A dribble of water sputtered out reluctantly, then turned into a torrent.

'There doesn't seem to be a fridge,' said Alex.

'It's in the pantry. Angus entertained here so often, and it was such a long drive to Paphos, he installed a cooling system inside the pantry itself too. And no, before you ask, there wasn't a freezer here in those days. The door is just to your left. Go and check the fridge is still there, will you? Angelina did say she'd leave us some milk and bread.'

'Sure.'

Alex wandered off and Helena, switching lights on as she went, found herself in the main hall at the front of the house. The worn stone floor, laid out in a chequerboard pattern, echoed beneath her feet. She looked up to the main staircase, the heavy curving banister built by skilled craftsmen from oak, which she remembered Angus had shipped over especially from England. Behind her stood a grandfather clock, sentry-like, but no longer ticking.

Time has stopped here, she mused to herself as she opened the door to the drawing room.

The blue damask sofas were covered in dust-sheets. She pulled one off and sank into downy softness. The fabric, though still immaculate and unstained, felt fragile beneath her fingers, as if its substance, but not its presence, had been gently worn away. Standing up, she walked across to one of the two sets of French windows that led outside to the front of the house. She drew back the wooden shutters that protected the room from the sun, unlocked the stiff iron handle and went out onto the terrace.

Alex found her a few seconds later, leaning on the balustrade at the edge of the terrace. 'The fridge sounds like it's got a bad attack of asthma,' he said, 'but there's milk and eggs and bread in it. And we've definitely got enough of this, that's for sure.' He waggled a huge pink salami at her. Helena didn't answer. He leant next to her. 'Nice view,' he added.

'It's spectacular, isn't it?' She smiled, pleased he liked it.

'Are those tiny lights down there the coast?'

'Yes. In the morning, you'll be able to see the sea beyond it. And the olive groves and vineyards falling away below us into the valley, with the mountains on either side. There's a gorgeous olive tree in the garden over there which, legend has it, is over four hundred years old.'

'"Old" . . . like everything seems to be here.' Alex looked down, then to his left and right. 'It's very, um, by itself, this place, isn't it? I can't see any other houses.'

'I thought it might have become built up round here, like it has down along the coast, but it hasn't.' Helena turned to him. 'Give me a hug, darling.' She put her arms around him. 'I'm so glad we're here.'

'Good. I'm glad you're glad. Would you mind if we got Immy in now? I'm worried she'll wake up, get frightened and wander off. And I'm starving.'

'Let's run upstairs and find a bedroom to put her in first. Then perhaps you could give me a hand carrying her upstairs.'

Helena led Alex back across the terrace, pausing under the vine-covered pergola that provided welcome shelter from the midday sun. The long, cast-iron table, its white paint flaking, the bulk of it covered with mouldering leaves shed from the vine above it, still stood forlornly beneath it.

'This is where we ate every lunchtime and evening. And we all had to dress properly, too. No swimsuits or wet trunks allowed at Angus' table, no matter how hot it was,' she added.

'You won't make us lot do that, will you, Mum?'

Helena ruffled her son's thick blond hair and kissed the top of his head. 'I shall count myself lucky if I manage to *get* all of you to the table, never mind what you're wearing. How times have changed,' she sighed, then held out her hand to him. 'Come on, let's go upstairs and explore.'

It was almost midnight by the time Helena finally sat out on the small balcony that led from Angus' bedroom. Immy was sleeping soundly on the vast mahogany bed inside. Helena had decided she'd move her tomorrow into one of the twin rooms, once she'd discovered where all the bedding was kept. Alex was along the corridor, lying on a bare mattress. He'd locked all the shutters to protect himself from mosquitoes, even though the resulting heat in his room was sauna-like in its intensity. Tonight, there wasn't a whisper of wind.

Helena reached into her handbag, drew out her mobile and a battered packet of cigarettes. She put both on her lap and stared down at them. A cigarette first, she decided. She didn't want the spell to be broken just yet. She knew William, her husband, wouldn't *mean* to say anything that would jerk her back to reality, but the chances were that he would. And it wouldn't be his fault either, because it made perfect sense to tell her whether the man had been in to fix the dishwasher and ask where she had hidden the bin bags because the garbage needed to go out for the bin collection tomorrow. He'd assume she'd be glad to hear he had everything under control.

And . . . she would be. Just not *now* . . .

Helena lit the cigarette, inhaled and wondered why there was something so sensual about smoking in the heat of a Mediterranean night. She'd taken her very first puff only yards away from where she now sat. At the time, she had guiltily relished the illegality of it. Twenty-four years on, she sat feeling equally guilty, wishing it was a habit she could finally break. Then, she'd been too young to smoke: now, at almost forty, she was too old. The thought made her smile. Her youth, encapsulated between the last time she had been in this house and smoked her first cigarette, and tonight.

Then, there had been so many dreams, the prospect of adulthood laid out before her. Whom would she love? Where would she live? How far would her talent take her? Would she be happy . . . ?

And now, most of those questions had been answered.

'Please, let this holiday be as perfect as it can be,' she whispered to the house, the moon and the stars. For the past few weeks she'd had a strange feeling of impending doom which, try as she might, she simply hadn't been able to shake off. Perhaps it was the fact that she was fast approaching a milestone birthday – or simply because she'd known she was returning *here* . . .

She could already feel Pandora's magical atmosphere closing around her, as if the house was peeling away the protective layers and stripping her down to her very soul. Just as it had done the last time.

Stubbing the half-smoked cigarette out then throwing it into the night, she picked up her mobile and dialled her home number in England. William answered on the second ring. 'Hello, darling, it's me,' she said.

'You've arrived safely then?' he asked, and Helena felt instantly comforted by the sound of his voice.

'Yes. How are things at home?'

'Fine. Yes, fine.'

'How's the three-year-old trainee terrorist?' she asked with a smile.

'Fred's finally subsided, thank God. He's very cross that you've all gone away and left him behind with his old dad.'

'I miss him. Sort of.' Helena gave a low chuckle. 'But at least with only Alex and Immy here, I'll have a chance to get the house organised before you two arrive.'

'Is it habitable?'

'I think so, yes, but I'll be able to see better in the morning. The kitchen's very basic.'

'Talking of kitchens, the dishwasher man came today.'

'Did he?'

'Yes. It's fixed, but we might as well have bought a new one instead for the amount it cost.'

'Oh dear.' Helena suppressed a smile. 'The bin bags are in the second drawer down to the left of the sink.'

'I was going to ask you where they were kept. The dustmen come tomorrow, as you know. Ring me in the morning?'

'I will. Big kiss to Fred and to you. Bye, darling.'

'Bye. Sleep well.'

Helena sat a while longer looking up at the exquisite night sky – awash with a myriad of stars that seemed to shine so much more brightly here – and felt the onset of exhaustion replacing adrenaline. She slipped quietly inside and lay down on the bed next to Immy. And, for the first time in weeks, she fell asleep immediately.

ALEX'S DIARY

11th July 2006

I hear him. Hovering somewhere above me in the dark, sharpening his teeth in preparation for his meal.

Which is me.

Do mosquitoes have teeth? They must do, because how else could they pierce the skin if they didn't? Yet, when I achieve the ultimate, and manage to squash one of the little buggers against the wall, there is no crunching sound, just a squelch of softness. No cracking of enamel, which is what I heard when I fell off the climbing frame at the age of four and broke my front tooth.

Sometimes, they have the cheek to come and whine in your ear, alert you to the fact you're about to be eaten. You lie there, arms swatting thin air, while they dance invisibly above you, probably giggling hysterically at their hapless victim.

I pull Bee from my rucksack and place him under the sheet next to me. He will be fine because he doesn't need to breathe. For the record, he is not actually a bee, he is a stuffed rabbit, a rabbit as old as I am. He is called Bee because he is 'B' for Bunny. That's what I named him when I was a toddler – Mum says it was one of my first words – and it's stuck.

She also said that 'someone special' gave him to me when I was born. I think she probably means my father. However sad and pathetic it is at the age of thirteen to still be sharing one's bed with an ancient toy bunny rabbit, I do not care. He – The Bee – is my talisman, my safety net and my friend. I tell him everything.

I've often thought that if someone could gather all the gazillions of cuddly child comforters together and interrogate them, they would know far more about the child they sleep with than any of the kids' parents. Simply because they actually listen without interrupting.

I cover the vulnerable parts of my body – especially my fat cheeks, which would give a mosquito breakfast, lunch and supper at one suck – as best I can with various articles of clothing.

Eventually, I fall asleep. I think, anyway. That is, I hope I'm dreaming, because I'm in a burning furnace, flames licking my body, heat melting the flesh off my bones.

I wake to see that it's still dark, then realise I can't breathe and find a pair of my underpants is covering my face – which is why it's dark and I can't breathe. I remove them, gulp in some air and see a ladder of light seeping in through the shutters.

It's morning. I am bathed in my own sweat, but it was worth it if that little bugger of an insect didn't get me.

I pull myself wetly from the mattress, tearing the sopping clothes off my body. There is a small, cloudy mirror over the chest of drawers and I stagger towards it to inspect my face. And see an enormous red bite-mark on my right cheek.

I swear, using words my mother would hate, wondering how it managed to manoeuvre itself beneath the underpants to get me. But all mosquitoes are part of an elite force, highly trained in the art of infiltration.

As well as the bite, the rest of my face is as red as the reddest side of a Cox's Pippin. I turn to the windows, open the shutters and blink like a mole as I step out onto the small balcony. I feel the heat of the morning sun burn me like the furnace in my dream.

When I've adjusted my vision, I see the view is amazing, just as my mother said it would be. We are very high up, perched on a mountainside, the yellow and brown and olive-green landscape below me arid and parched, like me. Far, far away, the blue sea shimmers in the sun. I then look down and focus on the small figure at the edge of the terrace below me.

My mother is using the balustrade as a barre. Her golden hair flows downwards as she bends the top half of her body back like a contortionist and I can see her ribs clearly out-lined beneath her leotard. She does this ballet routine every morning. Even on Christmas Day, or after she's had a very late night and a few glasses of wine. In fact, the day she doesn't do it, I'll know something is horribly wrong with her. Other kids get Coco Pops and toast at breakfast-time, with parents who are upright. I get my mother's head peering upside down at me from between her legs, as she asks me to put the kettle on.

She tried to get me to do ballet once. That's one way in which we are definitely not alike.

I am suddenly incredibly, unbearably thirsty. And I feel dizzy. The world spins slightly and I fall back into the room and onto the mattress and close my eyes.

Perhaps I have malaria. Perhaps that mosquito has done for me and I am in the last hours of my life.

Whatever I have, I need water and my mother.

β

Two

'Dehydration. That is all. Mix this sachet with water for salts now and then give him another before bed. And drink many fluids, young man.'

'Are you sure it's not malaria, doctor?' Alex eyed the diminutive Cypriot suspiciously. 'You can tell me, you know, I can deal with it.'

'Of course it isn't, Alex,' snapped Helena. She turned to the doctor and watched as he closed his medical bag. 'Thank you for coming so quickly, and I'm sorry to have bothered you.' She ushered him out of the bedroom and led him down the stairs to the kitchen. 'He seemed delirious. I was frightened.'

'Of course, it is natural, and it is no problem. I treated Colonel McCladden for many years. His death . . . so sad.' He shrugged and handed Helena his card. 'In case you need me again. In future, it is better for you to visit the surgery. I'm afraid I must charge you a call-out fee for today.'

'Oh dear, I doubt I have enough cash on me. I was

going to go up to the bank in the village today.' Helena replied, embarrassed.

'No matter. The surgery is just a few doors down from there. Drop the payment off with my receptionist later.'

'Thank you, doctor, I will.'

He stepped through the front door, and Helena followed him. Then he turned back to look up at the house. 'Pandora,' he mused. 'You must have heard of the myth?'

'Yes.'

'Such a wonderful house, but like the box in the legend after which it is named, it has been closed up for many years. Are you the one to open it, I wonder?' He smiled at her quizzically, showing a set of white, even teeth.

'Hopefully not so that all the evils of the world can pour out,' Helena said with a wry smile. 'Actually, this is my house now. Angus was my godfather. He left it to me.'

'I see. And will you love it as he did?'

'Oh, I do already. I came here to stay as a teenager and I've never forgotten it.'

'Then you will know that this is the oldest house in these parts. Some say there was already a dwelling here thousands of years ago. That Aphrodite and Adonis once came to taste the wine and spent the night here. There are many rumours in the village . . .'

'About the house?'

'Yes.' He met her gaze steadily. 'You remind me very much of another lady I once met here at Pandora, many years ago.'

'Really?'

'She was visiting Colonel McCladden, and I was called to treat her. She was beautiful, like you,' he said with a smile. 'Now, make sure the boy drinks plenty of fluids. *Adio,* Madame.'

'I will. Goodbye, and thank you.'

Helena watched him drive off in a cloud of chalk dust. Looking up at Pandora, despite the searing heat, a shiver ran up her spine and the strange feeling of dread suffused her once more. She forced herself to concentrate on the list of jobs in her head. The first was that she needed to check on the state of the swimming pool, so she walked briskly around the house and across the terrace, noting that it could do with some colourful plants in the currently empty, mouldering stone urns to enhance it, and adding that task to her mental list. The pool, which lay beneath the terrace down a crumbling set of steps, looked to be in surprisingly good condition, but would obviously need years' worth of grime cleaned from it before it was usable.

As Helena turned to walk back to the house, she glanced up, noticing how different Pandora looked from this viewpoint. The initial approach to the main entrance gave a somewhat austere impression and was unadorned, but the front of it was positively picturesque. As well as being softened by the long terrace with its pergola, each bedroom window was aproned by an ornate wrought-iron Juliet balcony, giving a bizarre impression of an Italianate villa. She wondered why she hadn't remembered it like this, but then realised that since she'd last been here, she'd actually lived for a while in Italy, so was now able to make the comparison.

She went back inside and walked upstairs to Immy's bedroom. Her daughter was standing in front of the mirror in her best pink party dress. Helena couldn't help but smile as she watched Immy admiring herself unseen, twisting her small body and throwing her glorious flaxen hair this way and that as she contentedly surveyed her reflection through wide, innocent blue eyes.

'I thought I left you to unpack, darling.'

'I have, Mummy.' With a sigh of irritation, Immy dragged herself away from the mirror and pointed to indicate that the clothes strewn all over the room were no longer in her case.

'I meant unpack into the *drawers*, not onto the floor. And take that dress off. You can't wear it now.'

'Why not?' Immy's rosebud lips drew together into a pout. 'It's my favourite.'

'I know, but it's for a party, not for running round a dusty old house in the heat.'

Immy watched her mother sweep her clothes into a pile on the bed and begin to stow them away. 'Anyway, the drawers smell funny inside.'

'They just smell of old,' countered Helena. 'We'll leave them open to air. They'll be fine.'

'What are we going to do today? Is there Disney Channel on the television here?'

'I . . .' It was almost midday now, and the morning had passed in a blur of panic trying to find a doctor for her apparently delirious son. Helena sat down abruptly on the bed, suddenly longing for the Disney Channel too. 'We have lots to do today, darling, and no, there isn't even a television here.'

'Can we buy one, then?'

'No, we can't,' she snapped, then regretted it immediately. Immy had been so good, both on the journey here and this morning, amusing herself quietly. She reached for her daughter and gave her a cuddle. 'Mummy's just got to sort out a few things, then we'll go exploring, okay?'

'Yes, but I might be a bit hungry. I didn't have no breakfast.'

'No, you didn't, so I think we'd better go shopping very soon. I'm just going to check on Alex, then we'll go out.'

'I know, Mummy!' Immy's face lit up as she scrambled off Helena's knee and began to root around in the small rucksack she'd carried with her on the plane. 'I'll make Alex a "Get Well" card to cheer him up.'

'That's a lovely idea, darling,' Helena agreed as Immy brandished paper and felt-tips triumphantly.

'Or . . .' Immy stuck a pen in her mouth as she thought. 'If he's not going to get well, do I pick some flowers from outside to put on his grave?'

'You could, but I promise you he is not going to die, so I think the card is a better idea.'

'Oh. He said he was when I went in to see him this morning.'

'Well, he's not. You start making it, and I'll see you in a few minutes.'

Helena left the room and walked along the corridor to see Alex, half of her wishing that her son would morph into a hoodie-wearing *normal* adolescent, one who enjoyed football, girls and hanging around shopping centres at night with his mates, horrifying the odd granny with their antics. Instead, he had an off-the-scale IQ, which sounded good in practice, but actually seemed to cause more problems than his high-voltage brain could ever solve. He behaved more like an old man than a teenager.

'How are you?' She peered cautiously round the door. Alex was lying in his boxer shorts, one arm slung across his forehead.

'Mmph,' came the reply.

She sat down on the edge of the bed. The ancient fan she'd dragged out of Angus' bedroom to lend a cool breeze to her son's burning forehead clanked with the effort of turning.

'Not a good start, eh?'

'Nope.' Alex did not open his eyes. 'Sorry, Mum.'

'I'm going to take Immy into the village to buy some supplies and pay the doctor. Will you promise to drink lots of water while I'm gone?'

'Yup.'

'Want anything?'

'Some mosquito repellent.'

'Really darling, Cyprus mozzies are perfectly harmless.'

'I *hate* them, whatever their nationality.'

'Okay, I'll get you some. And if you're feeling better tomorrow, we'll go to Paphos town. I've got a list of things to buy, including fans for all the bedrooms, bedding, towels, a new fridge-freezer and a TV with a DVD player.'

Alex opened his eyes. 'Really? I thought TV was off the agenda here?'

'I think a DVD player is just about acceptable for Immy and Fred, especially on hot afternoons.'

'Wow, things are looking up.'

'Good.' Helena smiled down at him. 'You rest today, then hopefully you'll be up for a trip out tomorrow.'

'I'm sure I'll be fine. It's only dehydration, isn't it?'

'Yes, darling.' She kissed him on the forehead. 'Try and get some sleep.'

'I will. Sorry about the malaria thing, by the way.'

'It's okay. See you later.' As Helena went downstairs, she heard her mobile ringing in the kitchen. Running through the hall, she managed to reach it just in time.

'Hello?'

'Is that you, Helena? Jules here. How are you?'

'Fine, yes, we're fine.'

'Good-oh. How's the house?'

'Wonderful. Just as I remembered it.'

'Twenty-four years ago? Goodness, I hope they've updated the plumbing since then!'

'Actually, they haven't.' Helena couldn't help a frisson of enjoyment as she gently taunted Jules. 'It definitely needs a bit of a facelift and a couple of new loo seats, but I think it's sound – structurally, at least.'

'That's something, then. Glad the roof won't fall in on us while we're sleeping.'

'The kitchen could do with some modernising, too,' added Helena. 'I think we'll be relying on barbecues more than the oven. To be honest, it may not be what you're used to.'

'I'm sure we'll manage. And of course I'll bring our own sheets with us – you know I always like to anyway. If you need anything else, just let me know.'

'Thanks, Jules, I will. How are the children?'

'Oh, Rupes and Viola are fine, but I've spent what feels like weeks doing prize-giving, governors' speeches and soggy strawberries. Sacha managed to wriggle out of all that kind of stuff, lucky sod.'

'Oh.' Helena knew Jules secretly loved it. 'How is Sacha?' she asked politely.

'Working all the hours God sends, drinking too much . . . you know what he's like. I've hardly seen him in the past few weeks. God, Helena, afraid I've got to dash. We're having a dinner party here tonight, so I'm frantic this end.'

'I'll see you in a few days' time, then.'

'You will. Don't get too much of a head start on the tan, will you? Pissing down here. *Ciao*, darling.'

'*Ciao*,' Helena mouthed into the mobile disconsolately as she disconnected the call and sat down at the kitchen table. 'Oh God,' she groaned, wishing with all her heart she hadn't allowed Jules to railroad her into coming to stay here for two weeks. She'd used every excuse she could think of, but Jules had simply refused to take no for an answer. The upshot was that the four members of the Chandler family – Jules, her two children and her husband Sacha – were descending on Pandora in a week's time.

Whatever dread Helena felt about the Chandlers joining them, she knew she must keep it to herself. Sacha was William's best and oldest friend; his daughter, Viola, was William's godchild. There was nothing she could do but accept the situation.

How will I cope . . . ? Helena fanned herself in the oppressive heat, seeing the kitchen and its dilapidated state through Jules' eagle eyes and knowing she wouldn't be able to bear the criticism. She reached for her scrunchie, abandoned on the kitchen table last night, twirled up her hair and wound it into a knot on the top of her head, relishing the sudden coolness at the nape of her neck.

I will cope, she told herself. *I have to.*

'Are we going yet?' Immy was behind her. 'I'm hungry. Can I have chips with ketchup at the restaurant?' Her small arms snaked around her mother's waist.

'Yes, we are.' Helena stood up, turned round and managed a weak smile. 'And yes, you can.'

The midday sun scorched through the windows of the car as Helena drove along the road that wound through the acres of grapevines. Immy sat illegally next to her in the front, the seatbelt worn across her like a saggy fashion accessory as she knelt up to look out of the window.

'Can we stop and pick some grapes, Mummy?'

'Yes, let's, though they don't taste quite the same as normal grapes.' Helena brought the car to a halt and they both got out.

'Here.' Helena bent down, and from under a fan of vine leaves, revealed a tight cluster of magenta grapes. She tore it away from the branch and broke a few off.

'Should we eat them, Mummy?' Immy asked, staring at them doubtfully. 'They don't come from a supermarket, you know.'

'They're not very sweet yet because they're not quite ripe. But go ahead, try one,' Helena encouraged as she put one into her own mouth.

Immy's small white teeth bit into the tough outer flesh cautiously. 'They're okay, I suppose. Can we take some back for Alex? Sick people like grapes.'

'Good idea. We'll take two bunches.' Helena began to break off another cluster, then stood up, instinctively feeling someone watching her. And caught her breath as she saw him. No more than twenty yards away, standing in the middle of the vines, staring at her.

She shielded her eyes from the glare of the sun, hoping irrationally that this was a hallucination, because this could not *be* . . . it just couldn't . . .

But there he was, exactly as she remembered him, standing in almost the same spot as when she'd first seen him twenty-four years ago.

'Mummy, who's that man? Why's he staring at us? Is it 'cos we stole some grapes? Will we go to prison? *Mummy?!*'

Helena stood rooted to the spot, her brain trying to make sense of the nonsense her eyes were showing her. Immy tugged at her arm. 'C'mon, Mummy, quickly, before he gets the policeman!'

Helena dragged her eyes away from his face and let herself be frog-marched back into the car by Immy, who took herself round to the passenger seat and sat expectantly next to her.

'Come on, then. Drive,' Immy ordered.

'Yes, sorry.' Helena automatically found the ignition, and turned the key to start the car.

'Who was that man?' Immy asked as they began to bump along the road. 'Do you know him?'

'No, I . . . don't.'

'Oh. You looked like you did. He was very tall and handsome, like a prince. The sun made a crown on his head.'

'Yes.' Helena concentrated on negotiating the track through the vines.

'I wonder what his name was?'

Alexis . . .

'I don't know,' she whispered.

'Mummy?'

'What?'

'After all that, we left Alex's grapes behind.'

The village had changed surprisingly little, compared to the ugly Lego-land below them that had sprung up higgledy-piggledy along the coast. The narrow high street was dusty and deserted, the inhabitants hidden away in their cool stone houses, avoiding the searing sun while it reigned at its most powerful high above them. The one shop had added a DVD library, which Helena knew would please Alex; but apart from a couple of new bars, everything else looked much the same.

Having stopped at the bank, then handed over some cash to the doctor's receptionist next door, Helena took Immy for lunch in the pretty courtyard of Persephone's Taverna. They sat under the shade of an olive tree, Immy enchanted by a family of skinny kittens that wound round her legs, mewing pitifully.

'Oh Mummy, can we take one home with us? Please, please,' Immy begged, feeding a kitten the last of her chips.

'No, darling. They live here, with their own mummy,' Helena replied firmly. Her hand shook slightly as she lifted a glass of young local wine to her mouth. It tasted exactly the same – slightly acrid, yet sweet – as she'd always remembered. She felt as if she had fallen through the looking-glass, back into the past . . .

'Mummy! Can I have ice cream or not?'

'Sorry, darling, I was daydreaming. Of course you can.'

'Do you think they have Ben and Jerry's Phish Food here?'

'I doubt it. I should think it's plain old vanilla, strawberry or chocolate, but let's ask.'

The young waiter was summoned by Immy, the deal with the ice cream done, and a Cyprus coffee, medium sugar, ordered for Helena, to dilute the glass of wine.

Twenty minutes later, they left the taverna and wandered along the dusty street towards the car.

'Look at the nuns, Mummy, sitting over there on the bench.' Immy pointed in the direction of the church. 'They must be very hot in those dresses.'

'They're not nuns, Immy, they are the old ladies of the village. They wear black because their husbands are dead and they are called widows,' Helena explained.

'They wear black?'

'Yes.'

'No pink? Ever?'

'No.'

Immy looked horrified. 'I don't have to do that when my husband dies, do I?'

'No, darling. It's a tradition in Cyprus, that's all.'

'Well, then, I'm never moving here,' Immy retorted, and skipped off towards the car.

The two of them arrived back at Pandora with the boot of the car loaded with provisions. Alex appeared at the back door.

'Hi, Mum.'

'Hi, darling, are you feeling better? Can you give me a hand with some of these shopping bags?'

Alex helped Helena unload the boot and took the bags into the kitchen.

'Gosh, it's hot.' She wiped her forehead. 'I need a glass of water.'

Alex found a glass, went to the fridge and poured out cold water from a jug. He handed it to her. 'There.'

'Thank you.' Helena gulped it back gratefully.

'I'm going upstairs for a rest. Still feeling a bit dizzy,' Alex announced.

'Okay. Come down for supper later?'

'Yes.' He walked towards the door, then stopped and turned round. 'By the way, there's someone here to see you.'

'Really? Why didn't you tell me when I first arrived?'

'He's out on the terrace. I told him I didn't know what time you'd be back, but *he* insisted on waiting anyway.'

Helena struggled to keep a neutral expression on her face. 'Who is he?'

'How should I know?' Alex shrugged. 'But he seems to know you.'

'Really?'

'Yes. I think he said his name was Alexis.'

ALEX'S DIARY

11th July (continued)

I'm standing at the window of my bedroom, peering round the shutters so I can't be seen from the terrace below.

I'm watching the man who has come to see my mother. He is currently pacing nervously, backwards and forwards, hands jammed into his pockets. He is tall and well built, his skin tanned a deep nut-brown. His thick black hair is slightly greying at the temples, but he definitely isn't an old man. I'd guess he's probably just a little older than my mum. And younger than my stepfather.

I noticed when he arrived and I saw him up close, that he has blue eyes, very blue, so perhaps he is not a Cypriot. Unless he is wearing coloured contact lenses of course, which I doubt. The upshot of all this man's combined parts means that he is definitely very good-looking.

I watch as my mother glides onto the terrace. She walks so gracefully it's almost as if her feet are not touching the ground, because the top half of her body doesn't move, even though her legs do. She stops a few feet away from him, her hands hanging loosely by her sides. I cannot see her face, but

I can see his. And watch as it creases into an expression of pure joy.

My heart is beating fast now and I know it's no longer dehydration. Or malaria. It's fear.

Neither of them speak. They stand where they are for what seems like hours, as if they are drinking each other in. He looks like he'd like to drink Mum, anyway. Then his arms stretch out and he moves towards her and stands in front of her. He takes hold of her small hands in his big ones and kisses them reverently, as though they are holy.

This is gross. I don't want to see it, but I can't help myself looking.

He finally stops the hand-lip thing, then takes my mother in his muscular arms and embraces her. She is so tiny and pale and blonde against his dark strength that she reminds me of a china doll being hugged to death by a large brown bear. Her head is thrown backwards at a funny angle against his huge pectorals as he squeezes her to him. His elbow seems to be round her neck and I only hope her head doesn't snap off, like Immy's china doll's did once.

Finally, just as I am running out of breath from holding it so long, he lets her go and I gulp in some air. Thank God. No lip-to-lip kissing, because that would have been rank beyond belief.

But it's not over yet.

He still doesn't seem inclined not to be holding some part of her anatomy, so he takes her hand again. And leads her towards the vine-covered pergola and they disappear beneath it, out of my sight.

Damn! I walk slowly back to my bed and throw myself onto it.

Who is he? And who is he to *her*?

I knew, as soon as I saw him standing on the terrace, looking like he owned the place, that he was something. Should I phone Dad? The dad that's not my dad, but as much of one as I've ever known? I knew he'd eventually come in useful for something one day.

Surely he wouldn't be happy about his wife being mauled on a terrace by a big brown Cypriot bear? I reach for my mobile phone and turn it on. What do I say?

'Come NOW, Dad! Mum's in mortal danger under the pergola!'

Christ. I just can't. He thinks I'm a weirdo anyway. I'm fully aware he has no choice but to tolerate me because he loves Mum, and I came as part of the package. Unfortunately I'm rubbish at most ball games, even though I'm enthusiastic. When I was younger, he tried to teach me, but I always ended up feeling I'd let him down by not getting into the firsts for anything. And then turning in golden ducks in front of him when he came to watch me, 'cos I was so nervous. Me being good at that kind of thing would have helped our relationship a lot, but at least he loves Mum and protects her against all the others that seem to want her.

Like the one currently under the pergola.

Ironic, really. There was me looking forward to some time alone with her without Dad, who makes me feel I'm always in the way, yet here I am, not twenty-four hours on, wishing he was here.

Maybe I *should* text him . . . I check my mobile, then discover I only have eighteen pence credit left, so I can't. And even if I did, what could he actually do?

There's no one else here but me. And Immy, but she doesn't count.

So . . . there's only one thing for it: I shall have to go it alone.

I will go into battle to save my mother's honour.

ψ

Three

'You look . . . just the same.'

'No I don't, Alexis, of course I don't. I'm twenty-four years older.'

'Helena, you are beautiful, just as you were then.'

Heat flew to Helena's already flushed cheeks. 'How did you know I was here?'

'I'd heard a rumour in the village. Then Dimitrios called me at lunchtime and said he'd seen a golden-haired lady and a child on the track leading from Pandora, so I knew it must be you.'

'Who is Dimitrios?'

'He is my son.'

'Of course! Of course!' Helena laughed in relief. 'Immy and I stopped on the way to pick some grapes and I saw him, staring at me. I thought it was you . . . how silly . . . he looks so like you.'

'You mean he looks like I *did*.'

'Yes. Yes.'

They lapsed into silence for a while.

'So, how are you, Helena?' he ventured. 'How has your life been all these years?'

'It's been . . . good, yes, good.'

'You are married?'

'Yes.'

'I know you have children, Helena, because I have already met your son and heard about your daughter.'

'I have three, but my little boy, Fred, is at home in England with his father. They're joining us here in a few days' time. You?'

'I was married, to Maria, the daughter of the old mayor here in Kathikas. She gave me two boys, but died in a car accident when Michel, my second son, was eight. So now, we three men live together and harvest our grapes and produce our wine, like my father and grandfather and great-grandfather before us.'

'I'm so sorry, Alexis. How absolutely awful for you.' Helena heard the triteness of her words, but couldn't think what else to say.

'God gives and he takes away, and at least my boys came out of it alive. And Dimitrios, whom you saw in the vines, is about to be married, so the generations continue.'

'Yes. I . . . So little seems to have changed here.'

Alexis' expressive face moulded into a frown. 'No, much has changed in Cyprus, as it has everywhere. But this is progress. Some of it is good, and some not so good. A few becoming very rich, and greedy, as always, for more. Yet here in Kathikas – for the present at least – we are an oasis. But the developers' greedy fingers will one day stretch into our fertile land. They have already started to try.'

'I'm sure they have. It's such a perfect spot.'

'Yes. And don't imagine that everyone in our village will resist the temptation, especially the young. They want their fast cars and their satellite dishes and the American way of life they see on their televisions. And why shouldn't they? We too wanted more, Helena. So, let us move on and stop sounding like our parents,' he chuckled.

'We *are* our parents, Alexis.'

'Then let us be the children we were, just for now.' He reached for her hand, just as Alex emerged onto the terrace.

Helena drew her hand away, but knew her son had seen it.

'Where's Immy?' he demanded rudely.

'In the kitchen, I think. Alex, you've met Alexis already.'

'We have the same name. It means "defender and protector of the people",' smiled Alexis congenially.

'I know. Mum, I hope Immy hasn't wandered off while you weren't looking. You know what she's like.'

'I'm sure she hasn't. Why don't you go and find her, and bring her out to meet Alexis? And put the kettle on, please. I'm desperate for a cup of tea.' Helena sank into a chair, feeling emotionally drained.

Alex eyed her defiantly, then turned to walk away inside.

'He is a good-looking boy,' remarked Alexis. 'Well built.'

Helena sighed. 'He is . . . unusual, that's for sure. And brilliant, and exasperating, and difficult and . . . oh, I love him to bits,' she said with a weary smile. 'Perhaps one day I'll tell you about him.'

'Perhaps, one day, we will tell each other about many things,' Alexis said quietly.

'Here she is.' Alex led a tear-stained Immy onto the

terrace. 'She was being chased around the kitchen by a large stripy hornet thing. With a killer sting, probably,' he added.

'Oh darling, why didn't you call me?' Helena opened her arms and Immy ran to her.

'I did, but you didn't come. Alex saved me. A bit.'

'She is so like you, Helena. She is, how do you say . . . your double,' Alexis smiled.

'I call her MiniMum. Get it, Alexis?' Alex barked. 'No, probably not. Never mind.'

'Would you like some tea, Alexis? I'll go and make it,' Helena butted in to defuse the situation.

'Yes, please. Why not share the English passion for a hot drink in hot weather?' he smiled.

'It's a well-known fact that a hot cup of tea cools you down. That's why they drink it in India,' remarked Alex.

'Nothing to do with the fact they all lived on tea plantations, then,' murmured Helena, with a grimace at her son. 'Come on, Immy, you can help me. I'll be back in a minute.'

Alex sat down in his mother's vacant chair, folded his arms across his chest and glared at Alexis. 'So, how do you know my mother?'

'We met, many years ago, when she was last here, staying with Colonel McCladden.'

'You mean Angus, her godfather? And you haven't seen her since?'

'Oh yes, I have, actually,' he said with a smile, 'but that is another story. So Alex, you like Cyprus?'

'I don't know yet. It was dark when we got here and I've been in bed all day due to possible malaria. It's very hot, with mosquitoes and stripy hornets everywhere. And I don't like those.'

'And the house?'

'It's cool. I mean, it's not at all cool, it's boiling, but I love history and this place has got lots,' Alex conceded.

'This is a very historical area. If you like history, you may know of the Greek myths. According to them, Aphrodite was born in Paphos, and spent her life with Adonis on the island. You can go and see his bath, only a few miles from here.'

'Let's hope he's taken the plug out or the water will be very stale by now,' Alex muttered under his breath.

'It is a beautiful waterfall in the middle of the mountains,' Alexis continued. 'You can jump from the high rocks into the water, which is clear and pure and very refreshing in the heat. I will take you there if you wish.'

'Thanks, but extreme sports aren't really my thing. So' – Alex eyed him – 'what do you do around here?'

'My family has run the local vineyard for hundreds of years. We make wine. It provides a good living for our family. And we are starting to export more and more abroad. Ah, here is your mother.'

Helena emerged onto the terrace and put the tray down on the table. 'I've settled Immy upstairs for a rest. She's exhausted from the heat and the hornet. Alex, do you want some tea?'

'Yes.' He stood up. 'You sit down, Mum, I'll pour. I've just been hearing about Adonis' Bidet.'

'You mean the waterfall? Oh, it's so beautiful, isn't it, Alexis?' Helena smiled at him as they both shared a memory.

'Perhaps Dad will take us all when he arrives,' Alex announced loudly. 'When is Dad arriving, by the way?'

'Friday, as you know perfectly well, Alex. Milk, Alexis?'

'No, thank you.'

'But it might be sooner, mightn't it, Mum? I mean, Dad might surprise us and just turn up here any time.'

'I doubt it, Alex, he's got work to do.'

'But look how he misses you. He's always calling you on the mobile. It wouldn't surprise me if he did arrive earlier, you know.'

Helena raised an eyebrow as she passed Alexis his tea. 'Well, I hope he doesn't. I'd like to get the house looking a little more welcoming before he does.'

'Do you need any help with it, Helena?' questioned Alexis. 'It has been empty for a long time.'

'Actually, I'd love it if you knew someone who could sort out the pool. It needs cleaning and filling.'

'What pool?' asked Alex, suddenly animated.

'There's a gorgeous swimming pool just through that gate and down the steps,' Helena indicated the location with her hand. 'Unfortunately, most of the olives seem to have fallen into it and there are a few broken tiles that probably need replacing.'

'Then I will send Georgios up to look at it,' said Alexis. 'He is the cousin of my wife, and a builder.'

'You're married?' asked Alex, suddenly animated.

'Sadly, no longer, Alex; my wife died many years ago. I will call Georgios now.' Alexis produced a mobile from his pocket, dialled and spoke in fast Greek. He put the mobile down and smiled. 'He will come here tonight, and maybe you will have a pool to swim in by the time your husband arrives.'

'That would be wonderful,' Helena said gratefully. 'I

was also wondering where I go in Paphos to buy a new fridge-freezer, an oven, a microwave . . . in fact, the whole nine yards, kitchen-wise. We have a heap of people arriving next week. Though I'm worried everything might take time to be delivered.'

'No need for delivery. I have a transit van for transporting my wine to the hotels and restaurants in the area. I can take you, and we can bring the items back here ourselves.'

'Are you sure you wouldn't mind?'

'Not at all. It will be my pleasure, Helena.'

'And would you know anyone in the village who could help me with the housekeeping? Perhaps do a little cooking?'

'Of course. Angelina, who left you the keys, worked for the colonel in his last year here. She is available, I am sure, and she loves children. I will contact her for you. She will come to see you.'

'Thank you, Alexis, you are a saviour,' said Helena gratefully, sipping her tea. 'Maybe I'll ask her whether she'd like to do a little babysitting, too, so we can go out in the evenings sometimes.'

'I can babysit, Mum,' put in Alex.

'Yes, I know you can, darling, thank you.'

'And what about the structure of the house?' enquired Alexis.

'It looks all right to me.' Helena shrugged. 'But then, I'm hardly an expert.'

'I will ask Georgios to look at it when he comes to see the pool. For example, the plumbing and the wiring . . . these things have not been touched for many years, and we must make sure they are safe.'

'I know.' Helena sighed. 'It really is a Pandora's Box. I hardly dare open it.'

'You know of the legend at this house?' Alexis directed the question to Alex.

'No,' he replied sulkily.

'It is a good legend, not a bad one. It is said that anyone who comes to stay at Pandora for the first time will fall in love while he or she is staying under its roof.'

'Really?' Alex raised an eyebrow. 'Does that apply to five-year-olds too? I noticed Immy looking rather dreamily at her toy lamb earlier today.'

'Alex! Don't be rude!' Helena reprimanded him, her patience finally snapping.

'Ah, he is a boy and afraid of love,' Alexis said with an indulgent smile. 'But when it comes, he will welcome it, as we all do. Now, I must go.' He stood up, and Helena followed suit.

'It is wonderful to see you, Helena,' he said, kissing her warmly on both cheeks.

'And you, Alexis.'

'I will be here tomorrow morning at nine to go to Paphos, yes? *Adio*, Alex. Look after your mother.'

'I always do,' Alex grunted.

'Goodbye.' Alexis nodded at him and strode across the terrace and out of sight.

'Really, Alex,' Helena sighed at him in frustration, 'do you have to be so obnoxious?'

'I wasn't, was I?'

'Yes, you were, and you know it! Why didn't you like him?'

'How do you know I didn't?'

'Oh come on, Alex, you went out of your way to be contrary.'

'Sorry, but I just don't trust him. I'm going down to see the pool, if that's okay with you.'

'Fine.'

Helena watched her son amble off across the terrace, glad he had left her in peace for a while . . . that they had *both* left, these two males who had the same name and held court in her heart. As the shock of Alexis appearing began to subside, she thought how he had been little more than a boy back then, only a few years older than her son. Now he was a middle-aged man, but his essence remained unchanged.

Helena rubbed her nose thoughtfully. No one forgot their first love – everyone believing their own experience was unique, unrivalled in its power, passion and beauty. And of course, that first summer here with Alexis had stayed in her memory for twenty-four years, like a butterfly caught forever in amber.

They'd been *so* young . . . she almost sixteen, he almost eighteen, and still, he knew nothing of the aftermath of their relationship, or of her life since then. And how their love had changed her life.

A sudden lurch of fear clutched at Helena's heart and she wondered again if coming back here was the worst possible thing she could have done. William would arrive in a matter of days, and she'd told him nothing about Alexis. What had been the point of him knowing about someone who was little more than a shadow from her past?

But Alexis was no longer a shadow. He was very much

alive and real. And there was no escaping the fact that her past and present were about to collide.

Helena's mobile rang just as she was placing supper in front of Alex and Immy.

'Answer it, will you, Alex?' she said as she lowered the precariously packed tray onto the terrace table.

'Hi,' he said. 'Yeah, hi Dad. We're all fine. Apart from the fact Mum is about to make me and Immy eat some pickled goats' testicles in a fish-poo sauce, from the look of things. Enjoy your pizza while you can, that's my advice. Yeah, I'll pass you to Mum. Bye.'

Helena raised her eyebrows with a weary sigh as Alex passed the mobile to her. 'Hi, darling. Everything okay? No, I'm not poisoning them. They're trying feta cheese, hummus and taramasalata. How's Fred?' Helena balanced the mobile between shoulder and chin as she unloaded the tray. 'Good. Have a word with Immy, and we'll speak later. Okay, bye. It's Daddy.' Helena passed the mobile to her daughter and Immy took it.

'Hi, Daddy . . . yes, I'm fine. Alex was dying this morning and Mummy and me saw a prince in a field while we were picking grapes but the police might have arrested us so we had to leave them behind but then we got them again on the way back and the prince's daddy came to see us here and had a cup of tea and was really nice. And I had ketchup and chips for lunch and it's very hot here and . . .' Immy paused for breath and listened. 'Yes, I love you too and miss you a bit. Okay, Daddy, see you soon.' She made sucking noises down the line to indicate kisses and expertly pressed the right button to end the call. She looked down at her plate. 'Alex is right. This looks yucky.'

Helena was still cringing at Immy's conversation with her father. She put two pieces of pitta bread on her plate and spooned on some hummus. 'Try it,' she encouraged.

'Can I please have ketchup with it, Mummy?'

'No, you can't.' Helena fed a small piece of bread and hummus into Immy's mouth. She waited whilst her daughter's taste buds whirred into action and eventually, the food received a small nod of approval. 'Good. I knew you'd like it.'

'What's the gloopy stuff made from?' Immy enquired.

'Chickpeas.'

'Chick's pees? Oooh,' Immy said with a shudder. 'You mean their wee-wee?'

'Don't be silly, Immy,' countered Alex, who was yet to put anything in his own mouth. 'Chickpeas are a kind of pea, they're just not green. Sorry, Mum' – Alex raised his hands in defeat – 'I haven't got my appetite back yet after this morning.'

'Okay.' Helena wasn't in the mood for a battle. 'So, it's good news about the swimming pool, isn't it? It should be filled by the time Daddy arrives. Here, have some taramasalata, Immy. And tomorrow in Paphos we can buy some sun-loungers and—'

'YUCK-EE!' Immy inelegantly spat the contents of her mouth out onto her plate.

'Immy!'

'I'm sorree, but that is wank!'

'*Rank*, Immy. And don't copy what I say, please,'

reprimanded Alex, trying to remain straight-faced. 'You're only five.'

'Yes, you are, and princesses do not use words like "rank". Do they, Alex?' Helena was also stifling laughter. 'Now, while I call Daddy back, why doesn't Alex take you upstairs and get you ready for bed? Then I'll come and tell you one of your favourite stories?'

'Okay. I want the one about when you were ballet-dancing in Vienna and a prince took you to his palace for a ball.'

'It's a deal,' Helena agreed. 'Go on, off you go.'

As her two children disappeared into the house, she picked up her mobile and dialled home.

'Hello, darling,' said William. 'Supper a success?'

'I'll leave it to your imagination.'

'Perhaps that's best. So, good day?'

'Eventful.'

'Sounds like it. Who's the prince Immy told me about?'

'Oh, just the son of an old friend.'

'Right.' There was a pause. 'Helena, darling,' said William, slowly, 'I want to ask you something.'

'What?'

'I . . . well, I'm not sure how to tell you this, but . . . it's Chloë.'

'Is she all right?'

'Oh yes, she's fine, apparently. Though I can only go on what her house-mistress at school tells me, as you know. However, I received a letter from her mother today.'

'A letter? From Cecile? My goodness!' Helena breathed. 'She actually put pen to paper? That's nothing short of a miracle for your ex-wife, isn't it, darling?'

'It is rather, but the thing is . . .'

'Yes?'

'She wants Chloë to fly over and spend some time with us in Cyprus.'

ALEX'S DIARY

11th July (continued)

This holiday, to quote my baby sister, gets ranker by the second.

Mosquitoes, heat, old houses in the middle of an arid field where they've never heard of broadband and a grape-stamper wanting to stamp himself all over my mother. Not to mention Jules, Sacha, Viola and Rupes – their Neanderthal, brain-dead son – coming to stay next week.

I wish I could start a campaign on behalf of all Kids of Parents Who Are Best Friends, to raise awareness for the kids' plight. Just because the oldies used to share sweeties and secrets when they were younger, then moved on to alcohol and eventually potty-training together, does not necessarily mean that the *children* of Best Friends will feel the same about their counterpart offspring.

My heart always sinks when I hear those immortal words, 'Alex, darling, the Chandlers are coming over. You will be nice to Rupes, won't you?'

'Well, yes,' I reply, 'I will try, Mother dearest.' But when Rupes thumps me accidentally on purpose in the bollocks during a 'friendly' rugby tackle, or goes screaming to his mum accusing me of breaking his PSP when he dropped it on the floor originally and I stood on it because I didn't know it was there, it can be pretty tough going.

Rupes is about the same age as me, which makes it really bad. And we're chalk and cheese. He's probably everything my stepfather William would like as a son: great at ball-sports, jocular, popular . . . and a right evil bastard when no one else is looking. He's also as thick as two short planks, thinks Homer is the star of *The Simpsons* and that's why he's famous for his philosophy.

We don't have a lot in common, Rupes and me. He has a little sister called Viola, all red hair, freckles and rabbity teeth, with a complexion that's so pale she fades into the background like a small ghost. Mum once told me she's adopted. If I was the Chandlers, I'd have stuck out for a child that at least vaguely resembled my gene pool, but maybe Viola was all that was available at the time. And due to Rupes' over-powering presence and her timidity, I can't really say I know who she is.

To cap it all, Mum's just informed me that my stepsister, Chloë, is coming to stay here too. I only remember her vaguely, because I haven't seen her for six years. The BFH – Bitch From Hell – as she is affectionately known in our household, who is my stepdad's ex-wife, stopped Chloë seeing her father when Mum got pregnant with Immy.

Poor Dad. He tried everything to see her, he really did. But the BFH had brainwashed Chloë into believing her father was the devil incarnate because he wouldn't buy her ice creams that cost over a pound – thinking about it, he still won't for us lot – and eventually, Dad had to give up. After numerous and bankrupting court cases to try and get access to her and losing, even the social worker said it was probably best, because Chloë was getting such a hard time from her mum if she ever mentioned her dad, and the battle was affecting her psychologically. So, for Chloë's sake, he did. He doesn't say much about it, but I know he misses her a lot. The nearest he gets to her is writing birthday and Christmas cards and a cheque to the very expensive boarding school she attends.

So . . . why her sudden reappearance?

Apparently, so Mum tells me, the BFH has got a boyfriend. Poor bloke. She is one scary woman. I admit to being terrified of her the one time I met her, because she is seriously, evilly mad and probably looks exceptionally good in black. She must have mixed something up in her cauldron to give to this poor boyfriend of hers, because he wants to take her away to the south of France for the summer. Apparently, he wants time with her by himself.

I hope his legs don't end up on a plate with the other frogs, that's all I can say.

Anyway, the upshot is, we get to have Chloë.

My mother looked distinctly nervous when she told me just now, but she was putting on a good show, saying how great it would be for Dad after all the years of not seeing his daughter. The most worrying thing of all was how she said it would be a bit of a squash, because Chloë should have her own room. And 'people' would have to share.

I know what she was insinuating.

I am sorry. But I absolutely will not, under any circumstances, share a room with Rupes. I will sleep in the bath or if necessary, outside or anywhere that isn't with him. I can cope with having my personal space invaded during the day, as long as I know I can have it back at night.

So, Mother dearest, it's a complete no-go.

She also said how we must make Chloë welcome, help her feel part of our family. Our whatever-is-the-opposite-of-nuclear family.

Christ. Dysfunctional or what? Someone should write a thesis on us. Or perhaps I should.

I lie on my bed, staring up at the ceiling, having nearly gassed myself with the Cypriot mosquito spray Mum got me from the shop – which is probably so full of banned pesticides, it will probably kill *me* into the bargain – and try to work out how many different bloodlines there are in our family.

The only thing is . . .

I wish I knew all of mine.

δ

Four

The following morning, Helena woke from a restless night's sleep. Her mind had flitted from one unsettling thought to the next as the hours dragged slowly towards dawn. Even though she felt exhausted, she was grateful for the distraction of the trip to Paphos and her long shopping list.

Alexis arrived in his transit van at nine, and the four of them climbed onto the wide front seat. Immy was enchanted to be sitting up high in the front, but Helena saw Alex sulking silently, staring out of the window as they descended down the winding road from their hilltop eyrie. She'd given him the option of staying behind at Pandora and helping Georgios sort out the pool, but he'd insisted on coming. She was under no illusions as to why – she was under surveillance.

'Wow, Mummy, it's like being on a helter-skelter, isn't it?' Immy said as they zigzagged down the hairpin bends towards the coast.

'You will not recognise Paphos town, Helena,' commented Alexis as he drove. 'It is no longer the quiet fishing port it once was.'

As they drove into the town, Helena was aghast at the seemingly endless stretch of neon signs glaring out from ugly concrete buildings along the roadside. Large billboards advertised everything from luxury cars to timeshare apartments to nightclubs.

'Look, Mummy! There's McDonald's! Can we go and get a cheeseburger and fries?' said Immy longingly.

'It is sad, yes?' murmured Alexis, glancing at Helena.

'Terribly,' she agreed, spotting an English-style pub with a garish banner outside, announcing televised football and all-you-can-eat roast lunches every Sunday.

They parked outside a cavernous homeware superstore, and Helena realised Alexis was right: Paphos had exploded into the kind of shopping experience any British town would be proud to call its own.

'Globalisation, I loathe it!' she muttered as she climbed out.

Inside the store a few minutes later, Helena picked a lace tablecloth up from a pile and read the label of origin. 'China,' she remarked to Alexis. 'Last time I was here, the lace was made by the local women and sold on market stalls. You offered them what you wanted to pay.'

'You are just sad because we are no longer "quaint". But we learned everything we know from you British during your occupation,' Alexis added with an ironic smile.

Two hours later, with a token stop-off at McDonald's to placate Immy, Alexis' van – laden with white goods and a mountain of other items Helena had bought – arrived back at Pandora. The shopping spree had cost a small fortune, but she'd used some of the money from Angus' bequest and hoped that her godfather would have approved of it being spent on refurbishing Pandora. It was certainly in need of updating.

Alex, who had hardly spoken a word all day, silently helped Alexis and his builder relative, Georgios, lug the boxes off the van and onto the wheeled trolley that Alexis had left at the house earlier.

As she spread pretty bedspreads, put cream silk lampshades on bases in place of fly-blown orange glass, and hung wispy pieces of voile at the bedroom windows, Helena reluctantly admitted to herself that there were some advantages to globalisation.

'The freezer is switched on, the new oven in and the old one out, and the dishwasher and washing machine await a plumber, who will come tomorrow.' Alexis had appeared at Helena's bedroom door and stood watching her making up the old wooden bed with crisp, white cotton sheets. He surveyed the room and smiled. 'Ah, a woman's touch . . . it is irreplaceable.'

'There's a long way to go yet, but it's a start.'

'And perhaps the beginning of a new era for Pandora?' he ventured.

'You don't think Angus would mind, do you?'

'I think a family is exactly what the house needs. It always did.'

'I'd like to paint this room, soften it a little,' she remarked, looking at the stark, whitewashed walls.

'Why not? My sons could start tomorrow. They would have it done in no time at all,' Alexis offered.

'Oh Alexis, you are kind, but they have work, surely?'

'You forget I am their boss. So,' he said with a grin, 'they will do as I say.'

'The time is flying already,' Helena exclaimed. 'My husband arrives on Friday with Fred.'

'Does he?' Alexis paused, then continued. 'So, you choose the colour and we will do the job.'

'Well, in paltry return for all your help, I shall open the bottle of wine you brought us.'

'Helena, you look pale. Are you tired?' Alexis put his hands tentatively on her shoulders. 'You are an English rose and cannot take the heat. You never could.'

'I'm fine, Alexis, really.' Helena broke free from his touch and hurried down the stairs.

Later, once Alexis and Georgios had left and Alex was setting up the DVD player with Immy dancing round him excitedly, Helena climbed guiltily into her new hammock, which Alexis had suspended between the beautiful old olive tree that stood proudly in the centre of the garden to the side of the terrace and another, younger upstart.

A delicious breeze rustled through the branches, gently blowing wisps of her hair across her forehead. The cicadas were practising for their sunset chorus and the sun had lost its midday glare, softening into a dappled, mellow light.

She thought about the imminent arrival of her unknown stepdaughter, Chloë. William had sounded decidedly nervous last night, and she knew he felt it was a lot to ask: both of her and of their children. She too was concerned. Alex was the resident cuckoo in the nest, after all. Was there really room for another? Helena wondered how *he* would react to Chloë's arrival, let alone the two little ones, who had never even met their sister. But how could she deny William the chance to spend precious time with his daughter, even if there was a good chance Chloë's presence would throw the family dynamic off-balance?

And Chloë herself: how would she feel about being thrown into a family she had been taught to loathe? Yet Helena knew that Chloë was the real victim of the situation: a child caught up in the maelstrom of an acrimonious divorce, used as a weapon by a woman scorned. Even though Cecile professed to protect her daughter from the apparently dangerous clutches of her father, the reality was that, through the lowest form of emotional blackmail, Chloë had almost certainly been scarred by not being allowed to have a normal relationship with her father as she grew up.

She was almost fifteen now – a difficult age for any girl, especially one who'd been forced to deny her love for her father, to satisfy a mother who would accept nothing less. Helena knew also that the heart beating inside her, which loved her husband and her children, had to extend yet further to include Chloë. The chambers were stretched already, providing the emotional support demanded of any wife and mother. Now, even more was needed from her, due to the complex ramifications of a second marriage.

She was the maypole around which her family danced. And tonight, Helena felt the ribbons very tight about her chest.

'I'm sorry, Mum, but it's a no. NO! NO! NO! Okay?'

'For goodness' sake, darling, it's a big bedroom! There's

easily enough space for the two of you. You won't be spending any time in it, anyway, apart from sleeping.'

Alex was sitting with his arms crossed and Helena could feel the metaphoric smoke coming out of his ears. 'Mum, that is not the point. And you know it. You *know* it.'

'Well, I really can't see any alternative, Alex.'

'I'll sleep with Immy and Fred, or get bitten to death by mozzies in a sun-lounger on the terrace rather than sleep with *him*. He smells terrible.'

'Yes, he does, Mummy. He farts all the time,' Immy added unhelpfully.

'For your information, so do you, Immy, but that isn't the point,' continued Alex. 'Apart from the fact he smells, which he does, I hate him. He's gay.'

'Don't be ridiculous, Alex! And so what if he was!' Helena was exasperated.

'Not *gay* gay, Mum, but "gay". In other words, a complete arseh—'

'Enough, Alex! I've had enough! Whether you like it or not, there's no alternative. I have to give Chloë her own room. She's a teenage girl and she doesn't know any of us except Dad and—'

'Why doesn't she sleep with *him*, then?'

'Oh for goodness' sake, Alex! Don't be facetious.' Helena stood up and began to pile the dirty supper plates together. 'I'm trying to do my best for everybody here and I was hoping I might be able to count on you to help me. Thanks a lot.' Carrying the plates into the kitchen, she clattered them into the sink, then thumped the drainer with her fist to release some tension.

'Here you are, Mummy.' Immy appeared behind her, brandishing a teaspoon. 'I'm helping you clear up.'

'Thanks, darling,' Helena said wearily. 'Can you ask Alex to bring in the rest?'

'No, 'cos he's gone.'

'Gone where?'

'Dunno. He didn't say.'

An hour later, Helena put Immy to bed, then indulged in a long bath in Angus' ancient but gloriously deep tub. Drying herself with one of the new fluffy towels she'd bought in Paphos, she put on her robe and padded back downstairs to sit on the terrace. She was just about to reach into her pocket and furtively light a cigarette when Alex appeared out of the gloom.

'Hi. I just came to say sorry,' he said as he slumped heavily into the chair. 'Really, I'm not being difficult, but I will do anything to avoid sharing with Rupes. I just' – Alex ran a hand through his hair – 'can't.'

'Okay.' Helena surrendered. 'Let me think about it. I'm sure we can sort something out.'

'Thanks, Mum. Well then, I think I'll go and enjoy my personal space whilst I can. Get an early night.'

'The pool should be filled by tomorrow afternoon. That'll be good, won't it?'

'Suppose so.' Alex nodded half-heartedly. 'So, is Mr "I Can Sort Out Any Problem For You My Darling Helena Just Ask Me" back here again tomorrow?'

'Alex, stop it!' Helena blushed despite herself. 'I am not his "darling" and besides, I really don't know what I'd have done without him.'

'You are his "darling", Mum. He fancies you rotten and

74

you know it,' Alex said flatly. 'It makes me feel sick to watch him watching you. He'd better look out when Dad comes. I don't think he's going to be too chuffed with Mr Fix-it hanging around all the time.'

'Alex, enough! Alexis is just a very old friend.'

'That's all?'

'Yes, that's all.'

'And you haven't seen him since you were last here?'

'No.'

'Well, he told me he *had* seen you since, so one of you is lying.'

'Right, that's it! I refuse to sit here and be grilled by my thirteen-year-old son. Whatever was in the past stays in the past. This is the present, and I am happily married to your stepfather. Alexis is very kindly helping me help Pandora – a house he's very fond of too, actually – come back to life. *End*. Okay?'

Alex shrugged. 'Okay. But don't say I didn't warn you. I don't like him.'

'I think you've made that perfectly obvious. I'm warning you, Alex, I will not tolerate rudeness to him from you any longer. Is that understood?'

'Yes, Mum. Night,' Alex muttered. He turned in the direction of the house, then paused and looked at her in afterthought.

'Mum?'

'Yes?'

'What's with this shared name thing?'

'Sorry?'

'What I mean is . . . it is just a coincidence that we share the same Christian name, isn't it? Me and . . . Alexis?'

'Of course it is, darling. I liked the name back when I knew him, I liked it when you were born and I still like it now.'

'Nothing more in it than that?' Alex probed.

'Why on earth would there be? There are thousands of men called Alex.'

'Yep, sure, it's just . . . nothing. Night, Mum.'

'Good night, darling.'

When she knew Alex had finally disappeared upstairs, Helena went to the kitchen and made herself a cup of tea, then returned to the terrace and studied the clear, starry sky in an effort to calm her jumbled emotions.

She knew it was getting closer by the day – the moment she had dreaded for the whole of her elder son's life.

It was a miracle Alex had never asked her directly before now, once he had understood that a father had a biological input in the creation of a child as well as its mother. William had filled that role since they had married when Alex was three. They'd both encouraged Alex to call him 'Dad', and her son had seemed to accept the status quo without questioning it.

Perhaps, thought Helena, there was a part of Alex that *didn't* want to know, in case the answer was too dreadful. Which, in truth, it was. Of course, she mused as she sipped her tea, she could lie, say his father was dead. Make up a name, a past . . . a moment in time when she had been in love with a wonderful man and they had conceived Alex because they had wanted him so very much . . .

Helena put her head into her hands and sighed deeply. The selfish parts of her only wished he *was* dead, but in reality, he was very much alive . . . and present.

She knew her son might be intellectually sophisticated enough to rationalise, but the emotional part of him would surely find the truth impossible to cope with. Especially at his tricky age, as he traversed the rocky road from boy to man.

Dealing with Alex in general had always been so difficult. Helena had known almost from the beginning that he was an unusual child; so bright, so very *adult* in the way he processed information. He could reason and manipulate like a seasoned politician and then, on the turn of a sixpence, slip back into his chronological age and become a child again. She remembered when he'd become obsessed by the dawning idea of death and had cried himself to sleep at the age of four as he came to terms with the thought of not being 'here' forever.

'But none of us are here forever,' Helena whispered sadly to the night sky, ablaze tonight with its millions of stars. They had seen everything, she thought, yet kept their wisdom to themselves.

William told her she indulged Alex, pandered to his whims, and perhaps she did. She alone read his vulnerability, knowing he had to cope with the isolation of feeling he was 'different'. His junior school had suggested Alex should be assessed when he was eight, as he was outstripping all his classmates academically. She'd done so reluctantly, not wanting to label him while he was still so young. He'd come out of the assessment as a 'gifted' child, with an IQ off the scale.

Helena had kept him at the local primary school, wanting to make sure his childhood was as normal as possible. Then, a year after starting at the local secondary school, the headmaster had called her in and suggested Alex should go for an academic scholarship to attend the most prestigious boarding school in England.

'Really, Mrs Cooke, I think we would both be doing Alex a disservice if he wasn't at least given the opportunity to try. We do our best here, but he needs to be stretched and there's no doubt he'd be better off with other boys of a similar intellect.'

She had discussed it with William, who had agreed with the headmaster, but Helena – having been sent off to boarding school so young herself – was reluctant.

'There's no guarantee Alex will get the scholarship, and with the best will in the world, we can't afford to send him if he doesn't,' William had argued. 'So why don't we let him at least try? We can always say no if he doesn't want to go.'

And then, Alex *had* won it, and everyone had been so excited that she felt she was being churlish not to seem excited too. After all, it was a huge achievement. And a wonderful opportunity for him.

When she'd asked Alex himself if he was pleased, he'd shrugged and averted his eyes so she couldn't read his expression.

'If you are, Mum – then so am I. Dad seems happy, anyway.'

Which had told her nothing.

William had been thrilled and proud, but Helena couldn't help wondering – however unfairly – if her husband's positivity was partly based on the fact Alex would be boarding.

She was very aware that William had taken Alex on because he had fallen in love with *her*, and her son came as part of the package. Whether he had actually wanted Alex or not, he'd had no choice but to accept that he would live under their roof. Those were the facts, however one wanted to dress them up. And Alex – being Alex – would not have missed the underlying semantics.

Her son read *her*, too . . . perhaps better than anyone else. It was as if he saw through her skin to the nub of her, no matter how tightly she wrapped the thick veil that shrouded her innermost thoughts around her.

Helena pulled the cigarette out of her pocket and lit it.

Alex *knew* her protestations about Alexis' motives were lies.

He *knew* there was far more to it than she was telling.

And the truth was, he was right.

By the following sunset, the master bedroom had been painted a soft dove-grey by Dimitrios and Michel, Alexis' sons.

As they'd arrived earlier that morning in Alexis' van, Helena had walked outside to greet them, unable to help noticing how genes made themselves evident in different ways. Both young men were blessed with dark wavy hair, tawny skin and athletic physiques, but while Dimitrios had Alexis' kind eyes and gentle manner, Michel, the younger son, reminded her of nothing less than a Greek god. His looks were subtly amplified to make him even more handsome than his father.

As the brothers got to work with paintbrushes and rollers, Helena had continued to spread her purchases through the house, blunting the male edges of Pandora with femininity. Immy had helped her cut flowers and branches of olive from the gardens, and they had improvised by using large stoneware jugs in which to arrange them. The windows in all the rooms had been thrown open and, as the sun blazed in, the musty smell of emptiness began to burn away into the past. Pandora began to come alive.

Earlier that morning an arresting, ebony-haired young woman had appeared in the kitchen and Helena had been surprised to discover she was Angelina, Angus' old housekeeper. Her image of a dour, Cypriot version of Mrs Danvers proved wide of the mark as Angelina scrubbed floors and hoovered energetically, her dark eyes full of laughter as she bantered playfully in Greek with Alexis' sons.

'Mum, the pool will be ready for swimming in about an hour,' Alex announced as he found Helena in the drawing room, beating the dust out of the cushions of the damask sofas. 'Georgios is filling it now.'

'Fantastic! We'll all go for an inaugural swim then.'

'It'll be very cold, as the sun won't have had time to warm the water, but I think it'll be refreshing,' Alex added hopefully.

'Just what I need to cool down after all this hard work.'

'Yeah, not much of a holiday so far, is it? I feel as though we've just moved in somewhere.'

'We have, I suppose,' agreed Helena. 'But it'll be worth it, don't you think? I so want Dad to like it here.'

'I'm sure he will.' Alex came towards her and hugged her spontaneously. 'I'm so excited about the pool.'

'Good,' said Helena, relieved that Alex's dark mood of last night had vanished and the sun had come out, lightening up him too.

'I'm going to swim every morning before breakfast and get fit,' he added. 'See you later.'

'Okay, darling.'

'Cup of tea, Madame?' Angelina was carrying a heavy tea tray through the drawing room towards the terrace, with Immy following in her wake like a handmaiden.

'Oh, yes please. And do call me Helena, Angelina.'

'Hokay, Helena, I try,' she replied in her broken English.

'Mummy, we baked biscuits in the new oven to try it out.' Immy was clasping a plate carefully in her small hands. 'Everyone must try one, 'cos they are yummy.'

'I'm sure they are.' Helena was glad to see Immy had taken to Angelina. With the hordes descending on her in the next few days, she would need all the help she could get. She followed them onto the terrace and flopped into a chair under the pergola. 'Thanks, Immy.' She took a biscuit and bit into it. 'Mmm, they are very good.'

'Well, Angelina helped me, but I actually made them, didn't I?'

'You deed, Immy,' Angelina agreed, as she chucked her cheek affectionately.

An hour later, they gathered at the pool for an inaugural swim. There was a unified screeching as Helena, Immy and Alex joined hands to jump in.

Leaving the children to splash around, Helena climbed out ten minutes later and lay on the side of the pool, warming her goosebumps in the late afternoon sun.

'Hello, Helena.'

She looked up as a shadow crossed her body.

'Hello, Alexis.'

'I see all is well here?' He squatted down on his

haunches next to her and Helena felt suddenly exposed in her skimpy bikini. She sat up and curled her knees to her chest protectively.

'All thanks to you and your family. I'm so grateful, Alexis, really.'

'It is no more than my duty. After all, Pandora was owned by my family for over two hundred years, until your godfather persuaded my father to part with it.'

'Well, it's most kind of you to help me.'

'Atcch! Do not be so formal and English with me! You speak as if we hardly know each other.'

'We don't.' Helena paused before she added, 'Not any-more.'

'Then let us get to know each other again. Will you come for supper with me tonight at my house?'

'I . . . Alexis, I can't leave Immy and Alex.'

'I have asked Angelina. She is happy to babysit.'

'You've done what?' Helena was suddenly angry. 'Per-haps it would have been a better idea to ask me about this first.'

Alexis was immediately contrite. 'I should have asked you. I apologise, Helena.'

'Well, I can't come, anyway. I have far too much to do here. William is arriving with Fred tomorrow.'

'Mummy! I'm getting cold. I need a towel 'cos I want to get out!'

'Coming, darling.' Helena stood up and made to move away. Alexis caught her arm before she could.

'At least let us talk soon, catch up on the missing years.'

She looked up at him, opened her mouth to speak, then shook her head wordlessly and pulled out of his grasp.

ALEX'S DIARY

13th July 2006

I am lying on my back, floating in the middle of the freezing pool – I can't hear any earth sounds as my ears are underwater. Here, as I look up from my water-bed, I can see the dark, curved dome above me, which is the roundness of the earth and sky. It isn't flat, but like a cave, the roof sparkling with un-mined diamonds. I listen to the gloopy noises in my ears, close my eyes and imagine this is the closest thing you can get to being back in the womb. Apart from the fact there are no on-tap chips and chocolate and coal, or whatever your mother cares to pass you to eat down the umbilical cord.

It's a miraculous process, really it is, the creation thing.

I'm feeling calmer tonight because I have a new womb . . . I mean, *room*, to call my own. Granted, I will have to curl up in the foetal position once I'm in it – when I reach out my arms, I can touch the mahogany shelves, lined with hundreds of leather-bound books on both sides – but I don't care. It is mine and mine alone and most importantly, a Rupes-free zone.

I'll also have enough reading material to keep me going for the duration of the holiday, for my new habitat is what my mother rather grandly, under the circumstances, referred to as 'the library'. It is, in fact, little more than a broom cupboard (and I'd bet it probably once was), placed just off the drawing room. I shan't be able to – for health and safety reasons – invite anyone else into it, as there may not be enough oxygen to sustain two pairs of lungs. Besides, they'd have to lie on top of me as there is no room to stand.

Mum has said she doesn't mind if I pile some of the books up onto higher shelves, so I can at least have somewhere to put my stuff.

It also has the luxury of a door I can lock and a small window placed high up. Creepy Mr Fix-it has managed to shoehorn a camp bed into it for me to sleep on.

I turn over and swim to the edge of the pool, then climb out and shake off the excess water. I pick up a towel, which is wetter than I am from previous use, and wrap its sogginess round my shoulders. I flop onto a sunbed and dry off in the still ridiculously hot night air, hoping I'm not the reason my mother looks so down in the mouth tonight.

She's hardly spoken a word to me since Mr Fix-it left a couple of hours ago. She was monosyllabic with Immy too, mind you, so perhaps we're both in the doghouse, for reasons unknown.

I hope . . . well, I hope it's not because Dad's arriving tomorrow. Spoiling her love-nest thing with Mr Fix-it. I don't think it is, because I'm sure she loves Dad, but I know how hard women's minds are to read. Where do they learn to be so contrary?

Immy is already cottoning on to the whole female thing. She'll blackmail me into playing some boring Immy-type game, which always involves her being a princess or a fairy and wearing a piece of pink netting over her jeans, and me being everything else from Wicked Uncle to a naughty elf. Then suddenly, without warning, she'll stamp her little foot, tell me she's not playing anymore and flounce off.

Like . . . she thinks I care?!

I kneel up on my sunbed and peer through the line of olive trees that borders the pool. If I crane my neck, I can see Mum sitting on the terrace. She is wearing a white kaftan; the moonlight bleaches her blonde hair and washes out the faint colour she has achieved in the sun.

She looks like an alabaster statue.

Or a ghost.

And I know as I watch her, that just now, she is in the past, reliving another life.

Five

Fred had finally given in and fallen asleep, his small head lolling on William's lap, small sticky hands still clutching his new aeroplane tightly. William licked his finger and clumsily tried to wipe off the worst of the chocolate from around his son's mouth. When they landed, he'd have to take Fred to the gents' and give him a serious hosing down before Helena saw him. Their son's skin seemed to be Velcro for dirt.

William closed his own eyes, grateful for a respite. The flight with Fred had been a humbling experience. He was usually the man in the suit trying to contain his irritation as some pint-sized monster dug their feet into the back of his seat, screamed, wriggled and stuck their face in between the seats, while a harassed parent struggled to control the child.

He tried to doze, but the Fred-inspired adrenaline still coursed round his body, so he gave up and focused instead on arriving in Helena's world. He'd been so busy tying up loose ends at his practice, he'd not had a chance to think about it very much.

Pandora . . . he'd realised from the faraway look on his wife's face every time she spoke of it, what it meant to her. And William knew he must not let her down by making any negative comments when he arrived. Even if the house and location were rather ordinary and Cyprus as arid a collection of escarpments as he imagined, he swore he would not let his feelings show.

Helena had certainly sounded distant and strange in the past few days. Perhaps walking back into her doubtless mentally honed vision of perfection had been a let-down. But he didn't know for sure. Where his wife was concerned, he knew nothing for certain.

Helena: even now, as they approached their tenth wedding anniversary, sometimes William felt she was still out of reach. There was an aura to her, an aloofness which meant that, even when he held her naked in his arms, when they were joined as close as two people could physically be, there was part of her that wasn't *there*.

And yet, she wasn't cold. She was as warm and loving as a woman could be. And her children adored her. *He* adored her. William wondered whether it was her beauty that inspired distance and awe. He'd watched the reaction of others to her closely over the years, both male and female. People were not used to being presented with physical perfection: they coped with their own flaws by seeing them mirrored in others. With her golden hair, pale, unblemished skin and exquisitely proportioned body, Helena was as near to his feminine ideal as one could get. The fact she was also a mother only added to her allure, making her *real* and not an untouchable ice-maiden. She often made him feel, through no fault of her own, that he was a mere mortal and she a goddess. Which then led to feelings of insecurity, because sometimes, he couldn't believe this amazing woman had chosen *him*.

He always comforted himself with the fact he provided her with the things she needed, was the yin to her yang. They were very different people: she was artistic, ethereal, dreamy, while he was grounded, solid and logical. They came from completely different worlds, and yet the past ten years had been the happiest of his life. He hoped she'd been happy too.

But since the letter from her godfather's lawyer had arrived, telling her she'd inherited an old house in some god-forsaken backwater of Cyprus, she'd become more distant. And in the past few weeks, he'd really felt that Helena was drifting away. Yet there was no evidence, nothing solid to back up this feeling. In essence, Helena had been the same as always; running their home, caring for their children, being there for him and the countless others who oscillated around the glow of his wife's warmth and humanity.

Not given to introspection, as the plane touched down on the tarmac at Paphos airport, William found it hard to quell his feeling of trepidation.

'Oh Immy, that is *soo* tacky. I'm not standing next to you if you're going to hold it up.'

'Alex, don't be mean. Immy spent all morning making it. It's lovely, darling,' Helena said to Immy. 'And Daddy will love it too.'

Immy's bottom lip quivered as she trailed the paper banner proclaiming, 'WELCUM TO SIPRUS DADDY AND

FRED' into arrivals. 'I hate you, Alex. You're the stinkiest brother ever.'

'Not as stinky as Fred, remember,' Alex pointed out, as they followed Helena into the throng surrounding the arrivals doors. Through which, at any moment, the two other members of their family unit would appear.

'Right, whilst we're waiting, I'm going to the car rental booth just over there to sort out swapping mine for the people carrier,' Helena said, feeling harassed. 'You two stay here and look for Dad and Fred to come through. Their plane landed twenty minutes ago, so they should be out soon. And Alex – keep a close eye on Immy,' she cautioned before disappearing into the crowd.

'Oooh! I'm so excited!' squeaked Immy, waving her banner over her head like a fan at a pop concert. 'Oh, look. There they are . . . DADDEEE!'

William appeared through the doors, pushing a trolley with Fred perched on top of the suitcases. Immy ran to him and threw herself into her father's arms.

'Hello, Immy darling,' William said, smothered under his daughter's kisses. He peeped out from behind her long blonde hair and smiled at Alex. 'Hello, how are you?'

'Fine thanks, Dad, yeah.' Alex took hold of the trolley and knelt down to see Fred. 'Hi there, li'l bruv. Give me five.'

''Lo, Alex.' Fred smashed his small palm against his brother's bigger one, then held up his toy plane. 'I gotta prezzie from Dad.'

'You did? Wow, you must have been a good boy.' Alex picked Fred up in his arms.

'Nope. I was bad.'

'On the plane? Did you like the plane?'

'Yep.' Fred nodded, his freckled nose wrinkling as he rubbed it. 'Where is Mummy?'

'Yes, where is Mummy?' William was beside them, scouring the concourse for his wife.

'Over there by the car rentals.' Alex gave Helena a wave as he spotted her walking towards them.

Fred wriggled out of his arms and ran towards his mother.

William watched his wife, as always when he hadn't seen her for a while, struck afresh by her loveliness. She was wearing a blue T-shirt and a pair of cut-off denim shorts, her long blonde hair tied carelessly back in a pony-tail, and looked no older than a teenager.

She walked towards him, holding Fred by the hand.

'Hello, darling.' He put an arm round her shoulder and kissed her.

'Hello.' She smiled up at him. 'Good flight?'

'Eventful,' he sighed, 'but we made it here in one piece, didn't we, Fred?'

'Yep. Can we go to Cipuss now, Mummy?' Fred asked.

'Darling, this *is* Cyprus, but yes, we can go home to our house.'

'But I just come here!' Fred looked confused.

'I mean our house here in Cyprus. The car's just through there.' Helena pointed to an exit.

'Then let's make a move,' said William.

'Helena, it's beautiful, it really is.' An hour and a half later, he stood on the upstairs balcony, gazing out at the view.

'Really?'

'Really. And the house . . . well, you've worked wonders, considering you've only been here for a few days.
Everything looks so fresh and bright.' He stepped inside
their bedroom, then stopped and sniffed the air. 'Can I
smell paint?'

'Yes.'

'Surely you haven't had time to decorate, on top of
everything else?'

'No. I got someone to do it for me.'

'I am impressed,' said William. 'It takes me weeks to
find someone to mend a pipe back in England, let alone
paint a house in a couple of days. Anyway, it looks lovely.
And not at all how I imagined it.'

'How did you imagine it?'

'I don't know. Just very . . . Mediterranean, I suppose.
Stark, a bit spartan . . . yet you could put this house in an
English country village, and it wouldn't look out of place.
It's more old rectory than Cyprus villa. It's got character.'

'It's a very old house.'

'And with lovely old cornicing.' William turned his
architect's eye over the proportions of the room. 'And high
ceilings.' He then ran his hands over the top of the polished
mahogany tallboy. 'I'd reckon some of the furniture is quite
valuable, too.'

'Angus wanted to create his little piece of England right
here,' Helena explained. 'He had everything shipped over,
down to the grandfather clock in the hall.'

'And it's all yours now.'

'Ours,' Helena corrected him with a smile.

'And probably worth quite a lot of money.'

'I'd never sell it,' she replied defensively.

'No, but there's nothing wrong with knowing how much it's worth. Perhaps you should get it valued.'

'Maybe.' Helena steeled herself not to mind that her husband could even *think* of Pandora in terms of pounds, shillings and pence. 'Come on, darling, I'll show you the gardens.'

The two of them joined the children in the pool just as the sun was setting, then Helena suggested they go up to Persephone's Taverna for an early supper. 'I'll show you the village,' she said as William negotiated the potholed track. 'And the kids can have chips and chicken nuggets for a change.'

Having wandered along the one street, with William professing an urge to go and look inside the pretty Orthodox church at some point, they walked into Persephone's.

'This is a very cosy place,' remarked William as they sat down at a table. He hauled Fred onto his lap in an effort to contain the child, who was long past tiredness and into hyperactive mode instead.

'Can I do blow on the candle, Dad?' Fred asked.

'No, you can't. Here, have your car instead.' Helena took a toy out of her handbag and zoomed it across the table to Fred. 'It's hardly changed at all since I was last here, and the food is really good.'

'We're not having any more of those chick's pees, are we, Mummy?' put in Immy.

'No, but Daddy and I are having the meze. You should try some,' Helena said as their wine arrived. She ordered for them all. 'Oh, and I've found a cleaner, William, who can also babysit. Yes, Fred, your food is coming. Here, have some bread to keep you going, Immy.' Helena adeptly conducted three conversations at the same time.

'One way or another, I think we'll need her,' answered William wearily, turning to Alex. 'So, what do you think of Pandora? Like it?'

'The pool's legend,' Alex said with a nod.

'And the house?'

'Yeah, it's okay.'

'England won the test match against the West Indies, did you know?'

'No. The TV here only has Cyprus channels.'

William gave up. When Alex was in non-communicative mode, it was best to surrender.

Thankfully, the food arrived swiftly and the children dug in hungrily.

'This meze is excellent,' said William. 'Try some, Fred?'

'Plaeeuuuaa!!' Fred covered his mouth and shook his head vehemently.

'I hope he's not going to live on chicken nuggets and chips for the whole holiday, darling,' William commented primly to Helena.

'Well, if he does, it won't kill him, will it?' Helena retorted, shovelling another forkful into her son's mouth.

'The Irish lived only on potatoes for years,' put in Alex.

'And they died in their thousands,' replied William.

'That was actually during the famine, when the potatoes were diseased and they starved. And half the world lives mainly on rice, you know,' Alex continued pedantically. 'Which is basically carbohydrate, with some fibre.'

'Mummy, I need the toilet and I want Alex to take me,' Immy broke into the conversation.

'Lucky me,' muttered Alex. 'Come on then.'

'Me too!' Fred climbed off his chair and trotted after his brother and sister.

A moment of calm descended on the table, and William poured them both some more wine. 'So, has Alex been okay?' he enquired.

'Yes, fine. Or at least, normal, for him.' Helena gave William a small smile. 'You know how he is.'

'I do. So, how has it been to be back here after all these years?'

'Lovely, yes, really lovely. I—'

'Mummy! Look who's here! It's your friend!' Immy appeared behind Helena. 'I told him he had to come and meet my daddy.'

Helena turned round and looked up into the deep blue eyes of Alexis.

'Hello, Helena,' he said, obviously uncomfortable. 'I am sorry to disturb your family, but your daughter insisted.'

'Of course you're not disturbing us, Alexis. This is my husband, William.'

Alexis managed to release his hand from Immy's iron grip and held it out across the table. 'I am glad to meet you, William.'

'And you. Alexis, is it?'

'Yes.'

There was a long pause, during which Helena desperately trawled through a hundred different ways to break the silence, none of which she felt were at all suitable.

'Alexis took us to Paphos in his big van, Daddy,' Immy piped up. 'He came shopping with us and he's been helping Mummy make the house nice for you and Fred.'

'Has he now? Then perhaps I should say thank you for your help, Alexis,' replied William evenly.

'It is no problem. How do you find Pandora?' he asked.

'I think it's a wonderful house, in a beautiful location.'

'Alexis' family owned the house before Angus bought it, and Alexis owns the vineyards that surround it.' Helena had finally managed to find her voice.

'You make wine?' enquired William.

'Yes.' Alexis pointed to the jug on the table. 'You are drinking it.'

'It's good, very good. Can I offer you a glass?'

'No, thank you, William. I must go back to my guest. He is a wine merchant from Chile, and I wish him to buy from me.'

'Then come round to Pandora and have a drink with us there,' William suggested.

'Thank you. I would like that. It is good to meet you, William. *Adio*, Helena, Immy.' He nodded and left the table.

Alex had spotted Alexis as he came out of the toilet with Fred, and hung back until he'd gone. 'What was *he* doing here, Mum?' he asked as he and Fred sat back down at the table, his voice dripping with animosity.

Which told William everything he needed to know.

When they arrived back at Pandora, Helena put the little ones to bed, then ran a bath. She felt exhausted; last night, she hadn't slept. Perhaps it was simply the tension of William and Fred arriving that had caused it.

'The DVD player is set up in the drawing room.' Alex wandered in to the bedroom without knocking, a habit Helena knew irked William.

'Good,' replied Helena. 'I'm just going to have a bath. You off to bed?'

'Yes. At least I've got a few books to choose from in my new library. Night, Mum.'

'Sleep well, darling.'

'Night, Alex.' William appeared in the bedroom as Alex was leaving.

'Night, Dad.'

William shut the door firmly behind him, then followed Helena into the bathroom. As she climbed into the tub, he sat down on the edge of it. 'Peace,' he said with a smile, running his hands through his dark hair and yawning. 'I think I'll sleep well tonight.'

'Five hours on a plane with Fred is enough to knock anyone out for the duration,' Helena agreed. 'He fell asleep halfway through his story. I just hope he sleeps in tomorrow, otherwise he'll be a nightmare for the rest of the day.'

'I think that's some hope,' William sighed. 'So, how do you know Alexis?'

'I met him when I was last staying here.'

'He's a handsome man.'

'I suppose he is, yes.'

'He must have been a knockout when you first knew him,' William probed.

Helena concentrated on soaping herself in the bath.

'So, come on then.' William gave up trying to be subtle. 'Was there ever anything between you?'

'Can you pass me the towel?'

'Here.' William handed it to her, marvelling at the way neither age nor childbirth seemed to have left their tell-tale marks on his wife's body. With the water running off her skin, she reminded William of a nymph, her small breasts still high and full and her stomach flat. William felt a stirring in his loins as he watched her climb out and wrap herself in the towel. 'So? You haven't answered the question.'

'We had a holiday romance whilst I was here, that's all.'

'And you haven't seen him since?'

'No.'

'So it was . . . innocent?'

'William,' Helena sighed, 'this was twenty-four years ago. It's not important, is it?'

'Is Alexis married?'

'He was, but his wife died.'

'So he's a widower, then.'

'Yes.' Helena roughly towelled her hair dry, then reached for her robe.

'Did you know he was going to be here?'

'I had no idea. I haven't spoken to him for twenty-four years.'

'Yes, you're right. It was a long time ago.'

'Yes, it was. Now, how about you jump in before the water gets cold? I'll go and close up downstairs. And speaking of downstairs, I was thinking that first thing tomorrow, I'd like to run into Paphos and pick up some plants for those lovely old urns on the terrace and that little flower bed next to the pool. Angelina's here, so she can babysit the little ones for a couple of hours. Will you come with me?'

'Of course I will.'

'Great. See you in a minute.'

William undressed and sank into the bath, berating himself for his questioning. He was being paranoid and unfair to Helena. As she rightly said, whatever had taken place nearly a quarter of a century ago had no bearing on *now*. But the way Alexis had looked at his wife earlier in the taverna . . . William knew instinctively it was the gaze of a man still in love.

ALEX'S DIARY

14th July 2006

To Dad: 'Hello, dahh-ling.'

    To Immy and Fred: 'No! darrrlings!'

    To me: 'Oh, darling!'

    So, we are all here and back to Peter Pan Land. We are the 'Darling' family and my mother is Mrs Darling. I'm amazed she hasn't employed a dog yet as our nanny, but give her time. Why did she bother naming any of us individually, when she uses one noun for all?

    It's especially difficult when she calls out a collective 'darling' from the kitchen and all of us respond from everywhere in the house, and stand there in the kitchen while she decides which 'darling' it is she requires. On the whole, I think she's a very good mother, but this 'D' business drives me nuts. It must be a hangover from when she was working on the stage as a ballerina. It's the kind of thing 'theatricals' say.

    We are a family of five, soon to be six when this Chloë person arrives, which is quite large by today's standards. Inside that family group, surely we need to maintain our individuality? And what is more personal to us than our names?

Fred has started copying her recently. I worry he'll get a seriously rough ride at school if he thinks it's okay to call the resident class bully 'darling'.

Anyway, as long as she doesn't start including Mr Fix-it on her 'D' roster, I can just about cope.

Of course, I was Number One 'Darling', once. I came first, before any of them.

And if I'm honest, sometimes I find it difficult to share her. She's like a soft, round cheese and when I was born I had the whole lot to myself. Then she met Dad, and a great big piece was sliced off, though I reckon I still had half left. Then along came Immy, who got a big chunk, then Fred, who got another. And I'm sure she'll need to cut off another sliver for Chloë, so my piece keeps getting smaller and smaller all the time.

It really struck me today, when Immy jumped into her father's arms at the airport, that I don't have one. A father, that is. William does his best, but put it this way: if there was a fire, I'd bet my entire Tintin memorabilia collection he'd save his real kids first. Which technically makes my chunk of the cheese half *again*, as Dad and Immy and Fred have bits of each other's.

Dad seemed very happy indeed when I won my scholarship to *that* school. He opened a bottle of champagne, and I was allowed a glass too. Perhaps he was celebrating the fact that in the future I'll be away from home most of the time and he won't have to put up with me anymore.

Why am I suddenly over-obsessing more than usual about this father business?

Perhaps because, up until now, my mother has always been enough. I haven't needed anyone else.

But just recently – and I read her very well – I've felt her slipping away.

She is not herself.

And nor am I.

Six

William and Helena spent the early part of the morning at a small garden centre that Helena had spotted on the outskirts of Paphos.

It was rare these days for them to have time alone together and despite it being a relatively mundane task, Helena enjoyed wandering up and down the sunny rows of plants hand in hand with William, picking out various brightly coloured geraniums plus several oleanders and lavenders, which she knew would withstand the arid climate. The garden centre owner also had a little stall out front selling fresh local produce, so they stocked up on fragrant, fat tomatoes, melons, plums and sweet-smelling herbs to take home with them, loading everything into the boot of the car before heading back to Pandora.

'Sadie for you.' William came into the kitchen to hand Helena her mobile as she prepared lunch.

'Thanks. Hello, darling, how are you?' Helena used the

chin-to-shoulder technique to hold the phone so she could continue washing the lettuce. 'Oh, no, really? . . . Oh, what a shit! Are you okay? No, I'm sure . . . Yes, it's lovely here. William and Fred arrived yesterday and we're all having an afternoon by the pool, enjoying the peace before the Chandlers arrive. Hold on two secs, Sadie.' She turned to William and indicated the tray of plates and cutlery. 'Can you take them outside, and tell the kids to get out of the pool and dry off ready for lunch?'

William left with the tray and Helena resumed her conversation with Sadie. 'Of course you'll meet someone else. I never thought he was "the one" anyway . . . What? Well, if that's what you'd like to do, but I really don't know where you'll sleep. We're already bursting at the seams. Okay,' Helena sighed. 'Well, chin up. Just let me know the time of your flight and I'll come and get you from the airport. Bye, darling.'

William had returned to the kitchen. 'The kids are drying off. Anything else to go outside to the table?'

Helena tipped the lettuce leaves into a bowl already half full of chopped tomatoes and cucumber, tossed it deftly with her fingers and handed it to William.

'So,' he said as he took it, 'how's Sadie?'

'Suicidal. Mark's told her it's over.'

'Right.'

'I know you didn't like him much, and to be honest, nor did I. But Sadie did.'

'So I gathered from the hours of calls, waxing lyrical in your ear.'

'Yes, but Sadie is my best friend and I have to be there for her. The thing is—'

'She wants to come and stay here, get away for a few days to mend her broken heart and cry on her best friend's shoulder,' William finished for her.

'In essence, yes,' Helena agreed.

'So, when is she arriving?'

'She's calling the airline now to try and book a ticket.'

'Very soon, then.'

'Probably. I'm sorry, darling, but she sounds dreadful.'

'She'll bounce back – she normally does,' he muttered darkly.

Helena grabbed a platter of cold meats from the fridge, glancing at William as she did so. 'I know it seems like an imposition, but you need to remember that Sadie and I are like sisters. We've known each other since junior school and she's the nearest thing I have left to family. I love her, simple as that, and I just can't say no.'

'I know,' William sighed in resignation. 'And I like Sadie, I really do, but I'm just worried this so-called holiday is threatening to become a few weeks of hard labour, with the house turning into a free hotel with me, and more to the point, you, running it.'

'Pandora was made to be full of people. It certainly was when I was last here.'

'Yes, and I'd bet it had a full complement of staff to cater to the guests' every whim,' said William. 'I don't want to see you run ragged, that's all. You look exhausted already.'

'I'll ask Angelina if she'll help out more, especially with the catering. She used to cook for Angus, and he was dreadfully fussy, so I'm sure she's very good.'

'Okay,' William acquiesced, knowing it was a done deal.

'Coming out?' He offered her his hand, and she followed him into the bright sunlight of the terrace.

The three children were already gathered around the table under the pergola in various states of undress, Fred completely naked.

'Mum, I'm sorry, but I don't want to spend my entire holiday minding Fred and Immy in the pool,' complained Alex, slumping into a chair. 'Immy just wants to jump in all the time and I can't leave her in case she hurts herself or drowns and it's just . . . boring.'

'I know, Alex. I'll come down after lunch and relieve you, promise,' said Helena, serving out salad onto each of the plates. 'Guess what? Auntie Sadie is coming to stay with us.'

'Another slice gone,' muttered Alex under his breath.

'What, Alex?' asked William.

'Nothing. Can you pass the pitta bread, Immy?'

'It does mean we're going to have to rethink the bedrooms yet again,' said Helena. 'I suppose we could clear out the box room, which is full of Angus' stuff, and Sadie could sleep in there. It's not a bad size, but it'll take some work to do it.'

'And a skip, from what I saw was in there. He was obviously a hoarder,' added William.

'You never know what you might find, Mum,' said Alex, brightening up. 'I'll help you. I love wading through old junk.'

'We've noticed, from the state of your bedroom,' remarked William.

'Thanks, Alex,' said Helena, ignoring him. 'We could do it this afternoon.'

'Daddy, when will you take us to the water park?' asked Immy.

'Soon, Immy, but I think the water park in our garden is good enough for now.'

'But it hasn't got no slides or things.'

'Eat your ham, Immy, don't play with it. Daddy's just arrived. Stop hassling him,' reprimanded Helena.

'Unless you want me to take them to the water park this afternoon, get them out of your hair while you clear out that box room?' offered William. 'And remember, Chloë's arriving tomorrow. I have to fetch her from the airport. And then the Chandlers arrive the following day, God help us.'

'YES! Daddy! Today! Today!' Fred joined in Immy's chorus, banging his spoon on his plate in tandem.

'Enough!' William barked. 'If you promise to eat everything on your plate, we'll go later on, when the sun's gone down a little.'

'You might be right about the skip,' mused Helena. 'But where on earth I get one from, I've no idea.'

'Can I have a drink of orange juice, Mummy? I'm thirsty,' Fred asked.

'I'll get it, Fred.' William stood up, glanced at Helena and gave her a wry smile. 'I'm sure your friend Alexis would know. Why don't you call him?'

Helena and Alex stood in the doorway of the box room, mainly because it was impossible to step inside.

'God, Mum, where do we start?' As Alex looked at the furniture and endless discarded brown boxes, stacked to the ceiling, he began to regret not joining the others at the water park.

'Bring the chair from Immy and Fred's bedroom, and we can stand on it and pull down some of these boxes and stack them all on the landing. Then at least we can get in.'

'Okay.'

Alex fetched the chair, stood on it and lifted the first box down to Helena. He climbed down to watch as she opened it.

'Wow! It's full of old photographs. Look at that one! Is that Angus?'

Helena surveyed the handsome, fair-haired man in full military regalia and nodded. 'Yes. And in this one . . . he's on the terrace here with some people I don't know, and . . . goodness, that's my mother with him!'

'Your mum was very pretty, she looked like you,' remarked Alex.

'Or I look like her, and yes, she was,' Helena smiled. 'She was an actress before she married my father. She did rather well, starred in a number of West End plays and was thought of as a real beauty.'

'Then gave up her career to marry your dad?'

'Yes, although she was well over thirty when she married him. She didn't have me until she was forty.'

'Wasn't having a baby so late unusual for those days?'

'Very.' Helena smiled at Alex. 'I think I might have been a bit of a mistake. She really wasn't the maternal type, your granny.'

'Did I ever meet her?' asked Alex.

'No. She died before you were born. I was twenty-three and dancing in Italy at the time.'

'Do you miss her now she's dead?'

'To be honest, Alex, not really. I was packed off to

boarding school at the age of ten, and even before that, I had a nanny. I always felt as though I was rather in the way.'

'Oh Mum, how awful.' Alex patted her hand in a show of sympathy.

'Not really.' Helena shrugged. 'It was what I was brought up to expect. My father was much older than Mum, nearly sixty when I was born. He was very rich, had an estate in Kenya and used to disappear off shooting for months at a time. They were what you might call socialites, my parents, always travelling, throwing house parties . . . a little girl didn't really fit in to their lifestyle.'

'I never met Grandpa either, did I?'

'No, he died when I was fourteen.'

'If he was so rich, did you get lots of money when he died?'

'No. My mother was his second wife. He had two sons from his first marriage and they inherited everything. And my mum was a real spendthrift, so there wasn't much left when she died either.'

'Sounds like you had a crap time growing up.'

'No, just different, that's all. It made me very self-sufficient, anyway.' Helena felt the usual sense of discomfort that welled up within her when she talked about her childhood. 'And determined to have a proper family of my own. Anyway, let's put this box to one side. If we're going to go through the contents of every one we bring out of there, we'll never get it cleared.'

'Okay.'

They worked solidly for the next two hours, pulling

Angus' past out of the room. Alex unearthed a trunk containing his old uniforms, and followed his mother downstairs to the kitchen wearing a khaki peaked cap and carrying a regimental sword.

'Very fetching, darling.' Helena poured them both some water and drank thirstily from her glass. 'This really isn't the thing to be doing on a boiling hot afternoon. But I reckon we're over halfway there.'

'Yeah, but what are we going to do with it all? I mean, you can't throw this away, can you?' Alex wielded the sword, which was extremely heavy.

'I think it might be an idea to hang that on a wall somewhere in the house, and we can store the boxes of photographs and other memorabilia in the outhouse until I get a chance to look through them. As for the rest . . . we do need a skip. I'd better call Alexis, as Dad suggested, see if he knows where I can get one.'

Alex made no comment as Helena dialled a number on her mobile, then disappeared onto the terrace to talk. She came back and nodded. 'Good news. He's going to come over with his truck, load up the rubbish and take it to the dump for me. We won't need a skip after all. Come on, let's get back to work. Alexis is coming at five.'

When William pulled up in the drive at Pandora, he saw Alexis carrying a large box into the outhouse. The back of the truck parked in front of the house was full of broken furniture, old lampshades and moth-eaten rugs. He left Immy and Fred asleep in the back of the car, with the doors open to let in the early evening breeze, and went inside to find Helena.

'Hello, darling.' Helena stood upstairs at the door of the empty box room with a broom, dusty but triumphant. 'Isn't it great? It's much bigger than I thought. I reckon we can easily get a double bed in here. Alexis says there's one in a spare room of his we can borrow.'

'Oh. Good.'

'It needs a coat of paint, of course, but it's got such a lovely view of the mountains and the floor isn't tiled, just boards, so I thought we could varnish them eventually.'

'Great,' said William. 'So, your friend's been helping you.'

'Yes, he came over with his truck about an hour ago. He's put all the boxes I want to look through in the out-house, and the rubbish on the truck to take to the dump.'

William nodded. 'I'm sure he's been very helpful, but you could have asked me to move those boxes, you know.'

'You weren't here, William, and Alexis offered, that's all.'

William didn't reply. He turned and walked back along the corridor towards the stairs.

'You're not cross, are you?' she called after him.

'No.' William disappeared down the stairs.

Helena thumped the door frame. 'Oh, for goodness' sake! You were the one who suggested I call him,' she muttered under her breath as she followed him downstairs to find Alexis standing in the kitchen.

'All is done. I will go now to the dump to take the rubbish.'

'Will you not stay for a drink with us?'

'No, thank you. I will see you soon.'

'Yes. And thank you so much, once again.'

Alexis smiled, nodded and left through the back door.

Having removed two grumpy, tired children from the car, fed them, then put them on the sofa in the drawing room in front of a DVD, Helena poured herself a glass of wine and went out onto the terrace. She could hear Alex splashing around in the pool, and saw William leaning on the balustrade at the end of the terrace. She sat down under the pergola, not inclined to announce her presence. Finally he turned towards her and walked back across the terrace to sit beside her.

'Sorry, Helena, that was churlish of me. It just feels odd, that's all, another man doing stuff that I'd usually do. I feel as though I've entered your world here and I don't belong.'

'Darling, you've been here less than a day. You're still adjusting to the place.'

'No, it's more than that,' he sighed. 'This is your kingdom, your house, your life from another time. Whether it's true or not, that's how I feel.'

'You don't like it here?'

'I think it's beautiful, but . . .' William shook his head. 'I need a drink. One moment.' He disappeared inside, and came back with a bottle and a glass.

'Top-up?'

Helena nodded, and he refilled her glass.

'This wine really is very drinkable. Your friend obviously knows what he's doing.'

'His name is Alexis, William, and yes, he does, but then, he was taught from the cradle.'

'Well . . . I suppose we should have him round for supper to thank him properly.'

'There really is no need.'

'Yes, there is. To be frank,' he said, taking another sip of wine, 'I'm probably uptight about tomorrow.'

'You mean Chloë's arrival?'

'Yes. This daughter of mine, whom I no longer know, who's only been taught what a shit I am . . . I have no idea how she'll be, but I'm as sure as hell that it wasn't her idea to come here. She's bound to be resentful about being shipped off to us, so her mother is free to be romanced in France without her. She might be very difficult, Helena. And' – William took a sip of his wine – 'I wouldn't blame her if she was.'

'I'm sure we'll deal with it, darling. And there'll be a lot of people here, which should dilute any tension.'

'Of which there's bound to be lots, from all sorts of angles.'

'We'll cope.' Helena reached for his hand, and squeezed it. 'We always do.'

'Yes, but . . .' William sighed. 'I had hoped that we might not just "cope". That this summer would be a chance for us to have some *fun*.'

'And I don't see why we can't. We've certainly got an interesting cast of characters on the guest list.'

'Have you heard from Sadie yet, by the way?'

'Yes. She arrives on the same flight as the Chandlers. I'm going to see if they can give her a lift here from the airport.'

'Christ!' William managed a wry smile. 'The notorious Jules and her browbeaten spouse, not to mention Rupes and Viola, a suicidal Sadie . . . and a daughter I hardly know.'

'Well, if you put it like that, it does sound completely

ghastly,' agreed Helena. 'Shall we give up and go home now?'

'You're right. I'm being negative, forgive me. By the way, have you mentioned anything about Chloë's imminent arrival to Immy and Fred?' William asked her.

'No. I've told Alex, but I rather thought you'd like to be the one to tell the little ones.'

'Right. I'd better get a move on, then. Any ideas as to how I put it to them?' he asked.

'Casually, I suppose, like it's no big deal. And remember that blood is thicker than water. Chloë is their half-sister, and they share fifty per cent of their genes.'

'You're right. It's just the other fifty per cent of Chloë that worries me. What if she's like her mother?'

'Then God help us all. How about we tell Immy and Fred together?'

'Yes.' William nodded his head gratefully. 'Thanks, Helena.'

The two little ones were, as Helena expected, unperturbed by the impending arrival of the sister they'd never met.

'Is she nice, Daddy?' asked Immy as she snuggled on William's knee. 'What does she look like?'

'Well, everyone used to say that Chloë looked like me.'

'She has short brown hair and big ears? Ugghh!'

'Thanks, sweetheart.' William kissed the top of his daughter's head. 'She's far prettier than I am, I promise.'

'Is Cowee comin' to live forever with us?' enquired Fred from under the table, where he was playing with one of his trucks.

'It's Chloë, Fred,' corrected Helena. 'No, just for the time we're here in Cyprus.'

'Does she live by herself, then?'

'No, she lives with her mummy,' explained William.

'No she don't, 'cos I never seen her in our house.'

'She has a different mummy to you, darling.' Helena knew it was pointless trying to rationalise the situation to a three-year-old. 'Anyway, time for sleep, chaps.'

The usual chorus of complaints ensued, but finally, both of them were tucked up in their beds next to each other. Helena kissed them gently on their sweetly sweaty foreheads.

'Night-night – don't let the bed bugs bite.' She pulled the door to behind her and bumped into Alex on the landing, taking his rucksack downstairs to his new sleeping quarters.

'Hi, Mum, okay?'

'Yes. You?'

'Yup.'

'You didn't have to move out until tomorrow, you know. Dad's not collecting Chloë until after lunch. That's plenty of time to change the sheets and get the room straight in the morning.'

'I want to.' He started down the stairs.

'Okay. I put a fan in there for you earlier. I don't want you getting heat-stroke again.'

'Thanks.' Alex stopped and looked up at her. 'Are you going to look through those boxes in the outhouse?'

'Yes, when I have time, which certainly won't be for the next few days.'

'Can I?'

'As long as you don't throw anything away.'

''Course I won't. You know me, Mum, I love history. Especially my own,' he added pointedly.

'But Alex' – Helena ignored the remark – 'a lot of it won't mean anything to you. Remember, Angus wasn't related to me. He was my godfather.'

'Still, I might find out things about him, which would be interesting, wouldn't they?'

'Yes, of course.' Helena didn't fail to notice the underlying sentiment. Alex was looking for clues, but she knew he wouldn't find any amongst Angus' boxes. 'Go ahead, but I don't want you festering away in there all day tomorrow. We have guests coming, and I'll need your help.'

'Course. Night, Mum,' he said, as they reached his new bedroom.

'Night, darling,' she replied, as Alex closed the door.

ALEX'S DIARY

15th July 2006

I am sitting on the bed in my tiny cell. The fan my mother has equipped me with is close enough to give me a blow-dry in one minute flat. In front of me is a box I have just dragged in from the outhouse, filled with letters and photographs, which may or may not be relevant to me and my past.

My mother is not stupid. She knows what I am searching for. She knows how much I want to know . . .

Who I Am.

Well, she didn't act as though she was worried that any key to the great mystery might be lurking in those boxes, so there's probably nothing of interest amongst Angus' stuff.

I wonder why she's so cagey about her own past? She hardly ever talks about her mother and father, or where she grew up, or how. She gave a lot of information out about it earlier today, for her.

It made me realise how most kids I know have a granny and grandpa present in their lives, or at least a strong memory of them. All I know for certain is that Helena Elise Beaumont is my mother and I was born in Vienna (she couldn't hide that as it's written on my birth certificate) and I lived there until I was three, after which she met Dad, then we came back to England and they got married. Apparently, I was a bilingual toddler. Nowadays, I struggle to count to ten in German correctly.

I lie back with my head resting on my arms and stare at the cracked, yellowing ceiling above me. And muse that my friend Jake – I use that term loosely, in that we communicate occasionally and he is less of a moron than the rest of them in my class – has a mother who is comfortably plump and homely-looking, like most mums with teenage sons seem to be. She works part-time as a secretary at a doctor's surgery and makes great cakes when I've been round for tea, and everything about her is . . .

. . . normal.

Her whole life is photographically displayed on the sideboard, side by side with her freshly baked scones. Jake knows all about his grandparents, and who his father is, as he sees him every day. The only mystery he has to solve is how to persuade his mum to lend him a tenner so he can buy the latest PlayStation game.

So why is my mother, and my past, such an enigma?

I breathe deeply and realise I am starting to seriously obsess again. Apparently, it's a normal characteristic for someone like me. A 'gifted' child. I loathe being a statistic, and do my best not to conform to it, but sometimes it's hard. To take my mind off things, I sit upright and begin to pull endless sepia photos of unknown people who are now almost certainly dead out of the box. Some of them have dates on the back, some don't.

Angus was very good-looking when he was younger, especially dressed in his uniform. I'm surprised he never married. Unless he was gay. He doesn't look it, but you never can tell. I've often wondered how you know if you are. I might be weird, but I'm definitely straight, in a bendy sort of way.

I have finally got to the bottom of the box, waded through the mounds of photographs and correspondence concerning shipments of whisky from Southampton and import duty on this painting or that piece of furniture. Then I pull out a bulging brown envelope addressed to 'Colonel McCladden' at Pandora and reach my hand inside it.

Out flutters a large number of flimsy blue airmail envelopes. I peer into one, and see its contents are still intact. I remove the letter and see there is a date at the top, *12th December*, but no year or address.

I read the first line:

'My darling, darling girl.'

Right. It doesn't take Holmes and Watson to deduce that this is a love letter. The writing is beautiful, in ink, scripted in the fluid way people were taught in those days.

I scan through it. It's a eulogy to an unknown woman known as 'Darling Girl' throughout. Lots of *'the days are endless without you and I long to have you back in my arms . . .'*

Not really my type of thing, all this soppiness. I'm more of a thriller man, myself. Or Freud.

Most irritating of all, when I reach the end, there is no signature, just an indecipherable flourish that could be any of perhaps twelve letters.

I put the letter back in its envelope and open a couple more. They read in a similar vein and reveal no more clues as to time or identity than the first one.

I look inside the big brown envelope to check it's empty, and find a folded piece of paper.

'I believe these letters are your property. As such, am returning to sender.'

That is all.

So the author of these was obviously Angus. Which would also solve one puzzle and confirm he was definitely not gay.

I yawn. I am tired tonight, having lugged all those boxes around in the heat. I will give these letters to my mother tomorrow morning. They are definitely more her kind of thing than mine.

I switch off the light and lie on my back, pulling Bee from under my pillow and placing him in the crook of my arm. I enjoy the breeze from the fan wafting across my face and wonder how a man such as Angus could command armies and shoot people, yet write letters like those at the same time?

It's a mystery to me so far – this 'love' thing – but I daresay I'll find out what it's like.

One day.

ζ

Seven

Where the *hell* was she?

William ran his fingers through his hair in agitation.

The plane had landed over an hour ago. Passengers had streamed out of arrivals and now the concourse was eerily quiet.

He tried Helena on her mobile, but she wasn't answering. He'd dropped her off with the kids at a local hire-car firm in Paphos, as it had been decided they would definitely need a car each. She'd said she might take the children to the beach. William left her a message to call him back urgently, then, having made another sweep of the arrivals area, he headed for the flight information desk.

'Hello, I'm wondering whether you could check if my daughter was on the morning flight from Gatwick. I'm here to collect her and she hasn't turned up yet.'

The woman nodded. 'Name?'

'Chloë Cooke, with an "e".'

The woman tapped on the computer, scrolled down and

finally looked up at him. 'No, sir. There was no one by that name on the flight.'

'Christ,' William swore under his breath. 'Is it possible to check if she arrived on another flight from the UK today?'

'I can try, but we have several, from regional airports around the country.'

'Has there been a flight from Stansted so far?' William followed a hunch.

'Yes, it landed half an hour before the Gatwick flight.'

'Okay, could you try that?'

More tapping, and the woman finally looked up and nodded. 'Yes, a Miss C. Cooke was on the Stansted flight.'

'Thank you.'

William walked away from the desk, a mixture of relief and anger coursing round his veins. His ex-wife had obviously changed the arrangements without letting him know. *Par for the course for her*, he thought furiously. He stifled his anger and went in search of his daughter.

Twenty minutes later, and on the verge of alerting the airport police to an abducted minor, William stumbled on a small bar next to the arrivals hall.

It was empty, apart from a teenage girl and a dark-haired young man sitting together smoking on bar stools. From a distance, he saw the girl had a mane of long, shiny chestnut hair. She wore a tight T-shirt and a miniskirt on her sylph-like frame, her endlessly long bare legs crossed as she flipped a flat pump on and off one heel. As he drew closer, he realised it was Chloë: a Chloë who in the past few years had changed beyond all recognition from a child into a beautiful young woman.

William recognised his daughter's allure, as – obviously – did the man sitting opposite her. He was resting a hand lightly on Chloë's bare thigh. William moved swiftly towards them, realising the man was older than he looked from a distance. Squashing down the primal urge to thump him, he stopped a few yards away.

'Hello, Chloë.'

She turned, saw him and smiled lazily. 'Hi, Daddy. How are you?'

Blatantly taking a last drag of her cigarette, she stubbed it out as William walked forward and kissed her formally on the cheek.

Like the stranger she was.

'Meet Christoff. He's been keeping me company while I was waiting for you.' Chloë turned her enormous, fawn-like brown eyes back to her suitor. 'He's been telling me all the cool places to go clubbing round here.'

'Good. Now let's go.'

'Okay.' Chloë slid elegantly off the bar stool. 'I've got your mobile number, Christoff. I'll give you a call and you can show me the sights of Paphos.'

The man nodded wordlessly, and gave a small salute as Chloë followed William out of the bar.

'Where's your suitcase?' he asked her, looking down at the small holdall she was carrying.

'I haven't brought one,' she answered airily. 'I won't need more than a couple of bikinis and a few sarongs here anyway. It's cool to travel light.'

'I'm sorry I wasn't here to meet your flight. Your mum gave me the wrong details, obviously,' he said as he led her out into the bright sunlight and towards the car.

'We thought we'd be in London, but then we ended up at the cottage in Blakeney and Mum discovered I could fly here from Stansted. She tried ringing you to let you know, but she couldn't get hold of you.'

William knew his mobile had been with him permanently, on red-alert for the usual last-minute change of arrangements that came hand in hand with collecting Chloë. He swallowed, knowing it was probably only the first of numerous occasions on which he'd have to bite his tongue for the sake of *détente*.

'I looked for you everywhere at the airport when I arrived, you know. It was only luck that took me into that bar. You're meant to be eighteen to go in, Chloë, I saw it on the door.'

'Oh well, you found me in the end. Is this your car?'

'Yes.' William opened the door.

'Wow, a people carrier.'

'I'm afraid so. There are a lot of us. Hop in.'

Chloë threw her holdall on the back seat, put her hands under her chestnut hair to draw it away from her swan-like neck, and yawned. 'I'm wrecked. I had to get up at half past three this morning. The flight left at seven.'

'Did Mum take you to the airport?'

'God, no. You know what she's like first thing in the morning. She booked me a taxi.' She turned to him and smiled. 'I'm a big girl now, Daddy.'

'You're fourteen, Chloë, and two years off the legal smoking limit, I might add.' William turned the key, started the engine and pulled the car out of the space.

'Fifteen next month, actually, so chill, Daddy. I only have the occasional ciggy. I'm not addicted or anything.'

'Well, that's okay then,' replied William, knowing his daughter would miss his irony. 'So, how's school?'

'Oh, you know, school really. I can't wait to leave.'

'And do what?' William was painfully aware that normally, a parent would *know* the answer to this question. The thought depressed him further.

'Dunno yet. I might go travelling, then do some modelling.'

'Right.'

'I've already been spotted by an agency, but Mum says I have to get my GCSEs first.'

'She's right. You do.'

'Girls start modelling at twelve now. I'll be past it at sixteen,' Chloë sighed.

William chuckled. 'Hardly, Chloë.'

'Well, you'll both be sorry one day, when you've lost me my chance of making shedloads of money and getting famous.'

'Your mum has told you about Immy and Fred, hasn't she?' William changed the subject.

'You mean my two baby siblings? Yeah, 'course she has.'

'How do you feel about meeting them?'

'Cool. I mean, we're not exactly unusual, are we? My best friend Gaia is the daughter of a rock star – Mike someone – he was really famous back in your day, and she has so many steps and halves she's lost count. Her dad's in his sixties and his girlfriend is expecting again.'

'I'm glad you feel normal, Chloë, that's good.'

'Yeah. As Gaia says, having divorced and remarried

parents is especially good at Christmas, 'cos they all buy you presents to win you over.'

'That's an . . . unusual way of looking at it,' William gulped. 'Helena's looking forward to seeing you again.'

'Is she?'

'Yes, and Alex, her son. Remember him?'

'Not really.'

'Well, I'm warning you that Alex is an unusual boy. He's been assessed as "gifted", which means he can come across as a bit odd. But he isn't. He's just got an intellect way beyond his years.'

'You mean he's a nerd?'

'No, he's just . . .' William struggled to find the words to explain his stepson. 'Different. The Chandlers, old family friends, are coming too, as is Sadie, Helena's best friend, so there's a houseful. It should be fun.'

There was no response from Chloë. William looked across at her and saw she was fast asleep.

No one was at home when he pulled the car into the drive at Pandora. He shook Chloë gently.

'We're here.'

Chloë opened her eyes and stretched lazily. She looked at her father. 'What time is it?'

'Ten past four. Come on, I'll show you the view.'

''Kay.' Chloë climbed out of the car and followed her father round the side of the house and onto the terrace.

'Cool,' she said with an approving nod.

'I'm glad you like it. Helena inherited the house from her godfather, so some of the interior needs updating,' added William, as Chloë stepped through the French windows into the drawing room.

'I think it's perfect just the way it is, like something out of an Agatha Christie movie,' said Chloë. 'Is there a pool?'

'Yes, just through the gate to the left of the terrace.'

'Great. I'll go for a swim, then.' Chloë promptly took off her T-shirt and skirt to reveal the skimpiest of bikinis underneath, and sashayed outside.

William watched her glide across the terrace and sat down heavily in a chair under the pergola.

Either Chloë was a consummate actress, or the fears he'd had about her attitude towards him were unfounded. He'd spent the past week rehearsing what he'd say to her when she accused him of deserting her, not loving her . . . preparing for the clusters of emotional mines that must have been carefully placed by her mother.

She was, in her own words, 'cool'. So cool, William realised, that perhaps her indifference towards him hurt just as much as the ingrained hatred he'd been expecting. She didn't seem to *care* that she hadn't seen him for almost six years.

But, he mused, could a fourteen-year-old really be as confident as Chloë seemed? Or was this all an act, to protect the frightened little girl beneath the veneer of self-assurance? William was painfully aware of his limitations as to the workings of the female mind. There was only one thing to do: he'd ask Helena when she returned.

Her new rental car drew up ten minutes later, spilling the guts of his family messily onto the terrace.

'Hi, Daddy!' Immy jumped into his arms. 'I made a big sandcastle then Fred knocked it over. I hate him.'

'I'll kill you!' Fred appeared on the terrace with a plastic water pistol.

Immy screamed and buried her face in William's shoulder. 'Get him away!'

'Put that down, Fred. You're frightening Immy.'

'No I not. She kill me on the beach first.' He nodded ferociously. 'Where Cowee?'

'*Chloë*, Fred.' Helena was draping wet beach towels over the balustrade. 'And yes, where is she?'

'In the pool,' William said, putting Immy down.

'*How* is she?' Helena asked him under her breath.

'Fine, absolutely fine. I think you'll find she's grown up a little since we last saw her. In *all* sorts of ways,' William said with a grimace.

Helena saw Alex lurking on the edge of the terrace, trying to peer through the olive trees down to the pool without looking as if he was. 'Well, shall we all go and say hello to her?'

'No need. I'm here.'

Chloë appeared on the terrace, her lithe body still glistening with droplets of water from her swim, and walked towards Helena. 'Hi there.' She kissed her on both cheeks. 'Love your house.'

'Thank you,' said Helena with a smile.

'And these two are my little sis and bruv, are they? Come and say hello, then,' she encouraged.

Immy and Fred were both staring silently at the exotic, long-limbed creature, and didn't move.

'Oh, they're so cute! Immy's the image of you, Helena, and Fred looks just like Daddy.' She walked towards them and knelt down. 'Hello, I'm Chloë, your big and very bad long-lost sister.'

'Daddy said you looked like him, but you don't have

big ears and you have lovely long hair,' Immy offered shyly.

Chloë smiled up at William. 'Right, that's okay then.' She reached out her hand to Immy. 'Will you show me round your lovely house?'

'Yes. Mummy and I put flowers in your bedroom,' said Immy, taking Chloë's proffered hand.

'I might have some sweeties in my bag as well.' She glanced back at Fred as Immy led her towards the house.

'Can I come too?' Fred hopped out from behind William, and ran on his plump little legs to join them.

'You're next to me, Chloë,' Immy's high voice could be heard from inside the house.

'And me,' said Fred. 'Where the sweeties, Cowee?'

Helena glanced at William and smiled. 'That wasn't too painful, was it? My goodness, she's pretty.'

'Yes, she is, and in my book, seems far too mature for a fourteen-year-old.'

'She's almost fifteen, don't forget. And girls tend to grow up more quickly than boys, darling. Would you mind terribly getting me a cold drink? I'm parched.'

'Of course, milady. I could do with one too.' William nodded at her, and went inside the house.

Helena turned and saw Alex standing behind her. 'Are you all right? You look as if you've seen a ghost.'

Alex opened his mouth, but no words came out. He shrugged instead.

'You didn't say hello to Chloë, Alex.'

'No,' he managed.

'Why don't you go upstairs with the others?'

He shook his head. 'I'm going to my room for a bit. Think I've got a migraine coming on.'

'Too much sun, probably, darling. Go and have a rest and I'll call you when supper's ready,' Helena suggested. 'Angelina's left us something in the oven that smells delicious.'

Alex grunted and went inside.

'Is he okay?' asked William, after passing Alex on the way out of the house, carrying two clinking glasses of iced lemonade. Helena was the only one able to divine Alex's mood.

'I think so.'

As William sat down, Helena walked behind him and massaged his shoulders. 'By the way, I only got your voice-message when we came up from the beach. Was everything okay at the airport?'

'Cecile changed Chloë's flight and didn't bother to tell me, that's all. I found her in the bar, eventually, smoking a fag with some slimy Cypriot she'd picked up en route.'

'Oh dear,' Helena sighed, flopping into a chair beside him and taking a sip of lemonade. 'Well, she's here now. She didn't seem at all perturbed by meeting us. She was as cool as a cucumber just then.'

'Can it be real, or is it all an act?' William shook his head. 'I just don't know.'

'Well, the good news is that she's obviously child-friendly. Immy and Fred took to her immediately. And I certainly didn't get the feeling she was harbouring some deep-seated loathing for you,' Helena added.

'If she isn't, I'm amazed, under the circumstances.'

'Darling, most children love their parents unconditionally, whatever they've done – or not done. Chloë's obviously a bright girl. If her mother's been metaphorically twisting a knife in your back, she'll understand why.'

'I hope so. At least these few weeks will give me a chance to establish a relationship with her, just in case I don't see her again until her twenty-first,' William replied morosely.

'Chloë's getting to be a big girl now. And no matter what her mother might do or say, she's going to start making her own decisions, which could well include having you in her life again when *she* wants it, not just to suit her mother's romances.'

'Let's hope so. Now, somehow, I have to adjust to a child I hardly know. The problem is, she isn't a child anymore, and I've no idea how far her mother lets her go or what her boundaries are. What if she wants to go out with this Cypriot she picked up at the airport? They were talking about meeting up. I don't want to come on like the heavy-handed father after not seeing her for years, but on the other hand, she is only fourteen.'

'I understand, but Kathikas is hardly the clubbing centre of Europe,' Helena comforted with a smile. 'I doubt she'll get into too much trouble up here.'

'Where there's men, Chloë is trouble,' sighed William. 'The local boys will be onto her like bees round a honey pot. The thought of some boy getting his slimy paws on my daughter . . .' He shuddered.

'A normal fatherly reaction, because you know what *you* were like when you were younger,' Helena chuckled as she stood up. 'Right, while I sort out supper, how about you go upstairs and rally the younger troops into the bath?

Chloë must be starving, and I thought it would be nice for us all to eat together.'

'Okay. I'm on my way.'

'Is Alex coming out?' Chloë asked Helena as she placed the piping-hot casserole dish on the table.

'No. He says he's got a migraine. He gets them regularly, poor thing.'

'That's a shame. He hasn't even said hello to me yet,' Chloë commented, managing to balance both Immy and Fred on her insubstantial lap. 'When I arrived, he just kind of . . . stared at me and didn't speak.'

'He'll be fine tomorrow after a good night's sleep. This smells divine.' Helena unwrapped the protective layers of waxed paper that covered the contents of the casserole dish, and began to serve the food onto plates. 'Angelina told me it's *kleftiko*, a kind of slow-cooked lamb.'

'Like Lamby sort of lamb?' questioned Immy. 'Nope, I can't eat it.' She shook her head and crossed her small arms across her chest. 'It might be Lamby's mummy or daddy.'

'Don't be silly, Immy, you know perfectly well Lamby is a toy. He's not real. Now sit down in your chair and eat your supper like a big girl,' snapped William.

Immy's bottom lip quivered as she slid off Chloë's knee. 'Lamby *is* real, Daddy.'

'Course he's real, sweetie.' Chloë stroked Immy's hair and settled her sister in the chair next to her. 'Horrid Daddy.'

'Yes, horrid Daddy,' agreed Immy triumphantly.

'Can you pour me a glass, Daddy?' asked Chloë, as William opened a bottle of wine.

William looked uncertainly at Helena.

'Does your mum let you have wine at home?' Helena asked her.

''Course she does. She's French, remember?'

'Okay, just a small glass then,' agreed William.

'Get real, Daddy. I was champion Bacardi Breezer drinker at the end-of-term ball at school.'

'Well, that beats winning the geography prize any day,' William muttered under his breath. 'Right, let's eat.'

After a relatively calm supper, the two little ones insisted Chloë take them upstairs and read them a story.

'And after that, I'm going to see Alex, say hi, then crash,' Chloë said as she was pulled by both arms inside. 'Night, guys.'

'Night, Chloë.' Helena stood up and began stacking the dirty dishes onto a tray. 'She's lovely, William, and so good with the little ones. And it's great to have an extra pair of hands.'

William yawned. 'Yes, she is. Let's leave the rest for tomorrow. I need to "crash" too. What time are Sadie and the Chandlers arriving?'

'Mid-afternoon, so we've got plenty of time.'

'Maybe even enough to have an hour by the pool. You never know your luck, do you, Helena . . . Helena?'

She pulled her attention back to her husband. 'Sorry, what did you say?'

'Nothing important. Are you all right?'

She answered with the warmest smile she could muster. 'Yes, darling, I'm absolutely fine.'

ALEX'S DIARY

16th July 2006

I take back all that I said in my last diary entry.

All of it. Every last word, thought and deed.

The 'one day' turned out to be TODAY: July 16th, at approximately twenty-three minutes past four.

The moment I Fell In Love.

Oh shit! I feel ill. I am now diseased. My heart, which has done a jolly good job of pumping the blood round my veins for the past thirteen years, has thrown a wobbly. It has let something in. And this 'something' is insidious. I can feel it swelling and growing and sending its tentacles round my body, paralysing me, making me sweat, shiver, lose control of . . . *me*.

I realise, only a few hours into this 'change of heart', that it no longer takes its lead from my physical body. It does not operate according to how fast or slow I am walking. It responds violently, pumping away, even though I am lying still, because I have thought about her: the Chloë person.

Forget Aphrodite, forget the Mona Lisa (who has a bad

receding hairline problem anyway), or Kate Moss. MY girl is mossier than the mossiest moss.

It's at it again – my heart – pounding the blood round my body as if I have just won the marathon or been attacked by a shark and left with bits of me hanging off.

The minute I think of her, it happens.

In fact, all sorts of things happen, but I don't think I'll go into those now.

At least I know for certain I'm not gay. Or saddled with an Oedipus complex.

I am loveSICK. I need a note from the doctor to sign me off from life until I have recovered.

But do you? Ever recover, I mean? Some don't, I hear. I might be like this for life.

I mean, for Chrissakes, I haven't even opened my mouth to speak to her yet. Although that's partly to do with my lips refusing to move when I'm in her presence. And there's no way I could eat in front of her, and try and talk at the same time. That would be too much. So, it looks like I might go seriously hungry this holiday. Or do a good line in midnight feasts.

How will I cope with seeing her every day, her butter-soft flesh tantalisingly close, but untouchable?

Besides, she's a relative, but at least she's not blood, so relatively speaking, it could be worse. I think it would be quite cool to tell the boys, 'Hey, I'm in love with my sister,' and watch their reaction.

As I stared at her today, and the heart-thing started, I could see she *did* look like Dad. And I thought how amazing genes are, to have morphed from him (male, average-looking, old, but at least with hair) to her: the ultimate female. She is simply perfection.

I take off my T-shirt and my boxers, but put my socks on. I've been bitten viciously on the ankles and the mozzies are not getting me tonight. I pull out the pair of 10 denier tights that I bought today from a supermarket near the beach Mum took us to. The woman who took my money gave me strange looks, but I don't care.

I open the packet and stretch the tights, feeling smug at my brainwave. I pull the thing they call a gusset onto my head and down over my face, and hit the pillow in triumph. I can breathe perfectly through them because they are sheer and it means that finally, I have foiled those little buggers for good.

As an added bonus, I realise that – like the stocking-masked villains in bank-heist movies – I can also *see* through the gauzy fabric. I promptly root under my bed for the envelope full of letters. I didn't give them to Mum this morning because she was so busy. And now my state of mind has changed so dramatically in the past twenty-four hours that I will look at these letters through new eyes.

I select a letter at random, insert my earphones beneath the stretchy nylon covering my head, and switch on my iPod. Then I lie back to enjoy spending time with someone whose heart obviously once beat as fast as mine has since I set eyes on Chloë.

For a few seconds, to the sound of Coldplay, which I rarely listen to but seems to suit my new mood better than Sum 41, I close my eyes, indulge myself and picture her in my mind.

When I finally open my eyes, I see I am not just picturing her in my mind. She is standing right there in front of me!

Crap!!

Her mouth is moving but I can't hear what she's saying because of the iPod. I switch it off, then realise to my horror I am bollock naked apart from my socks. I sit up and pull the sheet around me.

'Hi, Alex, I'm Chloë. I just came to say hello.' She smiles at me lazily.

Come on, you dick, make your lips move! I lick them with my tongue to give them encouragement, and manage a strangled 'Miiii.'

She is gazing at me very strangely. I've no idea why.

'You feeling better now? Headache gone?'

I nod. 'Yeah,' and then carry on nodding.

'I wanted to say thanks for letting me have your room. Immy told me. You sure you're okay in here? It's the size of a broom cupboard.'

'Yeah, fwine.' I nod some more. It's like an uncontrollable yet comforting twitch.

'Okay, well, maybe we could catch up tomorrow, yeah?'

'Yeah. Gweat.'

Oh crap! I can't stop nodding! Just call my best friend Big Ears . . .

'Night, then,' she says.

'Nwight.'

She's about to shut the door when she pauses and asks, 'You got earache or something?'

I give up and shake my head instead of nodding it.

'Just a headache?'

Back to nodding.

'Oh.'

She's nodding too now as she turns to leave, but then says, ''Cos I was just wondering . . .'

'Wop?'

'Whether that's why you're wearing a pair of tights on your head. Night, Alex.'

η

Eight

Helena woke filled with unease as the dawn rose the following morning. She willed herself to go back to sleep, because the day ahead would be so long, but the unsolicited thoughts crowding into her head made displacement activity vital. So finally she clambered out of bed, dressed in her practice clothes and let herself out onto the terrace.

The sun was rising slowly and sleepily as Helena warmed up with some *pliés*, using the balustrade as a barre, thinking how inappropriate it would be to mix sunrise colours in a room, yet how they seemed to meld so exquisitely together in the sky. She bent forwards, brushing the stone floor of the terrace with her fingertips, straightening then bending backwards as her arm formed a graceful arc above her head. When she was dancing, the physical movement of her body calmed her mind, enabling her to think more rationally.

This morning, she didn't know where to start.

What *should* she think?

A few weeks ago, the thought of coming here to Pandora with her family had been a wonderful one. Since then, circumstances had led to the state of high anxiety in which she found herself this morning. At this particular moment, it was all she could do not to run away; from her past and her present, and the ramifications of both on her future.

How she longed to unburden herself, to finally tell William and Alex, and remove the source of the pressure that lay upon her chest, day in, day out . . . but she knew that was impossible.

It would destroy everything.

So . . . she would do as she always had. And cope with the secrets alone.

She executed an *arabesque*, wondering grimly for how much longer her body would be capable of performing such fluid, easy movement. When she'd been younger, she'd had everything in her favour to achieve her dream of becoming a ballerina; a strong yet graceful, flexible physique that rarely let her down, a musicality that allowed her instinctively to interpret the notes, *and* the more unusual skill, which marked her out from the others: her considerable talent as an actress.

She'd risen swiftly through the ranks at the Royal Ballet, her name recognised across Europe as a talent to watch. She'd been wooed by the La Scala ballet in Milan, then at twenty-five, she'd moved with Fabio, her dance partner, to become a principal dancer at the renowned Vienna State Opera Company Ballet.

And then . . .

Helena sighed.

She had fallen in love. And everything had changed.

'Are you all right, Helena? You look tired. Couldn't you sleep?'

William stood behind her in the kitchen half an hour later, regarding her thoughtfully.

'I was thinking of all the things I have to do before the Chandlers and Sadie arrive, so I thought I'd get up and do them. I'd also like to plant out the flowers we bought at the garden centre before the sun gets too hot. I haven't had a chance yet and I'm worried they'll die if I leave them in their pots for much longer.' Helena retrieved the breakfast cereal from the cupboard and began to pile bowls onto a tray to take to the terrace.

'Darling, I feel very guilty. Not only have I foisted Chloë on you, but Jules and Co., too.'

'Hardly. Jules rang up and invited herself,' Helena said.

'I know she can be difficult, but Sacha's having a really rough time at the moment. Things aren't going at all well for him, business-wise.'

'Aren't they?'

'No. Look, darling, I promise I'll help out as much as I can. I thought Angelina was coming in today?'

'She is. I want her to make supper and give the bathrooms a once-over. You know how fussy Jules is.'

William walked over to his wife and massaged her shoulders. 'Christ, you're tense, Helena. Do try and remember that this *is* supposed to be a holiday.'

'I will. It's just with everyone arriving today, there's so much to do.'

'I know, but there's lots of us here too. You just have to ask us.'

'Yes,' she answered with a wan smile. 'Right, I'm going

upstairs to sort out towels. Could you give Immy and Fred their breakfast? Although I know Fred has already found the sweetie cupboard, because I found a trail of wrappers on the floor.'

William nodded. 'Of course. And if you want, I'll take them both out for a bit to get them out of your hair. We'll go exploring. I'd like to see a little more of the area anyway.'

'Thanks, darling, that would be a help.'

'Helena?'

'Yes?' She paused in the doorway.

He looked at his wife, then sighed and shrugged his shoulders. 'Nothing.'

She nodded at him and made her way upstairs.

By four that afternoon, the house was ready. Helena had even managed to hurriedly plant out the geraniums in the urns on the terrace and made a start on weeding the over-grown flower bed by the pool, ready for the lavender to go in. She switched on the kettle, arms aching with tiredness, and while it was boiling, went to find Alex. He'd announced he still had a migraine earlier that morning and had not emerged from his room all day. She knocked on his door, then opened it quietly, in case he was asleep. He was reading on his bed.

'Hi, darling. How are you feeling?'

'Okay.'

'Should you be reading if you have a headache?' queried Helena. 'And why don't you open the window? It's incredibly stuffy in here.'

'NO!'

'No need to shout. I was only making a suggestion.'

'Yup. Sorry, Mum.'

'And if it's to stop the mozzies, you're just being plain ridiculous. They don't come out until dusk.'

'I know that.'

'How's the head?'

'About seven out of ten, i.e. a bit better.'

'Then why don't you come and have a cup of tea with me outside?'

Alex looked at her nervously. 'Where's Chloë?'

'Down by the pool.'

'No thanks. I'll stay here.'

Helena sighed. 'Is there anything else wrong?'

'No. Why should there be?'

'Because you've been strange ever since Chloë arrived, that's why. She hasn't said anything to upset you, has she?'

'No, Mum! Really! I've just got a headache, that's all, please!'

'All right, Alex, I'm only trying to help.'

'God, Mum, you're really stressy today.'

'I'm not!'

'You are. What's up?'

'Nothing. I'll expect you out on parade when the Chandlers arrive.'

Alex nodded reluctantly. 'Okay, see you later.' And he buried his nose back in his book.

Helena wandered out onto the terrace with her tea, trying to regain some equilibrium, and gazed through the olive trees to see Chloë stretched out on her sunbed by the pool, headphones in her ears. She really was incredibly beautiful, her long limbs already suggesting she'd inherited her father's height. Although physically, Helena thought she resembled her mother, with her immaculate bone structure and straight, glossy hair. Cecile, William's ex-wife, had all the inbuilt elegance and arrogance that seemed to come hand in hand with Gallic ancestry.

There was no doubt William was drawn to challenging women. Even though he might outwardly present as straightforward, being an architect encapsulated his need for structure, but also, his creative flair and eye for beauty. And even though he might deny it, she knew he found mediocrity just as difficult as she did.

If only William knew just *what* a challenge he'd unwittingly taken on, she thought ruefully. But he didn't, and he hopefully never would, God willing . . .

The crunch of gravel on the drive told her the Chandlers had arrived. Taking a deep breath, Helena walked across the terrace to greet them.

'Good God, it's hot!' Jules Chandler swung her legs out from behind the steering wheel. She was tall and large-boned, attractive in a rather masculine way. 'Helena, dear, how are you?' Jules grasped her in a neck-lock that masqueraded as a hug.

'I'm fine. Welcome, Jules.' Helena smiled up at her, feeling, as always, waif-like and insubstantial beside her.

'Thanks. Come on, kids, get out,' she barked into the back of the car. 'Bloody awful flight, full of people with shaved heads wearing trainers. The men wore more jewellery than the women.' Jules swept a hand through the mane of thick light-brown hair she always had cut short, so she could run in and out of the shower after taking her habitual early morning ride.

'Hello, sweetie, how are you?' The softer grasp of Sadie, her closest friend, drew Helena into a further hug.

'I'm fine, Sadie. And you look great, for someone with a broken heart.'

'Thank you.' She pulled Helena closer. 'I had a "sod you, you bastard!" Botox sesh last week,' she whispered with a chuckle.

'Well, it looks like it's worked wonders.' Helena felt enormously comforted by Sadie's presence.

'Hi, Auntie Helena.' The recently acquired deep voice of Rupert, Jules' son, took her by surprise. As did his height and athletic physique, which gave the impression of the archetypal sportsman.

'Goodness! You've grown, Rupes,' she said as he leant his white-blond head down to kiss her.

'I'm thirteen now, Auntie Helena. I'm meant to grow.'

And so is my son. But he is physically still a child and you are already a man, she thought.

'Hi, Auntie Helena.' A pair of thin, white freckled arms wound round her neck and hugged her tight.

'Viola, darling.' Helena returned her hug. 'I think you've grown too!'

'No, I haven't. I'm exactly the same size, and they still call me "Ginger" at school, but what can you do?' Viola's small freckled nose wrinkled and she smiled, showing a protruding set of front teeth.

'Well, we all know you're strawberry blonde, and that they're all going to be so jealous when you're older and never need expensive highlights.'

'Oh Auntie Helena, that's what you always say,' giggled Viola.

'I say it because it's true, isn't it, Sadie?'

'Absolutely,' Sadie said firmly. 'I would kill for your hair colour, truly, sweetie.'

'Where's Daddy, Viola?' Helena asked as she peered into the car, confused.

Jules gave a snort, which sounded rather like the horses she owned. 'You may well ask. My dear husband isn't here, obviously.'

'Where is he, then?' asked Helena.

'At this moment? Probably propping up a bar some-where in the City of London.'

'You mean he isn't in Cyprus?'

'No. Something came up with work and he cried off at the last moment. Bloody typical.'

'Is he coming at all?'

'Tomorrow apparently, but I wouldn't bank on it. We don't bank on Daddy anymore, do we, kids?'

'Mummy, don't be so mean! It's not Daddy's fault he has to work so hard.' Viola, a pure daddy's girl, defended her father.

Jules raised her eyebrows at Helena. 'Anyway, I'm sure you can understand why I'm seriously pissed off.'

'I can.' Helena nodded faintly.

'And where is the adorable William?' asked Sadie.

'Out exploring with his two adorable children,' replied Helena.

'You do have him well trained. I struggle to get Sacha to come to Speech Day,' boomed Jules as she opened the boot to retrieve her luggage. 'I'll join you in a minute,' she said as the rest of the party began to follow Helena round onto the terrace.

Helena saw Chloë had walked up from the pool, a tiny sarong wrapped round her hips, her skin already turning golden brown from the sun. 'Hi guys, I'm Chloë.'

'I know you are,' said Sadie, walking towards her and kissing her on both cheeks. 'I met you once when you were about six, but you probably don't remember me.'

'No,' said Chloë. 'Isn't this place cool?'

'It's beautiful,' agreed Sadie, looking appreciatively at the view.

'And I'm Rupert, Jules and Sacha's son. Hi, Chloë.'

Chloë looked at Rupes approvingly. 'Hi. You seen the pool yet?'

'No.'

'Want me to show you?'

'Sure. I'd love a dip.'

'Then follow me.'

As the two of them sauntered off towards the pool, Sadie turned and raised her eyebrows at Helena, as Jules lugged one of her enormous suitcases onto the terrace. 'Right, where do I put this?'

Having shown Jules to her room, and Viola to the one she'd share with Rupes, Helena left her before she could lodge a complaint about anything that was not to her liking. Wandering along the corridor to Sadie's room, she found her kneeling up on the bed and staring out of the window.

'The view is just glorious,' she said, turning to Helena with a smile. 'I wish I had a godfather who'd pop his clogs and leave me a house like this.'

'I know. I'm very lucky to have it. Coming down for a drink and a chat?' Helena lowered her voice. 'I think Jules will be some time, given the size of that suitcase.'

'Wouldn't be surprised if she hasn't brought her own wallpaper and paste and redecorated the bedroom by dinner-time,' Sadie sniggered. 'She insisted on taking charge of my passport at the airport,' she added as they walked downstairs. 'I felt like one of her kids.'

'She likes to be in control, that's all. Tea? Or something stronger?' asked Helena as she led Sadie into the kitchen.

'The sun is threatening to pass the yard-arm at any second, so definitely the latter.'

The two of them wandered out onto the terrace with a glass of wine each, and sat down. 'God, I'm glad to be away. Thank you so much for providing this stunning port in my storm.' Sadie clinked her glass against Helena's and took a sip of wine. 'Where's Alex, by the way?'

'In his room, with a migraine.'

'Oh dear. And how is he generally?'

'The same, really.' Helena shrugged.

'How's he feeling about going away to school?'

'He doesn't really mention it. God, Sadie, I just hope I'm doing the right thing.'

'Sweetie, he's won a top academic scholarship to one of the best schools in England. How could you doubt it?'

'Because Alex may have the mind of Einstein, but emotionally and physically he's still very young. I looked at Rupes, who's only four months older than him, and it frightened me. You know how difficult Alex finds it to interact with his peer group anyway. It's hardly going to help if they're all three feet taller than he is. I'm terrified that he might get horribly bullied.'

'Schools these days are down on that like a ton of

bricks. Besides, he might be small for his age, but Alex isn't a wimp, Helena. Don't underestimate him.'

'I also don't want him to turn into an arrogant, upper-class twit.'

'Like Rupes, you mean?' Sadie said with a wry smile.

'Exactly. And also, I shall miss him terribly,' she admitted.

'I know the two of you have always been so close, but surely that's even more of a reason to send him away? He needs to cut the apron-strings, for his own sake.'

'That's what William says, of course. And you're probably both right. Anyway, enough of me, how are you?'

Sadie took a gulp of her wine. 'Thinking I might go on a course which shows me how to stop falling for messed-up commitment-phobes. Honestly, Helena, I don't know how I manage it, I really don't.'

Helena looked at Sadie's alabaster skin, her ebony hair and the long elegant fingers that curled round the stem of her glass. She was exotic rather than beautiful, a woman of nearly forty, whose slender frame still allowed her to dress like a young girl. Today she wore a simple cotton dress and flip-flops, and looked no older than thirty.

'I don't either, Sadie, but then, you were never going to fall for someone boring, were you? You enjoy the challenge of the unusual.'

'I know, I know,' Sadie agreed with a sigh. 'The "I can fix you, you poor broken puppy" scenario definitely has its appeal. The more damaged they are, the more I want to save them. Then they get well, feel strong, and bugger off with someone else!'

'And now your latest disaster has done the same.'

'Actually, he's gone back to his ex-girlfriend, the same woman who originally dumped him for being emotionally stunted. Ha!' Sadie's lips twitched, and she began to giggle. 'Perhaps there's some money to be made out of this. A bit like puppy boot camp: send me your man for twelve weeks and I'll knock him into shape and post him back to you fully trained, panting at your heels when you whistle for him. What do you think?'

'Fantastic idea. Except you'd want to keep all the sweetest puppies for yourself,' smiled Helena.

'True. Anyway, I've decided I shall be man-less for the foreseeable future. And as you know, I can never look more than a day ahead, so I'm safe for tonight! How is William, my all-time favourite man, doing?'

'He's fine. The same as always.'

'Adoring, well-off, steady, great with kids, barbecues and in the sack. Yep.' Sadie took a slurp of her wine. 'He's mine if you ever bin him, promise?'

'Promise.'

'Joking aside, Helena, I've got to get a move on with this finding a mate business, you know. My biological clock is not so much ticking as needing a skilled watch-mender to repair it.'

'Hardly. Women go on having babies well into their forties these days,' Helena said.

'Maybe kids just aren't in Big G's plans for me, and I shall end up settling for hundreds of godchildren and none of my own,' Sadie sighed.

'Immy says you're her favourite godmother, so you obviously do a wonderful job.'

'Yes, I stuff tenners inside cards with aplomb, but thanks anyway,' Sadie said.

'Hi, Mum, hi, Sadie.'

Alex had ambled out onto the terrace unnoticed.

'Alex, sweetie, how are you?' Sadie opened her arms to embrace him. Alex dutifully went to her and allowed himself to be hugged. 'How's my lovely boy?'

'Okay,' Alex grunted, straightening up and scanning the terrace nervously.

'If you're looking for the others, they're down by the pool. Why don't you go and have a swim?' suggested Helena. 'I'm sure some exercise would do you good.'

'S'all right, Mum, thanks.' He stood in front of them uncomfortably.

'Then would you go and get the bottle of white wine from the fridge, darling?' Helena suggested. 'I'm sure Sadie would like a top-up.'

'Sadie would, yes.'

Helena sighed as Alex headed indoors. 'It doesn't help that he hates Rupes. Maybe that's why he's been skulking in his room all day.'

'I'm afraid I'm with him, there,' Sadie whispered. 'Rupes is an arrogant cuss.'

'Ah, there you are.' Jules emerged from the house, attired in a bright yellow sarong. On Chloë it would have looked glorious, but on Jules it gave the impression of a wilting sunflower. She sat down heavily in a chair. 'All done. Glass of wine going spare for me?'

'Alex, get another glass for Jules, will you darling?'

Alex, who'd just appeared with the bottle, made a face and went back inside.

'My goodness, he's put on a bit of weight since I last saw him. What on earth have you been feeding him, Helena?' said Jules loudly.

'It's puppy fat, that's all. He'll lose it when he starts growing,' Helena replied calmly, hoping that her son hadn't overheard Jules' comment.

'One would hope so. Obese children are becoming so common these days. You'll have to put him on a diet if he gets any bigger.'

Seeing Helena's discomfort, Sadie swiftly changed the subject. 'Isn't the house dreamy, Jules?'

'It obviously needs some serious renovation and new bathrooms, but it's in a lovely position. Thank you,' Jules said as Alex returned with a glass. 'How's school?'

'I've left it.'

'I know that, Alex,' said Jules sharply. 'I meant, are you looking forward to starting your new one?'

'No.'

'Why not? Rupes can't wait. He's won the sports scholarship to Oundle, you know.'

'I don't want to go away from home, that's why not,' muttered Alex.

'Oh, you'll get used to it. Rupes loved boarding at prep school. He was head boy, and collected a raft of sports prizes at Speech Day.' Jules' eyes filled with motherly pride as she saw Rupes and Chloë walking up from the pool.

'Hi, Alex, how you doing?' Rupes gave Alex a hefty thump on the back.

'Fine, thanks,' he nodded.

'Chloë 'n' me were going to wander up to the village

later to see what's going on, weren't we?' Rupes smiled at Chloë and laid a hand possessively on her shoulder.

'No, thanks. I've got a headache. I'll see you later.' Alex turned abruptly and disappeared inside.

Jules frowned. 'Is he all right?'

'Yes, he's fine,' replied Helena.

'Always been a strange lad, hasn't he? You make sure you give him a pep talk about boarding, Rupes. He's very nervous, poor thing.'

'Yeah, we both will, won't we Chloë? Don't worry, Helena, we'll sort him out,' Rupes swaggered.

'I think I heard a car.' Standing up before she was sick into her wine glass, Helena crossed the terrace to greet William and the little ones.

ALEX'S DIARY

17th July 2006

Oh, woe is me, woe is me!

I've just counted the number of days that tosser is staying, then I counted the number of hours that made, and in one million, two hundred and nine thousand, six hundred seconds from now, he will be . . .

GONE.

Two weeks, two whole weeks of Rupes lording it over Chloë, touching her perfect skin and making jokes that aren't even funny, yet she laughs.

She can't fancy him, surely? He's as thick as a plank, and then some. I thought elegant, intelligent women like her preferred men with brains, not lolloping great lumps of arrogant, vapid muscle.

Supper tonight was a living hell. Rupes made sure he sat next to her, his Ray-Bans still on his head like a girly hairband, even though it was pitch-black.

He thinks he is – as Chloë says with alarming regularity – SOOOO cool.

And the way he laughs: a great choking sound like he's

swallowed a peanut and is trying to bring it up. His Adam's apple shakes in a revolting way and his neck and face go bright red as if he's drunk too much port.

Am I jealous because he has an Adam's apple?

Because he is six feet taller than me?

Because Chloë seems to like him?

Yes! Yes! Yes!

I thump my pillow, then look underneath it and realise I've just thumped Bee in the face too. I kiss the stuffing where his nose once was, and apologise to him. I hold his small grey paws in my small brown paws.

'You are my only friend,' I say solemnly. He doesn't reply, but then, he never does, because he is an inanimate bundle of old cloth and cotton wool.

I used to believe he was real once. Am I mad? I've often wondered if I am. But then, what is sanity? Is it a great blond thug of a boy who knows how to chat up girls? If it is, I'd prefer to be me . . .

I think.

I know I'm no good at small talk, and it's a disadvantage to feel unable to communicate. Perhaps I should join one of those monasteries where monks maintain permanent silence. That would suit me down to the ground.

Apart from the fact I don't believe in God, and I wouldn't want to wear a dress.

I don't think Dad thinks much of Rupes either, which is something. He pulled him up a couple of times when Rupes was spouting crap at the table, and corrected him and his inaccurate geography. 'No Rupes, Vilnius is *not* in Latvia, it's the capital of Lithuania.' I could have kissed my old man when he said that. Although personally I'm surprised Rupes even knew Vilnius was a city, rather than some overpaid celebrity footballer.

He's actually only four months older than me, yet he seems to think he's already joined the massed ranks of adults and they'll be interested in what he has to say. It's that grim mother of his that encourages it. She hangs off his every word and completely ignores poor old Viola, who's turned out to be rather sweet. She's almost eleven, which makes her only a couple of years younger than me, although she seems far younger, more like Immy and Max.

I've always liked little kids. I like the way they ask bizarre questions out of the blue. A bit like me, except I've learned to think them now, not say them out loud.

And she's bright, Viola. And she confided to me tonight at supper that she doesn't like horses very much. Which is a real shame, as her mother insists she sits on one every day of her life and makes her enter competitions and groom their manes and brush their fetlocks, whatever fetlocks are.

Jules reminds me of a horse. She has huge teeth and a big nose, and I'd just love to stick a bit in her gob to shut her up.

Anyway, none of this brings me any closer to solving my problem: how to tell Chloë I love her.

She spoke to me once tonight. She said, 'You okay, Alex?' And it was magic. She said it with feeling, total concentration, with an accent on the 'you'. Which must mean something, surely.

I couldn't reply, of course, because of this thing with my mouth refusing to work when I'm in her presence, but I think I nodded well enough. But if I can't actually *speak* to her, how can I tell her I think she is the most wonderful girl in the world?

At that moment, I glance at the brown paper envelope full of love letters lying on my bed. Then at *The Collected Poems of Keats* on the bookshelf above me.

And I see the answer.

θ

Nine

'Sweetie, there is the most fabulous-looking man walking down towards the house.' Sadie found Helena and William in the kitchen, setting up breakfast the next morning.

'That'll be Alexis, then,' William mumbled.

'Who is he?'

'Helena's old friend.'

'You kept him quiet, darling,' Sadie said. 'Well, is he local? Single?'

'Yes and yes. He lives a few miles away in the village and he's a widower.'

'Things *are* looking up. Shall I take him onto the terrace? Offer him coffee? A full body-rub?'

'Why not?' said Helena with a shrug.

'Good-oh. I'll just go and put some lippy on. Back in a tick.'

'Sadie is incorrigible,' said William with a smile. 'But I do love her. More than a certain other woman I could mention currently staying under this roof.'

'Jules is slightly . . . overpowering. She doesn't mean to be, though.'

'You're being too kind. Jules is an out-and-out Attila, and I'm sorry I've inflicted her on us for two weeks. She just has this unerring knack of always saying the wrong thing. How Sacha puts up with her on a daily basis, I just don't know. Perhaps she's an absolute goer in the bedroom, gives him the ride of his life. She gets enough bloody practice at it.' William sniffed. 'She bored me to death with running martingales and snaffles last night.'

'She told me that she'd rearranged the pantry when I came down this morning, and put everything in the fridge and the freezer, that leaving them out was a health risk,' Helena said. 'I tried to explain about Angus' cooling system, but she announced she didn't want to subject herself or her kids to E. Coli or salmonella.'

'Well, I'm glad you can take her behaviour so calmly, as I'm struggling already. At least she's gone out for the day and taken Viola and that bullish son with her. Rupes looked very put out at being dragged off with his sister to some ancient ruin. I think he was hoping to spend it sniffing round Chloë instead. So' – William turned to Helena – 'what do you want to do today?'

'I was thinking we could take the kids to Adonis Falls. It's tucked away in the mountains and the waterfall is amazing. You can jump off the rocks into the pool below.'

'Okay. A family outing it is, if we can tear Immy and Fred away from the DVD player. They're back in front of the TV again this morning.'

'At least they're not fighting, and it's very hot outside.' Helena gazed out of the kitchen window.

'Well, let's take the coffee out to the terrace and see if Sadie has pounced on Alexis yet.'

Helena followed William outside.

Alexis, sitting with an animated Sadie at the table, smiled in relief at their arrival. '*Kalimera*, Helena, William. How are you?'

'We're good,' she nodded.

'Alexis has just been telling me he makes wine,' Sadie said, as William set the coffee tray down. 'I've assured him I am his ideal end-user. Coffee, Alexis?'

'Thank you, but no, I am not staying. Helena, I came to bring you this.' Alexis pointed to a small wooden box he'd placed on the table. 'I found it in a drawer of a broken chest as I was putting it on the rubbish dump. I thought it too pretty to be thrown away.'

'And quite fine.' William studied the box. 'It's made of rosewood, and that is a very intricate mother-of-pearl inlay.' He traced his fingers over it. 'I'd say it's quite old, judging by the colour of the wood. Perhaps it's a jewellery box.'

'Any forgotten emeralds tucked into the lining?' quipped Sadie, as William opened it. She reached across the table and stroked the green felt that covered the inside. 'I can't feel anything.'

'Thank you for rescuing it, Alexis. It's beautiful, and I shall put it on my dressing table,' said Helena.

'Of course! It's Pandora's Box!' smiled Sadie. 'You'd better be careful, sweetie. You know how the legend goes.'

'Yes,' Helena agreed. 'So you'd better close it quickly before all the evils of the world jump out.'

'I also came to ask you all if you would be kind enough

to attend an engagement party I am throwing for Dimitrios, my eldest son, this Friday. I would be honoured to have you there,' said Alexis.

'That's very kind, but there are rather a lot of us,' replied William. Helena immediately wondered if he was searching for an excuse.

'That is not a problem. It is a big party, and everyone is welcome. You know how we Cypriots like to celebrate.'

'I think it sounds like fun, and we'd love to come. Thank you, Alexis,' said Helena, shooting William a defiant glance.

'And what about you joining us for supper tonight?' urged Sadie. 'We're down a man and poor old William could do with some support to cope with all these women, couldn't you, sweetie?'

'I could, yes,' agreed William flatly, knowing he'd been out-manoeuvred.

'Then, thank you, I will see you later.' Alexis nodded at them. 'Goodbye.'

'Right, if we're going out, I'd better start rounding up the kids. Chloë and Alex haven't even got up yet.' William was about to leave the terrace when Helena clapped a hand to her mouth.

'Oh God, I've just realised that the engagement party is on the night of our tenth wedding anniversary!'

William paused and looked at her. 'Well, we don't have to go.'

'But we've just said we would.'

'You mean *you've* just said we would,' he corrected her.

'Sorry, darling. But won't it look rude to renege, especially after all the help Alexis and his family have given us? And who knows, William – it might actually be nice to go out to a lovely party for a change, and have a night off catering here for the masses.'

'If you say so,' said William tersely, then set off inside to rally the children.

Sadie glanced at his departing back, then lowered her voice as she spoke. 'So, tell me all about Alexis. Was there ever anything between you two?'

'Why on earth should you think that?'

'From the way he looked at you, of course. You can't miss it. And I'd say William can't either. Come on, Helena, spill the beans.'

'Really, Sadie, it was nothing more than a teenage romance when I came to stay here with my godfather.'

'Was it a love thing?'

'He was my first boyfriend. Of course I thought it was something special. Everyone does.'

'He's obviously still holding a candle for you, even after all these years.' Sadie stretched dreamily. 'How unutterably romantic.'

'Apart from the fact I'm happily married to someone else.' Helena ran her fingers along the delicate mother-of-pearl pattern on the box. 'Oh, and I have three children.'

'Tell me honestly: do you still feel anything for him? Because I just get the feeling there's something you aren't telling me.'

'I'm fond of him and the memories we shared, but no, Sadie, there's nothing more.'

'Really? I mean, is it total coincidence your first-born son shares a name with that of your first love?'

'Sadie, for goodness' sake! I just happened to like the name, that's all.'

'And you swear you haven't seen him since?'

'Please, Sadie, you're like a dog gnawing at a bone. Can we just leave it alone?' Helena begged her.

'Okay. Sorry, sweetie.'

Helena stood up. 'I'd better go and help William round up the kids. Do you want to come to Adonis Falls with us, or are you happy to laze around the pool?'

'I'll stay here and get ready for dinner with our very own Adonis, thanks,' Sadie said with a wink as she watched Helena leave. 'See you later.'

The journey to the waterfall through the mountains was rocky and hazardous, just as Helena remembered it. The road was very narrow, full of huge potholes and steep inclines.

'Thank God this isn't our car,' declared William, as he steered skilfully through the clouds of dust. 'There'd be nothing left of the tyres, not to mention the suspension.'

'It's like being on a roller-coaster, Mummy,' shouted Immy excitedly as she bumped along unperturbed on the seat behind. Alex sat next to her with his hands grasping the edge of the seat tightly, white-faced and staring straight ahead. In the seats at the back, Chloë had her eyes closed with her earphones in and Fred was, incredibly, asleep with his head resting on her arm.

'Did you drive along here when you came before?' asked William.

'No,' Helena said with a laugh, 'I was on the back of a moped! Can you believe it?'

'I'm amazed you survived to tell the tale. Who was the driver?'

There was a short pause before she said, 'Alexis.'

William gripped the steering wheel a fraction tighter. 'Perhaps later, you would have the grace to tell me exactly what went on between you and him,' he said, lowering his voice to a grim whisper. 'It's obvious he thinks there's unfinished business between the two of you. And I'm not particularly keen on the feeling that I'm being cuckolded right under my very nose!'

'William, please! The children might hear you!' Helena whispered back desperately.

William jammed on the brakes, and brought the car to a sudden halt. 'Right, kids, looks like we're here.'

They were deep in a valley, the mountains rising majestically on either side of them. Helena got out and helped Immy and Fred from their seats, trying to swallow down the lump in her throat, so they wouldn't see she was near to tears.

William had already marched off ahead of them to the entrance, and she knew to leave him alone. She was used to his sudden bursts of anger, and normally he cooled down quickly and was apologetic and repentant. Besides, after her chat with Sadie, she understood why. William was feeling threatened, and she knew she needed to put his mind at rest.

'Has everyone got their towels? Okay, let's go.'

Helena took hold of Fred's hand, Immy clung on to Chloë, and Alex brought up the rear alone.

William had already bought their tickets. He picked up Fred and hugged him. 'You ready to go jump into some very cold water, little chap?'

'Yes, Dad, I ready.'

They bumped fists and set off for the waterfalls.

Slithering down the precarious rocks, Helena found herself up to her middle in clear, icy-cold water as her little ones paddled around her. William and Alex had swum to the edge of the pool and were now climbing the rock so they could jump in. Chloë was sitting sunning herself on the edge, attracting admiring glances from the male population around her.

'I'm jumping in – watch!' Alex waved at her from the slippery ledge, twenty feet above the pool, then jumped and landed with a huge splash.

'Go, Alex!' clapped Chloë excitedly as he resurfaced. 'That was SO cool.'

'I'm going up to the next rock above,' he called as he swam back towards it.

Helena looked up and saw how high it was. 'Please take care, Alex,' she shouted to him, as William prepared to take the plunge from the lower rock. She thought how youthful he was for forty-five; yet to gain a single grey hair on his dark head, and his slim body was lithe and toned.

'Go, Daddee!' shouted Immy, splashing around with Fred excitedly. William waved at them, then jumped, and his children cheered him.

'Me jump now, Mummy,' said Fred, starting to paddle towards the rocks. Helena pulled him back. 'When you're bigger, darling.'

'Wanna go now!'

William swam up to his son and held him aloft. 'You want to jump in?'

'Yes!'

'Okay, here goes!' He lifted Fred high above his head,

and let him go. Fred's water-wings stopped him from going under, and he yelped with happiness.

'Look, Helena, Alex is going to jump from that really high rock,' Chloë shouted from behind her. 'Will he be okay?'

'I hope so,' she said, as Alex leapt off. Chloë shrieked and clapped as he came up from under the water and swam towards them.

'Rupes said Alex was a wimp and a nerd, but I'd like to see *him* doing that,' said Chloë to Helena.

'Alex is neither. He's got incredible courage, in all sorts of ways,' Helena said as he swam towards them, panting but triumphant.

'Did you see me, Mum?' Alex asked her.

'Yes. You were fantastic, darling.'

'You were. I was wondering' – Chloë bit her lip, looking gorgeously vulnerable – 'if I tried from the lower rock, would you hold my hand as we jump, Alex?'

''Course. Come on, then.'

Helena noticed the look of pride on her son's round face as he led Chloë towards the rocks. And suddenly, she realised why Alex had been acting strangely over the past couple of days; he obviously had a crush on Chloë.

There was an enormous splash as they jumped off together, and a cheer from the crowd watching below.

Twenty minutes later, Immy had had enough. 'Mummy! My hair is wet and I'm shivery and thirsty, and I want to get out,' she wailed.

'You stay with Fred,' Helena called to William as she dragged her daughter out of the pool. 'I'll get some drinks, and meet you up on the terrace.'

Helena collected some cans from the car, and sat down with Immy on a shady bench under an olive tree. She closed her eyes for a moment, remembering the time long ago when Alexis had brought her here. Then, it wasn't so much of a tourist attraction, simply a place of beauty, known mainly just to the few locals who lived close by. They too had jumped off the rocks together and swum in the deep, clear water.

And here, on the edge of the deserted pool, in a place of legend, Helena had crossed the threshold into womanhood.

'Mummy? Are you listening to meee?'

'Of course I am, darling.' Helena dragged her attention back to Immy.

'I said, I'm hungry and I need a packet of salt and vinegar crisps.'

'We'll be having lunch soon, so you'll have to wait. Look, here come the others.'

'I can show it to you if you like,' Alex was saying to Chloë. 'It's a wicked book, and the copy Angus has is a first edition.'

'I'd love to see it.'

'Great. I'll find it when we get home.'

'Cool.'

Alex was so different today, Helena thought. His lovely eyes were sparkling and his animated face shone with happiness as he chatted with his stepsister, glancing at her furtively with obvious adoration.

'Wow, look at that,' Chloë giggled, pausing by a statue of a naked Adonis and Aphrodite in an embrace. 'He's . . . er . . . quite impressive!' She read out the words engraved in English on the stone plaques beside it. 'Adonis and Aphrodite, the god and goddess of love and beauty. Legend has it that they lived here together with their many children. Ladies born infertile who wish to become pregnant must touch Adonis' appendage, and will have many children thereafter.'

'Don't you dare, Chloë,' William said, bringing up the rear with Fred. 'And don't let your mum anywhere near it either, Alex. That's the last thing we need, isn't it, darling?'

Helena swallowed hard, and nodded.

'Absolutely.'

ALEX'S DIARY

18th July 2006

I flew today!

But I wasn't on a plane, and nothing but my arms were propelling me through the sky. I flew through the air, as the One I Love watched me, then cheered and clapped as I landed, *plop*, in the water.

No matter that my tummy is now covered in red marks where my flab made frictional contact with the water, or that I've twisted my ankle from losing my footing on those slippery rocks. Or the massive bruise on my face that I've no idea how I got, but it might have been her elbow making contact as we held hands and jumped off together.

Pain is meaningless against the joy of the look on her face. I am her hero. I am her protector. She thinks I am COOOOL.

She *likes* me.

And it helped that the paralysed-lips thing seemed to vanish in the ball-petrifying coldness of Adonis' Bidet. Perhaps there is some magic in that water as, when she spoke to me, for the first time, I could actually speak back.

So, we talked and it turned out that she likes reading. She wants to be a fashion journalist if she can't be a model and is very up on all the latest editions of *Vogue* and *Marie Claire*.

Very soon, she will be stepping into my Broom Cupboard to see the copy of *Far from the Madding Crowd* I have found on the crowded shelves of Angus' library. She says she's reading it for GCSE. Well, she says she's not got that far into it, but she likes the film with Alan Bates and Julie Christie and she really rates Terence Stamp as 'Captain Troy'. (I'd go for Alan Bates as 'Gabriel Oak' myself, but there's no accounting for taste.) I wish I could give her the book as a present. But my mother might not be too chuffed as it's a very old copy and probably worth a fortune.

And . . . she'll have got my poem by now.

I nipped upstairs and put it in her bedroom whilst she was in the shower when we got back from the waterfalls.

She's probably reading it right now.

I didn't sign it, of course, but she'll know who it's from. I paraphrased from the love letters I found in Angus' photograph box and borrowed some metaphor from Keats. Personally, I think it sounded pretty good.

I'm also comforting myself that size isn't everything. Look at that Formula One goblin and his seventeen-foot-tall wife. Or all those tiny jockeys with their supermodel girlfriends. If you love someone, you don't care how big or small they are.

Besides, I have lots of room for future growth, and some money stashed away in a building society which could buy me some trainers with serious lifts until I do. I suppose it helps if you are as rich as Croesus, but like size, money isn't everything. And I have plenty of room for growth in that department too.

It turns out that her school isn't so far from the one I am going to in September. Perhaps we could meet for tea on a Sunday, having written to each other feverishly during the week, professing our undying love . . .

Suddenly things are starting to look up.

And perhaps this holiday won't be the nightmare I thought it would be only this morning.

Oh, help. There is someone knocking on my Broom Cupboard door. It must be her. I take a deep breath and hobble over to open it.

Ten

'Hi, Alex. I've come to see that book you told me about. I brought Rupes, too.'

Chloë smiled up at Rupes and led him into the tiny room by the hand.

'Oh, er, right.' Alex reached up to take the book from the shelf, then handed it to Chloë.

'Wow, it's beautiful. Isn't it, Rupes?' Chloë turned the fragile, leather-bound book over in her hands.

'S'pose so; not really my kind of thing, books.'

'Really?' Chloë looked up at him. 'I thought you were quite into . . . poetry?'

Rupes shrugged. 'More of an outdoor man myself.'

Chloë giggled. 'Don't be coy, Rupes. It's good that a man has a sensitive side to him and you can't deny that you have.'

Rupes looked nonplussed. 'Er, yeah, s'pose.' He glanced at Alex's bed and picked up the ragged rabbit lying on the pillow. 'And what have we here?'

'Sorry, could you put it down? I don't like people touching him,' said Alex sharply.

'Think you'd better lose that before you go to boarding school, mate.' Rupes raised his eyebrow at Chloë and gave a short 'tssk', as he dangled the rabbit by its ears. 'The other lads might give you a rough time. Am I right, Chloë?'

Alex snatched the rabbit from Rupes' fingers and held it to him defensively. 'To be honest, Rupes, I couldn't give a shit, but thanks for the warning, anyway.'

'Lots of girls in my dorm still have teddies and stuff,' said Chloë kindly.

'Exactly. They're girls. Hear you jumped from a high rock today, Alex. That how you got that bruise?'

Alex shrugged mutely.

'Well, I'm gonna set up some pool Olympics for us kids. Then you can show us all how great you are in the water. You on for it?'

'Maybe.'

"Kay, see you later. You coming, Chloë?'

'Yes. Thanks for showing us the book, Alex.' She smiled at him. 'See you at dinner.'

'You're looking very nice tonight, Sadie,' William said, finding her alone on the terrace, knocking back a vodka.

'Thank you, kind sir. One does one's best,' she said with a smile.

'Mind if I join you? Helena's taking a shower.'

'Of course. I'd love to spend a few exclusive minutes with one of my favourite men,' she said as he sat down next to her. 'Look at that sunset. Just glorious.'

'Yes. Amazing, isn't it? In fact, the whole place is far

more beautiful than I thought it would be, especially the house.'

'It's incredibly atmospheric and Helena's done a fabulous job of making it feel like a home.'

'Actually, while I've got you to myself, I wanted to ask you how you think Helena seems at the moment.'

'She looks tired, but that's probably because she's been running round trying to get Pandora sorted for everybody.'

'And . . . in the past few weeks?'

'To be honest, William, I've hardly spoken to her. Work's been so frantic, quite apart from my turbulent private life. Why? Do you think there's something the matter?'

'I just don't know. Helena's an expert at keeping her thoughts to herself. Even though we've been married for so long, she's still something of an enigma. Especially on the subject of her past.'

'And surely that's part of her charm?' Sadie reminded him. 'Helena is the least neurotic woman I know. Perhaps inside she's a seething morass of neediness, but she'd never allow anyone to see it.'

'Exactly. She's always in control.' William took a sip of his wine. 'But how can you possibly live with someone for all this time, and yet feel as if you still don't really know them? That's how I'm feeling about Helena right now. Has she ever spoken to you about this Alexis chap?'

'You mean the Alexis who is arriving here at any second, and whom I'm going to do my best to seduce?' She gave a wicked grin. 'Apparently, they had a bit of a fling when she was staying at Pandora years ago, but I really don't think it was much more than that.'

'Really?' William frowned. 'I know you wouldn't tell me, Sadie, even if she'd told you about it in gory detail.'

'You're right, I wouldn't, but on Girl Scout's honour, in this case I have nothing to tell.'

'All I know is she's even more distant than usual, and . . .' He shook his head and sighed. 'I just feel there's something wrong.'

'Hello, campers!' Jules appeared on the terrace. 'Bloody water's stone cold. Could you ask the manager of this establishment to sort it before tomorrow?'

'Hardly a problem in this heat, surely?' said Sadie.

'No, but it's obvious the entire plumbing system is buggered. My loo doesn't flush properly either.'

'There are bound to be problems, Jules. It's a very old house,' William replied evenly.

'Which will cost an arm and a leg to renovate, never mind the upkeep. Helena's not expecting you to shell out for it, is she?'

'Helena is a woman of means now. With Angus' legacy, she's quite capable of covering all the costs herself. By the way, have you heard from Sacha today?' William changed the subject. 'Has he said when he's coming?'

'I haven't switched on my mobile. I'm on holiday, even if he isn't,' Jules replied, with an edge to her voice.

'I'm sure he wants to be here, Jules, but perhaps he's under a lot of pressure. Things aren't as easy in the City as they used to be. And Sacha did a very brave thing by setting up on his own when he came back from Singapore.'

'*Kalispera*. Good evening, everyone.' With timing as immaculate as his freshly laundered white shirt and brown chinos, Alexis arrived on the terrace. He placed two bottles of wine and a large bunch of white roses on the table. 'Sadie, William,' he smiled at them in turn. 'And may I be introduced?' He held out his hand to Jules, who visibly lost a layer of frost as she allowed him to take her hand in his. 'Alexis Lisle.'

'Jules Chandler. Are you Cypriot or English?'

'I am Cypriot, but my family line was begun by an Englishman, who came here in the eighteenth century and married my seven-times-great-grandmother. So, we still bear his surname.'

'Drink, Alexis?' William offered him a glass of wine.

'Thank you. And as you English say, cheers.'

The assembled company raised their glasses as Helena joined them, looking lovely in a simple white cotton dress. 'Hello, Alexis.' She greeted him, but did not move to kiss him. Instead, she turned to William. 'Darling, would you pop upstairs and say good night to the little ones?'

'Of course. Anything need to be done in the kitchen while I'm up?'

'No, apart from telling the older ones that supper will be ready in fifteen minutes.' She touched him lightly on the arm as he passed.

'Could you chivvy Viola up to bed whilst you're at it? She's watching a DVD inside. Tell her she can read 'til eight, then lights out,' called Jules.

William nodded and went inside.

'So, Alexis, come and sit.' Sadie patted William's vacated chair. 'I want to hear more about your wine business.'

Helena half listened as Alexis explained the workings of his vineyard. Jules was saying something to her about the awful plumbing, but she wasn't paying attention.

'Yes,' she said, absently, hoping it was the right answer.

'You're not going to renovate the bathrooms, then?'

'To be honest, I haven't really thought about it. Excuse me, Jules, I have to go and check on supper.' Helena stood up and went to seek sanctuary in the kitchen. She stirred the pork casserole Angelina had left for them in the oven, checked the rice that was simmering on the hob and drained it.

A hand snaked round her waist from behind. 'Our little ones are in bed, and I took Viola upstairs too. Poor little thing – could her mother not even make the effort to go up and say good night? I do sometimes wonder why they bothered adopting her in the first place,' William commented. 'Pretty obvious who the favourite child is in that family.'

'Jules can be a little harsh with her, but Sacha absolutely dotes on her,' Helena equivocated.

'I seriously don't know how you can be so kind about Jules, when her behaviour irritates the hell out of everybody else. Anyway, I think Viola's a sweetheart, and as she's my goddaughter, I'd like her to have the best time possible now she's here. '

'I agree. I'll certainly try to give her as much attention as I can. She's a little lost soul,' said Helena thoughtfully, tipping the rice into a large serving bowl. 'And she definitely needs some TLC.'

William swung Helena gently round to face him, then kissed her on the forehead. 'Sorry about earlier.'

'Really, it's okay. It's my fault too. I understood after I spoke to Sadie that it's . . . difficult for you.'

He swept a strand of blonde hair away from her eyes.

'Yes, it is. And really darling, I'd appreciate it if at some point you told me exactly what happened between the two of you.'

'I will, I promise, but not now,' Helena said as she turned back to the hob. 'Anyway, Sadie looks as though she's in for the kill out there with him, so I wouldn't worry.'

'You don't mind, do you?'

'Of course not!' Helena snapped. 'I—'

'Hi, Daddy. How's tricks?' Chloë sauntered into the kitchen, wearing a turquoise sarong masquerading as a dress.

'Fine,' William sighed. 'You?'

'I'm cool. Is it okay if me and Rupes walk up to the village after supper? Check out some of the bars?'

'As long as you don't drink alcohol and you're back by midnight, then yes, I suppose so,' he said resignedly.

'Thanks, Daddy. Mmm, something smells good.' Chloë peered into the cast-iron pot that Helena was now lifting from the oven. 'By the way, who's that bit of beefcake out-side on the terrace?'

'His name's Alexis. He's . . . a neighbour,' added Helena.

'He's quite fit for an oldie. Sadie's getting stuck in, anyway,' she giggled. 'See you guys later.'

'Hold on a minute.' William stopped her as he lifted the covered dish from the countertop and held it out to her. 'Make yourself useful and take out the rice, please.'

'Have you seen Alex, Chloë?' asked Helena, as she followed them both outside and placed the casserole on the table.

'I think he's in his room. Want me to go and get him?' offered Chloë.

'Yes please.'

'No probs.'

'Is that your daughter, William?' asked Alexis, watching Chloë retreat back into the house.

'Yes.'

'She is very beautiful. You must be a proud father.'

'I am. But like all fathers, worried she's growing up too fast. More wine, Alexis?'

Alex came hobbling out with Chloë a few minutes later, looking glum.

'Why don't you sit next to Sadie, darling?' said Helena.

'Thanks.'

'Your father says you jumped from Adonis Falls today, Alex,' said Alexis as he sat down.

'Yep.'

'You are brave, especially from the high rock.'

'Even I wouldn't jump from that one,' remarked William, as he handed round steaming plates of pork and rice.

'We ought to go, too,' interrupted Jules. 'Rupes was the school diving champion.'

'It is not a good idea to dive from that height. Even though the pool is deep, there are rocks at the bottom. Your feet touch them, okay, but your head, no, it is not good,' warned Alexis.

'I'm sorry I didn't come. It sounds wonderful. Would you take me there some time, Alexis?' asked Sadie.

Alexis stared at Helena for a moment, then averted his eyes. 'Of course. And anyone else that wishes to come.'

'I do.' Rupes appeared, reeking of aftershave and sitting himself down next to Chloë. 'This looks good, thanks, Auntie Helena,' he said as a plate was put in front of him.

'I think it's time to drop the "Auntie" now you're thirteen and officially a teenager. Please, do start, everyone,' said Helena, finally sitting down herself.

'I'd like to propose a toast to the hostess, who has worked so hard to make Pandora comfortable for us all. To Helena.' William raised his glass.

'To Helena,' everyone chorused.

After dinner, Rupes and Chloë disappeared off to the village, armed with mobiles and a torch. Alex scuttled off back to his room and Sadie insisted she would do the clearing-up, corralling Jules into helping her.

Which left Helena, William and Alexis on the terrace.

'Brandy, Alexis?'

'Thank you.'

William passed him a glass. 'So, tell me, how is your business competing with the New World wines? Which, from what I saw in the supermarket, are very popular here?'

Helena half listened as the two of them discussed business. William was on his best behaviour, no hint of his earlier anger in his demeanour. They were both good men, she thought, and there was no reason why they shouldn't become friends. As long as neither of them ever learned the truth . . .

Alexis left an hour later. Jules had already gone up to bed, and Sadie sat back and yawned sleepily.

'Alexis was telling me earlier about his wife, and how hard his boys took it when she died. She was only thirty-four, poor thing. The good news is, even though he's had such a rotten time, he doesn't seem needy, or a bastard. He's a thoroughly nice man, which at the very least has helped restore my faith in the male sex. Right, I'm for the sack. All this sun knocks it out of you. Night.'

'She's right. Alexis is a nice man,' William mused when Sadie had left. 'But I can't quite see those two getting together.'

'You never know. Stranger things have happened.'

'Perhaps, but it's obvious Alexis isn't ready to let go. Not of his wife, might I add, but you.' William checked his watch. 'Where on earth have Chloë and Rupes got to? It's almost one o'clock.'

'I'm sure Rupes won't let anyone harm her.' Helena was relieved he'd changed the subject.

'Actually, I'm far more worried about the harm he may want to inflict on her *himself*,' William muttered, as the sound of a car crunching along the gravel lane leading to Pandora made them both turn. 'Christ, I hope they haven't got themselves arrested for underage drinking. Perhaps we shouldn't have let them go out alone.' William stood up and strode towards the drive, with Helena following in his wake.

As the car drew closer, they realised it was a taxi. Once it had drawn to a halt, the rear door opened and a creased figure emerged, clutching a holdall.

'Thanks.'

Slamming the door, the figure walked towards them.

'Hello, chaps. I finally made it.'

'Sacha! Why on earth didn't you let us know you were here? We'd have collected you from the airport. Good to see you, old boy!' William gave his best friend a 'man hug' that involved much clasping of forearms and back-slapping.

'I did leave a message on Jules' mobile to ask her to

pick me up from the airport, but she obviously didn't get it, so I grabbed a taxi. Hello, Helena. How are you?'

As he kissed her cheek, Helena flinched at the stench of alcohol on Sacha's breath.

'Come round onto the terrace and have a coffee. You must have had a long day,' said William.

As they stepped into the soft light emanating from the terrace, and Sacha slumped into a chair, William saw his skin was as white and dry as parchment, a raft of lines etched deep on his forehead and on either side of his nose. His normally shiny, unruly mass of auburn hair was greasy and noticeably greying at the temples.

'I'd rather have some of that brandy than a coffee,' Sacha said, pointing to the bottle on the table.

William poured a small amount of the dark-gold liquid into a glass.

'Come on now, Will, fill her up,' urged Sacha.

William exchanged a look with Helena as he reluctantly topped up the glass.

'Shall I tell Jules you're here?' Helena asked.

'God, no,' said Sacha, downing a large slug of brandy. 'To coin a phrase, let's let sleeping dogs lie.' He chuckled at his own tasteless joke.

'Well, I'm off to bed. It's getting late.' Helena stood up, desperate to leave and rationalising that this was definitely a man-to-man moment. 'Good night.'

'Night, Helena,' muttered Sacha.

'I'll be up soon, darling,' William said as his mobile bleeped to tell him he had a text.

on wy hme. all cool c n r x

He grimaced. 'That was from my darling daughter, telling me that she and your son have finally decided to come home, some two hours later than promised.'

'Of course! Chloë is here.' Sacha had already drained his glass and reached for the bottle to pour himself another. 'How is she?'

'A typical teenager, desperate to grow up. You can imagine that I was expecting the worst, given her mother, but actually, she's delightful. If I'd had a hand in her upbringing, I'd be very proud.'

'Come on, you were there during her formative years and it's not your fault that cow you married was unhinged.'

'Chloë's also stunning, even with fifty per cent of my genes. Your son obviously thinks so too,' said William, hearing the slur in his friend's voice and trying to lighten the darkening mood. He knew Sacha was already very, very drunk.

'I'm sure. Bloody women, eh? They're all the same, using their charms to trap us poor hapless men. Then once they've got us, spending the rest of their lives complaining. Look at Jules. In her list of favourite people, I probably rank somewhere between Hitler and the Devil.'

'You don't mean that, Sacha.'

'Oh, I do,' he said vehemently, then let out a bitter, mirthless laugh. 'In fact, that's the only thing cheering me up; the thought of Jules' face when she finds out.'

'Finds out what?'

Sacha looked at William, his face a picture of despair. He shook his head and chuckled harshly.

'I suppose it's pointless trying to keep it a secret any longer. From anyone.'

'What on earth is it?'

Sacha took another gulp of brandy. 'Well, let me see: I've remortgaged the house twice now, and taken out numerous private loans to keep afloat. But it's all over, Will. My business is bankrupt. And the consequence is that my family and I have lost everything.'

ALEX'S DIARY

19th July 2006

It's past one in the morning and I lie here hardly daring to breathe in case I miss the sound of footsteps.

I have to know Chloë is home and safe.

I heard a car and thought it was them. But then I heard a voice and it's Sacha who's arrived. And then . . . I'm not certain, but soon after that, I thought I could hear the sound of a man crying. Perhaps they're watching a DVD in the drawing room or something, because I can't think that either Dad or Sacha would be sobbing their eyes out like a pair of girls. It's not the kind of thing boys do in front of each other.

Our tear ducts are programmed from conception only to Operate In Private. And On Special Occasions, of which there are only two categories: births, and deaths.

Even then, it's dodgy, as from what I've seen, a man has to be 'there' for the woman in his life. She can fall apart all over the place and everyone thinks how amazing (birth) or caring (death) she is. Whereas, the moment we shed a public tear, we are girly and that's the end of it.

I once went to hospital, having fallen off my bike and

managed to grind the tarmac deep into my kneecap. I cried, automatically, because it bloody hurt! Did I get sympathy as Cruella De Nursey picked out each tiny, hideously painful piece of path from my knee with a pair of tweezers? Did I hell! Even though I'd left behind a piece of skin large enough to equip the nearest toad with a full-body graft, I was ordered by Cruella to be a 'big boy'.

Now, now, dear, big boys don't cry . . .

No wonder men are ridiculed by women for not being 'in touch' with their emotions. How can we be, when we are not even allowed to send our feelings a letter, let alone call them on the telephone, or – horror of horrors – actually 'visit' them in person by allowing our tear ducts to open?

Yet who is it that mainly brings the boys of this world up? YES!!

The women!!

I pause in my philosophic ramblings and wonder whether I have just discovered some enormous, world-shattering conspiracy. One day, will my name be mentioned alongside Aristotle? Hippocrates? Homer Simpson?

The point is this: what exactly do women want from us?

Whatever it is, I am unable to continue to consider it, as I hear familiar voices from along the corridor.

She is home. Thank God. I can now relax, get some sleep, knowing Chloë is safely tucked up in bed a few feet above me.

I can hear the patter of her delicate feet as she walks into her room and begins to do whatever it is girls do before they retire for the night. Taken out of context, it sounds as if she is on patrol, marching backwards and forwards. In reality, she is

probably getting undressed, hanging her clothes in the wardrobe, finding her nightwear, brushing her hair, reaching under
the bed for her lost copy of *Heat* magazine. Et cetera.

I switch off the light, tell her I love her, and prepare to
nod off. Just as I am doing so, there is a knock on my door.

It opens, without waiting for a response from me.

'You awake, Alex?'

'I am now.'

What does *he* want?

I sit up as Rupes enters my space.

'Hi.'

'Hi.'

Rupes squeezes his muscles through the narrow entrance
between the end of the bed and the door, then closes the
door behind him, which is a worrying sign.

'I want to ask you something.'

'Yeah? What?'

'Did you write Chloë a poem and leave it in her room this
morning?'

I am aghast he knows about this. 'I . . . might have done.'

'Thought so. She liked it.'

'Really?' My spirits rise. Has she sent Rupes here as a
romantic emissary, being too shy to confront me herself?

'Yeah. Problem is, she thinks I wrote it.'

What?!

How could she?! Rupes isn't eloquent enough to copy out
a nursery rhyme, let alone compose the kind of poetry Words-
worth himself would be proud of.

'Yeah,' he chuckles as he looms above me. 'She got very
friendly with me tonight. All that slush obviously did the trick.
So I was wondering if you and I could strike a deal?'

I remain silent in the darkness.

'Like, if I paid you, you could write me some more. Say, a fiver a letter?'

I am not silent on purpose anymore. I am simply struck dumb.

'Let's face it, you're never gonna get off with her. You're her little stepbrother. It would be, well . . . incredulous.'

'You mean "incestuous".' His pathetic command of the English language unlocks my jaw. 'No, it wouldn't be. I am not related by blood to her so there is no reason why not, if we . . . chose to.'

'Unfortunately it's me she's got the hots for, not you. So, will you or won't you?'

'Under no circumstances would I even consider the possibility. Forget it, Rupes. It's a no.'

'You sure?'

'I'm sure.'

I hear him sucking air in between his big front teeth. 'It's unfortunate you couldn't see fit to help out a mate, especially when there was something in it for you. Oh well, daresay you'll change your mind. Night.'

As he leaves the room, I wriggle back down into my bed, panting with the tumult of emotions suffusing my brain.

No! No! No!

My poor, fair Chloë. You have been brainwashed, hypno-tised . . . you've taken leave of your senses! I will save you, I will protect you, for you know not what you do.

I now know that this is out-and-out war, and I lie there plotting my campaign.

It is some time later when I dream my door is opening

and hands are rummaging under my armpit and pulling something away from me.

In my dream, I am too tired to wake up and stop them.

ια´

Eleven

'Cup of tea for you.'

William put the mug on Helena's bedside table and sat down, watching her stir.

'What time is it?' she asked sleepily.

'Just gone seven.'

'You're up early. And you didn't come to bed until well after three.'

William sighed. 'Sacha's in a dreadful state. Sorry to wake you, but I thought we should talk before the others get up.'

'What's happened?' Helena sat upright and reached for her tea.

'His business is about to go under.'

'Oh God, William,' she breathed. 'Well, perhaps he can start another one or go back to being an employee.'

'I'm afraid it's a bit more serious than that. What I'm about to tell you must go no further, for obvious reasons.'

'Of course.'

'Sacha's done something understandable, but completely reckless. When the business needed some cash urgently to keep it going, he remortgaged the house, and then took out personal loans to keep it afloat.'

Helena groaned. 'No.'

'Oh yes,' William confirmed. 'I won't go into detail, but the upshot is, the moment the company declares itself insolvent, he'll lose the lot. Including the house. He's sold all his shares too, so in his words – albeit drunken ones – the Chandlers are currently destitute.'

'Surely the banks will let him keep the roof over his head? Jules must legally own half of it, at least.'

'No. She doesn't. Sacha told me last night that because it's his ancestral home – the only thing his parents left him when they died, but worth a fortune – and it's been in the family for a couple of hundred years, it was never put into Jules' name alongside his. As well as paying off the enormous mortgages, it's a saleable asset against his other debts, not to mention the contents. And as such, the bank will repossess it.'

'Oh God, William.' Helena was horrified. 'Is there any way you can help?'

'What he needs is an insolvency lawyer, but he's brought his laptop so at least I can look through everything with him calmly. Although, from what he said last night, he's already explored every loophole and thinks the result is inevitable.'

'He was very drunk last night. Maybe it's not as bad as he thinks.' Helena sipped her tea.

'I think it almost certainly is. He's going to show me the figures this morning, but putting aside how awful it is for him for a moment, I wanted to chat through how this is going to rebound on our holiday here.'

Helena leant back against her pillows with a weary sigh. 'Can you imagine Jules' reaction to all this?'

'I can, and I don't relish the thought one iota. One would like to think she'd stand by her man in his hour of need, whatever he's done and however it impacted on her, but somehow I can't see that happening, can you?'

'I've no idea how she'll react. Does she know anything at all?'

'Nothing, apparently. However difficult I find Jules sometimes, to be told you've lost everything overnight is going to be a terrible shock.'

'What about the kids?'

'Sacha says they can kiss goodbye to their private education, not that it'll do Rupes any harm to be taken down a peg or two. There's an outside chance he might qualify for a financial bursary, because he's already won a scholarship. Sacha's also convinced Jules will walk. Let's face it, there won't be an awful lot to stay for.'

'For richer, for poorer and all that. They've been married for eighteen years, after all.'

'Yes, but let's be honest, these days they're almost certainly together for the kids and lack of an alternative, rather than love.'

'Dearie me,' Helena said with a shudder. 'So, what do you think the rest of us should do today? If Sacha is going to tell Jules, I want everyone safely out of harm's way. Having removed anything breakable from Pandora first,' she added wryly.

'Don't worry, he won't tell her today. I'm going to spend

some time with him checking his maths, but my bet is that he'll have to go back to London immediately to call in the official receiver. He's just got to face it and get on with it.'

'We'll just have to hope there's a last-minute reprieve.'

'It will take a miracle, from the sound of things. So with regards to Pandora, we'll have to try to carry on as normal. I just thought you should know the score, and perhaps divert Jules from too many snide comments about her husband spending the first day of his holiday shut in the study with me and his laptop.' William took her hand in his. 'I'm sorry to inflict all this on you, darling.'

'It's hardly your fault, is it?' She smiled weakly at him. 'It's life, and reality, that's all.'

'Mummy! There you are! Come and watch me jump in, pleeease!'

'I'm here, darling, I'm here.' Helena had been about to sit down for a couple of minutes to drink her coffee, but she wandered down to the pool instead. Immy, in a fluorescent pink bathing suit, was standing impatiently on the side.

'Are you watching?'

'Intently,' replied Helena.

'Here I go.' Immy held her nose and jumped. Helena clapped enthusiastically.

'Well done, darling.'

'Can we go to those rocks and I can jump in like Alex and Daddy? I'm good enough, aren't I?'

'Of course you are, but it's a bit dangerous for a little girl.' Helena sat down on the edge of the pool, dangling her feet in the cool water. Chloë, ostensibly on lifeguard duty, was with Fred, who was giggling as he tried to push her off the lilo.

'Hello, Auntie Helena.' Viola appeared and sat next to her.

'Hello, darling. You okay?'

Viola shrugged. 'Sort of.'

Her freckled face was pale and wore a tense expression. Helena reached for her hand. 'Want to tell me about it?'

'Yes.' Viola sat down next to her. 'You know Daddy's arrived?'

'Yes.'

'I found him on the sofa in the drawing room when I got up to watch a DVD this morning.'

'That was probably because he arrived so late, he didn't want to wake Mummy up,' Helena explained.

'No, that wasn't it. He sleeps in the spare room at home all the time. He looked terrible when he woke up. His eyes were all red and he, he looks sort of . . . saggy. And he shouted at me when I kissed him good morning and told me to go away,' Viola sighed. 'Do you think I've done something wrong?'

'Darling, of course you haven't.' Helena wrapped an arm round Viola's thin frame and hugged her. 'Sometimes, we grown-ups have problems which are nothing to do with our children. Just like when a teacher tells you off at school, or one of your friends says something to upset you. That's nothing to do with Mum and Dad, is it?'

'No. But I don't get cross with them just because I'm upset.'

'True,' Helena agreed. 'But, I promise neither of them

are cross with you. Daddy's just got a few problems at work, that's all.'

'Well, if he told me, maybe I could help, just like he helps me with being teased about my hair.'

'I think that all Daddy needs from you is to know that you love him.'

'Well, of course I do. I love him best of all.'

'Tell you what, how would you like to come with me to a beautiful beach I know? I'll ask the others and we could have a swim and some lunch there. What do you think?'

'Yes, Auntie Helena, that would be nice,' Viola said wanly.

'I'm up for it,' shouted Chloë from the pool. 'I'd love a swim in the sea.'

'Me too!' said Immy.

An hour later, Helena had managed to corral the kids into the car. Even Alex had decided to come, having realised that Rupes was out with his mother – apparently helping her shop for new pillows, after she'd decreed Helena's were too thin.

'Why can't we wait for them to come back, Helena?' Chloë asked. 'I'm sure Rupes would love to come with us.'

'If we don't go now, it'll be too late,' lied Helena, wanting to leave before they returned.

'Wait for me!' Sadie came running towards them just as Helena was reversing the people carrier out of the drive. 'I'm coming too.'

'Hop in.' Helena smiled as her friend climbed in next to her.

'I'm taking cover with the rest of you. The atmosphere

in that house is heavy with the pall of a storm about to break.'

'A wise decision,' agreed Helena.

'What on earth is going on, sweetie?' Sadie lowered her voice to prevent Viola hearing, even though the giggles and screams from the back of the car would drown out any conversation. 'Sacha's been locked in the study all morning with William, and Jules has been patently ignoring him for misdemeanours unknown, then stalked out dragging a sulky Rupes with her.'

'I'll tell you later, but it's not good news.'

'I gathered that, at least. Oh dear, it's such a shame that whatever it is has happened here at Pandora. We can't let it spoil the holiday.'

'No, it's not ideal, but it won't be for long. It looks like Sacha will have to go straight back home to England,' Helena said under her breath.

'Will Jules go with him?'

'That, Sadie, is the million-dollar question.'

Lara Beach was in the National Park, designated an area of outstanding natural beauty: rugged, rocky and still as nature had originally made it, due to the ban on any form of development. After another bumpy drive over an unmade road, Helena steered the car onto the low headland above a horseshoe-shaped beach, the clear water sparkling in the midday sun.

Everyone poured out, carrying buckets and spades, towels and rugs, and made their way down the steps to the golden sand.

Having covered all the children in factor 50, put hats on

heads and water-wings on arms, Sadie and Helena finally sat at the water's edge watching them splash and scream in the shallows.

'Isn't it just great the way Immy and Fred have taken to Chloë? And vice versa. She's very sweet with them and they adore her. Just look at them all . . . even Alex looks happy today,' said Sadie. 'They've managed to bond like a proper family.'

'Our disparate set of kids, you mean?' said Helena with an ironic smile. 'Yes, that part of things couldn't have gone better. William and I were both worried about how Chloë would be. But maybe who we are and how we react to situations is simply destined from birth. Chloë was obviously born with a sweet, relaxed nature. She really doesn't seem to harbour any resentment towards William. Or me, for that matter.'

'Not that she should, given the circumstances, but I know what you mean. Better watch out, Helena, she might like being part of the family so much, she'll decide she wants to stay for good. And how would that make you feel?' Sadie grinned at Helena as she stood up. 'Right, I'm going in for a dip with the kids. You joining me?'

'In a second. You test the temperature and I'll follow.'

Sadie ran in, squealing at the coldness of the water. Helena tipped her face up to the sun, thinking about the Chandler family. And wondered whether, if one made a pact with the Devil – when there was deception from the start – life would always find a way of making one pay the debt. If that was true, then hers was yet to be settled . . .

'Hi, Mum. The water's fantastic. You coming in?' Alex

shook himself like a dog, then plonked himself down on the rug next to her.

'Yes, in a moment.'

'By the way,' Alex said as he made patterns in the sand with his feet, 'I haven't had a chance to tell you 'cos you've been so busy, but I found some old letters in one of those boxes. I don't know for sure, but I'm pretty sure they were written by Angus, to a mystery woman.'

'Really? How exciting. You must show them to me. Any clues as to who she was?'

'No, I've read most of them and he never mentions her by name. Do you know if Angus had a . . . girlfriend?'

'Certainly not when I came to stay with him. I presumed he was a confirmed bachelor, but who knows what he might have got up to? I'll look forward to reading those, darling, when I have more than a minute to myself.'

'Not much of a holiday for you, is it, Mum? All you've done is slave since you got here.'

'That's my role, and I enjoy it.' She shrugged equably. 'Are you enjoying it?'

'Yes and no. I prefer it when it's just us family and I know you don't like me saying so, but Rupes really is an arseh—'

'You don't need to say it again, Alex. What do you think of Chloë? You two seemed to be getting on really well yesterday.'

Alex paused, cleared his throat and dropped his head to prevent his mother from seeing him blush. 'I think she's great.'

'Good. So do I.'

'I like Viola too. What a sweet kid she's turned into,

though I feel very sorry for her. Jules seems to ignore her all the time. By the way, Mum, did Angelina go into my room this morning to make my bed?' he asked her.

'Probably, why?'

'I couldn't find Bee when I went to get my beach stuff. I'll have another look when I get back, but I wondered if she might have thought Bee belonged to Immy or Fred and put him upstairs in their room?'

'Maybe. Anyway, he can't have gone very far, and knowing your propensity for losing things that are right under your nose, you'll probably find him staring up at you from the pillow when you get back. Okay. I'm going into the sea. Coming?'

Helena stood up and held out her hand to her son, and the two of them ran into the waves.

Later, they ate a glorious lunch of barbecued fresh fish at the rustic taverna overlooking the bay.

'I tired, Mummy.' A sandy Fred snuggled up onto her knee after he'd finished eating, and stuck his thumb in his mouth.

'It's all that falling over in the waves.' Helena stroked his poker-straight brown hair, so like his father's.

'We're going back in,' said Alex, as he and Chloë stood up. 'Wanna come, Viola?'

'Yes, please.'

Alex reached out his hand and Viola took it, followed immediately by Immy, who took Chloë's hand.

'Viola seems to have taken quite a shine to Alex,' commented Sadie as she watched them.

'He's always been caring with the younger ones,' said Helena, draining her wine glass. 'Sometimes a little too much. He'll find me in the kitchen at home and demand to know exactly where both Immy and Fred are, in case they're lost or in trouble. It's part of his overblown adult sense of responsibility, so the child psychiatrist told me when he was assessed.'

'Helena' – Sadie paused and eyed her – 'has he ever asked you about his father?'

'No. Well, not directly, anyway.'

'Well, I'm amazed, given his mental maturity. Put it this way, he must have thought about it,' Sadie reasoned. 'So, beware; sooner rather than later would be my guess.'

'Perhaps he doesn't want to know,' Helena replied, looking down at Fred, dozing contentedly in her arms.

'Does William know who he was?'

'No.'

'Has he asked?'

'Yes, when we first met. I told him it was someone I'd met in Vienna and who I'd prefer to forget, that the chapter was closed. He respected that, and he still does,' she answered abruptly. 'It's nobody's business but mine.'

'And Alex's.'

'I know that, Sadie. And I'll just have to cross that bridge when we come to it.'

'Sweetie, I love you dearly, but I've never understood why his father's identity is such a closely guarded secret that you haven't even told *me*. Surely, whoever he was, it can't be that bad?'

'I promise you, it can. Sorry, Sadie, I'm really not up for talking about this. Believe me, I have my reasons.'

'Okay.' Sadie shrugged. 'I know how private you are, but as your best friend, all I'm doing is warning you that the day of reckoning isn't far away. And you will have to face it, for the sake of your son. Now, I'm going in for a last dip.'

Unable to move, as Fred was fast asleep on her knee, Helena watched as Sadie joined the others in the sea. Even though she hated Sadie's probing, she understood her motives – and knew she was right.

ALEX'S DIARY

July 19th (continued)

I knew it was too good to last.

A lovely day out with my love and I arrive home to the worst, the absolute worst.

My mother said Bee might be staring up at me from my pillow, that I might have missed him earlier. Well, she was partly right. He was staring up at me from my pillow.

Except it wasn't him in the flesh – or in scrappy bits of old material, to be more precise – it was his celluloid image, a printed-out black-and-white photo of him. Blindfolded (with a sock, from the looks of things) and hung by his ears from an olive tree. Fred's toy water pistol is pressing into his tummy.

On the bottom of the photo is a message.

'Do as I asked, or the bunny gets it. PTO.'

I turn it over and see more words.

'Tell anyone, and you will never see him again.'

Part of me wants to slap Rupes on the back for coming up with such an imaginative form of blackmail. I didn't know he had it in him. And part of me wants to scratch his eyes out, scream and howl and bite like a banshee until he returns my most precious possession.

So, I have a hostage situation on my hands. I must remain calm and think rationally, weigh up the various options I have at my disposal.

Option 1:

I can go straight to my mother and show her the photograph. She will be furious with Rupes and demand the bunny back.

Result: The note has told me I will never see Bee again if I tell anyone. Rupes is a hardy adversary, and will almost certainly carry out his threat. He may well dispose of Bee before he is placed safely back in my hands.

'It was only my little joke, Auntie Helena, a bit of a jape, but unfortunately, I now seem to have mislaid the rabbit. He's vanished. Sorry and all that, but surely it was only a TOY.'

Urgh. I feel sick at the thought. That route would certainly achieve the result of my mother having to finally cut the crap and agree Rupes is an out-and-out tosser, but I doubt it would bring my poor little friend back to me safe and sound.

It would also make me appear to be the mummy's boy Rupes believes I am. And as I have ten days left with him here, I dread to think of all the ghastly forms of mental and physical torture he may come up with.

My life may well be at risk, let alone my little friend's.

'Oops! So sorry, Auntie Helena. I was standing right next to Alex on the terrace, and I watched him as he leant just a little too far over the balustrade. I did my best to pull him back before he tumbled one thousand feet to his grisly death, but it was just too late.'

I shudder. Am I being paranoid here? Rupes might be a bully and a toerag, but is he a murderer?

Possibly. So . . .

Option 2:

I can agree to his request.

Result: Bee is saved, I am saved and Rupes gets to snog Chloë.

Perhaps the last option is worse than me and my bunny's joint execution. To say the Sword of Damocles is hanging over me would be a grave understatement.

Come on, Alex, think! Surely this is where your super-duper, top-of-the-range-with-added-torque-and-spoilers IQ comes in? The pain-in-the-bum 'gift' – 'Oh, Alex's intellect separates him, makes him abnormal, a nerd, a boffin, a plonker' – that God has saddled me with?

Just for the record, I am none of the above. I am crap at figures, and Einstein's Theory of Relativity reads like Serbo-Croat to me. When Serbo-Croat existed, which it doesn't anymore, except probably in secret underground dens across what used to be Yugoslavia. But isn't any more.

And finally, after eating two slightly melted Crunchie bars I'd been saving for emergencies in my rucksack, a plan is taking shape in my agile brain.

I know I cannot outwit Rupes the Ruthless physically. He could pluck me and string me up next to my poor little friend with a couple of index fingers. Even though the branch would probably break if he did so.

But I can write a mean essay. In at least a couple of differ-ent languages.

ιβ'

Twelve

Having arrived home and left Immy and Fred eating delicious freshly baked buns in the kitchen with Angelina,
Helena found William upstairs in the bathroom, still wet
from a shower. 'How are things with Sacha?'

'He took a taxi to the airport about an hour ago to fly
to London. He'll be in the office first thing tomorrow to
call in the official receiver.'

'What's Jules had to say about that?'

'I haven't seen her. Angelina says she came back here at
lunchtime, then went out again with Rupes.'

'Is Sacha going to call her?'

'He has. Or at least, he's left a message on her mobile
saying there's a problem and he's had to return home. She's
obviously still got her mobile switched off. To Sacha, at
least.' William sighed as he dried himself. 'He's not in good
shape at all.'

'I'm sure. How long will he be gone?'

'He said he'd call tomorrow evening to let me know the score.'

'But surely he's got to talk to Jules face to face as soon as possible?'

'I agree, but what can we do? To be fair, he did try to speak to her this morning, but she said she hadn't got time to chat and flounced off in the car with Rupes.'

'So,' Helena sighed, 'this means we have to pretend everything is fine, while secretly knowing they're all about to be homeless and penniless?'

'It looks like it, yes.'

'How will Jules feel if she finds out we knew and she didn't? She's a woman who likes to be in control.' Helena switched on the shower to find only a meagre trickle of lukewarm water.

William buttoned up his shirt. 'Hopefully, he'll call her tomorrow when he's done the dirty deed. And she and the kids will have to fly home. By the way, Alexis called round earlier. He wanted to know if we'd mind if he brought his grandmother to see Pandora. She's very old and fragile apparently, and used to work here a long time ago.'

'She did.' Helena nodded as she stepped under the trickle. 'She was Angus' first housekeeper – in situ when he bought the house, and still going strong when I came here last time. Angus told me that she and Alexis' grandfather met across a crowded vineyard.'

'I asked them round for a drink at seven. I felt I couldn't refuse.'

'Thanks. She seemed ancient when I knew her. God knows how old she must be now. From what I remember' –

Helena shivered slightly – 'she's a little . . . strange. Right, I'd better get a move on.'

Chloë had offered to bath the little ones, and when Helena arrived downstairs, all three of them were snuggled on the sofa together watching *Snow White*.

Helena kissed her clean, sweet-smelling son on top of his shiny head.

'You okay, darling?'

Fred didn't bother to remove the bottle of milk he was drinking. He shifted it to the corner of his mouth like a smouldering cigarette. 'Wanted Power Ragers, not girls' storwee.'

'I said it's your turn to choose tomorrow night,' Chloë said to him firmly.

'Not fair.' Having made his protest, Fred twirled his hair round his finger and sucked away contentedly.

'Thanks, Chloë,' Helena said gratefully.

'No probs. I love Disney films anyway. I'll put them to bed when it's finished.'

'See you at dinner.' Helena walked onto the terrace to find Jules back from her travels, with a heap of glossy brochures on the table in front of her.

'Now this one has the most spectacular view,' she was saying to Sadie. 'Even better than the one here, I think. It's set in an acre, has four bedrooms and a stunning twenty-metre pool.'

William, who had appeared behind her holding a tray of glasses and wine, raised an eyebrow at his wife. 'Anyone for a drink?' he said as he set the tray down on the table.

'Absolutely,' said Jules eagerly. 'Hello, Helena. Viola says you had a lovely day at the beach. Thanks for taking her.'

'We did. You?'

Jules grinned. 'I've been house-hunting.'

'Have you?' Helena held onto her fixed smile as she took a glass from William.

'I mean, I have a little money put aside from my late mother's bequest, so why not use it to buy something here? I can put the cash towards a deposit and Sacha can damn well take out a mortgage from one of the brokers he spends so much time with in the City and stump up for the rest. All our friends have a house abroad but Sacha has always refused to contemplate it. He says it's too much hassle if something goes wrong. Which means we end up every year having to rely on friends in places that aren't up to scratch. And I do so hate being a guest.'

No one could think of a thing to say in response to this, so Jules continued obliviously, 'I've decided it's time *I* made a decision. So, we're going to buy a house. Cheers!'

'Cheers!' The others toasted with her and took hefty, fortifying gulps of their wine.

'The property market is doing so well here, and it's not much different from buying at home, especially as all the rules are changing now Cyprus has joined the EU. A charming young man explained it all to me this afternoon. They manage the property for you when you're not here and let it out. So you get an income and, with the capital growth, it's got to be a good investment, don't you think, William?'

'I don't know the market here, Jules. I'd have to study it before I could give you an answer.'

Jules tapped her nose. 'Trust me, I have a good instinct for these things. Remember I was a successful estate agent before I had Rupes. Besides, it'll give our family what we need – our own house in the sun, where we can entertain *our* friends.'

'Have you spoken to Sacha about this?' William managed to croak.

'No,' Jules responded airily. 'I've decided to count him out of the holiday altogether. If he comes back, he might be in for a bit of a surprise. Who knows?' She laughed loudly. 'Anyway, I'm off for what I hope is a hot shower. Viola's in the pool with Rupes. Keep an eye out, will you?'

When Jules had left, the three of them sat in silence for a while, lost for words.

Eventually Sadie said under her breath, 'She really is a piece of work, that one.'

'I'm sure she doesn't mean half the things she says,' said Helena, standing up. 'I'm just going in to check on supper. You two carry on.'

'Sacha is one of the *most* charming men I've ever met,' said Sadie in a low voice. 'What on earth did he see in Jules? You should know, William. You're his oldest friend.'

'I agree. He was always a sucker for a pretty face, ever since our schooldays together,' he mused. 'When we were at Oxford, he was surrounded by endless gorgeous blondes. Then he left university and met Jules a year or so later, when she was already working as an estate agent. She was the antithesis of his past girlfriends: sensible, bright and grounded.'

'If he wanted someone to take him in hand and sort him out, he definitely made the right choice,' murmured Sadie.

'I think that's exactly what he wanted. She was actually rather sweet and attractive when she was younger,' William continued. 'And she adored Sacha, would have done anything for him. She basically bankrolled his ambition to become an artist after he left Oxford, when his parents refused to give him another penny.'

'Well, something must have gone horribly wrong for her to have become so bitter,' Sadie remarked.

'If I remember, it all seemed to go wrong when Jules got pregnant with Rupes and couldn't work full-time anymore, meaning Sacha had to get a proper job. He should never have gone into the City, to be honest. He couldn't even keep track of his own expenses, let alone look after other people's money. They gave him a job simply because he was charming and had aristocratic connections.'

'I'm sure that's what made him so appealing to Jules. She's obviously socially aspirational,' said Sadie.

'She was incredibly ambitious for them, yes,' William agreed, 'and thrilled when he got offered a position in Singapore. Unfortunately, it's dog-eat-dog in the City these days – more of a meritocracy. The old school tie's been locked back in the trunk where it belongs. You stand or fall on ability alone. And Sacha has fallen big time.'

'Jesus, what a mess,' said Sadie, turning at the sound of footsteps. 'Oh, look who's here.'

'*Gia sas*. I hope I do not interrupt you.'

Alexis stood behind them. Leaning on his arm was a tiny, shrivelled lady, bent double with arthritis and old age. She was dressed in traditional Cypriot black – Immy's nightmare – and Helena, reappearing from the kitchen, walked forward to greet her.

'Christina. It's been such a long time.' Helena bent down and kissed the old woman on both cheeks.

Christina looked up at her, and put a claw-like hand round Helena's. She mumbled something in Greek, her voice thin, strained, as though it was an effort to speak. Then she looked up at Pandora and smiled, revealing an incomplete set of blackened teeth. She raised a shaky hand and whispered to Alexis.

'She is asking if you would mind stepping inside with her, Helena,' he translated.

'Of course not. William, would you pop inside and check whether Chloë's taken the little ones upstairs yet?' Helena was reluctant to let Immy or Fred see Christina just before bedtime, given that she bore more than a passing resemblance to a witch.

'Absolutely,' said William, understanding immediately and moving swiftly towards the house.

'I'll go and chivvy Viola out of the pool,' Sadie suggested, standing up. 'She must be prune-like by now.'

Alexis and Helena helped Christina slowly across the terrace towards the drawing room.

'How ill is she?' asked Helena quietly.

'She says she is tired of living, that her time here on Earth is up. So she will die soon,' Alexis said, matter-of-factly.

They walked into the recently emptied drawing room, and Helena pointed to one of the high-backed winged chairs. 'I think she would be the most comfortable in that.'

The two of them settled Christina into it, then sat on either side of her. Her eyes flitted around the room and Helena could see their alertness, which belied the fragility of the body in which they were housed.

Her gaze came to rest on Helena. She stared unwaveringly until Helena had to avert her eyes; then she began to speak in fast Greek.

'She says you are very beautiful,' Alexis said, 'and that you look very like someone she once knew, who came here to stay very often.'

'Really?' Helena said. 'Someone else said that to me recently. Who was she? Can you ask?'

Alexis held up his hand as he concentrated on what his grandmother was saying.

'She says a secret is harboured here and . . .' Alexis paused, and looked down at his hands.

'What?' Helena urged him.

'That it is kept by you,' he murmured, embarrassed.

Helena's heart began to pound steadily against her chest. 'Everyone has secrets, Alexis,' she said softly, but he wasn't listening. He was staring at his grandmother, his eyes troubled as she continued to talk. He said something to her in Greek, shaking his head as Christina continued to babble. Suddenly, the old woman's energy seemed to dissipate and she crumpled back into her chair, silent now, and closed her eyes.

Alexis pulled out a snowy-white handkerchief and mopped his brow. 'My apologies, Helena. She is a very old woman. I should not have brought her here. Come, we must take you home,' he said gently to Christina.

'Please tell me, Alexis, what was it she was trying to say?'

'Nothing, it was nothing. The ramblings of a confused old lady, that is all.' Alexis reassured her as he half walked, half carried Christina towards the French windows. 'You must take no notice. I am sorry to disturb your evening. *Antio*, Helena.'

As she watched them leave, Helena hung on to one of the doors for support. She felt faint, breathless, sick . . .

'Darling, are you all right?' A strong arm supported her round the waist.

'Yes, I . . .'

'Come and sit down. I'll get you a glass of water.'

William helped her to the sofa and while he went to the kitchen, Helena tried to regain her composure. Angus had always said, years ago, that Christina was mad. He'd tolerated her strange ways for her wonderful housekeeping skills, plus the fact she spoke no English and was therefore unable to repeat gossip from the house locally.

William came back with the water and took her hand in his. 'You're freezing, Helena.' He felt her forehead. 'Are you ill?'

'No, no . . . I'll be fine, really.' Helena sipped the water he'd given her.

'What did she say to upset you?'

'Nothing, really. I think I'm just . . .'

'Exhausted.'

'Yes. Give me a few minutes and I'll be okay. I'm feeling better already, honestly.' She looked at him and nodded, then stood up. As she did so, her legs wobbled beneath her and she clutched at her husband's arm.

'Right. That's it. I'm taking you upstairs and putting you to bed. And I don't want a word of protest out of you.'

He lifted her easily into his arms and carried her towards the stairs.

'But what about supper? I've got to check the moussaka . . .'

'I said I didn't want a word of protest out of you. In case you didn't already know, I am actually capable of putting a meal on the table. And I have a willing band of helpers who can damn well pitch in, too.' William laid her down gently on the bed. 'Just for once, darling, trust me. Pandora's world is able to turn for a few hours without you. You need some rest.'

'Thank you, darling,' she said, still feeling horribly faint.

'Helena, you really are pale. Are you sure there's nothing wrong?'

'No. I'm just tired, that's all.'

'You know,' he said, gently kissing her forehead, 'if there was something, whatever it is, I can cope with it. I promise.'

'I'm sure I'll feel better tomorrow. Don't tell the kids anything, will you? You know how Alex goes into a panic the moment I'm not one hundred per cent.'

'I'll say you're having an early night. That is allowed, you know.' He smiled and stood up. 'Try and get some sleep.'

'I will.'

William left the room and walked slowly towards the stairs, knowing that however much his wife denied it, the old woman had said something to upset her. He only wished to God she would open up to him, tell him what she thought and felt.

There was no doubt Helena hid secrets; for example, the identity of Alex's father. And, given Helena's underlying tension and the almost constant presence of Alexis, it didn't take a rocket scientist to put two and two together and come up with what the likely scenario was.

That would technically mean his wife was a liar, as she'd sworn she hadn't seen him since her stay here twenty-four years ago.

Here at Pandora, it seemed Helena's past had collided with her present – and for that matter, *his*. Surely he now had a right to know?

He'd leave her be for now, but as William descended the stairs, he decided he wouldn't leave Pandora without knowing the truth.

ALEX'S DIARY

July 19th (continued)

Well.

That was a fun evening.

Dante's Inferno without the excitement of the Inferno. Everyone sat at the table and looked as if their genitals were about to be barbecued. Granted, we were eating Dad's chicken wings (he'd forgotten to take out the moussaka, which burnt to a crisp, and he had to resort to the one method of cooking he knew). But they weren't that bad, just a little on the charcoaled side.

It's not often I feel like the life and soul of the party, so the fact that I did gives a fair indication of the general mood. I could say it was Jules' fault, for wittering on about what a dick she had for an absent husband – which then upset Viola – or that it was down to Rupes sulking because Chloë went off on a date with some chap she'd met at the airport. Or Sadie, who was having a bad day about her ex, apparently, so decided to share all the gory details with us. Or Dad, whose expression resembled the Grim Reaper as he doled out his burnt offerings.

I could cite any of these reasons for the pall that hung over the table like the lingering smoke from the barbecue, but none of them would be accurate.

It's because Mum wasn't there.

She's like super-glue, really. She invisibly binds the household together.

Yet you don't notice this until she isn't there, and all the bits drop off.

I went to check on her earlier, the minute I'd heard from Dad she'd 'gone for a rest'.

'Gone for a rest' is a patronising euphemism adults use with their offspring, who are meant to accept it at face value.

Mothers do not get 'tired'. It's not in their remit. They stagger on until they sink, shattered, into bed at the appropriate time. E.g., after the washing-up.

So, in my experience, 'gone for a rest' does not mean my mother is tired. It means anything from too many gin and tonics to terminal cancer.

I studied her closely, smelling her breath as I hugged her and confirmed she was definitely not suffering from overindulgence. As for the terminal cancer, that is a possibility I suppose, but as I was with her today in the sea, and she was swimming and splashing and looking as fit as a flea, her decline would have to have been miraculously fast.

She might have been pale beneath her tan – but I've always wondered how on earth does one see the paleness when one is tanned? Another ridiculous, useless saying, like 'suck it and see'. Suck what, exactly? And if you did, and it was full of arsenic, you wouldn't be seeing anything for the rest of eternity.

I digress. My instincts tell me my mother is not about to depart this world, so I'd have to deduce that it was that weird nun who came with Mr Fix-it who said something to upset her.

That man is trouble with a capital T. I wish he'd keep away from us, but no, he keeps turning up like a bad penny at the merest hint of an opportunity. If I was Dad I'd be getting seriously pissed off by now. Because it's obvious what he wants.

And it's not available.

ιγ′

Thirteen

Helena had given in at midnight and taken a sleeping tablet. She kept two in her wash-bag for emergencies and they'd sat there for the past three years, ever since she'd been pre-scribed them just after Fred was born.

Last night *had* been an emergency. She'd lain upstairs listening to her family eating downstairs and felt like a caged animal: trapped with her own thoughts, which paced relentlessly round and round in circles in her head.

She'd taken the tablet just as she heard William coming upstairs to bed, and pretended to be asleep. Then, finally, she'd fallen into a blissful blankness.

The joy of waking to find the bright light of morning rather than the grey gloom of dawn made her understand how easy it would be to become addicted. She stretched, feeling her muscles struggling to accept being jump-started, and looked at the clock in surprise. It was half past nine – the longest lie-in she'd had in years.

She saw there was a note on the bedside table, propped up against a mug of tea.

'Darling,

Hope you're feeling better today. Cleared everyone out of the house to give you some peace. Make the most of it and NO housework! See you later, W x'

Helena smiled as she folded the note, but as soon as her lips formed the shape, she remembered last night and what the old woman had said to her. 'Oh God,' she whispered to herself, and sank back onto the pillows.

The silence was deafening. No screams or giggles or muffled Disney soundtracks emanated from anywhere in the house. She reached for the mug of tea, her mouth feeling dry, and sipped it, even though it was lukewarm.

William made her a cup of tea every morning. Despite the fact he could no more work the tumble dryer than take the controls of a spaceship, and watched the cricket on television when he was meant to be watching the children, in a hundred different ways he tried to show her he cared.

Because he loved her. He'd walked into her life ten years ago and saved her. Helena's stomach turned involuntarily at the thought. If he knew the truth, he would never forgive her. And she would lose him and the wonderful family they had created together.

Over the years, there had been months at a time that had passed without her thinking about it. But last night, Helena had felt as though the old woman had looked into her soul and knew what lay there. As if what had lain hidden was slowly rising, on its way to the surface. Helena bit her lip as tears pricked her eyes.

What should she do? What *could* she do?

'Get up, for a start,' she murmured, sensing the whiff of self-pity and hating it. Her family needed her and she must pull herself together.

Deciding to swap her normal half-hour of dance exercises for the exhilaration of twenty lengths in the pool, which might help expel the after-effects of the sleeping tablet, Helena changed into her bikini and wandered downstairs. Angelina was in the kitchen, clearing up from last night's supper.

'I'm sorry, it's such a mess.'

'No, eet is what I am paid for,' Angelina said with a smile. 'My work. Your husband he say you must rest today. I am in charge. I like,' she added.

'Thank you.'

Helena made her way to the pool, dived in and swam up and down, feeling her senses slowly return to her as the repetitive physical motion calmed her. She went back upstairs to take a shower and noticed the old envelope full of letters that Alex had left on her bedside table when he'd come up to check on her last night.

Picking it up, she went back down to the pool, lay on one of the sunbeds and pulled out a letter at random.

April 20th

My darling girl,

I am sitting under our tree and thinking of the last time you were here with me, lying beneath it in my arms. Even though it was less than a week ago, it feels like a lifetime. Not knowing when I will see you again makes our parting so much harder.

I have been giving serious consideration to the

idea of a move back to England, but how much more would I see of you? I know your life takes you away so often, and at least my work here occupies the empty spaces between your visits.

Besides, living in the greyness of London and being stuck in an Admiralty office, pushing papers around a desk, does not appeal. Here, I have the brightness of the sun to help me through my darker moments, when I have to accept that that which I hold so very dear can never be mine.

My darling, you know that I would do anything to be with you. I have money. We could go where no one knows us, begin again, start a new life.

I accept and understand, of course, that the reasons you are not here in my arms are valid, but occasionally I ask myself if you really do love me the way I love you. If you did, then . . .

Forgive me, but sometimes my frustration over-whelms me. I am having the darkest of moments. Without you, life feels little more than a long, hard trudge towards Calvary. Forgive me, darling girl, for my misery. I long to write of the joy we might share if life were different.

I will wait for your next letter with my usual eagerness.

And send you my heart, full of love,

xxx

A

Helena folded the letter and replaced it in the envelope. The lump of emotion the words had engendered felt like a hard piece of apple in her throat. She found it difficult to believe that her godfather, a man who had seemed so controlled, could have written such a passionate letter. There was something very moving about the way that even *he* had succumbed to the most basic and uncontrollable human emotion: love.

'Who was she?' Helena whispered to herself. She turned over onto her stomach, and glanced up at the house.

Pandora knew.

Helena walked into the kitchen two hours later to find a goat's cheese salad that Angelina had prepared for her. Adding a glass of water to her tray, she walked out onto the terrace to eat. A good night's sleep plus the bonus of a rare relaxing morning had slowed her heart rate, if not solved her problem.

And reading the rest of Angus' letters, searching for clues as to whom his paramour might have been, had comforted her. No one's life was spotless, however they chose to present themselves to outsiders. Chance and coincidence played havoc with everyone at some stage. The feeling she'd had when younger of being blown like a leaf wherever the winds of fate took her was probably far more common than she imagined. Angus' letters had shown that in spite of his powerful position in charge of hundreds of men – and on occasion, their very *lives* – he had not been any more in control of his destiny than she was.

And it was a sad fact that, whoever this woman was – and from the letters, Helena was convinced she'd been married – Angus had spent his last years alone. And besides that, the letters had obviously been returned to him, judging by the terse note that accompanied them. Perhaps, she pondered, by the woman's husband . . .

As she ate, Helena wondered if it *had* been a mistake to come back here. Last time, Pandora had changed her life and begun a chain of events that had shaped her destiny. And subsequently brought her to where she was now, feeling as though invisible snakes were coiling around her brain, and there was no escape, whichever path she took.

'I should have told him years ago,' she murmured, tears again filling her eyes. 'I should have trusted in his love.'

Moving to the hammock, she clambered in and dozed, relishing the blissful peace. Opening her eyes at the sound of footsteps, she saw Alexis crossing the terrace towards her.

Rolling herself out of the hammock, she walked slowly towards him.

'Hello.'

'Hello, Helena.'

'I'm just going to make a cup of tea. Would you like one?' she asked, walking past him and up the steps.

'Where is everyone?'

'I have no idea, but they aren't here,' she said as they crossed the terrace and entered the house. 'William thought I needed a break, so he took them all out for the day.' Helena looked at her watch. 'It's almost four, they should be back at any moment.'

'He is a good man, your husband,' Alexis said, as Helena filled the kettle and switched it on.

'I know.'

'Helena, I came to apologise for my grandmother. She is mad, her words meaningless.'

'She might be, but she was also right.' Helena turned to him and, with a sudden sigh of resignation, gave him a wan smile. 'There have been too many secrets, Alexis. So, maybe now it's time I began the process and told you the truth.' She poured the boiling water into the teapot and stirred its contents. 'Come and sit with me on the terrace. There's something I need to tell you.'

Alexis stared at her in shock, his teacup suspended between the table and his mouth.

'Helena, why did you not tell me? You know I would have been there for you.'

'There was nothing you could have done, Alexis.'

'I would have married you.'

'Alexis, the truth is that I wasn't sixteen until September of that year. You may even have been charged for having a relationship with a minor. And it would have been my fault for lying to you, saying I was older than I really was. I told you I was seventeen, remember? I am so sorry, Alexis.'

'Helena, whether you had told me your true age or not, I would have loved you anyway. The fact you were younger makes it worse for you, not me.'

'Well, that summer here certainly shaped my future. Isn't it amazing how every decision we make then affects the next one?' Helena murmured. 'Life is like a set of falling dominoes; it's all linked together. People say you can discard your past, but you can't because it's part of who you are and who you will become.'

'You say that summer shaped your future. Well, it has shaped mine too. Because Helena, no woman has ever matched up to you,' he added sadly. 'At least I understand now why you did not contact me when you went back to England all those years ago. I thought . . .' Alexis' voice was thick with emotion. 'I thought you no longer loved me.'

'Of course I loved you!' Helena wrung her hands. 'I thought I might die from the awfulness of cutting off contact with you, but I didn't want to trap you, put you through the pain of making the decision. I'd told you I was taking care of that kind of thing when I wasn't, and didn't even know how to! I was so naive. I . . . it was so unutterably awful, I . . .'

'You know I would have been there with you if you had told me. But you did not. So all I can do now in retrospect is share the pain and regret the outcome,' Alexis said gently.

'At least you went on to marry and have two beautiful sons.'

'Yes. My wife was a good woman, and I give thanks every day of my life for the sons she bore me. But of course, it was a compromise. I could never feel for her as I did for you.'

'But life *is* a compromise, Alexis. That's what you learn with maturity.' She shrugged. 'And we are both mature now.'

'You don't look a day older than you did then.'

'That's sweet of you, but of course I do.'

'Have you told William of this?' he asked her.

'No. I've always been too ashamed of it, of what I did.'

'Perhaps you *should* tell him, now you have told me. He is your husband and I can see he loves you. I'm sure he would understand.'

'Alexis, there are *many* things I've never told William,

secrets that I keep to protect all of us.' Helena shuddered suddenly in the heat.

'You can tell me anything and I would not think less of you, because the love that was then . . . is now.'

Helena looked at him, at the tears in his eyes. She shook her head helplessly. 'No, Alexis, I'm no longer the innocent girl I was when you met me. I've weaved a web of deceit and lies that's affected everyone. I killed our child when I was sixteen. You can't know how many times since I've wished to God I'd just given in to fate and come and lived here and married you. I can never forgive myself for it, never.'

'Helena, Helena . . .' Alexis stood up and moved towards her. He pulled her up into his arms to comfort her. 'Please, you must not blame yourself. You were so young and you also chose to carry the burden alone. It was unfortunate, but these things happen. You are hardly the only woman in the world to have made the terrible decision.'

'I don't care about other women! Every time I look at my children, I think of the missing one. I look at the empty chair . . .'

Helena cried onto his shoulder then, her tears soaking his shirt as he stroked her hair silently, murmuring endearments in Greek.

'Mummy! Mummy! We're back! Are you better? Daddy says if you are, we can go out for chips and ketchup tonight in the village! I think you will be, don't you? Hello, Alexis.'

Helena pulled away abruptly from Alexis' embrace, turned slowly, and saw William standing behind Immy.

'Hello, darling,' he said to her coldly.

'Oooh, Mummy, you still don't look well. Your eyes are

all red. Daddy, I don't think Mummy is better, but maybe a plate of chippies might help,' Immy continued, oblivious to the tension.

'I will leave you. Goodbye, Helena. Goodbye, William.' Alexis walked across the terrace past William, who pointedly ignored him.

'Had a peaceful afternoon?' he asked her, sarcasm dripping like slowly poured honey from his words.

'Yes, thank you. Where did you go?' she asked, desperately trying to pull herself together.

'The beach.'

'Which one?'

'Coral Bay. Think I'll go for a swim in the pool.' He turned away from her.

'Yes. I'm fine to look after the kids and . . . William?'

'Yes?'

'Thank you for giving me some time to myself.'

'I can see you made the most of it.'

'William?' She walked towards him. 'Can we talk?'

He waved her away dismissively with his hand. 'Not now, Helena, please. Okay?'

With a sinking heart, Helena watched him disappear down the steps to the pool.

ALEX'S DIARY

20th July 2006

Oof!!!

What has happened in this house in the past twenty-four hours? I wish someone would tell me what is going on. Because something is.

Tonight at the restaurant it was Dad's turn to look as though, rather than a French fry – or a Cyprus fry, to be more precise – he'd swallowed a snake that was slowly eating his innards away and breathing poison through his veins. I don't know about Mum being ill, but Dad looked seriously rough.

Mum was valiantly doing her 'everything is absolutely fine, kids, and aren't we having a thoroughly jolly time on holiday?' impression, which probably fooled everyone else, but not me.

And even though I am feeling happy due to Rupes becoming the Incredible Sulk over Chloë's detailed and incisive description of her snog with Airport Guy last night (if also suicidal about her snogging someone else), I can't sweep away the feeling that something has gone seriously wrong in our household.

Dad seemed so wrapped up in his own woes, he didn't even complain that Chloë was meeting Airport Guy again tonight. Or that Fred painted himself and the table with chocolate ice cream and had a temper tantrum when he wasn't allowed any more to daub with.

Dad drank a lot more than usual, too. For that matter, so did Mum, who hardly drinks anything normally and had three glasses without leaving any dregs at all. And then Dad got up from the table and said he'd take Fred and Immy home to bed, and went off without a word. Leaving Mum, Sadie, the ghastly Jules, the Incredible Sulk and sweet little Viola behind.

Talking of which, I do like Viola. For a ten-and-a-half-year-old, she is extremely well read, even if a lot of the books she reads have 'thongs' and 'snogging' in the title. However, I hope I've managed to convince her to focus her literary hunger on *Jane Eyre*, of which there is a very nice copy in my Broom Cupboard Library. I think it will suit her. She is a waif and stray herself.

I digress. Shortly after Dad left, the conversation became even more strained. Jules continued to talk about the house she is going to buy, with no mention of the fact her husband even exists or that he is currently AWOL.

I've always rather liked Sacha. Even though he is an alcoholic and bears more than a passing resemblance to Oscar Wilde with all that entails, and everyone in both his family (other than Viola) and mine raise their eyebrows and sigh when they make reference to him as if he were a naughty but indulged toddler, there's no doubting he's bright. And under that City suit, an eccentric bursting to break free.

God help me if finance ever becomes my fate. I wouldn't so much break the Bank of England as shatter it into a million pieces.

Anyway, back to today. Just after we'd arrived home from the beach, I was in the boot clearing out the endless soggy towels, when Mr Fix-it stomped past me looking grim.

He'd obviously been visiting Mum whilst we were all out.

A horrible thought is lurking in the recesses of my mind, but I refuse to acknowledge it. That would make it real and it just can't be.

It just can't.

So instead of that, I am focusing my considerable brain-power on my own problem: the successful rescue of my bunny.

The letter is finally complete. I'm taking a chance, I know, but as with all missions of this nature, there has to be some element of risk.

I read the letter back to myself and allow myself a chuckle at its cleverness. Colette meets 'The Three Little Pigs' meets Alex the Great.

All in French.

I've tested Rupes' prowess without him knowing. He can't count to *cinq* without getting stuck. Chloë, on the other hand, being half French, is fluent.

She'll understand.

I've pushed a note under his door to say the letter's ready for him to take delivery and designated the swimming pool at eight tomorrow morning for the 'drop'. I know how these kidnap plots can go horribly wrong, so I've suggested he puts the bunny on the floor in front of him so I can see him, and only then will I hand over the letter.

He will read it and the French words will mean nothing to him. So he will be happy.

Just in case of disaster, I'm hiding Immy in the olive trees and priming her to scream her sparkly flip-flops off for 'Mummee!' if there is one false move from my adversary. For example, if he recaptures the bunny and makes off with the letter.

It's cost a fortune in sweeties to bribe her, but who cares as long as it works? Then my dearest and oldest friend will have to suffer the indignity of a Safe (Dog)-House, i.e., an old kennel which I found in the back of the shed, for the duration of Rupes' stay.

I pull the gusset over my face and switch the light off. I close my eyes but I just can't sleep. Adrenaline flows through me at the thought of my rescue mission tomorrow, but also at the thought of something else.

Could it be? Oh God, please, I would even – gulp – sacrifice Bee to make it *Not* Be.

Mum cannot love *him*.

She just . . .

Cannot.

ιδ'

Fourteen

'*There* you are. I've been looking all over the place for you.'

Helena turned as Sadie poked her head round the door of the study.

'Sorry. I was just going through Angus' desk to see if I could find anything more about this mystery woman I mentioned to you last night, who he seems to have been in love with.'

'Any luck?'

'No, but there's a locked drawer here and I can't find the key.'

'You'll probably have to force it. The key could be anywhere. You must find out who she is, Helena. It's such a romantic story.'

'I don't want to break into the desk if I can help it, it's so lovely.' Helena ran her hands over the smooth green leather covering the top of it.

'Apart from making sure you were okay, I just came to alert you to the fact that something very odd was going on at the pool this morning.' Sadie perched in front of Helena on the edge of the desk. 'I was gazing out of my bedroom window earlier, and I saw Rupes and Alex standing on opposite sides of it, squaring up. Looked like pistols at dawn to me,' Sadie said with a giggle. 'Then there was a big splash and some shouting, and everything went quiet.'

'Oh God! Have you seen them both since?' Helena asked anxiously.

'Yes. Rupes was marching up the stairs to his bedroom as I was coming down, then I saw Alex disappearing into his broom cupboard. He looked as if he'd been for a swim fully clothed.'

'Really? I hope Rupes isn't bullying Alex, but you saw them both afterwards so they're obviously still alive.'

'They were, yes.'

'I'll go and check on Alex now.' Helena made to stand up. 'I've been in here since seven and I didn't hear a thing.'

'Are you hiding?' Sadie asked Helena as she reached the door.

'What do you mean?'

'You *know* what I mean. You're usually at the centre of everything at breakfast-time, not ferreting around in the study. Have you and William had a bust-up?'

'No. Why?'

'Last night, he hardly spoke to you. Usually he's so . . . attentive.' Sadie crossed her arms. 'Something's pissed him off.'

'Well, I've no idea what.'

'And you . . . sorry, but you look terrible, sweetie.'

'Thanks.'

'You seem to have a permanent frown. Helena . . . why don't you open up and tell me what's going on? I'm your closest friend, remember? Not the enemy.'

'Really, I'm fine. I just . . . haven't felt great in the past few days, that's all.'

'Okay, have it your way,' Sadie sighed. 'But you could cut the atmosphere in this house with a knife.'

'Could you? I'm sorry, Sadie. I'm obviously being a terrible hostess.'

'Nonsense! You're being wonderful and you know it, so please don't manufacture a guilt-trip, because that really isn't the point. It's nothing to do with Alexis, is it?'

'Why do you ask?' Helena's hand was still clutching the doorknob.

'William was on great form yesterday afternoon at the beach, then we all came home and he walked round to the terrace to find you. And the next thing I see is Alexis marching away down the path. He'd obviously been here whilst we were all out.'

'He had, yes.' Helena sighed in resignation.

'Which I'm sure didn't please your husband.'

'No, but I can't *make* him believe there's nothing going on between us if he chooses to think there is. Anyway, I have to go and see if Alex is okay.' Helena opened the door and left the room.

After a few moments, Sadie followed suit and found William in the kitchen making toast. 'Morning,' she greeted him. 'Another effing beautiful day in paradise. Did you sleep well?'

'Fine, thanks. Coffee?'

'Lovely. By the way, what's the form for the party tonight?'

'What party?' asked William.

'The engagement "do" for Alexis' son. Remember? He invited all of us. It might be fun,' said Sadie.

There was an awkward pause before William spoke. 'I *had* forgotten . . . And the fact that it's our tenth wedding anniversary today. Well, under the circumstances, perhaps the rest of you should all go. I'll stay here and babysit the kids. It's going to be far too late for them and they'll no doubt behave appallingly,' he added morosely.

'I think Helena's already asked Angelina,' Sadie commented as he handed her a coffee. 'And of course you must come. It's a special night for the two of you.'

At that moment Helena walked into the kitchen. 'What have I asked Angelina to do?'

'Look after the little ones whilst we go to Alexis' son's engagement party,' repeated Sadie. 'And happy anniversary, you two, by the way,' she encouraged.

'Oh. Yes, thanks Sadie.' Helena cast a quick glance at William, who had his back to her.

'I'm taking my coffee onto the terrace. Coming, Sadie?' he said eventually, standing up.

Left alone in the kitchen, Helena sank into a chair and put her head in her hands. William had studiously ignored her since the previous afternoon. By the time they'd arrived home from the village last night, he was already in bed, ostensibly asleep. And he hadn't even wished her happy anniversary just now, or mentioned the card she'd left on his bedside table. How ironic that it was today of all days.

Fighting the urge to pack a suitcase, grab her children

and run from a haven that was rapidly becoming a hell on earth, Helena looked heavenwards for inspiration.

And found none.

With Jules, Rupes, Sadie and Chloë tanning themselves by the pool, and William determinedly absorbed in a book, Helena made her escape. She shoehorned her three children and Viola into the car, and headed for Latchi. Sadie was right – despite outward appearances, the atmosphere at Pandora currently felt like a ticking time bomb.

Alex was unusually morose, even for him. He sat silently next to her as they drove towards the coast.

'Your eyes look red, darling. Are you sure you're feeling all right?' she asked him.

'Fine.'

'Probably the chlorine from your swim this morning. Is there a problem between you and Rupes?'

'Mum, I told you earlier there wasn't.'

'Okay, if you insist.' Helena was too exhausted to argue.

'I do.'

'Anyway, you'll love Latchi town,' she said with false brightness. 'It's very pretty, and there are lots of souvenir shops around the harbour. You can spend your holiday money on your usual selection of quality local merchandise.'

'A euphemism for the crap I always buy, you mean?' Alex pulled a face. 'Charmed, I'm sure.'

'Come on, Alex, I'm only teasing. You can spend your money on whatever you like.'

'Yeah.' He turned away and stared out of the window.

'What's wrong?'

'I could ask you the same thing,' he fired back.

'I'm fine, but thanks for asking.'

'Could have fooled me,' he muttered. 'I'm as "fine" as you are.'

'Okay,' Helena sighed. 'Let's call it quits, but in case you've forgotten, I'm the adult and you're the child in this relationship. If you have a problem, please promise you'll come and talk to me.'

'Yep.'

'Good. Now, let's find somewhere to park.'

Helena sat at the water's edge, watching the children playing in the sea. Relieved that she'd run from the cloying atmosphere of Pandora, where her life felt as if it was held at the central point of the compass and any direction was a possibility, she did what she always did during difficult moments in her life: counted her blessings.

In front of her were three happy, healthy children. If the worst happened, Pandora was hers and would provide a roof over their heads, with Angus' financial bequest funding their living costs for at least a few months. Maybe she'd have to sell Pandora, move back to England and start teaching ballet classes – something she'd been thinking about recently. The point was, they would survive, *she* would survive. After all, she'd done it before. She could do it again. But she hoped with all her heart it wouldn't come to that.

'Look, Daddee! Mummy bought a prezzie for me!'

Fred plonked the toy car onto William's oiled and browning stomach.

'Wow! Another car! Aren't you lucky?' He smiled, ruffling his son's hair.

'And I got a sticker book,' Immy added, promptly sticking a shiny pink fairy onto William's forehead. 'That's for you, Daddy.'

'Thanks, Immy.'

Immy floated off round the pool to present the other sunbathers with the fruits of her generosity.

Chloë, woken from her slumber by Immy, sauntered across to her father and sat on the bottom of his bed.

'Hi, Daddy.'

'Hi, Chloë.'

'You know this party tonight?'

'Yes.'

'Do I have to come?'

'You do. We've all been invited and I'd like you to be there.'

''Kay. Then can I bring Christoff?'

'The guy you met at the airport?'

'Yeah. He was taking me out again tonight so I thought he could hook up with us.'

'No, he couldn't "hook up". He's not been invited and this is a family party.'

'Oh Dad, I'll tell him not to eat much.'

'No. And that's my final word.'

Chloë sighed heavily, then shrugged. 'Whatever.' She stood up and wandered off in the direction of the house.

There was a knock on Helena's bedroom door as she emerged from the shower.

'Come in.'

'Only me.'

It was Jules, sporting a badly peeling nose.

'Hello.' Helena gave a ghost of a smile and slipped hastily into her robe as Jules sat down on the bed.

'I was wondering, Helena, whether tomorrow you'd come and look at this house I'm thinking of buying. I did ask William, but frankly he didn't seem that interested.'

There was a moment's hesitation before Helena replied, 'Of course I will.'

'Thanks.' Jules nodded gratefully. 'I'd like another opinion before I sign on the dotted line and put down the deposit.'

'Which is due when?'

'Next week some time.'

'Goodness, that's fast. Will you tell Sacha before you sign?' she asked carefully.

'*Who?*'

'You haven't heard from him, then?'

'Yes, I have, he's left a couple of messages on my mobile. But I think it's about time I made some decisions without him, don't you?'

'Jules, it's none of my business, really it isn't.'

'No.' Jules was studying her nails. 'I know it isn't.' Then she looked up at Helena and smiled brightly. 'Well, if I do buy it, we'll almost be neighbours. It's only on the other side of the village. That would be fun, wouldn't it?'

'Yes. Of course it would. By the way, you haven't forgotten about this party tonight, have you?' Helena changed the subject.

'William reminded me. I'm looking forward to it. It'll

give me a chance to meet some of the locals.' Jules stood up, then gazed around the bedroom. 'Bet you can't wait to give this house a decent paint job. The grey colour in here is just *too* depressing. See you later.'

At six thirty, everyone gathered on the terrace for pre-party drinks. Sadie had alerted the household to the fact that it was Helena and William's anniversary, and had arranged for Angelina to serve local sparkling wine and canapés she'd made earlier.

'Chloë, is that a pelmet you have slung round your hips?' asked William, staring in horror at the tiny leather skirt, which barely covered his daughter's bottom.

'Oh Dad, don't be such a prude. We're all practically naked during the day here, so why should the evenings be any different?' She swung her sheet of shiny hair and flounced off to talk to Rupes, who was wearing a lurid pink shirt that only served to exacerbate his sun-enhanced complexion.

'You look nice, Mum,' Alex offered, emerging onto the terrace. 'Happy anniversary, by the way.'

'Thank you, darling,' Helena said gratefully.

'Doesn't she look nice, Dad?' urged Alex.

William turned round and studied the cornflower-blue silk dress his wife was wearing. It was one of his favourites, matching the colour of her eyes. With her freshly washed, sun-bleached hair hanging loose around her face and her skin subtly tanned, William thought with immense sadness that she had never looked more beautiful. 'Yes.' He nodded. And turned away.

*

An hour later, everyone was piling into the cars to take them up to Alexis' house when a taxi turned the corner and began making its way down the hill.

'Well, I never! It's the prodigal returned,' said Jules, resplendent in a gold top with a matching headband worn Greek-style across her forehead.

'It's Daddy!' Viola shouted delightedly, running towards the oncoming car.

'Hello, lovely.' Sacha clambered out of the car as his daughter threw herself at him. He hugged her tightly.

'We've missed you, Daddy.'

'And I've missed you.' He looked up at the assembled company. 'Well, this is a nice welcome! You all look smart. Are you off out somewhere?'

'We're going to a party, Daddy,' said Viola.

'Ahh,' Sacha responded with a nod. 'Can I come?'

'Of course you can, can't he, Mummy?'

'Never one to miss a good bash, were you darling? You probably smelt the alcohol from London,' Jules replied sarcastically.

'Why don't the two of you stay here? We'll take the kids with us, give you a chance to say hello to each other, then you could both follow us up a little later?' William suggested hopefully, trying to provide the opportunity for Sacha and Jules to talk alone.

'*He* can follow us up, if he wants. *I'm* going now. Come on, you lot. We're going to be late. See you later, *sweetheart*,' Jules drawled as she ushered her children into her car.

Sacha shrugged helplessly as he watched his wife snap the driver's door shut.

'Okay, change of plan,' William said to Helena. 'I'll stay here with Sacha, let him change and have a wash, then drive him up. You lead the rest.'

'Do you know where to go?' she asked him.

'Vaguely. I'll find it.' William turned his attention to Sacha, 'Come on, old chap, let's go and have a chat.'

ALEX'S DIARY

21st July 2006

It's not often I feel anger. The deep, burn-through-your-heart-and-set-your-soul-on-fire sort.

I understand now how men can kill in moments of high emotion. This was what I felt by the pool this morning.

I should have known at the start it would not go to plan.

My faithful sidekick Immy had a humongous tantrum about not being able to put on her favourite dress to be a spy.

An overgrown woodland pixie in a voluminous piece of lurid pink netting and chiffon, wearing sparkly flip-flops and a pair of yellow sunglasses shaped like stars, just might have been noticeable in the olive trees and given the game away.

I'll bet James Bond never had this kind of trouble with Moneypenny. So I had to leave her be and face the consequences alone.

Rupes appeared at the allotted time. He was wearing those hideous Ray-Bans of his and trying to look cool.

'Got the letter?' he asked me, from the other side of the pool.

He stood legs akimbo, arms folded, looking like he was having his team photo taken as captain of the Rugby First XV. He didn't frighten me. Much.

'Got the bunny?' I replied.

'Yeah. Let's see the letter then.'

'Let's see the bunny.'

Rupes unfolded his arms and turned to retrieve a plastic bag from under a sunbed mattress. Damn! He'd obviously planted Bee there earlier and I could have come and got him without all this palaver. I saw Bee's precious head sticking out of the plastic. And nodded. I held up the envelope.

'It's in French, as promised.'

'Read it to me.'

'Of course.'

I cleared my throat.

'"Ma chèrie Chloë. Prendre vers le bas la lune!"'

'In English, you muppet!'

'Sorry. "Cancel the stars! There is a new light in the firmament! You shine like a new-born angel, fresh against worn-out planets! You have eyes like sma—"'

'Okay, enough.' Rupes looked as if he was going to be sick. 'Give it to me.'

'I want the bunny at the same moment. We'll walk towards each other and do the exchange.'

Rupes shrugged and started walking round the pool. We met at the edge of the deep end.

I could see he was sweating. I was as cool as a cucumber. 'Here.' I reached out one hand which contained the letter and the other to grab the bunny bag.

His hands came towards me. He clasped the letter and I clasped the handles of the bag.

Then, quick as a flash, he wrenched the bag out of my hands and threw it into the pool.

There was an almighty splash. I gasped in horror as, having expected it to float, I realised that it wasn't going to. My precious Bee sank slowly out of sight.

'Cheers for this.' Rupes was waving the envelope and chuckling manically. 'You can practise your apparently magnificent diving skills, saving that old bit of fluff. Sorry Chloë's not here to cheer you on!'

'Bastard!' I screamed, unzipping my shorts in preparation to jump in, then realising I had no underpants on underneath and doing them up again.

'Come on then, let's see you!' taunted Rupes as I jumped in, heavy Bermudas with days' worth of un-emptied crap in the pockets weighing me down.

I took a gulp of air and went under, feeling the chlorine burn my eyeballs (I never swim underwater without goggles as I emerge looking like a close relative of the Devil) and searched around in the murk for Bee.

He couldn't have gone far. He was light, so why on earth hadn't he floated? I came up for air, my vision blurred, to see Rupes laughing his socks off. (If he'd had any on. Which he didn't. Another ridiculous turn of phrase, but this was not the moment to analyse the English language.)

I drew breath again and swam down, and down, my lungs bursting with fury and panic and lack of oxygen. And there, right at the bottom of the seven-foot-deep deep end, lay Bee.

I came up again, wishing I could take my shorts off, but knowing the ignominy of remarks about the Lilliputian state of my privates would be too much to bear. Off I dived again, and managed to grab the top of the bag and pull. Then I pulled some more.

I couldn't move it. About to expire, I swam to the surface, my head spinning. I was gulping for breath so heavily I could not speak. I swam to the side and held on as I let my lungs fill. The thought of Bee drowning at the bottom, the chlorine eating into the remains of his delicate, un-furry fur, spurred me on. Taking a last gargantuan breath, I dove under the surface again, clasped the ear of my little friend and gave an almighty tug. And thank the Lord, he shifted. The swim up to the surface, dragging myself, my Bermudas and what felt like a two-ton sack of coal, will go down in history as the most harrowing moment of my life so far.

I could have drowned. My worst enemy and my best friend could have killed me.

When my hand came out of the water and I groped for the side of the pool to haul myself up the last few agonising inches, coughing and choking, I saw Rupes laughing away above me.

'Just doing as my dear mama asked; getting you ready for boarding school. See ya, Alex.'

With a wave and a smirk, he was gone.

My legs shaking like unset jelly, I pulled myself and my bunny up the steps and collapsed onto the side of the pool.

I turned and looked at the pitiful pile of soaking fur lying next to me. And saw the big rock that was tied to his paws. The ear by which I had pulled him up was now hanging on by one tiny thread.

I don't know how I've got through today, but I have. My fury and humiliation have known no bounds. I have contemplated running away, taking the next flight to Marrakech where I could work as a snake-charmer, if I could learn to conquer my intense phobia of snakes, but that would punish my mother and so wouldn't be fair.

Instead, I must go to this party, and live with the fact that my adversary will be there too. I comfort myself with the idea that he looks like a large pink pig in that shirt and also with the fact that Chloë is now completely ignoring him. I will use the time to make a plan which will be – and do not doubt me here – a fitting and just revenge.

Fifteen

The engagement party was taking place in the large court-yard at the front of the ancient, vine-smothered winery, which stood at one of the highest points in the village, overlooking a deep valley. The courtyard was bedecked with strings of fairy lights woven through the branches of the silvery olive trees that surrounded it, their glow augmented by the dozens of lanterns that had been lit all around.

A group of cheerful local women served out platefuls of food from behind a line of trestle tables, which were loaded with an enticing medley of delicious-smelling dishes: stuffed vine leaves, spit-roasted pork and lamb, *spanakopita* and grilled fish, accompanied by huge bowls of rice and salads.

By the time the Pandora posse arrived, the evening was already in full swing. A three-piece Cypriot band was play-ing in the corner, drowned out for the most part by the chatter of the two hundred or so guests. Wine was poured into glasses through a tube, straight from an enormous oak barrel.

'An alcoholic's paradise,' breathed Jules, taking a glass of white. 'Sacha would love it,' she added as she wandered off to circulate.

'Can I have a glass of wine, Mum?' asked Alex as he watched both Chloë and Rupes help themselves.

'Yes, a small one,' Helena agreed, taking a sip of her own and feeling oddly alone. She couldn't remember the last time she'd been to a party without William beside her. The situation was made all the more poignant by the fact that tonight should have been a celebration of their own marriage.

'Look, Alex, there's a man eating fire over there.' Viola, left stranded by Jules, pointed to another corner of the courtyard. 'Can we go and watch?'

'Why not?'

They pushed through the crowd, who were all dressed in their best, towards the fire-eater.

'Do you think my daddy is okay?' Viola reached up on tiptoe to speak into his ear.

'I don't know, Viola, but I should think so.'

'He's not. I know something is wrong with him.'

Alex reached for her small hand and tucked it into his own. 'Viola, parents are funny things. Try not to worry. I'm sure whatever it is will sort itself out. In my experience, these things usually do.'

'William's not your real dad, is he?'

'No, he isn't.'

'Did you know that my daddy isn't either? Or my mum?'

'Yes, I did.'

'I love him like he is, though. He's always been there, you see. It doesn't matter really, does it?'

'What?'

'Whether you have their genes. I'm sure my real father could never have been as nice and kind as the one I got. Do you love William? I think he's lovely.'

'I . . . yes, I do.'

'I'm glad he's my godfather. Alex?'

'Yup?'

'Do you think they love us the same as if we *were* theirs?' she asked uncertainly.

"Course they do, Viola. Probably even more. I mean, you got chosen by them especially.' He gave her a clumsy hug, then pointed to the fire-eaters. 'Hey, look how high they're throwing the fire sticks up in the air.'

'Wow,' she said, distracted, her face full of wonder.

'There you both are.' Helena appeared behind them.

A waitress was passing with a tray of wine and Helena drained what was left of hers, then took another.

'Mum! Be careful. You know you can't drink more than a couple without getting squiffy.'

'Alex, you are not my minder, and this is a special occasion,' Helena snapped at him.

'Sorr-*eee*. Come on, Viola, I'll take you to the front so you can see better.'

Left to herself again, Helena drifted through the mass of people, listening to the excited chatter of a crowd in which everyone was almost certainly distantly – if not directly – related to someone else, through years of intermarriage. She gazed at the throng gathering around the band, a few couples beginning to dance. Dimitrios and his fiancée, Kassie, were at the centre of it, their faces animated with happiness.

Helena thought it unlikely that their lives would ever

take them far from this place, and she imagined they would probably produce a new generation of strapping boys who would one day take over the winery. They would find their pleasure through each other, their children and the close community that supported them.

Helena felt suddenly envious. And terribly sad.

'How are you this evening, my Helena?'

She was momentarily startled by the voice at her shoulder, and turned to find Alexis standing behind her.

'Hello.' She gathered herself together, thinking that she mustn't spoil the celebration with her own self-indulgent melancholy. 'This is a wonderful party – thank you so much for inviting us all.'

'It is my pleasure, and my son's. I only wish to know that you are enjoying yourselves.'

'Oh, we are.' She hesitated for a moment, not wanting to broach the subject, but feeling she must. 'Alexis, please forgive me for my outburst yesterday.'

He gave her a sad smile. 'No apology necessary. I only wish you had told me years ago. But what is done is done. The important thing now is that we learn and move forward. Speaking of that, where is William? I have not seen him tonight.'

'He's coming later, with Jules' husband.'

'I see.' Alexis let out a sigh. 'I fear he is unhappy because he saw me holding his wife in my arms.'

'He is. And it just happens to be our tenth wedding anniversary tonight.'

'Then Helena, I think you must explain to him the circumstances. William should know the truth. It will help him to understand you. And me.'

If only it was as simple as that, thought Helena, as a cheer came up from the crowd watching Dimitrios and his fiancée dance.

Alexis looked across at them and smiled. 'I wish that we were them, beginning our lives together. But' – he shrugged – 'it was not to be. And I want you to know I now accept it will never be. You belong to another, and I can see that he loves you very much. Truly, Helena, I wish to apologise both to you and to him. My behaviour has been unacceptable. I have struggled to adjust to the fact you are no longer mine . . . but I must. Now, come and let me introduce you to some faces from your past.'

He stretched out his hand. After a moment's hesitation, she held out her own. 'Yes. Thank you, Alexis.'

Alexis' friends – mere boys when she first knew them – were now fathers with wives. They clasped Helena to them, greeted her warmly, telling her she was still beautiful and asking her questions about her family and Pandora. She enjoyed their attention, but with Alexis' sage words still ringing in her brain, she couldn't help wondering whether William would actually come, or whether she'd spend the night of their tenth anniversary alone.

Which was no more than she deserved . . .

The dancing had begun in earnest and the guests were all taking to the floor to dance the traditional Cypriot steps, passed down through generations. Helena saw Jules and Sadie in the crowd, their arms above their heads, trying to follow their partners' movements.

'Papa! Papa! You must dance *Zorba* for us.' A sweating Dimitrios clapped his father on the back.

'Yes, Alexis! Dance for us! Dance!' The crowd took up the refrain.

'And Helena, you must dance with him, like you danced together here before!' It was Isaák, an old friend of Alexis'.

'Yes, let's see you strut your stuff. It's meant to be what you do, after all!' Jules shouted from the crowd, as multiple hands pushed Helena forward to join Alexis in the centre of the huge circle that had formed around them, everyone grasping each other's shoulders in preparation.

'Remember this?' He smiled at her gently. 'My eighteenth birthday party, held right here.'

'How could I ever forget?' she whispered.

'Shall we begin?'

He clicked his fingers above his head, the signal that they were ready, and the bouzouki player struck up the ponderous opening chords.

As the circle began to move around them, so Helena and Alexis did too, the steps precise, clipped. They danced separately, but together, and even though Helena had not danced these steps for almost a quarter of a century, they were imprinted on her memory. And now, the music and her body commanded her. She was no longer a nearing-forty wife and mother, but a free-spirited fifteen-year-old, dancing in a sun-filled field of grapes with the boy she loved.

The steps, so simple when they were slow, became more complicated as the music raced on, faster and faster, Helena twirling and swooping around Alexis. As the tempo increased, the crowd circling them began whooping and stamping their feet. Alexis caught her in his arms and lifted her high above him, spinning her round and round until they were a whirling dervish of passion and excitement.

Above him, Helena opened her arms wide and threw back her head, trusting him completely. Flashes of colour were all she could see around her, the sound of cheering ringing in her ears.

She was *dancing*! She felt alive, exhilarated, *wonderful* . . .

Then the music slowed, and Alexis let her down gently, her body brushing close against his on its journey to the ground. He took her hands in his and kissed them, then spun her away from him so she could curtsey and he could bow.

The cries for an encore were relentless. Eventually, Alexis quietened the crowd. 'Thank you, thank you.' He took a handkerchief out of his pocket and wiped the sweat from his forehead. 'It is all too much for an old man.' The crowd protested, but Alexis held up his hands again for silence. 'Tonight we are here to celebrate the engagement of my son and his beautiful fiancée.'

Helena slipped away into the crowd as Alexis ushered his son and future daughter-in-law to stand next to him.

'Auntie Helena, you were really great.' Viola caught her hand, her eyes full of admiration.

'Wow, sweetie! Amazing!' said Sadie, as a small crowd formed around them.

'I didn't know you could dance like that,' said Rupes.

'Nor did I,' said a voice behind her. Helena turned on her heel.

'William, where on earth have you been?'

'Sorting out Sacha. Anyway, seems as though you've been getting on perfectly well without me.'

'Yes, I've had a lovely time,' she said defiantly. 'Now, I need a drink of water.'

'Shall I get you one?' he offered.

'No, I'll get one myself, thanks.'

William followed her. 'What the hell is going on?'

'Nothing! I was dancing, that's all.'

'For God's sake, Helena, you're my wife!'

'Yes, I am. So what was I doing wrong?'

'Helena, I'm not an idiot! Everyone who was watching saw it. It sticks out a mile.'

'What does?'

'Christ! Do I really have to spell it out? I've given you the benefit of the doubt time and again, tried to ignore the fact that every time I'm out of the house, *he's* there, like a rat up a drainpipe, sniffing around.' He grabbed a glass of wine from the table, took a gulp, then, noticing the two fascinated waitresses standing behind it, pulled Helena away into a quiet corner.

'Mr Bloody Perfect! Mr Helpful! "Mr Fix-it", as your son calls him! Even yesterday, after I'd taken the kids out because I thought you needed a rest and some time to yourself, who do I find on the terrace when I arrive back, clasping you to his chest? *Him!*'

'He came to make sure I was all right,' Helena replied quietly.

'I'm sure he did. And on top of that, I arrive here tonight and see the two of you dancing, looking as though you . . . *belonged* together! For once, just tell me the truth! You're still in love with him, aren't you? For *CHRIST'S* sake, just say it, Helena.' He took her roughly by the shoulders. 'TELL me!'

'Stop it, William, please! Not here, not now . . . we'll talk later, I promise.'

He looked at her, then gave a sigh of exasperation and defeat. Dropping his arms from her shoulders, he shook his head. 'But I'm telling you now that I don't want to be with someone who doesn't want to be with me. Happy anniversary, Helena.'

Then he turned and made his way swiftly into the crowd.

Feeling tearful, she walked back to the wine barrel and refilled her glass. She was about to take a large sip when someone put an arm clumsily round her shoulder, spilling the wine everywhere.

'Hello, lovely girl.'

'Sacha. You made it,' she said apprehensively.

'I did.' He brandished a brandy bottle at her, and took a swig.

Even though Helena had drunk more than she normally would, she was sober enough to recognise just how drunk *he* was. 'You look dreadful.'

'Probably,' he agreed, swaying slightly, 'but as a matter of fact I feel fantastic. You see, my angel, I have cause for celebration.'

'Really?'

'Oh yes.'

'Why?' She almost didn't want to know the answer.

'Because, in a few minutes' time, I will be free! And you know what that means, don't you, my sweetest Helena?'

'No, Sacha, I don't.'

'It means . . . well, you know what it means. But now, I

must go and find my lovely wife. And impart the good news.'

He gave her a wobbly mock-bow, then swayed back into the crowd. Helena watched as he pushed his way into the centre and went to stand next to Alexis, who had just finished speaking. Her eyes searched wildly for William, but she couldn't see him anywhere.

'Ladies and gentlemen! Do forgive me for butting in like this,' Sacha slurred. 'My name is Sacha Chandler, and I would like to add my own congratulations to those of this gentleman here. What is your name, sir?'

'I am Alexis.'

'Alexis. What a great name.' Sacha slapped Alexis hard on the back. 'Are you married?'

'I was, yes.'

'Oh dear. Did it all go pear-shaped? A trip down divorce drive?'

'No. My wife died,' said Alexis quietly, looking at the ground.

The crowd was still now, hushed, holding its breath as one. William appeared suddenly at Sacha's side and laid a hand on his shoulder.

'Come on, old chap, time to go home.'

'Go home? But I've only just got here!' shouted Sacha, shaking William's hand off. 'And anyway, I have an announcement of my own. Where is my lovely wife, Julia?'

'I'm here, Sacha.' Jules spoke up from the back of the throng.

'Right, I need to tell you something.' Sacha took another swig of his brandy. 'You see, I've got to do it now, or else I'll never find the courage. So, here goes, my love: my company

257

has not so much been liquidated, as nuked off the planet. I no longer have a single sou to my name. Oh, and no house either, because I mortgaged it to the hilt, so the bank'll snaffle that *tout de suite*. We are destitute, my angel, and have nothing but the clothes we stand up in. No more poncey schools for the kids. They'll have to move to the local comp, and those nags of yours in the back paddock will probably end up in a wok in the local Chinese take-away.'

Sacha laughed harshly at his own tasteless joke. Holding the bottle aloft, he toasted his horrified but rapt audience. 'So, ladies and gentlemen, there we have it! A double cele-bration! The start of one union, the end of another. Cheers.' He took a swig from his bottle.

The crowd began whispering, many of the non-English-speakers asking their neighbours to translate. William finally managed to grasp hold of Sacha's arm and pull him away.

Helena, who up until now had been paralysed by Sacha's drunken oration, raced to William's side, their earl-ier conversation on hold in the drama of the moment. 'Christ. What do we do now?' she whispered desperately.

They both looked at Sacha, who was hanging on to William for support.

'Go and look for Jules,' he suggested. 'See what she wants to do.'

Helena did so, but although she searched the entire party, both Jules and Rupes seemed to have vanished into thin air. She eventually found Viola sobbing into Alex's chest.

'What's going to happen, Mum?' mouthed Alex over Viola's Titian curls.

'I'm going to drive us all home as soon as possible. Let me just go and round everyone up. You take Viola to the car. It's open.'

'Okay. Don't be too long,' he whispered urgently.

'I won't.'

Helena hurried off and eventually found William and Alexis sitting on a wall, with Sacha doubled over between them.

'Jules has disappeared along with Rupes, but I want to take Viola and Alex home.'

'I have suggested William and Sacha stay here with me tonight,' said Alexis. 'Perhaps it is better, until the dust settles.'

Helena looked quizzically at William, who nodded in agreement.

'I'm gonna puke. Sorry chaps,' moaned Sacha, then promptly did so.

'You go home to the kids, Helena, there's nothing you can do here,' said William, getting out his handkerchief to clean Sacha up, while Alexis leapt up and ran off to fetch some water. 'Let me know if Jules turns up. I'll stay and make sure my oldest friend doesn't choke to death on his own vomit.'

'Are you sure you'll be okay staying here?' she asked her husband, hoping the expression in her eyes told him how she felt for his situation.

'Alexis and I had a chat just now and he says he has spare rooms. I don't want the children – any of them – seeing Sacha like this. It's not fair on them. Apart from the fact Jules might get violent. And has every reason to do so,' William sighed.

'Okay.' She tried to read his expression, but it told her nothing. 'Keep in touch.'

'I will,' he said, and turned his attention back to Sacha.

ALEX'S DIARY

21st July (continued)

Ahem.

Well, gosh! And all that. What can one say? I am . . . speechless, or wordless, as the case may be.

Unlike others, who made quite . . . umm . . . dramatic speeches tonight.

It was a seminal moment. Not quite up to Winston's level, but to give Sacha credit where it's due, he was very drunk and yet he didn't stumble over his words once.

So much for a quiet, relaxing holiday.

It is one o'clock, or thereabouts, and I am holed up in my hole. And because of the evening's Greek tragedy, played out for the entire village to witness and applaud, then hold their breath in horror, I too have been affected:

I am now feeling guilty. Dreadfully guilty.

They say you should be careful what you wish for, because you might not like it when you get it. And I don't.

Earlier today, when I was pegging my bedraggled bunny by the feet on a piece of string I'd managed to hang across my small window to catch the air (I couldn't risk leaving him on the line outside as he might have disappeared again), I asked God to employ a just punishment for Rupes, as I myself could not think of one heinous enough. In time it would have come to me, but my brain was addled by chlorine and emotion.

And, hey presto! Big G comes up with a pearl: Rupes is homeless and penniless. Penis-less would have been better, but let's not be churlish about this.

And best of all, he will probably have to face the prospect of some sink-estate comprehensive. If those exist on the out-skirts of Godalming, which they may not. But as they're near broke, they'll probably have to move to somewhere revolting anyway.

Rupes will duly be annihilated by a hoodie-wearing, knife-carrying gang of thugs, who will pulverise the public school out of him, and then some.

Oh! The joy!

On the other hand, I realise suddenly, he might gain con-trol, become leader of the pack and end up saving his family's fortunes as a drug pusher, insisting his gang swap the trainers and hoodies for brogues from Lobb and overcoats from Aquascutum. Though to be fair, I equivocate: he's cer-tain to get caught eventually, because he is a victim of his own arrogance, and will probably end up doing time in the clink with rapists and perverts for neighbours.

However, as much as I am overwhelmed by my prayers being answered – and so promptly, to boot – the look on little Viola's face was enough to make me feel like a complete heel.

A six-inch stiletto, in fact.

So, it's a Pyrrhic victory, as these things usually are.

Jules and Rupes vanished into the night like erstwhile lovers, leaving poor little Viola sobbing her heart out all over me.

When we arrived home, Mum, who'd sobered up considerably since her Dirty Dance with Mr Fix-it – puke! – took Viola off upstairs to bed, and told me and Chloë to follow suit.

We had a quiet chat at the bottom of the stairs before we parted for the night. Chloë seemed to think the whole thing was a complete hoot, but then I think she'd had more to drink than Mum, a habit that will have to stop once we are affianced. She was far more interested in telling me all about the dreamy Michel, Mr Fix-it's younger son, and how gorgeous he was . . . *also* a habit that will have to stop.

She was cross 'cos Mum had insisted she leave the party and come home with us, as Michel had already offered her a lift on his scooter later. And also because Sadie *did* stay on. She'd found a ten-year-old bloke she was hanging off, who'd also offered her a lift home on his scooter later.

I know she's Mum's best mate and she's great fun, but isn't there a time when you admit you've had it? That you're past it? Like, at twenty-five?

Sadie's miniskirt was competing with Chloë's for lack of length and I really think someone, like Mum, should take her in hand and tell her she should adopt a more mature approach to her attire. Preferably based on a nun's habit, and definitely no knees on show.

Mutton dressed as lamb . . . now, that cliché *does* make sense. And is, in my opinion, what Sadie looked like.

I saw *The Graduate* once. I didn't get it, I really didn't.

I divest myself of my shorts and T-shirt and sink into my bed, to find myself in a soggy puddle.

Dammit!

I look above me and see Bee still trying to break the world record for the longest time a rabbit can hang upside down, and realise he has spent the past few hours dripping all over my pillow and sheets. I stand up on the bed and unpeg him. He is relatively dry. Not surprising, as all the water now resides in my bed.

I manage a U-turn and move to the other end of it, so it's my feet that will get pneumonia, not my chest.

And I close my eyes and try to sleep . . . but adrenaline is pumping round my body, my heart making my body believe it is on a five-mile uphill run. In temperatures of over a hundred and forty degrees. I cannot still its beat enough to relax, and I know why.

Leaving Rupes and his weird family aside, all is not well with my own.

That dance. Him and *her* . . .

The ramifications are, frankly, terrifying. The linchpin, the safety-pin that is my mother, seems to have unpinned herself from Dad. And if she has, that might mean she unpins us all from our . . . *life*.

The fact I have a stepdad, that we have no choice but to tolerate each other, that he won't buy ice creams over a pound, and that I know he thinks I'm weird for preferring Plato to Pelé, is hardly perfect.

But I've realised tonight that he isn't that bad. In fact, he's quite a decent bloke. He's . . . safe, compared to other alternatives I could mention. Which are not . . . *he* is not . . . an alternative.

There is a timid knock on my door.

'Alex, are you awake?'

It's Viola. Oh, crap. 'Er, no, not really.'

'Okay.'

Then I hear her little feet padding away. And feel so guilty that I manoeuvre myself to standing and open the door. 'I am now,' I say to the shadowy ghost in her white nightgown. 'You okay?'

She shakes her head. 'I just heard Mummy come in with Rupes, but she's locked her bedroom door and told me to go away,' she whispers desolately.

I reach out my hand to her. 'Want to come into my Broom Cupboard for a bit?'

'Thank you.' And she takes my hand and follows me inside.

Sixteen

It was five thirty in the morning when William woke to bright sunlight streaming through unshuttered windows. It took him a few seconds to realise that he was not in bed at Cedar House back in Hampshire, or at Pandora. He was in one of the guest rooms at Alexis Lisle's elegant old house, which stood adjacent to the winery.

Slowly, the events of last night began to filter into his drowsy brain, and he groaned softly.

What a mess.

He shook himself fully awake, then clambered out of the single bed and peered at the figure lying in the other bed next to him. Having satisfied himself that Sacha was breathing steadily and sound asleep, and knowing that the chances of dropping off again himself were negligible, he dressed and crept downstairs into the cool, tiled hallway.

There were no other sounds of activity in the house, so he let himself out by the front door and wandered aimlessly down the long drive, across the rough track at the end of it, and into the dusty rows of vines in the vineyard beyond.

As he walked in the soft, misty light of the early morning, he tried to make sense of what had happened at the party. Quite apart from Sacha's alcohol-fuelled revelations, he suspected that he too had behaved badly.

Helena . . .

He'd been consumed by a red-hot lava of jealousy when he'd arrived to see her dancing with such abandon in Alexis' arms. His anger had finally exploded, after days of slowly burning resentment and confusion over the exact status of Helena and Alexis' relationship.

And the fact it was their tenth wedding anniversary had only exacerbated the situation.

William plucked a bunch of grapes from a vine and ate a couple, knowing their juicy flesh would not placate his growing thirst. The heat was already overpowering, and he needed some water. As he turned back and began to retrace his footsteps, he mused on Helena's general reluctance to open up emotionally to him.

Why did he feel that she always held back? Stood just a heartbeat away from truly being *his* . . . ?

Was it to do with Alexis?

Well, he decided, there was only one way to find out. And that was to confront the man himself.

Letting himself into the house, he heard sounds of activity from a room at the far end of the hallway. Making his way towards it, he tentatively opened the door to a large, sunlit kitchen, where he found Alexis busy brewing coffee.

'How are you, William? Did you sleep well?' Alexis turned and gave him a sympathetic smile.

'For a short while, yes, thank you. Alexis, I must apologise for putting upon you like this. And for that very unfortunate scene last night.'

'These things happen, William. I checked on Sacha just now and he's still out cold.'

'It will do him good to sleep. I doubt he has for a long time.'

'Coffee?'

'Yes – and some water, please, Alexis.'

Alexis poured water and then two cups from the coffee pot on the stove, and set them on the table. 'Please, my friend, be seated.'

The two of them sat opposite each other and concentrated for a few moments on sipping the hot, reviving liquid.

It was William who eventually broke the silence. 'Alexis, forgive me if it's not an appropriate time to have this conversation, given what happened last night, but I have to ask you bluntly, as I don't know any other way . . . what exactly *is* the story between you and Helena?'

Alexis paused for a few seconds, then nodded slowly. 'I am glad you ask me. And that we have an unexpected opportunity to talk in private. I was going to make sure that I engineered one myself. So . . .' he sighed, 'I think it is no secret that Helena and I had a summer romance when we were younger. When she left here, I saw her only once after that.'

'But she told me she hadn't laid eyes on you after her last summer here.'

'She tells the truth. I went to watch her dance with the

La Scala ballet at the amphitheatre in Limassol. She never even knew that I was there.'

'I see,' murmured William.

'And I will admit now that when I heard she was returning to Pandora after all these years . . . well, I cannot deny that there was a part of me that wondered if our old feelings for each other might reignite. But I tell you truthfully, William, that I know now there can never be more than memories and friendship between us. Because it is obvious she loves you, and she has told me so. Please forgive me, William. And you must not doubt her feelings for you. And if I have given you cause to, then all I can do is apologise wholeheartedly. It is no fault of Helena's, I swear.'

'Thank you.' William swallowed hard, fighting to control his emotions as a wave of relief washed over him. 'But I can't help feeling there's more to it than she's telling me. Is there, Alexis?'

'That, my friend' – Alexis glanced at him – 'is something you must ask your wife.'

Helena looked at the clock, gasping when she saw it was past nine o'clock and wondering why the little ones hadn't climbed into bed with her, as they often did if she was still sleeping. Grabbing her robe from the back of the door, she left the bedroom and made her way downstairs to the kitchen.

'Hi, Mummy! You weren't up, so I made Fred and me some breakfast,' Immy announced proudly.

Helena looked around at the devastation. She picked up a half-eaten bar of cooking chocolate and an upturned pot of olives from the floor. There was flour and sugar all over the table and floor, which would soon summon the local massed armies of ants.

'Hello, Mummy,' said a voice from under the table.

Helena pulled up the tablecloth, took one look at Fred's mouth and knew immediately where the other half of the cooking chocolate had gone.

'Hello, Fred,' she replied wearily, deciding she couldn't even begin to start clearing up until she'd downed a cup of coffee, and she filled and switched on the kettle.

'Can Immy make me breakfast every day, Mummy? She does it really good. Better than you,' he added gleefully.

'I'm sure she does. Why didn't you come in to wake me up like you usually do?' she asked.

'We did, Mummy, but you didn't wake up. You must have been very tired. Here's a drink for you.' Immy smiled and handed Helena a plastic cup full of some rank-smelling green gunk. 'I made it. Taste it. It's got lots of good things in it.'

'I . . . will, in a minute.' Helena almost gagged on the smell, feeling the effects of last night, which had prompted an alcoholic and emotional hangover. 'Thank you, Immy,' she managed as she put the cup down.

'Where Daddy?' asked Fred from his hidey-hole.

'He went with Uncle Sacha to do some . . . business. He'll be back later.' Helena decided to forget the coffee, and went to the fridge to pour herself a pint of water instead. She took a large gulp as the kitchen door opened and Angelina came in.

'Good morning, leetle ones.' She peered under the table at Fred and kissed Immy. 'You have good time last night, Helena?'

'Yes, thank you.'

'My friends tell me eet was good party. And you dance beautiful with Mr Alexis.' Angelina's dark eyes sparkled.

'Did you dance, Mummy?' Immy asked, wide-eyed.

'Yes, I did, Immy. Everyone did. Angelina, I was wondering whether you could take them both down to the pool and watch them whilst they have a swim? Would you like that, you two?'

Fred was out from under the table like a shot. 'Yes, please!'

'I will take them. But first' – Angelina put her hands on her hips and surveyed Immy and Fred – 'who make this mess in my tidy kitchen?'

'We did! We did!' Fred started jumping around excitedly, as Immy looked on guiltily.

'Then first we tidy together, then we swim? Hokay?'

'Hokay,' they agreed in unison.

Gratefully, Helena took the opportunity to exit the kitchen and take a shower.

'Hello, Auntie Helena. I was just looking for you.' Viola was standing at the top of the stairs as Helena made her way upwards.

'How are you, darling?' she asked.

She looked down at Helena and shrugged miserably. 'Was it all a bad dream?'

'Oh Viola, I'm so sorry, but we both know it wasn't. Do you want to come with me into my bedroom? We could sit and have a talk together.'

'Okay.' Viola followed Helena into the bedroom, and onto the little balcony. 'Mummy's door is still locked. I just tried it.'

'Perhaps she's still sleeping, but I'm sure we can wake her up if you want to see her.'

'No, she'll just say horrid things about Daddy. I'm sure it's not all his fault, but she'll blame him anyway.'

'Darling Viola.' Helena's heart went out to her. 'You have to understand that she's as upset and as shocked as you are.'

'Will they get divorced, do you think? Alex said they might.'

'I really don't know what will happen. They need to talk, that's for sure.'

'But they never *do* talk! Daddy tries, but then Mummy just shouts at him. She never listens to him, ever. What will happen to me, Auntie Helena?'

'Darling, you'll still have your mum and dad, and Rupes, but maybe you'll need to move somewhere else, go to a different school, that's all.'

'I don't care about that. I hate my school anyway. But if Daddy and Mummy divorce, I'm living with Daddy, so there!' Viola buried her face in her hands. 'I still love him, even if Mummy doesn't.'

'I know, darling, and he loves you.'

'If I can't live with Daddy, can I live with you instead? You're so kind, and so is Alex. And I'd help with Immy and Fred, I promise,' Viola offered desperately.

'We'd love you to live with us, but I think your mum might not want you to.'

'She won't care. She'll just want her precious Rupes. I think *they* should get married, they love each other so much.' Viola let out a small, strangled chuckle.

'Oh Viola, don't say things like that. Mummy adores you.'

'No she doesn't, Auntie Helena. I don't know why she adopted me in the first place.'

'Because she loved you. And *still* loves you.' Helena struggled to find the right words of comfort.

'Besides' – Viola's face darkened – 'she's a liar.'

'Why do you say that?'

'Mummy has money that she's never told Daddy about.'

'How do you know?'

'I saw her bank statement in her handbag once, just after Granny died. It had noughts on the end of the number.'

'Did it?' Helena remembered Jules mentioning the amount her mother had left her the other night. 'Well, surely that's good news? Maybe things aren't so bad, after all?'

'She might not share it with Daddy, though. Which is wrong because he shares all his money with us. Do you think I should tell him?'

'Not for now, no.'

'Okay.' Viola rubbed her nose distractedly. 'Do you think he will come and see us today?'

'I really don't know. I think that's up to your mum and dad to decide.'

'But what about me?'

'Oh, darling.' Helena reached for Viola, and pulled her gently onto her lap. 'I'm so sorry for what's happened, but you're safe here with us for now, and I'm sure your mum and dad will sort things out. They've both had a big shock too.'

'I want to see Daddy, Auntie Helena. He needs a hug.'

'I know he does, and I'm sure you'll be able to give him one soon. Now, how about finding your bathing costume and coming downstairs with me and Immy and Fred for a swim?'

'Okay,' Viola said with a defeated shrug. Pulling out of Helena's embrace, she padded miserably out of the bedroom.

By eleven, Helena was feeling much better. A swim, coupled with the exuberance of her children, had revived her, although she was still distracted by what was happening up at the winery between William, Alexis and Sacha.

Alex emerged to join them, as did Chloë, and the two of them organised games to keep the little ones amused. Helena was relieved to see Viola shouting and screaming with the rest as Alex chased her up and down the pool.

'Helena.' Angelina sidled up to her, smiling. 'I clean house this morning, but when I finish may I take little ones to the village? My parents wish to meet them. We will have tea together. And Alexis . . . I mean, *Alex*, and Chloë and Viola with the lovely hair too, if they wish.'

'I'm sure they'd love to come with you, Angelina, but please don't go to any trouble.'

'Eet is no trouble! We love the childrens here, you know that. Maybe one day, I have some too, but for now, I adopt yours instead.'

'That's absolutely fine by me,' Helena said with a grateful smile.

As she walked back up to the house to change out of her wet bikini, she found Rupes sitting alone on the terrace.

'Hello, Rupes,' she said tentatively.

'Hi.'

'How are you?'

He shrugged listlessly.

'Seen your mother yet this morning?'

He nodded in reply.

'How is she?'

'How do you think she is?'

Helena sat down beside him. 'Not so great, I'm sure.'

'She's too ashamed to come out of her room. She says she can't face anyone at the moment.'

'I can understand that. Would it do any good if I went to talk to her? Tried to make her see that no one's judging her? That none of this is her fault? We all just want to help. If we can.'

'Dunno if it'd do any good or not,' Rupes shrugged. 'It's her pride, you see.'

'Of course.' Helena laid a hand on his arm. 'It'll be all right, you know. These things always are.'

'No, it won't be all right.' Rupes shook her hand away. 'Dad's ruined all of our lives. It's as simple as that.' He stood up and walked across the terrace and around the house, heading for the sanctuary of the vines. Helena knew it was because he didn't want her to see him cry. She walked into the kitchen and saw her mobile was blinking.

It was a text from William.

'*Hi. Sacha not good. Call u later.*'

Helena studied the text, realising what was missing. There was no kiss.

After lunch, Angelina loaded the children into her car to drive them up to the village. Rupes was still off on his own, and Sadie hadn't yet returned to Pandora at all. Taking a deep breath, Helena went upstairs and knocked softly on Jules' bedroom door.

'It's Helena. Can I come in?'

There was no response.

'Jules, I can quite understand you might not want to see anyone, but can I at least get you something to drink? Tea? Coffee? Triple vodka?'

Helena was just about to walk away when a voice said, 'Oh, what the hell! Why not? If you promise to make the vodka a quadruple. Door's open.'

Helena turned the handle and walked in. Jules was sitting cross-legged in the middle of the bed, still wearing the gold top from the previous night. There were clothes flung everywhere, and the enormous suitcase lay half packed on the floor.

'Are you leaving?' Helena asked.

Jules shrugged. 'I thought I would, so I started packing, then I remembered . . .' she choked back a sob, 'I don't have anywhere to go.'

'Oh Jules.' Helena went to her and put an arm round her. 'I'm so, so sorry. For everything,' she added.

'How *could* he have let it get so bad without telling me?' she cried. 'I'm not an ogre, am I, Helena? I mean, unapproachable? I've tried so hard to get him to talk to me about work, but he just clams up and pours himself another drink.'

'Of course you're not, and I'm sure Sacha didn't mean not to tell you. I suppose that things reach a point when you've lied so much that another lie doesn't seem to matter.'

Helena sighed. 'He was very stupid not to share it with you, and none of this is your fault. You must remember that.'

'I've tried, but every time I think of him standing there, drunkenly parading our dirty washing in front of all those strangers, I think what they must have thought of me: a woman whose husband couldn't turn to his wife in his hour of need. I've tried to be a good wife, I really have. And my God, it's been hard sometimes.' She shot a look at Helena. 'Sacha is not a William, as you know.'

'No, I'm quite sure he isn't. Listen, all the kids are up with Angelina in the village. The house is empty, so why don't you freshen up, then come downstairs and we'll have something to eat on the terrace?'

Jules nodded. 'Okay. Thanks, Helena.'

Ten minutes later, Jules was sitting at the table on the terrace, devouring a chicken sandwich that Helena had hastily prepared, and drinking a large glass of wine.

'I'm literally speechless, to be honest. I just don't know what to think or say. I suppose I must take what Sacha said at face value and assume everything's gone.'

'You really need to sit down and have a proper talk with him, find out exactly how things stand.'

'I know how things will stand if I set eyes on that idiot at the moment: he won't have any teeth left to talk *with*! No' – Jules shook her head – 'I really can't face him just yet. And if he calls you, please tell him not to come near me until I say so.'

'If it's any consolation, I doubt he's feeling any better than you are.'

'He's not getting an ounce of sympathy from me ever again. Things are bad enough, but why the hell he had to publicly humiliate not just me, but the children as well, I really don't understand. What got into him, Helena?'

'Desperation, fuelled by booze, I would think.'

'Oh, I know he's got a drink problem – has done for years. But I've rather given up, as if I even mention it, he calls me an old nag. Like my horses, the poor things,' said Jules, taking a gulp of her wine. 'So, what can you do? Until he accepts he's got a problem, it's a road to nowhere. A bit like my future looks right now.'

'I know it must feel that way, but there's always a solution, Jules.'

'Forgive me, Helena, I know you're trying to help, but I'm not in the mood for wholesome Pollyanna-type platitudes. The truth is, he never loved me, and God only knows why he married me in the first place.'

'Don't say that, Jules, please! Of course he loves you.'

'No, he doesn't and he never has. *Fact*. I've always known it. The trouble is, I let him get away with blue murder for years just so I could hang onto him, grateful for any small nugget of affection he cared to throw my way.'

'I'm sure—'

'Don't even waste your breath,' Jules snapped. 'I know it's made me bitter, but if you only knew what I've had to turn a blind eye to, you wouldn't believe it . . .' Jules paused, then turned away and stifled a sob. 'Really, I've tried everything, from supporting his ambition as an artist, having children – even adopting the baby girl he always said he wanted when we couldn't seem to make one of our own – to a comfortable home and a hot meal on the table every night. I even tried a full selection of Agent Provocateur undies, but it hasn't made any difference. You can't force something when it just isn't . . . *wasn't* there.'

Helena said nothing, knowing all she could do was listen.

'I think Sacha was looking for someone to "fix" him,' Jules continued. 'I was always grounded, and he was a dreamer, with his head up in the clouds. I brought him down to earth, I suppose, organised him. Responsibility has never been his strong point, as you know so well,' Jules sighed. 'But you know what really galls me?'

'What?'

'It's the way everyone feels sorry for *him*! "Poor old Sacha, having to live with that dreadful woman!" And don't tell me you and William don't think it, Helena, because I know you do. You all do!' Jules thumped the table and Helena just caught the bottle of wine before it toppled over. 'Even now, I'll bet the sympathy's with him, not me. And even Viola, my own daughter, protects and defends him against me. I know there'll be a certain element who will be thrilled to see me getting my just reward.'

'Jules, I'm sure that's not true.'

'Oh come on, Helena!' Jules rounded on her. 'You and William tolerate me so you can see him! I'm not a complete idiot, you know, and I'm sick to death of it! I really am.'

Jules topped up her glass again as Helena looked on. 'God, I wish I was like you.'

'Why on earth would you want to be like me?'

'Because everyone adores you, Helena. You glide round in your golden light, gathering people to you, bathing them in your glow, so that when they've been near you, they feel as though a little of the Helena magic has rubbed off on them. But I *don't* have empathy or natural charm like you. I'm awkward, not comfortable socially, *shy* if you must know, so the things I do and say often come out wrong. Whereas I'm sure that even if you *have* done wrong, you know what to say and do to put it right.'

'I promise you, I don't, Jules. I've made some terrible mistakes,' Helena said with feeling.

'Haven't we all?' Jules looked away and took another large gulp of wine. 'And maybe . . . just maybe,' she breathed, 'this is the best thing that could have happened. Perhaps I need a fresh start. God, Helena, I just want someone who loves me. It's as simple as that. Anyway, I know I'll have to face Sacha and talk the situation through, but not yet, not until I've got my thoughts into some kind of order. There's only one thing I know for certain; our marriage is over. *Finito*, dead and buried. And please don't tell me it isn't, because I promise you I shall scream.'

'I won't, I promise.'

'And don't worry, I won't be here for much longer. My family has already wrecked what should have been a relaxing holiday for you all. Just give me a couple of days to think what to do, okay?'

'Really, Jules, there's no rush. Of course you can stay as long as you want.'

'You know what, Helena? You really are a sweetie, despite everything . . .' Jules sighed. 'Right, I'm going to go up and try and get some sleep. That wine's done the trick. I didn't get a wink last night.'

'I'll be here when the kids get back. Don't worry about them.'

'Thanks. And no matter what's happened in the past,

you've been a good friend to me. I really value that.' Jules squeezed Helena's hand so tightly, it was all she could do not to wince.

With a heavy heart, Helena watched as Jules walked across the terrace and into the house.

And wondered which of the two of them was feeling worse.

ALEX'S DIARY

22nd July 2006

Forgive me, but . . .

I just have to say it. I've been holding out, and can't do it any longer. So here goes . . .

This afternoon was fun. An entire family of Cypriot strangers, offering us revolting cake, inedible biscuits and coffee with bits of grit added for extra substance.

They talked to us – and boy did they talk – but there was only one little problem . . .

It was all Greek to me.

Hah! I've said it now.

And I won't say it again.

Halfway through the Mad Hatter's tea party, Chloë disappeared. She said she was popping along to the shop. I begged her to let me go with her, but she said she needed to buy 'ladies' things', which is a total no-no as far as I'm concerned.

That whole secret area of a girl's life is another world to me. At my old school, the female members of the class spent hours in corners chatting away about 'stuff'. As soon as myself or another male approached them, they'd giggle and whisper and tell us to 'eff off'.

It's such a shame, really, when the great male and female divide happens at the onset of puberty. Up until the age of eleven, one of my best friends was a girl called Ellie. We used to chase each other round the playground and share lunch together, and secrets. She'd confide in me who she fancied, and I'd confide in her that I fancied no one. Year six at my local school was not exactly bursting with Scarlett Johanssons or Lindsay Lohans.

They say beauty is only skin-deep. That's a bit like saying you'd choose the most hideous sofa to sit on for thirty years just because it was comfy. You'd still have to look at it every day of your life, and be embarrassed when your friends came round and thought you had dreadful taste.

I would have chosen the elegant, uncomfortable version, every time.

Maybe I'm shallow, but Chloë is the metaphorical chaise longue of the female world. She is narrow, with an exquisitely carved back, delicately turned arms and so slender that you'd no doubt fall off occasionally when you dozed. But she would always be a thing of beauty, and would be auctioned off for thousands at Sotheby's in a hundred years' time.

She's a bit like my mother, I suppose. They're not blood-related, and yet they share definite qualities.

And I hope one of those, for everyone's sake, is fidelity.

Going back to my friend Ellie, I always had a sneaking suspicion it was *me* she fancied. Those were the halcyon days when I didn't need a ladder to look my female classmates in the eye.

In fact, one could say that I was the stud of my class. At

the after-show party for the school production of *Oliver!* – during which I had given such a moving rendition of 'Where Is Love?' it had apparently reduced our boot-faced headmaster to tears – they were literally lining up behind the art block for a snog. I had to get them to form an orderly queue.

I learnt then that fame is a powerful aphrodisiac.

That was just before all the girls grew into giantesses in year eight and morphed into strange, secretive creatures from another planet. When bra sizes and lip gloss and . . . yuck! . . . those monthly things that sound disgusting beyond belief combined to become a world my gender couldn't begin to comprehend. It was like our hormones separated us out of a mixed scramble and formed a huge gulf between us, never to be closed.

It's nearly midnight here.

Dad and Sacha are still 'away' and won't come back until Mum has hidden every sharp object in the house to prevent Jules killing her husband. Jules swept Rupes and Viola off for supper in the village earlier tonight and Sadie is still AWOL, though she has texted Mum to report the hideous details of her 'shag-fest'.

(Mum should know by now that if she leaves her mobile lying around I'll read her messages. She hasn't worked out yet how to add a lock-code on it, and I'm certainly not going to tell her.)

It was actually very nice to have supper with Mum and the little ones with no added extras. I'd also sneaked into Mum's bedroom earlier and checked there were no suitcases packed. By either of them. So Dad hasn't left her. Yet. And over supper, she didn't sound as though she was thinking of leaving him either.

Yet.

She was far more concerned with Chloë texting her, saying she's with Michel and will be home 'later'. So that's where she snuck off to during the tea party this afternoon! Oh dear. I know I must grit my teeth, that Chloë must be allowed her freedom until we are wed, but sometimes it's hard. And it's especially hard knowing she's with Mr Fix-it's son . . .

Having said that, on the way back home from the tea party, Viola begged Angelina to pull in at Mr Fix-it's house, so she could at least run in and give her daddy a cuddle. (Talk about ironic; a bankrupt alcoholic taking refuge in a winery!) And she elected me to be her wing-man.

As we emerged from the car, Mr Fix-it came out of the barrel room, all smiles. He told Viola that Sacha was out with William, but he would let him know she had been to see him. Then he took us to the barn to see some kittens as a consolation prize.

'This must be very hard for her. It is good she has you,' he whispered to me as Viola bent down in ecstasy and took a tiny fluffy kitten onto her knee.

'I'm not sure Viola sees it like that,' I mumbled.

'Don't underestimate yourself, Alex, you are a kind and thoughtful young man.'

We left then, after Mr Fix-it said Viola could come up any time she wanted to see the kittens.

Anyway, it was nice to get a compliment. It threw me somewhat. And the other good news is that, even though Dad is staying under his roof, they haven't killed each other yet. Unless Mr Fix-it was lying, and Dad and Sacha are buried in a shallow grave somewhere in the grapevines . . .

There is a knock on my door. I stand up to open it.

'Alex? Are you awake?'

It's Mum. 'Yes.'

She tries the door, which of course I've locked in case of further intrusion from unwanted sources.

I'd better let her in.

ιζ'

Seventeen

'I'm worried about Chloë. She's not home yet,' Helena said as she peered round the door of Alex's room.

'She's always late back, Mum.'

'I know, but without Dad here, I'm responsible for her and I've got no idea where she is. She isn't answering her mobile either. You haven't heard from her, have you?'

'Nope, sorry. She's with Alexis' son, isn't she?'

'Yes, but I can't go to bed until she's home, and I'm tired.'

'What about ringing Alexis and seeing if he knows where they've gone?'

'It's almost one in the morning and I'm sure he'll have had an early night after the party. It wouldn't be fair to wake him. No,' Helena sighed, 'I'll just have to wait up for her. Sorry to disturb you, Alex. Sleep tight.' She smiled at her son wearily as she shut the door and walked back along the corridor to the kitchen.

She made herself a peppermint tea and went to sit on

the lounger on the terrace to await Chloë's return. And tried not to think about what was being said between the three men up at the winery . . .

Helena jumped at the sound of a moped buzzing over the gravel on the drive. She looked at her watch; it was half past two, and she realised she must have dozed off. It was a good ten minutes before she heard the tiptoeing of Chloë's feet on the terrace behind her.

'Evening, Chloë. Or should I say, good morning?'

Chloë jumped and turned at the sound of Helena's voice.

'Wow! You're still up,' she breathed.

'I was waiting for you to come home. Come and have a cup of tea with me in the kitchen.'

It was not a suggestion. It was an order. Chloë followed meekly behind Helena. 'Actually, can I just have a glass of water?' Chloë said as she sat down at the table. 'Am I in for a bollocking?'

'Yes, and no.' Helena poured some water for both of them, forgetting the tea. 'But I am *in loco parentis* while your father isn't here. And I was worried about you.'

'I'm really sorry, Helena. Is Dad coming back any time soon?' Chloë skilfully changed the subject.

'We're going to speak tomorrow and he'll tell me what Sacha is going to do. Jules is upstairs and refusing to see him.'

'I'm not surprised. Wasn't last night the most embarrassing thing you've ever seen?'

'It wasn't great, I agree. What did Michel have to say about it?' Helena asked, trying to steer the conversation back on track.

'That it was the best free show the village has had for years. Everyone was talking about it today.'

'Is that where you were tonight? In the village?'

'Yeah. We went to that new bar on the corner opposite the bank.'

'I know you've been drinking, Chloë. I can smell it on your breath.'

'Helena, *everyone* drinks at fourteen these days. And I only had a couple of glasses of wine. It was such a good night. Michel introduced me to all his friends. They're cool, even if their English is limited.'

'Until two o'clock in the morning? Surely the bar closes at eleven?'

'Michel took me for a drive on his moped afterwards.' Chloë blushed.

'Chloë, darling, Michel is eighteen, you're fourteen. Isn't he a little old for you?'

'I'm fifteen next month, remember? That's nothing. There's nearly six years between you and Dad. What's the big deal?'

'At your age, Chloë, it's a huge deal. He's an adult and you are still a child. Legally, if not in other ways.'

'Boys my age bore me,' Chloë stated arrogantly. 'Take Rupes, for example. What a douche-bag! He wrote me this love letter in French and it was terrible! He called me his "darling little pig" – he must have got *cocotte* confused with *cochon*. And he said I had eyes "like tiny bits of burning coal". Besides,' she added dreamily, 'Michel is the coolest person I've ever met. He's different from all the other boys I've known.'

'Is he?'

'Oh yes. He's so gentle, and clever and he talks to me like an adult. And I could listen to that accent all day.' Chloë gave a small shiver of pleasure. 'Like, usually I feel I'm in control. I know boys want to go out with me, but I've never really cared about them *enough*, if you know what I mean.'

Helena did know. 'Does he want to see you again?'

'He says he's going to borrow his dad's car tomorrow to take me to see Aphrodite's birthplace and then for lunch.'

'Chloë, I don't want to lecture you, or try to be like your mother . . .'

'Then don't, Helena.'

'Okay. But, *please*, be careful.'

'I will. I'm not stupid. For your information, I still *am* one, if you know what I mean. Most of my friends aren't.'

'Then just make sure you keep it that way. And if you don't, then for heaven's sake, come to me and we'll . . . organise something.'

'Thanks, Helena. You're really cool.'

'Believe me, I'm not condoning it, Chloë, but it's better to be safe than sorry. And do try and remember, this can never be anything more than a summer romance.'

'Why not? Michel was talking tonight about how much he wants to come and live in England when he's finished his degree at university in Limassol.'

'Yes, I'm sure he does. Anyway, this is a silly conversation. You only met him last night—'

'But it feels like I've known him forever.'

'I understand, but if you *are* going to see him regularly, we have to agree some ground rules, okay?'

'Sure,' she shrugged. 'But please can I go out with him tomorrow?'

'I'll have to talk to Dad about it first. And if Michel is as mature as you say, he'll understand that we need to know where you are. You're still a minor.'

'Okay.'

'And one of the ground rules will be that you're back by midnight, so we can go to bed knowing you're home safe and sound. Which is where I'm headed now.'

'Tell you what, if I'm going to be out all day, I'll get up for the little ones tomorrow morning and make them breakfast, then you can have a lie-in. How about that?'

'Deal. It must be love,' Helena said with a smile.

'Thanks. See you tomorrow.'

Helena lay in bed a few minutes later, so tired she was past sleep, thinking how short a time it felt since she too had crept back to Pandora in the early hours. Only to be caught and given a thorough dressing-down by Angus, who'd been burning the midnight oil in his study.

And here she was, having a modern version of the same conversation with her stepdaughter, about the son of the man she had once loved.

As Chloë had pointed out, things were different now. There was a freedom which hadn't been there for her and Alexis. The barriers had tumbled down on so many levels; socially there were far fewer restrictions, ease of travel and communication had been revolutionised since her day . . .

Perhaps, if they wanted to, Chloë and Michel *would* make it.

Helena realised with an ironic smile that any union

between their children would make her and Alexis relatives.

Just not in the way they had both once imagined.

Helena was upstairs helping Angelina change the sheets the following day when Alex appeared, clutching her mobile.

'Dad for you,' he said, handing it to her.

'Thanks, Alex.' She took the handset from him and put it to her ear. 'Hi, darling, what's going on? I've been worried about you.'

Alex was hovering behind her, so she walked away and onto the balcony.

'Hi,' William replied. 'I just need to know if Sacha's with you?'

'No, I thought he was with you?'

'Shit!' William sounded agitated. 'He seemed calmer when he surfaced this morning, a little more rational. Alexis and I fed him breakfast and had a talk with him. I've told him he's got to fly back to England as soon as possible and deal with the banks. Then he said he wanted to go for a drive to have some time alone, so I let him take the car, making him promise he'd be back in a couple of hours. He hasn't turned up yet and it's almost two o'clock. I thought he might have gone to Pandora to see Jules, who, incidentally, turned up here earlier to see Alexis and apologise for the other night.'

'No, Sacha's not here. When did he leave you?'

'Around ten, so he's been gone almost four hours and he's not answering his mobile. I should never have let him take the car. What if he's been drinking again and had a crash?'

'He was sober when he left, wasn't he?'

'Yes, but that doesn't guarantee anything now,' William sighed.

'What does Jules think about her husband's disappearance?'

'She left with Alexis, who wanted to show her something. She said she didn't give a damn where he was. How are the kids, by the way?'

'They're all fine. Perhaps you already know that Chloë's out for the day with Michel, Alexis' son? I texted you about it. He came to pick her up this morning and promised to look after her.'

'Yes, I saw him leave earlier.' There was a pause. 'Anyway, I'll hang around here for a bit longer, just to see if Sacha turns up, then I might as well come home.'

'Okay.'

'Bye, Helena. See you later.'

She took a couple of deep, calming breaths, dreading the conversation that would have to ensue once William was back. Alex was still hovering in the bedroom as she walked inside.

'Everything okay?' he asked.

'Fine. Dad's coming home in a while.'

'Good. How's Sacha?'

'Currently AWOL, but I'm sure he'll turn up.' Helena walked over to Alex and gave him a hug. 'Sorry it's all been so difficult here in the past few days. And thanks for being so great with Viola.'

'Truthfully, Mum, are you and Dad okay?'

'Of course we are. What makes you ask?'

'I saw you at the party. He was cross with you for dancing with Mr Fix— I mean Alexis, wasn't he?'

There was no point in lying. 'Yes. But everyone had had far too much to drink, and things got blown out of proportion, that's all.'

'Yeah, right. Mum?'

'Yes?'

'Can you promise, can you absolutely swear to me that you're not going to run off with Alexis?'

She took his bronzed apple cheeks gently between the palms of her hands and smiled down at him. 'I absolutely swear, darling. He's an old friend, nothing more.'

'Are you sure?'

'Completely. I love William, *and* our family. You all mean everything to me, promise.'

'Oh.' Alex's shoulders sagged in relief. 'Good. And . . .'

'Yes?'

There was a pause as Alex seemed to mentally prepare himself. 'I . . . need to ask you something else?'

'Spit it out, then.'

'And I want you to know that I won't be pissed off, but I just need to know. The thing is . . . is *he*, is Alexis, my—'

'Helena! Are you up here? Ah, yes, you are!' Jules bounced into the bedroom, looking flushed and bright-eyed. 'Guess what?'

Alex rolled his eyes at Helena and slunk out of the bedroom.

'What is it, Jules?'

'I went up to see Alexis at his house and he invited me in for a glass of wine. I apologised to him about the party and he couldn't have been sweeter, assuring me that most of the guests either didn't speak English or were too merry to understand anyway,' Jules said breathlessly, 'which as you can imagine, made me feel heaps better. I ended up pouring out the whole sorry tale over lunch.'

'Did it help? You certainly look better for it.'

'Oh yes. I mean, he probably knew most of it from William, but he was so sympathetic and understanding. He asked me what I was going to do next and I said I didn't know, because obviously my house in England would be sold, but that I didn't want to impose on you and . . .' Jules finally managed to take a breath between words. 'Then he said he had a house here we could borrow, while I sorted myself out. Isn't that just too sweet of him?'

'Wow! Yes, it is.'

'I mean, I offered to pay him some kind of rent – I told you I have a small amount from my mum – but he wouldn't hear of it. He said it was standing empty, then he took me to see it and to be honest, I was expecting some ramshackle old thing like Pandora, but guess what? It's brand new! He built it for himself last year to retire to when his son needs the big house for himself and his family. Helena, it's gorgeous! Just down a narrow track from the winery, beautifully furnished, and with a huge pool. Alexis said he chose the spot because he believes it gives the best view in the village. He says I can have it for as long as I need, with as much wine as I can drink thrown in. So' – Jules sank, exhausted, onto Helena's freshly made bed – 'what do you think of that?!'

'It sounds as though you've found your white knight coming over the hill to rescue you,' said Helena, as warmly as she could manage. 'I'm so glad, Jules. You know you're welcome to stay here, but I can understand if you want your own space for a while.'

'That man is an old-fashioned, *bona fide* gentleman. I shall have to have him round to supper to say thank you. He's only going to be up the track anyway.'

Helena saw that Jules was sparkling like a young girl. The years seemed to have dropped from her face overnight. Alexis had obviously given her some of the attention she craved.

'Right.' Jules stood up. 'You look shattered, Helena. I'm going to take all the kids down to the pool and give you some peace. Okay?'

'Okay.'

In an uncharacteristic display of affection, Jules threw her arms around Helena's shoulders. 'And thank you for everything.'

Helena retreated to her hammock as Jules swept the children off to the pool. She needed time to think before William arrived back.

She was just dozing off when she heard footsteps on the dry leaves that covered the ground.

'Hello, lovely.'

She felt a gentle kiss on her forehead, opened her eyes and saw Sacha.

'What are you doing here?' Helena shot upright. 'William's been worried sick about you.'

'I just needed some time away, you know. To think. Where's Jules and the kids?'

'Down by the pool.'

'Oh.' Sacha nodded. 'I came to say goodbye to them. I'm flying home today.'

'Right.'

'I have a lot of stuff to sort out in England, as you can imagine. In my head, and practically.'

'I'm sure. Viola's devastated.'

'Yes, and she has every right to be. Look, I just want to say, while I've got the chance, that I'm sorry for . . . everything.'

'Thanks.' Helena climbed out of the hammock. 'You should go and see your wife. Wait here for five minutes so I can get the kids out of the pool and into the house before they see you. You need to talk to Jules alone.'

'I know.' He put his hand on her arm. 'But just let me take a moment to say that I know my life has gone horribly wrong. I've been so selfish. I've hurt and abused a lot of people, including you and Will. And there's no one else to blame but myself. I can't change the past, but maybe now I want to try and make amends.'

'For your children, if nothing else.' Helena faced him, arms folded.

'Yes. I . . . Helena, before I go, there's one thing I want to ask you. I . . . Helena, please!'

But she was already walking away.

Less than half an hour later, Jules walked back to the house and found Helena in the kitchen, feeding Viola and the little ones the home-made lemonade and cakes that Angelina had made earlier.

'Okay?' Helena asked tentatively.

'Yes. Viola? Daddy's down by the pool,' said Jules. 'Would you like to go and see him?'

Her face lit up. 'Ooh, yes! Can I leave the table, Auntie Helena?'

'Of course.'

'Can we?' chorused Immy and Fred.

'No,' replied Helena, as Viola ran from the kitchen.

'Glad that's over and done with, anyway,' said Jules brusquely when Viola had left. 'I told him I wanted a divorce.'

'Are you absolutely sure, Jules? Wouldn't it be better just to let the dust settle a little?'

'No, it wouldn't. Mind if I have a glass of wine? It's past six.'

'Of course not.'

'Anyway, he said he'd agree to whatever I wanted. At least he seemed sober, which makes a change.' Jules giggled as she poured some wine into a glass. 'Unlike his almost-ex-wife.'

'He told me he was going back to England,' said Helena.

'He is, and I've told him I'm staying here with the kids for the rest of the summer. He can organise the house and fight with the bailiffs over what we're allowed to keep. The horses should be worth something, and at least they're in my name. I've told him to sell them and get the best price he can.'

'Good idea.' Helena felt a sudden admiration for Jules.

'Rupes is refusing to see his father. He's furious with him, Helena. Oundle was his dream. I'm going to call the Bursar first thing tomorrow morning. See if there's anything he can do to help.'

'It must be worth a shot.'

'Yes. Anyway, the divorce won't take long, as there's virtually nothing left to split. The money my mother left me will at least tide me and the kids over for a while and put some kind of roof over our heads. And I think a completely fresh start is in order. I need to think about what's best, but my life is suddenly an open book. Viola's going to be devastated when Sacha tells her we're divorcing, but, in the long run,' Jules said with a slow nod, 'it's probably all for the best.'

ALEX'S DIARY

23rd July 2006

I hope, when I arrive at *that* school, they don't ask me to write the standard 'What boring things I did on my holiday' essay. As mine wouldn't be. Boring, that is. They'd think I'd made it up. That I was a fantasist. Which, to be fair, I've been accused of being in the past.

A quick update on who is in residence at Pandora and who is not:

Sacha arrived, then left.

Dad arrived, then left with Sacha for the airport. Then arrived again.

Jules left, then arrived.

Chloë arrived.

Michel arrived with her, then left.

Dad is about to leave again.

Mum is leaving with him.

Sadie hasn't arrived, or left.

And nor have I.

Jules is babysitting all us kids so Mum and Dad can go out to dinner together. A belated tenth wedding anniversary celebration after the fiasco of the other night, which is a very good sign. Considering Jules and Sacha are doing the Big D, she looks as happy as a sandboy tonight.

What is a sandboy, I wonder?

And at least Chloë's at home tonight. He with the girly name brought her back an hour ago in time for supper.

He's a good-looking sod, old 'Michelle', there's no doubt about that. I had a good look at him today as he sat at our table on the terrace, Chloë all coy and holding his hand underneath it. He's tall, slim and dark-skinned, with his father's blue eyes. He looks nothing like me, and I'd be truly surprised if it does turn out we're half-brothers.

Not that looks mean anything in the great genetic lottery. You often see achingly beautiful children walking along the road with a parent who resembles a character from the Addams Family.

I was so nearly there earlier today.

I'd worked up the courage to actually say the words. I had my mother cornered, and I think she was about to tell me. Then that silly cow Jules walked in, and the moment was gone.

Rest assured, Mother dearest, it will come again. I want to return home knowing exactly who I am.

An awful thought has crossed my mind recently:

What if my mother genuinely doesn't know?

What if, horror of horrors, I was the result of some drunken one-night stand?

Or more accurately, a one-night lie-down?

The thought appals me, but one has to ask the question as to why half of my genes seem to be a more closely guarded secret than the denouement of the final Harry Potter book . . .

It can't be that bad, can it?

But as usual, I suppose I'm letting my imagination run away with me. It's only recently I've seriously started to obsess. And today was the first time I've almost managed to ask her directly. Maybe all I need to do is to sit down with her calmly, mother to son, and ask her outright.

Yes.

Apart from that, I am happy tonight. In fact, I am ecstatic. My mortal enemy is moving out tomorrow morning. No longer will I have to lock myself into the Broom Cupboard and wait for the first stink of aftershave to waft through the keyhole and alert me to his marauding presence. The bunny has finally dried out, as have my sheets, and if anything, he looks better for a damn good bath. I'd forgotten he was once white.

Jules was twittering about the charms of Mr Fix-it tonight, and there has to be a possibility that if she manages to close her mouth for longer than a couple of seconds, he might, with a blindfold on, and a couple of bags over her head, fancy her.

Okay. Now I'm really fantasising.

At least Mum swore to me she wasn't going to run off with him, and I have to believe her. I hope she's telling Dad the same thing tonight.

And if this thing with 'Michelle' doesn't turn out to be another Chloë fad, I will have to engineer ways to make it one. But for the moment, I am happy to let it run its course.

So everything is calmer tonight, at least. The only fly in the ointment is poor Viola, who is wandering around the house like a sad little ghost. She seems to have attached herself to me – not surprising, given that her mum keeps telling her to 'buck up', only a few hours after Sacha told her that her parents were getting a divorce.

Chloë's been sweet with her too – took her into her bedroom and they had a girl-to-girl chat. After all, she's a child of divorce too. Viola arrived outside my door afterwards, though at first I thought it was Chloë, from the gorgeous smell of the strong perfume she wears, which seems to permeate the entire house. Chloë had given her a little bottle of it, and a little bracelet to cheer her up.

Viola told me tonight that I make her feel better, which was nice. I've done my best with cuddles and stuff, and letting her cry; so much so that I worried my bed was going to get soggy again, just after it had dried out.

I gave her another book to read from the library, which I've now organised into alphabetical author order. I chose *Nicholas Nickleby* – at least it might help Viola realise that some people have an even more horrible life than she does. Although admittedly hers is pretty awful just now.

There but for the grace of God go I, and my family.

I can only pray that tonight's dinner is a success.

Eighteen

'Night, darling, see you in the morning.' Helena kissed Fred on the forehead and moved across to Immy's bed.

'Where are you going?' Her daughter eyed her suspiciously. 'You've got lipstick on.'

'Out with Daddy.'

'Can I come?'

'No. It's just Daddy and me. Chloë's here, and Alex, and Jules.'

'Don't like Jules. She smells,' said Fred.

'Okay, you two, shush now.' Helena walked to the door and switched the light off. 'Sweet dreams.' Collecting her handbag from the bedroom, she heard her mobile ringing inside it.

She dug around and actually managed to catch the caller before he or she rang off.

'Hello?'

'Helena! *Mia cara!* How are you?!'

It was a voice from the past, but so recognisable she'd have known it anywhere.

'Fabio!' Helena's face broke into an excited smile. 'My goodness! How wonderful to hear from you!'

'It is a surprise, yes?'

'Just a little! It must be, I don't know . . . over ten years?'

'I think it is at least that.'

'Where have you been? *How* have you been? And how on earth did you get my number?'

'It is a long story, *cara*, which you know I will enjoy telling you.'

Helena heard William calling her from downstairs. 'Fabio, I'd love to chat all night, but we're about to go out for dinner. Can I take your number and call you back? Where are you? Still in New York?'

'No, I am back in Milan these days, but travelling on and off with the La Scala ballet company. And you are in England?'

'Well, mostly, but I'm actually in Cyprus at the moment. My godfather died and left me his house, so I'm here with my family for the summer.'

'But I am coming to Limassol in three weeks' time! Remember how we danced together on a hot summer's night in the wonderful amphitheatre? It must be fifteen years ago now.'

'How could I forget?' Helena's eyes glinted with emotion at the memory. 'Actually, we're not that far from Limassol and Fabio, I'd adore to see you.'

'And I you, *mia cara*. It has been too long.'

'Yes, it has.'

'Then I will see if I can arrive in Cyprus earlier than I had planned and impose myself upon your hospitality for a day or two,' he announced.

'Wonderful. Is this the best number to call you on?'

'*Si*, it is my mobile number, you can reach me on it day or night. So, my Helena, we will speak tomorrow and arrange everything. *Ciao*.'

'*Ciao*, Fabio.'

Helena sat for a moment, her mobile in the palm of her hands, remembering.

'Who was that, Mum?' Alex was standing at the door.

'That, darling, was my old dancing partner, whom I haven't spoken to for at least ten years. And I'm so very pleased to hear from him.' She smiled and kissed Alex on the top of his head. 'Now, I must go. Dad's waiting for me downstairs.'

As William drove the car up the hill, Helena sat next to him, his close proximity and the fact they were finally alone making her stomach flutter with nerves.

'Okay, where to? I'd prefer not to go to Persephone's Taverna, if you don't mind,' he said.

'Well, there's always Peyia, it's a nice enough town a few miles away towards the coast. Not as pretty as Kathikas, but I do remember a little taverna just outside it. Angus took me there once. It used to be famous for its amazing view.'

'Sounds good to me. We can drive to Peyia and ask for directions.'

After a few wrong turns, they arrived in Peyia, which was bursting at the seams with residents and tourists. William pulled over and went to quiz a local shop owner about the restaurant Helena had mentioned.

'We're in luck, the shopkeeper knew exactly the place you're talking about, and even drew me a map,' said William as he got back into the car, brandishing a scrap of paper.

Eventually they arrived at the taverna and, at the top of a flight of steps, emerged onto a curved stone terrace, the candlelit tables sheltered by a vast wooden pergola abundantly covered in old vines. The terrace was busy with diners, but they managed to get a table beside the low wall that edged the terrace, with a stunning sunset view towards the coast.

'Well, this makes a change,' he said, ordering a carafe of the local red wine. 'Hello, Helena. My name's William. Good to meet you again.' He put his hand across the table to her and she shook it politely.

'You're right. It does seem a long time since we did this.'

'One way and another, this holiday hasn't quite turned out the way we expected, has it?'

'No.'

'Well, let's hope that now Sacha is on his way back to England, and Jules and Co. are off to Alexis' villa tomorrow, things will calm down. Have you chosen?'

'I'll have the chicken souvlaki.' She was not in the slightest bit hungry.

'And me, the fish.' William called the waiter over and ordered. He lifted his wine glass to hers. 'Cheers. And a belated happy anniversary, darling.'

'Thank you. And to you,' she replied tensely.

'So, you mentioned in the car that the famous Fabio is coming to Cyprus,' said William. 'It seems all Helena roads, past, present and future, lead to Pandora.'

'It is rather a coincidence. The La Scala ballet company are doing a week of special performances at the amphitheatre in Limassol. They did the same thing once when I was still dancing with them.'

'I wish I could have seen you dance.'

'You do. Every morning.'

'And the other night,' he added with a rueful smile. 'I meant on a proper stage, standing on your toes and wearing that net ruff around your middle.'

'You mean a tutu.'

'Yes, that's the one.' William paused to take a sip of wine, then said, 'So, how have you been in the past couple of days?'

'Fine. Just busy looking after everyone.'

'That's not what I meant.'

'No.' Helena fiddled with a piece of bread from the basket on the table, then swiftly changed the subject. 'Can you believe Sadie hasn't come home yet? She's still staying up in the village with this chap she met at the party. He's twenty-five and a carpenter apparently, with the best body she's ever seen.'

'How nice for her, but darling, we really do need to talk.' William firmly steered the conversation back. 'Alexis and I had a chat while I was staying with him. He apologised to me profusely, said his behaviour towards you, and me, had been inappropriate. Admittedly, it's not particularly pleasant having another man lusting after your wife, but I've accepted his apology. And I have to admit that he's a decent chap. He was good with Sacha too, and gave him plenty of sensible advice. So that's *his* side of things. What about you, Helena? Are you still harbouring some deep-seated passion for Alexis, as he admitted he has been for you?'

'No, William, I swear to you I'm not. Of course, seeing him again reminded me of when we were younger, but nothing more than that, I promise. I can't make you believe me,' she sighed, 'but it's true.'

'I do believe you. If I didn't, where would we be then? I was wrong to doubt you. We both know trust is everything in a marriage, though to be frank, I sometimes feel you don't. Trust me with your innermost thoughts, that is.'

'No,' Helena agreed. 'I'm so sorry, William. I just find it difficult.'

'Alexis also told me you had something you should tell me yourself.'

'Did he?' Helena gulped, and her heart started to pound.

'Yes. In other words, he thinks you *need* to tell me, for your own sake.' William reached across the table and put a hand on hers. 'So, darling, what was it? What happened?'

'I . . .' Tears sprang to Helena's eyes. '. . . can't . . .'

'Yes, you can—' They were interrupted at that moment by the waiter bringing their food, giving Helena a moment to regain control of herself.

When the waiter withdrew, William took her hand again and continued. 'Darling, I've had time to think about it in the past couple of days and it doesn't take a genius to guess, so I'll make it easy for you. Did you get pregnant by Alexis?'

'Yes.' Helena felt sick to her stomach, but the word – and the truth – was out there, and she couldn't take it back.

'So, what happened to the baby?'

'I . . . aborted it.'

'Did Alexis know?'

'Not at the time. I only found out I was pregnant when I got back to England.'

'Did you tell him?'

'Not originally, no. It was only recently, on that afternoon you took the children out to the beach to give me a break.'

'Christ, no wonder you both looked so odd when we got back. I knew something had happened, but I didn't know what, so I suspected the worst. Although now I know what it was, I'm not surprised he was comforting you. Just as I would have done if you'd ever have trusted me enough to tell me.' There was a hint of anger in his eyes, but also sympathy. 'So, what did you do?'

'I knew I couldn't keep the baby. I was a boarder at the Royal Ballet School by then, so I had to wait until half-term to do anything. I found the name of a clinic in the Yellow Pages and booked myself in. When I got home afterwards, I told my mother I had a bad stomach upset and spent the rest of the week in bed recovering.'

'So you went through the whole thing by yourself?'

'I couldn't tell anyone, William. I had just turned sixteen and I was terrified.'

'You never thought to tell Alexis? Surely you could have written to him? He obviously loved you, though what he was doing forcing you into an adult relationship when you were still only fifteen, I don't know. Part of me wants to wring his neck, as you can imagine.'

'William, he didn't know I was underage. I told him I

was nearly seventeen. I lied to him, because I knew if I didn't, he wouldn't touch me.'

'And you wanted to be touched.' William winced. 'Sorry, Helena, forgive me for finding this conversation so difficult.'

'Which is why I've never told you,' she whispered.

'Is this why you were so tense before you came here to Pandora? The thought that Alexis might still be here, and the truth would come out?'

'Partly, yes,' she agreed, 'but I didn't think you'd notice.'

'Of course I did. Everyone has. We've all been worried about you.'

'Have you? I'm sorry. I just . . .' Helena shook her head, and tried her best to stem the tears she had no right to shed. 'I didn't know what to do.'

'Personally, I find the truth – however painful – always works the best. Anyway, darling, now at least I know and I'm so sorry you had to go through that alone, and so young.'

'Please don't apologise, William. What I did has haunted me ever since. I can never truly forgive myself.'

'Well, you have to try, Helena. We all do what we think is best at the time and even you must realise that, in retrospect, it was the right thing,' William added gently. 'Unless, of course, you really wanted to come back here and marry Alexis.'

'It was a summer romance . . . I . . . *we* were from two different worlds, and so young. I cut off contact with him completely. I thought it was better that he never knew.'

'So you kept this secret all these years, and never told anyone?'

'Yes.'

'And you had no contact with Alexis afterwards?'

'I just said . . . I couldn't.' Tears came to her eyes. 'You can't imagine the shame I felt . . . *still* feel.'

'Well, hopefully now the secret is out, it might help you to heal. And realise you simply had no choice. I'm really sorry for what happened to you, darling. You were just a girl – scarily, not much older than Chloë – and probably not even as worldly-wise as she is. What a shame you couldn't tell your mother.'

'God, William!' Helena looked horrified at the thought. 'She would probably have kicked me out of the house and disowned me. She was very proper and old-fashioned. More like a grandmother, I suppose.'

'Well, maybe not having had a mother you could confide in is why you find it more difficult than most to rely on others. And more to the point, trust them. Please, darling' – William gently squeezed her hand – 'try to believe I'm here for you. I really am.'

'I know you are. And I'm so sorry.'

'So, just one more question while we're clearing the air . . .'

'What?'

'Are you sure you don't want to tell me who Alex's father really is? Having convinced myself it was Alexis – and I'm sure Alex has, too – I'm now back to square one.'

'William, please! I've told you before, it was just some nameless guy I had a one-night stand with,' Helena said, her brow furrowed with tension.

'I know you have. And equally, knowing you as I do – and especially after what you've just told me – it just doesn't make sense. It's not in your nature to have a one-night stand, Helena. Unless you were a very different person back then.'

'A slapper, you mean?' she sighed. 'After tonight's revelation, I'm sure that's exactly what you think I am.'

'Of course I don't. You were twenty-nine when I married you – naturally you had a past that involved men. My track record with women was hardly spotless, as you know, so please don't think I'm judging you, because I'm not. I've been married to you for ten years and I'd just like to know the truth, that's all.'

'Can we leave it, William? I've told you what you wanted to know, and . . .' Tears of exhaustion and frustration finally sprang to Helena's eyes.

'Okay, enough,' he said gently, seeing her despair. 'Thank you for telling me about the baby, darling. The worst is over now.'

If only it was, Helena thought sadly.

William held her hand across the gear-stick on the way home, like he used to when they first knew each other. His face had lost a lot of its tension, and he looked far more relaxed. He pulled the car into the drive of Pandora, switched off the engine and turned to her.

'I love you, Helena, please believe me. Whatever you've done before me is irrelevant. You're a wonderful wife, mother and human being, so stop torturing yourself, please.' He kissed her gently on the lips and stroked her hair. 'I want to take you to bed, right now. Let's sneak in through the kitchen door so we don't get sidetracked.'

They walked hand in hand towards the back door.

William opened it as quietly as he could, and they tiptoed across the darkened hall and up the stairs.

Later, Helena lay in William's arms, feeling the cool breeze of the fan blowing across her naked skin. William, as always, had fallen asleep straight afterwards. She had forgotten, in the tension of the past few weeks, what comfort lovemaking could bring. She felt calm, and thankful that she'd told him, even if there was so much more he couldn't know.

For a fleeting moment, Helena wondered if the rest of her story could stay hidden – if finally she might be able to let it all go, stay like this for always, safe in William's arms. Not waiting for the moment when he discovered the truth. And left her.

Helena closed her eyes and tried to relax. Tonight he was with her, and they were close once more. For that, she must be grateful. And finally, she slept.

'Mummy, are you awake?' Immy's silky hair tickled her nose.

'No, I'm fast asleep.' She knew Immy was staring down at her, studying her intently.

'Oh, but you're talking, so you must be awake.'

Fred punched her arm and she jumped. 'Ouch! Don't do that!'

'I waking you up,' he announced logically. 'I want milk.'

'Morning, darling.' William snaked a hand past Immy and stroked Helena's shoulder. 'I'll go downstairs and make some tea.' He was already up and reaching for his boxer shorts. 'Come on, you two,' he said to Fred and Immy. 'You can help me.'

'Daddy, why have you and Mummy got no clothes on?' Immy asked as she trailed behind him.

'It was very hot last night,' Helena heard him reply as the three of them left the room.

'Well, I really think you should keep your pants on in bed, Daddy.'

'Me too,' said Fred.

Helena lay back and smiled at the exchange. She felt refreshed this morning, as though a storm had passed over, bringing calm fresh air in its wake.

'Now perhaps we can really have a holiday,' she murmured to herself.

August 2006

Departures

ALEX'S DIARY

8th August 2006

The last couple of weeks have been just what a family holiday should be.

There has been no more Greek Tragedy, Bunny Boilers, Grape-Stampers, Divorces or Drunkards.

And after all the excitement and tension, it's been pleasant.

Actually, I hate that word. 'Pleasant' is a neat house in a suburb, it is matching anoraks going for a walk in the country on their matching owners. Who own one well-behaved dog and drive a Nissan Micra. It is middle-class mediocrity. It is most of the western world.

No one thinks they are ordinary, of course. If they did, they'd shoot themselves. Because we all aspire to be individuals. We are not ants, whose massed colonies and superb organisation when they are staging an attack on a tiny piece of chocolate Fred has dropped on the kitchen floor never ceases to amaze me.

They remind me of the Nazis, or the Russian Socialist Revolutionary Party, or Chairman Mao's gang of millions: precision-trained and brain-dead.

I think how much I'd like to meet the ants' leader. And imagine he is probably – like all psychopathic dictators – short and ugly, with a penchant for facial hair.

Perhaps I'd have a career path if I grew a moustache . . .

Talking of shooting oneself, nothing in the garden is ever totally rosy, as Michel and Chloë are still together. In fact, they are rarely apart. Sadly, he's a nice guy, and I really like him as these things go: he's gentle and bright and polite.

He adores her and she adores him.

The only saving grace is that Chloë has to leave here soon to join her mother on holiday in France. I will miss her dreadfully of course, but at least she'll be out of harm's way. And next time we meet, I'll be back on home – or at least, school – territory.

And that's another current fly – or even ant – in the ointment. When I arrived here, I had the whole of the summer before *that* school really reared its ugly head. Suddenly, it's August. We are no longer at the beginning of the holiday. We are on the downhill run to the end.

I heard my mother on the telephone to Cash's the other day, ordering my name tapes. 'Alexander R. Beaumont'.

I refuse to reveal what the 'R' stands for. All I can say is it's horrendous beyond belief. As is the uniform onto which it will be attached. I have also refrained from mentioning in this diary the actual name of the school I am to attend. All I can say is that you eat breakfast in white tie and black tails and that generations of British kings have been educated there.

I won an academic scholarship. Let's face it, I'd never get in on my hereditary credentials, given I only know the provenance of the ovary, rather than the sperm that sired me.

I wonder if they know I'm illegitimate?

At least, on one level, it goes to show how times have changed. Having said that, given the history I've read on our royal family, me and my unknown gene pool will apparently be in good company.

What is seriously scary is that my name is all my classmates will know of me. I will have to prove myself to a set of strangers with whom I must cohabit for the next five years, like it or not. My touchstone, the one person who understands me, will be miles away. My bedroom at home will be empty for weeks at a time.

Fred has already asked for my goldfish when I go, Immy for my portable DVD player. They are like tiny vultures, feasting on the prospect of my departure. I'd like to think they'll miss me, but I know they'll soon get used to me not being there. The family bucket of water: take out one glass (me) and it would still look quite full. Apparently, my new one has a whole lake to itself.

And what if they're all like Rupes? I could be dead by Halloween.

I'm starting to seriously panic now at the thought of starting at my new school in less than a month – I mean, I'm just a boy from a middle-class family who's never been on a grouse-shoot, and thinks 'polo' is a mint with a hole in it. My local school was so short on facilities that they bussed us once a week to the local pool.

It was meant to be up to me whether I went or not. But when I won the scholarship, everyone just forgot to ask me and assumed it was what I wanted.

On the plus side, at least Chloë will be just a few miles down the road. Her school and mine have 'dances' together, apparently. Christ, perhaps I'd better get practising my waltz and my American Smooth, given it's all I can do to bend my knees up and down to 'Crazy' by Gnarls Barkley.

Although it breaks my heart to see her with 'Michelle', the thought of her being so near to me when I go away glues it back together. And out of sight is often out of mind, so they say. That, and the fact Chloë is obviously impressed that I've won a scholarship there, is currently all that provides comfort for my black-tailed, lonely future . . .

I'm lying on my Broom Cupboard bed – I hasten to add that there is a spare room upstairs now, but when my mother asked me if I wanted to move back, I declined the offer. Bizarre that I want to stay down here, but I feel comfortable. And I'm never short of anything to read.

Tonight I choose Keats' poems and read, er, 'Fanny'. Not a title I would personally go for myself, but the words are lovely and it's a truism that misery loves company. It makes me feel better to know that someone else once felt like I do.

'Yourself – your soul – in pity give me all,
Withhold no atom's atom or I die.'

Then I hear two sets of tentative footsteps along the corridor – one male and one female – and a tear comes to my eye.

And I know all too well the pain of unrequited love.

ιθ′

Nineteen

Helena stretched forward, her left leg executing an *arabesque*. She held the position for a few seconds, then pirouetted fast across the terrace and flopped into a chair, sweating profusely.

At eight thirty, the sun was already searingly hot. As July had spun gently into August, the temperature had risen noticeably, and Pandora's occupants had visibly relaxed and given in to a heat-induced torpor. Even the little ones were comparatively languid, their usual frenetic activity levels tempered by the relentless sun. They had started sleeping in until past nine, and the whole pace of the house had slowed with them.

This was how Helena had imagined their time at Pandora would be: days were spent by the pool or on the beach, broken by lunch, then a siesta for all. William had metaphorically shrugged off his jacket and tie, spent time with his family and begun to relax. Since the night she'd told him about her lost baby, they had become closer too, both physically and mentally. And Helena knew she had never felt more contented – or loved – than in the past few days. Having seemingly wreaked havoc initially, Pandora was now weaving her magic spell on all its inhabitants.

The long, hot evenings were spent on the terrace *en famille*, or with added guests. Michel, Chloë's boyfriend, had become an almost permanent fixture at the house, both Helena and William deciding it was far better to welcome him and keep some semblance of control over Chloë, rather than isolating them both. As Helena pointed out, parental opposition and the thrill of the forbidden provided a potent mix.

And if William struggled with the thought of his daughter being romanced by the son of the man who had once been involved with his wife in very similar circumstances, he did a good job of controlling it.

Alexis had been round again for supper, this time at William's invitation. The tension that had existed before seemed to have dissipated and Helena felt the two men had developed a genuine, if guarded, liking for each other. Sadie and Andreas, her amorous young carpenter, had also joined them occasionally in the evenings. Even though Andreas' conversation had been almost non-existent due to his limited English, they seemed blissfully happy. As Sadie said, they communicated in the place where it mattered. Even Helena had to admit that 'Adonis', as the two of them had jokingly but aptly nicknamed him, *was* gorgeous.

'I will live for today and pay the price tomorrow,' Sadie had said with a shrug when Helena had asked where the relationship was heading. 'Even if I knew, I wouldn't be able to tell him,' she'd chuckled. 'And that suits me just fine.'

They'd not seen much of Jules since she and the children had left Pandora to take up temporary residence in Alexis' villa. But Viola, who turned up regularly on the bicycle Helena had suggested she borrow, said her mother seemed okay. She made a mental note to call Jules today. She didn't want her to feel abandoned, but equally, neither was she keen on encouraging anything that might disrupt the currently peaceful atmosphere at Pandora.

Having recovered her breath from her exertions, she got to her feet and strolled along the shady length of the terrace, stopping at regular intervals to admire and deadhead the flowers she'd planted in the weathered stone urns that had stood there since Angus' day. As she picked off the odd wilted bloom and automatically tested the soil for moisture with her fingertips, she was pleased to note that everything was thriving. Pink and white geraniums, twice the size of any she'd grown back home in their garden in Hampshire, jostled for attention alongside fragrant gardenias and gorgeous red hibiscus.

As she reached the end of the terrace, she leant on the balustrade and surveyed the rest of the gardens as they fell away towards the olive groves. With help from Anatole, a relative of Angelina's from the village, she'd begun to populate the beds with oleander, lavender and solano that would, with luck, survive year after year in the fierce heat. As she drank in the view, a butterfly drifted past, a shimmer of yellow against the backdrop of dazzling azure sky; the silence was only interrupted by the gentle background chorus of cicadas.

Helena wandered back across the terrace and into the kitchen. In retrospect, she now realised William had been right; that the build-up to this holiday, with all its complexities, had been extremely stressful. Apart from anything else, she had not known before she arrived how she might feel if she saw Alexis again – and if she did, what she would tell him about her disappearance all those years ago after the summer they'd spent together. Now, she had to believe the eye of the storm had passed and if anything, blown away a few cobwebs, leaving the main structure intact.

The rest of the messy jigsaw puzzle, created both by fate and her own clumsy hands . . . well, who knew?

She would live for today. And today was beautiful.

'Morning, darling.' William appeared and kissed her on her bare shoulder as she filled the kettle. 'What's on the agenda today?'

'Nothing too stressful. I must ask Angelina to get the guest room ready for Fabio, he'll be arriving in a couple of days.'

'Well, I'm sure you're looking forward to seeing him, but I have to admit, it's been lovely being just us.' He put his arms round her waist and kissed her neck.

'Yes, it has, but you're right: I feel like an over-excited child. It's been so long.' Helena broke away from him to reach for the cereal bowls. 'Don't forget that you need to drag Chloë away from Michel for a few hours and take her out to lunch before she leaves. You should have a good father–daughter bonding session while you can.'

'I'll do my best, but convincing her to have lunch with her ancient dad, compared to the youthful charms of Michel, will be a toughie.'

'Oh, and I've been meaning to ask you whether you

could have a look at that drawer I told you about in Angus'
desk? I don't want to ruin it by breaking the lock, but I'm
desperate to know what's inside.'

'Let me take the kids for a morning swim, then I'll see
what I can do.'

Helena checked her watch. 'It's almost ten o'clock! I
never thought I'd hear myself say this, but could you go
and wake up Immy and Fred or we won't get them into bed
before midnight this evening.'

Helena hummed as William left and she pottered round
the kitchen. Glancing out of the window, she saw the
oddest sight. Cycling down the hill was Rupes, precariously
balanced on Viola's small borrowed bicycle.

He drew to an ungainly halt beside the back door, and
walked towards the house.

'Come on in, it's open,' called Helena.

Rupes appeared, his face red and his T-shirt drenched
with sweat.

'Hello Rupes. You look boiled, do you want some
water?'

'Yes please, Helena. Christ, it's hot! I'll be glad to get
back to Blighty. The air conditioning in the villa's on the
blink and I can't sleep.'

'The newspaper said yesterday it's the hottest summer
here for almost a hundred years.' Helena went to the fridge,
poured a large glass of water and handed it to him. 'How's
your mum?'

'She's okay.' Rupert gulped back the water in three
swallows. 'Better than she was, anyway. Mind you, she
couldn't have been much worse, could she?'

'No. Well, it's nice to see you anyway.'

'Yeah. I've come with a message. Two things: Mum wants to ask you all over for dinner tonight, if you aren't busy.'

'Oh, that's nice of her. I was just about to call and ask her the same. I'll have to check with Angelina about babysitting, as it will be too late for Immy and Fred, but the rest of us would love to.'

'And also . . . er . . . is Alex around?'

'Somewhere, I should think. Shall I call him for you?'

'Thanks.'

Helena walked into the hall. 'Alex? Someone here to see you, darling.'

'Coming,' groaned a sleepy voice.

'He'll be along in a second. I'm afraid we've all started lying in quite late,' Helena apologised. 'How's Viola? She didn't come to see us yesterday.'

'She's okay. Missing our father, and the heat's getting to her, too.'

'It would, with her colouring.' Helena was struggling for conversation and was glad when Alex appeared. She watched his face fall as he saw who the visitor was.

'Hi, Rupes,' he grunted.

'Hi, Alex.'

'What can I do for you?'

'Well, umm, the thing is . . .'

'I'll leave you to it, shall I?' Helena said quickly, realising she wasn't wanted. 'See you tonight, Rupes. Eight-ish?'

'Yeah, sure.'

'Well,' Rupes cleared his throat when Helena had left

the kitchen. 'You, er, know . . . what's happened to our family?'

'Yes.'

'The problem is, my parents can't afford to send me to Oundle now, even with my sports scholarship. It's only twenty per cent of the fees, you see.'

'I do see,' Alex agreed.

'Mum got in touch with the Bursar to explain, and he's said they might consider giving me a full financial bursary, means-tested of course. They still want me for the rugby, you see. I'm trialling for the England under-18s team in a few weeks.'

'That's good news, isn't it?'

'Sort of, yeah.'

'So?'

'Well . . . my Common Entrance exam score wasn't that great. To be honest, I didn't really work that hard, because I knew they wanted me for the sport. But to get the bursary, they want me to sit their own academic exam in a week's time.'

'Oh,' said Alex. 'Right.'

'The thing is, if I don't pass, I'll be off to a local comprehensive somewhere.' Rupes hung his head.

'Okay, I get it. But where do I fit in?'

'Where do you think?' Rupes waved his hands in agitation. 'We all know you've got a brain the size of Russia.'

'Russia's actually far smaller than it used to be these days, but thanks anyway.'

'Alex.' Rupes put his palms flat on the table. 'I've got to pass this exam, but I'm crap at English, worse at French and just about passable at maths and science. I need some extra coaching in the humanities. Will you . . .' He cleared his throat. 'Will you help me pass?'

Alex whistled. 'Blimey, Rupes, you want me to teach you?'

'That's about the size of it. Mum's had some test papers sent over. Can you go through them with me?'

Alex rested his chin on his hand and sighed. 'To be honest, Rupes, I'm not sure I'm the right person to ask. I've never taught anyone before.'

'You're all I've got. I'll pay you, if you want. I have a few quid stored away, even if my parents don't. In fact, I'll do anything. You are my only hope.'

'There's no guarantee I can get you through. It'll be down to you in the end.'

'I'll work and work. Anything you say. *Please.*'

'Okay,' Alex said with a slow nod, 'but I don't want your money. Just an apology for behaving like a prick.'

'Fine.' Rupes puffed up his chest and winced as he breathed out. 'I'm sorry.'

'For behaving like a prick,' prompted Alex.

'For behaving like a prick,' muttered Rupes.

'Right. When do you want to start?'

'As soon as possible.'

'No time like the present.' Alex stood up. 'This afternoon I want you to write me a five-hundred-word comprehensive essay on how you believe bullying can be stamped out in schools, and how the bullies should be punished. I will mark it accordingly, then go through it with you to look at your mistakes. Okay?'

Rupert reddened, but nodded in agreement. 'Okay, deal. Now I'd better go.'

''Course. See ya, Rupes.'

'Yeah, see ya.'

'Darling, I've finally managed to open that drawer,' William announced as he came into the bedroom that evening.

'Really?' She turned to him, her face full of anticipation. 'And?'

'I'm afraid it's empty, although I think we ought to get the desk treated for woodworm. The little blighters are eating it alive.'

'Oh,' she said, disappointed. 'I really thought there might be a clue to Angus' lost love in there.'

'Well, at least I managed to get in without breaking the lock.' William looked at his watch. 'Ready to go? It's nearly eight o'clock.'

'Jules, you look fantastic! Doesn't she, Helena?' said William.

'Absolutely,' Helena agreed. Jules had obviously lost weight in the past two weeks, and her newly defined figure had given her a statuesque elegance and accentuated her toned, tanned legs. Her normally nondescript brown hair now shimmered with sun-induced auburn highlights, and hung softly around her face. A pair of chiselled cheekbones had appeared and her dark eyes shone with a new-found confidence.

'Flatterers,' Jules replied coyly as she led them onto the terrace of the villa. 'I just haven't been hungry recently. It seems trauma is the best diet on the market. And it's free,' she said with a little laugh. 'Chloë not here?'

'No. Surprise, surprise, she's gone out with Michel,'

answered Helena. 'They only have a couple of nights left together before she has to go to France.'

'He's a nice lad, Michel,' Jules acknowledged. 'He came down here to mend the air conditioning earlier on. Drink, anyone?'

'Hello, Auntie Helena, Uncle William.' Viola kissed her godfather, then clasped Helena around the waist.

'Hello, darling. How are you?' she asked.

'I'm good.' She nodded excitedly. 'Guess what? Mummy's let me adopt a kitten!'

'Has she?'

'For the holiday only, Viola,' corrected Jules. 'Alexis will look after it when we leave.'

'Will you come and see her?' Viola pulled on Helena's arm. 'She's sleeping on my bed and she is *so* cute!'

'I'd love to, darling.'

'I've called her "Aphro" after the goddess, and also 'cos she has all this long frizzy hair,' Viola explained as she led Helena by the hand into the villa.

A few seconds later, Rupes appeared at the entrance to the terrace. He beckoned to Alex, who nodded and followed him inside.

'So, William,' Jules said, handing him a glass of wine, 'what do you think of this place?'

He walked across the vast terrace, obviously recently laid with immaculate cream stone. 'It's got a view to rival Pandora's, that's for sure,' he said as he paused to take in the vista.

'Alexis built it specifically so it had the best view of the sea.' Jules pointed across the valley. 'Right between those two hills. I love it here. Everything is new and fresh and comfortable. I wish I could stay for longer.'

'How *are* things?' William asked. 'I haven't heard from Sacha since he went to England, though I've left him a number of messages.'

'We've been communicating by email. He's told me they've given him six weeks to pack everything up at the house and get out. And I've said I'm not going back to help him. To be honest, William, I just couldn't face it. If he'd only put the house in my name originally as well, it might have been a different story.'

'I'm sure,' William acknowledged. 'What will happen to all your things?'

'I've asked him to put them in storage until I've decided where the three of us are going to live.'

'Any ideas?'

Jules shrugged. 'The jury's out at present. I'm still hoping Rupes can get the Oundle bursary, *if* he can pass the academic test, that is. And if I do go back to England, I'll probably move close to his school and rent somewhere. Viola would have to go to a local junior school for now.'

'That all sounds sensible.'

'Well, there's part of me that never wants to see England again, as you can imagine. I love it here, but I'll have to work from now on, of course. '

'What will you do?'

'I was a pretty good estate agent before I gave it all up to look after Rupes, remember? I'm sure I can find someone to employ me on the back of my experience.'

'Well, I'm glad you've started to move on, Jules,' said William. 'It's been a tough old time for you.'

'I don't have a lot of choice, do I? Sink or swim, I'd say. And Alexis has been fantastic. He's the polar opposite of Sacha, in every way. He's really looked out for me since I moved in here and nothing is too much trouble. He's joining us for dinner, but he had to go to Limassol today, so he said he might be a little late.'

'Mummy, Auntie Helena loves the kitten,' said Viola as she and Helena emerged through the French windows.

'Who wouldn't? She's adorable.' Jules smiled at her daughter. 'So, shall we eat?'

William, Helena and Alex left just before midnight to drive home.

'Fancy a brandy on the terrace?' asked William, as Alex said good night and wandered off upstairs to bed.

'No thanks, but I'll keep you company if you like,' replied Helena, sitting down under the pergola as William went inside to get the bottle.

'Another completely clear sky,' she remarked, as he returned and sat down next to her.

'Yes. The stars here are truly amazing.'

'Jules was different tonight. She seemed . . . softer, somehow.'

'I know what you mean,' William agreed. 'Ironically, just when she had every reason to be bitter, the hard edge has gone, and she looks happier and more relaxed than I've ever seen her. Did you . . . see what I saw tonight?'

'You mean Jules and Alexis?' replied Helena.

'Yes. They seemed very comfortable with each other. I can't speak for Alexis, but I think she's definitely fallen for him.'

'Who knows? They could both use some love and companionship, that's for sure.'

'A few weeks ago, the thought wouldn't have crossed my mind, but it did this evening,' William mused. 'Even if it's only a fling, I doubt it would hurt either of them.'

'Alexis isn't the type to hurt anyone. It'll be interesting to see what happens.'

'And . . . if it does go further,' he said, 'how would you feel about it?'

Helena reached for William's hand and held it tight. 'I promise, I would feel absolutely fine.'

ALEX'S DIARY

9th August 2006

I understand now why those in control become power freaks and lose the plot.

Henry VIII, who dumped God and decided he'd take over the job instead.

Stalin, Hitler, Mao, who were the Devils Incarnate.

Bush, who wants *his* god to be Top Dog.

And Blair, the puppy, who's lost his hair and his good intentions along the USA way.

Tonight, while I was reading through Rupes' essay – which was abysmal to say the least and wouldn't get him into nursery, let alone a top British boarding school – I had a sudden glimmer of that same feeling.

As he looked at me, desperately searching my face for a positive reaction, I knew I could make or break him.

It was magic! For a few seconds, at least.

Then I felt sorry for him. My kind heart is what will stop me ever attaining a position of serious authority, because I can't bear to see anyone suffering. A girly trait, I know, but I was born to it; to see the other side of the story.

If I'd been presiding over Saddam Hussein's first trial, I know what would have happened: even though I loathe the evil bastard for all the suffering he brought to so many, I'd have seen him sitting there in front of me, a sad, mad, broken old man.

All he'd have to have said is something like 'My mother didn't love me,' and I might have sent him off to a comfortable prison cell to spend the rest of his days having counselling and watching reruns of *Friends*.

It does make me wonder whether at heart I am destined to vote Liberal Democrat.

So even Rupes, my sworn enemy, who's caused me more pain than Chinese water torture and mosquito bites combined, got to me today. I saw his vulnerability.

He's a thick, thick-necked rugger-bugger, whose future really *is* buggered if I don't lend a hand. And of course I will.

He needs to learn to spell *tout de suite*. I have left him poring, or, as he would undoubtedly put it, 'pouring', over the Oxford Dictionary. I have written out a list of impressive-sounding adjectives he is to learn by heart, which can be slotted in ad hoc to jazz up an essay.

His French is a nightmare. Tonight we are at the *'un, deux, trois'* stage, and I think I may have to enlist some expert help if we are even to get close. I will make the ultimate sacrifice and ask the fluent Chloë to lend a hand with the French letters . . . I mean, lessons, tomorrow. That is, if she promises to wear a yashmak while she works on his verbs so that he can keep his mind off his French Mistress as she does so.

Rupes, dear boy, you have set me the ultimate challenge.

And however much I want to walk past you in the gutter

337

one day, homeless, with only a rabid, scabby dog for company, I know I cannot be party to your downfall.

I also feel that 'academic tutor' will look good on my future CV.

Eventually, I settle down and try to sleep. Rupes is coming for tuition at eleven tomorrow morning, and I lie here thinking how I will plan the lessons. And I suddenly feel grateful to my still unknown gene pool for providing me with a brain that seems to function fairly effortlessly.

This brings me back to another 'subject': that of my own history. Whilst I've enjoyed the past couple of weeks of stress-free living, I haven't forgotten the question that I swore to myself I'd get an answer to before I leave Pandora.

Beware, Mother dearest, you are not off the hook.

I *will* ask it.

κ'

Twenty

'Morning, Dad.' Chloë drifted sleepily into the kitchen and pecked her father on the cheek. 'Did you have a good night?'

'Surprisingly, it was actually very pleasant. Jules was on really good form.'

'Cool.' Chloë went to the fridge, pulled out some orange juice and swigged it straight from the carton.

'Actually, Chloë, I want to talk to you.'

She swung round, suddenly animated. 'And I want to talk to you.'

'Good. Then let's go out for lunch.'

'Just you and me?'

'Why not? You're leaving in a couple of days, and I feel as if I've hardly seen you recently.'

'Yeah, that's what I want to talk to you about.'

'What?'

'Me and leav—'

''Lo, Chloë. Where Meeshell?' Fred bounced into the

kitchen and grabbed hold of her legs affectionately. 'He said he bring a real gun to show me that he shoots rats with.' Fred careered off round the kitchen, killing imaginary rodents with an imaginary weapon and shouting 'BANG!' at the top of his voice.

'He'll be here later, sweetie,' Chloë said, over the noise.

'Let's go out around noon and have a quiet lunch, okay?' suggested William.

''Kay, but I'll need to be back for three o'clock. Michel's taking me to Adonis Falls.'

'You'll be back in time,' William answered, grabbing a squirming Fred round the middle and plonking him in a chair at the table. 'Right, young man, let's get some break-fast into you.'

William took Chloë to the restaurant just outside Peyia where he and Helena had eaten, not trusting the tiny pop-ulation of Kathikas – most of whom Chloë now knew by name – to leave them undisturbed if they lunched in the village.

'So, what was it you wanted to ask me?' William sipped his lager, Chloë a Coke.

'Whether you'd speak to Mum about me staying here for the rest of the summer.'

'I see. That's quite an ask.'

'I don't want to go to France. Mum'll be with the awful Andy, there'll be nothing to do and I don't know anyone there. I'd *soo* much prefer to stay here with you.'

'Darling, you've been here for nearly a month already. Don't you think your mum'll want to see you?'

'She will for the first few hours, but then she'll ignore

me and I'll be in the way of her love-fest. Andy doesn't like me, and besides, he's a real creep. You'd hate him. Mum has crap taste in men.'

'Thanks!' William chuckled.

'I didn't mean you, Daddy, you know that.' She shrugged amiably. 'Anyway, will you talk to her?'

'To be honest, talking and your mother have never gone together. The chances are she'd slam the phone down on me when I'd barely opened my mouth.'

'Daddy, please try, for me,' she begged. 'I really don't want to go.'

William sighed. 'Look, darling, I've been down this road with your mother time and time again. She'll just accuse me of emotional blackmail and think I'm trying to score points because you want to stay. I'm sorry, Chloë, but there it is.'

'Don't be sorry. I know how difficult she is. I mean, I love her – she is my mum, after all – but I'm not surprised you divorced her. I probably would have too, the way she treats all her boyfriends. She has to be centre of their attention 24/7.'

William refrained from agreeing. 'All I can say is that I did my best, darling. And I'm so sorry I failed you.'

'I also know she made it hard for you to see me after you married Helena.'

'It certainly wasn't for lack of trying, that's for sure. But I want you to know you've never been far from my thoughts.'

'Oh, I sussed her out when I found a birthday card you'd sent me torn up in the bin. That's when I knew you still loved me, and hadn't forgotten me. But I had to play the game with Mum. You and I both know how volatile she is, and she was sooo jealous of Helena – got angry just 'cos I once said I really liked her. I'm cool about it, Daddy, really.' Chloë reached a comforting hand across the table and patted his.

'Well, I'm not "cool" about it, Chloë,' William sighed. 'I'd always hoped you could be kept out of our problems, and not used as emotional currency, but that wasn't the way it worked out.'

'Well, I don't care what happened between the two of you. You're my dad and I'll love you whatever.'

'And I'm so lucky to have such a level-headed and beautiful daughter.' William felt choked with emotion. 'I missed you so much when you were growing up, it physically hurt. I even considered kidnap a couple of times.'

'Did you? Awesome!' Chloë chuckled. 'Anyway, Daddy, that's all over now. I'm fifteen soon, and old enough to make my own decisions. And one of them is that I want to see a lot more of you and my family in the future, whether *she* likes it or not.'

'We both know she won't.'

'Yeah, well, it's not up to her, and if she gives me any grief, I'll threaten to come and live with you. That should sort it,' Chloë said with a grin. 'Besides, if she marries Andy the arsehole—'

'Chloë!'

'Sorry, but he is one. If she does, I don't want to be around much anyway. So, perhaps we could both ask her if I could stay on here instead of going to France?' she urged, steering him back to the subject at hand.

'Look, it's lovely that you've enjoyed being with us,

Chloë, but let's be honest, I don't think it's just us you want to stay in Cyprus for, is it?'

'Oh Daddy, don't say that.' Chloë looked offended. 'I've had such a cool time here with you all. I love the little ones, and Alex is so sweet and Helena's been so kind and . . . it's like, well, a proper family. To be truthful, I wasn't looking forward to it at all. I thought it would be really dull, but it's been the best few weeks of my life.'

'And meeting Michel has helped.'

'Yes, it has, 'course it has,' she admitted.

'He's a nice chap,' offered William, 'but there'll be lots more like him in the future, I'm sure.'

'Not like him.' Chloë shook her head defiantly. 'I love him.'

William, following Helena's advice, refused to be drawn. 'Yes, I'm sure you do,' he answered feebly as their meze arrived. 'Now, let's dig in.'

'Should I talk to Cecile or not?' William was perched on the end of Helena's sunbed. The moment they'd arrived home, Chloë had disappeared off in a cloud of dust on the back of Michel's moped.

'It's a tough one. If you ask her, she's bound to say no just to spite you.'

'Exactly.'

'But if you don't talk to her, Chloë will feel you're being unsupportive. So, how about some kind of compromise?'

'Like what?'

'Well, how about you call Cecile and tentatively suggest that Chloë comes back here for a few days at the end of the holiday in France? That way, Cecile gets to see her as planned, but it allows a bit of time for Chloë to hang round her mother and the boyfriend, bored stiff and pining for Michel. I'm sure that by then, Cecile will be only too glad to pack Chloë's bags and send her back to us.'

'Brilliant, darling!' He kissed her on both cheeks. 'Thank you. I'll tell Chloë.'

'It might not be exactly what she wants to hear, but it's probably the best solution, all round.'

'You know, Chloë really is a great kid. Very logical and clear-headed. She seems to have got her mother sussed, anyway, which is more than I ever managed.' William sighed.

'She's certainly grown up on this holiday.'

'I don't want to go there, thanks,' William muttered.

'I didn't mean it like that.' Helena sat upright on the bed, arms around her knees. 'We had a good chat and she knows what she's doing, so don't worry.'

'Phone, Mum!' Alex shouted up from the terrace.

'Coming, darling.'

Half an hour later Helena was sitting in the taverna in the village, opposite Sadie. She'd been expecting the worst when she'd received her SOS call; the end of another beautiful relationship, a Sadie in bits. Yet Sadie seemed anything but traumatised. Her eyes were sparkling and she looked radiant.

'So, where's the fire?' asked Helena, confused.

'I have news, sweetie.'

'So I gathered.'

'Good, or bad?'

'Depends on how you view it, I suppose. A bit of both, maybe.'

'Come on then, spit it out.'

'Okay, okay, I will. One minute . . .'

Sadie fumbled in her capacious handbag, finally draw-ing out a white plastic stick and handing it to Helena.

'Look at this. What do you think?'

'It's a pregnancy test.'

'I know that much. Read it.'

'I am. There are two pink lines, which means . . . oh my God! Sadie!'

'I know!' Sadie clasped her hands together. 'It does say I *am*, doesn't it? You've got more experience at this than me.'

'Well, they're all different, but' – Helena studied it – 'there's a definite line in the other box.'

'So I *am*. Pregnant, I mean.'

'According to that, yes. Wow.' Helena looked up at her friend and tried to literally read between the lines as to her state of mind. 'Are you happy?'

'I . . . don't know. I mean, I only found out a few hours ago. It must have happened on that first night we slept together, after the apocalyptic party at the winery. We were both quite drunk and weren't careful, if you know what I mean. I just can't believe it. Quite honestly, I'd given up hope of it ever happening. After all, I'm thirty-nine. But it has, it *has*!' Sadie's eyes filled with sudden tears. 'I'm going to have a baby, Helena. I'm going to be a mother.'

Helena thought back to the days when they'd been girls together, dreaming of meeting their Princes Charming, the pretty houses they would live in and the babies they would have. She had heard Sadie mention often in the past few years how sad she was that the latter had never happened for her. But the reality of it happening now – especially in

345

Sadie's current situation – was something altogether different.

'And what about Andreas? How does he feel?'

Sadie paused. 'I don't know. I haven't told him yet.'

'I see.'

'In fact . . .' Sadie drew in a breath. 'I haven't actually decided whether to tell him or not.'

'I think he might notice on his own in a few months' time, don't you?'

'Not if I'm back in England, he won't.' Sadie's fingers circled the rim of her glass.

'Have you fallen out?'

'God, no. It's actually quite difficult to argue in two different languages. We're fine.'

'So, what's the problem?'

'Isn't it obvious? He's a carpenter in a tiny Cypriot village, speaks barely a word of English and is fourteen years younger than I am. I mean, I've got to be realistic about this; can you honestly see us having a future together playing happy families?'

'Do you love him?'

'No.'

'That sounds pretty conclusive, then.' Helena felt blindsided by Sadie's honest response.

'I'm very fond of Andreas, really I am. He's such a sweet young man. And physically, it's been the best ever.'

'That's quite a statement, coming from you.'

'The point is, he's been a wonderful summer escape. You know I was really low when I arrived, and Andreas has provided the most fantastic ego massage. But I've always known I've got to go back to England. I've got a big work project starting next week. My affair was going to be a wonderful souvenir I could take home with me.'

'Darling, if you go ahead with the pregnancy, you'll have a living, breathing souvenir of this holiday for the rest of your life,' Helena reminded her. 'To be honest, I'm in shock. I really don't know what to say.'

'Well, I do. The bottom line is that I've decided I'm keeping the baby. This is probably my only chance of ever having one, and I know how much I'd regret it in my old age if I got rid of it.'

'Yes,' Helena said with feeling, 'maybe you would.'

'The *real* dilemma is, whether I tell Andreas I'm pregnant before I leave. You don't think it's illegal, do you? He can't accuse me of stealing his sperm or anything, can he?'

'I've no idea, Sadie. Although if he found out, he could probably demand access to the child.' Helena took a sip of her bitter coffee. 'Look, I don't want to burst your bubble, or patronise you, but as you know, I've been there.'

'Where?'

'Single and pregnant. And it's difficult, on all sorts of levels.'

'I don't know what it was like for you, Helena; you've never really told me about your time in Vienna when Alex was a baby. But how hard can it be? I'm financially independent, I own my own home and I work freelance. I'll hire a nanny, it's simple.'

Helena took a calming breath, thinking that Sadie made it sound as though having a child was merely a minor inconvenience solved by recruiting extra staff. She could feel herself becoming agitated, induced by the memories of the dark days she had suffered on her own solitary path.

'Sadie, it's not just the practical and domestic side of things – it's the emotional, too. You'll have to go through the pregnancy and birth without any support. And then, every time the baby cries in the middle of the night, or gets ill, *you* will be solely responsible for it, maybe forever.'

'Yes, I will. But Helena, I'm pregnant! Whatever it takes to do this, I'll cope, I really will.'

'I'm sure you will. I'm preaching, sorry. It's wonderful you're happy about it, it really is. All I'm trying to say is, think carefully before you dismiss Andreas completely. And for the record: morally, I think he has a right to know.'

'Maybe. I'll get back to England – put some distance between us – then decide whether to tell him or not. But spending my life with someone purely because I got pregnant by him is going back to the dark ages, and wrong for everyone concerned. I can do this by myself, I know I can.'

'Well, good luck.' Helena dredged up a smile. 'You know I'll be there for you as much as I can. When are you going home?'

'Sooner rather than later, under the circumstances. I might ask William to give me a lift to the airport tomorrow, if I can get a seat on a flight.'

'Andreas is going to be devastated.'

Sadie eyed Helena in surprise. 'Really?'

'Yes!'

'Nonsense! He'll probably mope around for a while from hurt pride, but as soon as the next pretty – and no doubt younger – face appears on the horizon, he'll forget all about me.'

'Personally, I wouldn't bank on it. From what I've seen, he's completely smitten.'

'Do you *really* think so?' Sadie's face suddenly registered panic. 'Oh my God, you don't think he'd do something daft and follow me to England, do you?'

'He might. Who knows?'

'Isn't that just bloody typical? I seem destined to be in love with men who don't want me! And then when they do, I don't want them! Sorry, I need to go to the bathroom. I'm feeling horribly sick.' Helena watched as Sadie stood up, looking green. 'Back in a tick.'

As she ran to the ladies', Helena sat wondering why she felt vaguely depressed. After all, Sadie was obviously overjoyed.

Then she realised what it was: Sadie was behaving like a man.

ALEX'S DIARY

11th August 2006

The Kleenex police have been on extra duty here at Pandora today.

We've had Sadie arriving with her suitcase; then the tear thing started as she said goodbye to Mum and went off with Dad to the airport. I can only deduce that the wood-chopper's chopper is off the agenda and Sadie's heading off to carve out a new future back in London. Then Mum started too as she waved Sadie off. I asked her why she was crying, but she did that thing she does and said 'I'm fine,' even though tears were pouring down her cheeks and she was so obviously not.

Chloë has literally dripped around the house for the past few hours. She is inconsolable about the fact she has to fly to France to her mother tomorrow and isn't allowed to stay on here for longer. Even though she is hoping to come back here before the end of the summer, it seems this is no comfort to her. And to be fair, it's unlikely to happen, given the logistics and her mother's mindset.

'Michelle' has since arrived to say goodbye, and they

have locked themselves in her bedroom. There is currently a small puddle of water collecting outside her door.

I myself have stood in it and added my own little tear over this situation. I will miss Chloë dreadfully.

Immy has stubbed her toe getting out of the pool, and there was blood. Add that to the lack of any Barbie plasters in the house, and the tear-duct explosion became inevitable.

And Fred, feeling left out of the general mood I should think, decided to have one of his humongous mega-strength tantrums. No one's quite sure what set it off, but we think it had something to do with a piece of chocolate. He's been sent to bed in disgrace by Mum and is still screaming his rocks off upstairs.

Fun, fun, fun.

I am currently sitting on the terrace all alone. Mum has gone upstairs for a bath and I think Dad – who's come back from the airport now – went with her. I am marking Rupes' French essay and correcting his appalling grammar, having decided this was not the time to ask Chloë to be his French Mistress for the night. So I am working overtime myself and trying to keep my mind off her imminent departure.

I rest my pen on the table and stare up at the stars. We have a whole two weeks left here, so why does this feel like the end of the holiday, when it isn't?

'Hi, Alex.'

I jump, turn round and see it's Mum. She's wafted down silently like a spirit in her white kaftan thingy.

'Hi, Mum.'

'Can I join you?'

''Course.'

She leans over me. 'What are you doing?'

'Helping Rupes with some work. He has to take an exam to get his bursary.'

'That's awfully sweet of you,' she says as she sits down.

'Has Fred stopped wailing yet? I can't hear him any more,' I say, trying to keep the conversation neutral. I can sense she is in a state about something.

'Yes. He gave up eventually and fell asleep. My goodness, that child can scream,' she sighs. 'Are you okay, darling?'

'I should be asking you that.'

'I was just upset to see Sadie go, that's all.'

'You'll see her in England, won't you?'

'Yes. I suppose it was the fact it felt like the holiday is coming to an end.'

'Just what I was thinking. But it's not.'

'No.' She looks at me. 'Sure you're okay?'

'Yep. I'll miss Chloë, mind you.'

'You're very fond of her, aren't you?'

I nod, then pick up my pen and pretend to carry on marking Rupes' essay.

'Fabio, my old dancing partner, is coming to stay tomorrow,' she says out of the blue. 'I have to pick him up from Paphos airport at lunchtime. He's huge fun, or at least, he was eleven years ago. You probably can't remember him. You were only two last time he saw you.'

I think back into the grey fuzz of faces and images. 'No, I can't.'

'He gave you Bee, your bunny.' She smiles in remembrance.

I gulp. 'He did?'

'Yes. He visited us in hospital after you were born and put the bunny in your cot next to you.'

'But . . . I thought . . .'

'MUM-MEE! I need yooou!'

'Come out here, Immy. I'm on the terrace with Alex.'

'Can't. My toe's bleeding again. HELP!'

My mother rises from her seat.

'Mum!' I call out to her in protest.

'Sorry, Alex, be back in a moment.'

Damn Immy! I must not let this moment pass. I grab her arm as she floats past. 'I thought my fath—'

'MUM-MEE!'

'Two ticks, darling.'

And she is gone, inside. And I know she won't return for ages. Her 'two ticks' means sympathy, more plasters, a glass of milk and probably a story. Knowing Immy, the *Complete Works of Hans Christian Andersen*, volumes one to sixty.

Crap! Shit! Bugger!

I give Rupes one tick, then ten crosses, out of sheer frustration.

I was so nearly there just now. I am almost certain she told me before that the bunny came from my father. Which is why I have almost died trying to save its furless backside.

So, if I'm right, then the missing piece of my personal jigsaw is arriving back in my life in a few hours' time: Fabio. It's a poncey name, but at least he's not called Archibald, or Bert.

There is a photo on the wall at home of him dancing in some ballet with Mum. She has a leg wrapped round his back and a knee against his groin. They were certainly intimate, although he has more make-up on than she does, so it's a bit difficult to see his features, not that I've ever looked that closely.

353

Rest assured, I will tomorrow.

But the question remains: if Fabio is my Daddio, why has she never told me?

κα

Twenty-one

Helena was up at half past five the following morning, full of nervous energy and apprehension. Fabio had called late last night to say he would be arriving from Milan into Paphos at lunchtime. She was going to pick him up. Once again, she had hardly slept, wondering what had possessed her to agree to him coming here to Pandora.

The fact they had lost touch over the years was directly down to her. Even though she could have searched him out through the New York City Ballet, she hadn't. Simply because it was too dangerous. She'd wanted to leave her past behind when she'd left Vienna. And that, sadly, had meant Fabio too, because he simply knew too much.

However, he *was* coming, and Helena was torn between terror and excitement.

She decided she must take him for lunch first. She had so much to tell him, facts that he *must* know before he met her family. One slip of the tongue from him and . . . she shuddered . . . the consequences would be too dreadful to contemplate.

Yes, it was a risk; but the truth was, she wanted to see him so desperately – the one person who had stood by her and supported her when she'd needed him. She knew he would struggle to believe what had happened since they'd lost touch. She struggled to believe it herself.

As she walked downstairs, she heard the back door close and the crunch of gravel from outside. Entering the kitchen, to her surprise she saw Chloë, quietly crying on a chair.

She looked out of the window and saw Michel running away up the hill.

Helena sighed, then went to switch the kettle on. 'Tea?' she asked.

'Will you tell Daddy, Helena?' Chloë looked up at her anxiously.

'About Michel still being here at dawn? Well, as far as I'm concerned, I haven't seen him.' Helena pulled some mugs out of the dishwasher.

'God, thanks, Helena. I've . . . we've never done that before, but it was our last night together, so Michel pretended to leave last night, parked his moped at the top of the hill in the vines, then came back when—'

'I'd really prefer not to know, Chloë.'

'Oh Helena, he's gone. He's gone and I don't know when I'm going to see him again.' Chloë wrung her hands in despair. 'How can I live without him? I love him. I love him so much.'

Leaving the half-made tea, Helena put her arms around

Chloë, who sobbed into her chest as she stroked the girl's long, silky hair.

'I don't want to go to France. I don't want to go back to England. I want to stay here with Michel,' she cried. 'Don't make me go, please!'

'I know, darling, I really know. First love is always the worst.'

'No, it's the best and it's for always, I know it is!'

'Well, if it is, then surely out of a lifetime, you can cope with a few days apart?' Helena pulled a chair out so she could sit down next to Chloë.

'But what about after the summer? I have to go back to school, like . . . *forever*.'

'There are holidays, and I'm sure Michel will be able to come and see you in England.'

'Mum won't ever let him stay with us! She'll think he's some Cypriot peasant. She wants me to marry Mr Goldman, or Mr Sachs or someone with lots of money!' Chloë looked at Helena. 'Would Dad and you let him stay at your house if he came over to see me?'

'I don't see why not. After all, Michel's been virtually living with us here.'

Chloë reached for Helena's hands and grasped them tightly. 'Thanks, Helena. Oh God!' She shook her head sorrowfully. 'How am I going to deal with this?'

'You are going to remember that Michel is feeling as awful as you. And that if it's meant to be, it will happen.'

'Do you really think he's feeling awful?'

'Absolutely. I promise you, Chloë, the one who's left behind always feels the worst. Now, how about that cup of tea?' She made to stand, but Chloë clung on to her. 'God, I wish you were my mother, Helena. I think you're legend. I really do.'

'Oh Chloë.' Helena put her arms around her stepdaughter and hugged her tightly. 'I wish you were my daughter too.'

An hour later, Helena took William a cup of tea.

'You're leaving for the airport in forty-five minutes. Chloë's taking a shower.'

'Thanks, darling. So, as I'll be at the airport, would you like me to hang around and pick up Fabio?'

'No thanks. I've got some shopping to do in Paphos anyway, and it might be nice for Fabio and me to catch up over lunch before we come back home.'

'Okay. At least you'll get some peace for a couple of hours before you leave. All the kids want to come with me to say goodbye. Even Alex. I think he has a crush on Chloë. What do you think?'

'Yes, he does,' Helena agreed, refraining from making any kind of derogatory 'it's only taken you how many weeks to notice?' type of remark. 'It's great they all want to say goodbye to her. She's a lovely girl.'

At the airport, William checked in his subdued daughter, accompanied by her equally miserable band of step- and half-siblings.

'Well, I guess this is it.' Chloë knelt down and hugged Fred.

'Don't go, Cowee, stay here, wiv us. We love you!'

'And I love you too, li'l bruv. Wish I could stay.'

'Who'll watch Disney films with us now?' said Immy plaintively.

'Alex will, won't you?' Chloë turned to him.

'Er, okay. I'll . . . er, give it a go.'

'Thanks. Bye, Alex. I'll miss you.'

'Will you?' he said in surprise.

'Course I will. You are sooo cool and cute and clever.'

'Am I?'

'Yes!' Chloë gave him a quick peck on the cheek. 'You know you are.' She then turned her attention to William and hugged him. 'Bye, Daddy. It's been awesome. Thanks for everything.'

'Bye, darling. We'll all miss you, won't we?'

'YES!' they chorused.

'I'll be back if Mum lets me, but I doubt it,' she said, her eyes filling with tears again. 'Bye, everyone.' With a final wave, she disappeared through the doors into security.

'Want Cowee to come back,' wailed Fred. Immy was crying too, and Alex wiped a hand surreptitiously across his cheeks.

'Okay, chaps.' William's voice was gruff with emotion. 'How about we head for the nearest McDonald's to cheer ourselves up?'

An hour later, Helena was also at the airport, waiting on tenterhooks for Fabio to appear.

'*Bella!* Helena!'

'Fabio!' Helena ran towards him and he caught her by the waist and twirled her round, much to the fascination of passers-by. Laughing as he set her down, he embraced her.

'It's so good to see you,' Helena said, his familiar smell

evoking so clearly another time in her life that she found tears in her eyes.

'It is wonderful to see you too, truly.' Fabio's dark brown eyes appraised her. 'And you look wonderful, *cara*, a little heavier than when I threw you around the stage all those years ago, but, pouf!' He shrugged. 'We are both getting old. Can we eat now? I am very hungry. I have had nothing since I left Milan at seven this morning. You know I cannot eat the plane food.'

They drove into Paphos town and found a restaurant at the quieter end of the bustling harbour-front, where they secured an outdoor table with a lovely view of the sparkling sea through the palm trees that lined the harbour wall. Fabio ordered half a bottle of Chianti and a Coke for Helena, then took out a pair of reading glasses and spent an age debating what he would eat. 'I hate this Cypriot food! They do not know how to cook,' he complained loudly.

'Then have a salad. They really can't go wrong with that.'

'You would be surprised. So! I have decided.' He clicked his fingers for a waiter, then explained to him in great detail exactly what he wanted.

Helena watched him with amusement, remembering his eccentricities, not all of which were endearing. He looked well, still toned and fit from daily classes, but his hairline – always a source of worry to him in the old days – had receded considerably.

'Why do you stare at the top of my head?' he asked her as the confused waiter was finally released. 'You notice I have lost my hair?'

'Well, maybe a little. Sorry.'

'I have. I hate it! I am the paranoid middle-aged man and I am having the transplant next year.'

'Honestly Fabio, it's not *that* bad. You look fantastic.'

'It is like the tide going out, but never coming back in. So, I fix myself. See?' He bared his teeth. 'I have new ones last year in LA. They are good, yes?'

'They are . . . impressively white,' nodded Helena, trying not to giggle.

'Also, my forehead.' Fabio pointed to it. 'It is smooth, *si*?'

'Very.'

'Botox. You must have some, Helena.'

'Why? Do I need it?'

'You must start before others notice.'

'Right,' she agreed with mock-seriousness. 'I'd forgotten just how incredibly vain you are.'

'Well, it is much worse if you were beautiful boy, like me, to grow old. Every time I look in the mirror, it hurts. So, now, *cara*, I will drink some wine and we will tell each other of our years apart.'

Helena put her hand across the table and rested it on his. 'Fabio, before we spend the next two hours reminiscing and going off at tangents, I need you to listen to me.'

He looked at her and frowned. 'Your expression tells me it is serious. You are not ill?'

'No, I'm not, but because you're about to meet my family, there is something you really have to know.'

'Will I need to drink?'

'Oh yes.' Helena nodded with feeling. 'And I would too if I wasn't driving. I'm warning you, you will not believe it.'

Fabio took a large gulp of his Chianti. 'Okay,' he said. 'I am prepared.'

William lay by the pool whilst the little ones watched a Disney film inside. The heat was intense, and he felt relaxed and sleepy.

The past three weeks had been wonderful, after the hurricane of the Chandlers and Helena's revelation. Which, although so difficult for her to admit, had in fact – to him, at least – seemed milder than the other scenarios his imagination had conjured up.

Of course, he was under no illusions that she had told him everything. When he'd first met her eleven years ago in Vienna, she'd had an air of mystery about her. What, he'd wondered at the time, was this beautiful, elegant woman – who spoke in a clipped British accent that betrayed her privileged background – doing working as a waitress in a café? He'd been enchanted from the first moment he'd laid eyes on her.

Then they'd begun to chat and on impulse, he'd invited her to have a drink with him after she'd finished her shift. She had refused, as he'd expected her to, but as always with him, perseverance had won the day. From then on, he'd ignored taking in the wonderful Vienna sights, instead sitting in the café with a book when he knew she was on duty. And eventually, she had agreed to the drink.

She'd told him then that she was an ex-ballerina, and had stopped dancing three years ago when she'd become pregnant. She had a son, apparently, and from the way her eyes shone as she talked about him, William could tell that little Alex was the centre of her universe.

He'd tried to probe more deeply, but it had been obvious from the start that Helena was closed on the subject of her past, and Alex's father. Even as their relationship had deepened and, step by tiny step, William had pursued her with grim determination (a scenario that had involved months of exhausting weekend commutes from London to Vienna), Helena had remained reluctant to discuss the details. Finally, after nine months, he had persuaded her to accompany him back to England, and installed her and little Alex in the poky Hampshire cottage that he'd rented in haste after his divorce.

He remembered her on their wedding day, looking exquisite in ivory satin – the perfect bride, as everyone had commented. Yet, when she had arrived next to him at the altar, and – formalities completed – he had lifted her veil to kiss her, rather than the anticipated joy in her eyes, he could have sworn he'd seen a flash of fear . . .

William heard the crunch of tyres on the gravel, and pulled himself back from his thoughts.

'Mummy's back, Daddy!' shouted Immy from the terrace. William shrugged on his shirt and went to join her.

'Daddee, he's got pink shorts on and a scarf thing round his neck and he walks like a girl,' Immy whispered as she peered round the corner at the man getting out of the car.

'That's because he's a ballet dancer, Immy. Now shush,' William ordered, as Fabio walked towards them.

'*Ciao*, William! After all these years I finally meet you. It is a pleasure.' Fabio gave William a neat bow of respect.

'And for me, Fabio.'

'Hello, leetle one,' Fabio bent down to kiss Immy on both cheeks. 'You are miniature version of your mamma, yes? I am Fabio. And this must be signor Frederick. Helena has told me a lot about you both.'

'It's nice to meet you, Mr Fabio. Were you and Mummy famous?' asked Immy, gazing up at him with wide blue eyes.

'Once, we were unstoppable, were we not, Helena? The next Fonteyn and Nureyev . . . aah, well,' he said with a shrug. 'Your mamma has done something more worthwhile with her life than chasing a dream. She has a beautiful family.' Fabio looked around. 'Where is Alex? I have not seen him since he was a toddler.'

'In the house somewhere. I'll call him. Cup of tea, Fabio?' William asked him.

'Coffee would be good, but I take only decaf.'

'I think we have some somewhere. Tea, darling?' William smiled at Helena, whom he thought looked strained and rather tired.

'Yes please. Hello, monster.' She smiled as she picked Fred up. 'Come and sit down, Fabio, and enjoy the view.'

'It is stunning,' he pronounced as he seated himself gracefully in a chair. 'William is a handsome man. I hate him. He has more hair than me,' he whispered loudly to her.

Immy sidled up to him. 'Are you really a dancer, Mr Fabio?' she asked him shyly.

'Yes, I am. I have been dancing all my life.'

'Did you dance with Mummy in Vienna when she met the Prince?'

'Ahh, the Prince.' He smiled at Helena. 'Yes, I did. We were dancing *Giselle*, Helena?'

'*La Sylphide*, actually,' she corrected him.

'You are right,' Fabio said, before turning his attention back to Immy. 'And then one night, your mamma had bouquet from him.'

'What's a bouquet?' enquired Immy.

'They are flowers given to beautiful ladies who dance the leading roles, but this bouquet has inside it a diamond necklace. Am I right, Mamma?'

'Yes, you are.'

'And then, he invites her to a ball at a real palace.'

Immy was enraptured. 'Ooh,' she breathed, 'just like in *Cinderella*.' Then she turned to Helena and put her hands on her hips accusingly. 'So why aren't you married to him now?'

'You mean why aren't you Princess Immy, and why do you live in a normal house instead of a palace, and have to put up with me for your old dad?' said William with a grin as he brought the tea tray out.

'I didn't love him, Immy,' replied Helena.

'I'd have married him for the diamond necklace and the palace.'

'Yes, *you* probably would, Immy,' agreed William. 'Coffee for you, Fabio.'

'*Grazie*, William.'

'So, did the two of you have a chance to catch up over lunch?' William asked.

'We have only, as you English say, scratched the surface, have we not, Helena?'

'I did most of the talking, so there's a lot I still don't know about Fabio.'

'Helena said you went off to the States just before I met her. Is that right?' asked William.

'Yes. I was there for almost ten years. I dance with the New York City Ballet, then last year, I think, Fabio, it is time for you to come home. So, now I am back at La Scala. I take the morning class and play the character parts suitable for a man of my age.' He shrugged. 'It is a living.'

'Fabio, you must be a good few years younger than me and yet you talk as if you were drawing your pension,' William chuckled.

'It is the dancer's life. It is so very short.'

'Did you tell Alex to come out to see Fabio, darling?' Helena asked William.

'Yes. He said he's coming, but you know he's a law unto himself.'

'I'll go and chivvy him along and check on dinner.' Helena stood up and walked inside.

'I was only saying to Helena just recently that I wish I had seen her dance.' William sipped his tea.

'She was exquisite! Certainly the best partner I have ever had. It is a terrible waste she felt she could not continue once Alex was born. She would have been one of the greats, I am sure of it.'

'I've always wondered why she stopped. Surely women can continue dancing once they've had babies, can't they?'

'It was a difficult birth, William. And she was alone and wanted to be there for her baby.' Fabio sighed. 'Our partnership was very special. It is rare to find that kind of empathy. And, for sure, I never found it again, or the success I had with Helena.'

'You were such a big part of her life. I admit it feels odd that I know almost nothing of it.'

'Just like I did not know of you or of your children's

existence until Helena and I speak a few weeks ago. We lost touch soon after I leave for New York: when I call her apartment in Vienna, she no longer answers the telephone. No one knows where she is. Of course,' Fabio said with a shrug, 'she is in England with you.'

'So how *did* you find her?' William asked.

'It was fate, nothing less. I am in the press office at La Scala and there is a great pile of envelopes on the desk, to post off to the mailing list with details of the forthcoming season. And there, on top, is envelope addressed to Ms Helena Beaumont! Can you believe it?' Fabio said excitedly. 'I scribble down the English address, then find her mobile on the La Scala computer records. There!' Fabio slapped his toned thighs. 'It was meant to be.'

'My wife rarely talks about her past,' William mused. 'And you are the first person I have met from it, apart from someone she knew here in Cyprus. So forgive me if you feel I am quizzing you.'

'Sometimes, it is better to draw the veil over the past and get on with the future, *si*?' Fabio feigned a yawn. 'I think I will retire to my room, if you do not mind. It was a very early morning.'

As he stood up, Alex appeared on the terrace.

'Hello, Fabio, I'm Alex. Pleased to meet you.' He stepped forward shyly with his hand outstretched. Fabio ignored it and pulled Alex to him, kissing him on both cheeks.

'Alex! My boy! It has been so many years since I saw you, and now you are all grown up!'

'Well, not quite,' said Alex. 'At least, I'm hoping for a bit more of the growing bit, anyway.'

Fabio held him by the shoulders and his eyes glittered with tears. 'Do you remember me?'

'Er, perhaps,' Alex muttered, not wanting to be rude.

'No, you don't, do you? But you were so young. Your mother says you are very clever boy, but maybe not dancer.' Fabio scanned Alex's torso. 'Rugby player instead, yes?'

'I like rugby, yes,' agreed Alex.

'You must excuse me now, but I am off for a siesta. We will talk much after I have slept, get to know each other again, *si*?'

Alex managed a smile. '*Si.*'

ALEX'S DIARY

12th August 2006

Do I think about the good news or the bad news first?

Do I hug myself with joy every time I remember the last words Chloë spoke to me?

'Cool' . . .

. . . and 'cute' . . .

. . . and 'clever'.

Wow!

There. That's the good news.

Now, for the bad: And it's *bad*.

I have met the man (and I use that word loosely) who may well turn out to be my father. No matter he is Italian. Italian is good. I like pasta and ice cream. No matter he is a dancer. Dancers are fit and strong with good muscle definition.

The thing that matters is this: everything about him, from his clothes, to the way he sweeps his hand through what's left of his hair, to the way he speaks and walks, indicates one thing and one thing only to me:

Fabio is . . .

Oh crud . . .

Oh bugger . . .

GAY!! And nothing will convince me otherwise.

I am prepared to accept that a certain level of effeminacy can still mean a man is a man and can do to a woman what a man does, but Fabio is a *screaming* queen!

I am trying to think this new information through calmly, but coming to some pretty dreadful conclusions.

Like . . . what if, once upon a long time ago, Fabio was in the 'undecided' category when it came to his sexuality?

So, there he is, partnering my mother, spending his days becoming familiar with parts of her body that usually only doctors have access to. They duly fall in love and start having a relationship. My mother gets pregnant with me, Fabio is still standing by her and is there when I am born, playing the dutiful daddy.

Then, suddenly, one day, bingo! Fabio realises he bats for the other side. And he doesn't know what to do. He still loves my mother, and me, hopefully, but he can't live a lie. So he sets off to the States to begin a new life, leaving my mother alone and devastated in Vienna with me.

Which would explain why she didn't go with him to New York and never danced again.

And it *also* explains the really big question: Which is why my mother has never told me who my father is.

'Er, Alex, darling, you see the thing is, your father, er, well, he's a raging homosexual, actually, but if you'd like to go and spend weekends with him and his male lover, and watch Liza Minnelli films with them, that's fine by me.'

She knows I'd be mortified. What boy wouldn't? Just thinking of my mates at school if Fabio ever arrived at a rugby game to announce himself as my dad, executing a

quick *entrechat* on the touchline whilst he watched me con-
vert a try, brings me out in a cold sweat.

The real problem is this:

Is homosexuality genetic? Oh crap!

Who can I ask? I *have* to know.

At this juncture, I must also stringently point out I am *not*
a homophobe. I have no problem at all with other people
living their lives as they see fit. They can let it all hang out,
and as often as possible for all I care, and Fabio seems like a
great bloke; funny and bright and G . . . A . . . Y.

He can be just as he likes. Just as long as he's not like *me*.
Or me like him.

κβ

Twenty-two

That evening everyone except the two little ones, who had been put to bed early, gathered on the terrace for drinks. Fabio arrived freshly showered, wearing a peacock-blue silk shirt and a pair of tight leather trousers.

'Isn't he going to sweat in those, Dad?' Alex asked William as they loaded trays in the kitchen to take outside.

'He's Italian. Maybe he's used to the heat,' William replied.

'Dad, do you think Fabio is, um, you know?'

'Gay?'

'Yes.'

'He is. Mum told me he was.'

'Oh.'

'Does that bother you, Alex?'

'No. And yes.'

'In what way?'

'Oh, no way in particular,' shrugged Alex. 'Is this tray ready to go out?'

With Fabio fully briefed over lunch, Helena had finally relaxed and was having a lovely time. During dinner, she and Fabio reminisced. Alex and William listened, fascinated, to the details of a part of Helena's life they'd never known.

'We met, you see, when I came to the Opera House at Covent Garden,' explained Fabio. 'Helena had just been promoted to soloist and I arrived from La Scala for a season. She is with this *terrible* partner who throws her, then forgets to catch her—'

'Stuart wasn't that bad. He's still dancing, you know,' Helena interjected.

'So, I arrive as guest artist and Stuart is off with the flu and they partner me with Helena, in a matinee of *La Fille mal gardeé*. And' – Fabio shrugged theatrically – 'the rest is history.'

'So then you followed Fabio back to La Scala?' asked William.

'Yes,' said Helena. 'We were there for two years. Then the Vienna State Opera Ballet offered us a contract as principal dancers with the company. And we couldn't refuse.'

'Remember I was not happy to begin with. It is too cold there in the winter and I get sick,' shivered Fabio.

'You really are the most appalling hypochondriac,' Helena remarked with a giggle. 'When we were on tour with the company, he had a suitcase just for his medicine,' she told William. 'Don't deny it, Fabio, you know it's true.'

'Okay, you win, *cara*. I am paranoid about getting the germs,' he agreed affably.

'So, will you stay now at La Scala, Fabio?' William topped up their glasses.

'I hope so, but it depends a lot on Dan, my partner. He

is set designer in New York. I miss him, but he hopes to get a position soon in Milan.'

'I'm so glad you finally found your soulmate, Fabio.' Helena smiled at him.

'As I am that you have found yours.' Fabio nodded gallantly towards both of them. 'Listen, I have brought with me photographs of Helena and I when we dance together. You want to see, William? Alex?'

'We'd love to see, thanks, Fabio.'

'*Prego*, I will get them.'

'And I will make some coffee,' added William.

As they both went inside, Helena glanced over at Alex. 'You're quiet, darling. Are you okay?'

'Fine, thanks,' nodded Alex.

'What do you think of Fabio?'

'He's, er, a very nice man.'

'It's so good to see him,' said Helena as first William reappeared with a tray and then a few minutes later, Fabio.

'Here we are.' Fabio waved a bulging envelope of photographs and sat down. 'There, Alex, it is your mother and I dancing *L'après-midi d'un faune.*'

'The afternoon of a faun,' translated Alex. 'What's that about, then?'

'It's about a girl who is woken up when a faun jumps through the window of her bedroom,' said Helena. 'Not a great story, but a wonderful part for a male dancer. Fabio loved it, didn't you?'

'Oh yes. It is one of my favourites – a ballet when the man can show off, not the woman. Nijinsky, Nureyev . . . all the greats danced it. Now, William, this is your wife in *La Fille mal gardée.* Isn't she beautiful?'

'Yes, she is,' agreed William.

'And this is us taking the curtain call together after *Swan Lake*.'

'Immy should see that one, Dad,' said Alex. 'Mum's wearing a tiara and holding lots of bouquets.'

'And this is us in our favourite café in Vienna with . . . do you remember Jean-Louis, Helena?'

'Oh my goodness, yes! He was a very strange man – he'd only ever eat muesli, nothing else. Pass me that photo, Alex,' she added.

'And this is Helena at the café again . . .' Glancing at the photograph as he handed it to William, Fabio suddenly blanched. In a moment of panic he tried to pull it back from William's grasp. 'But it is unimportant. I will find another.'

William held the photograph fast. 'No, I want to see them all. So there's Helena, and . . .'

Fabio stared at Helena in horror, his eyes signalling impending disaster.

William looked up at her in confusion. 'I . . . I don't understand. When was this photograph taken? How could . . . *he* have been there?'

'Who?' asked Alex, leaning over to see the photo. 'Oh, yes. What is *he* doing there with you, Mum?'

'But . . . you didn't know him then. How could he have been there with you and Fabio in Vienna?' William shook his head. 'Sorry, Helena, I don't understand.'

All eyes turned to Helena as she stared at her husband and son in silence. The moment she had always dreaded, had always known must come, was finally here.

'Go to your room, Alex,' she said quietly.

'No, Mum, I'm sorry, I won't.'

'Do as I say! Now!'

'*Okay!*' Alex stood up and marched off inside.

'Helena, *cara*, I am so sorry, so sorry.' Fabio wrung his hands. 'I think it is best I retire to bed for the night. The two of you must talk. *Buona notte, cara.*' Looking close to tears himself, Fabio kissed Helena on both cheeks, before retreating into the house.

William waited until Fabio had gone, then pointed to the bottle on the table. 'Brandy? I'm certainly having another one.'

'No, thanks.'

'Okay.' William poured himself a glass, then picked up the photograph and waved it at her. 'So. Are you going to tell me how you came to be gazing into the eyes of my oldest friend, several years before I even met you?'

'I . . .'

'Well, darling? Come along now. Spit it out. There must be a reasonable explanation, surely?'

Helena sat completely still, gazing into the distance.

'The longer you stay quiet, the more my mind conjures up thoughts that . . . Christ, they're unbearable, just unbearable!'

She continued to maintain her silence, until eventually he spoke again. 'I'll ask you again, Helena: What is *Sacha* doing in this photograph with his arm around you? And why on earth have you never told me you knew him before we met?'

Helena felt her lungs constricting, hardly able to breathe. Finally, she managed to make her lips function.

'I knew him in Vienna.'

'Well, that's bloody obvious. And . . . ?'

'I . . .' She shook her head, unable to continue.

William studied the photograph again. 'He looks pretty young in this photograph. So do you. This must have been taken years ago.'

'I . . . Yes.'

'Helena, I'm running out of patience here. For Chrissakes, tell me! Just how well did you know him, and why the hell have you never told me about this before?!' William banged the table hard, making the plates rattle and sending one of the coffee cups spinning to the stone floor, where it shattered. 'Christ! I don't believe this! I want some answers now!'

'And I'll give them to you, but first let me say I'm so, so sorry . . .'

'This photo makes me realise I've been deceived for years, by my best friend and my wife! Jesus, how much worse could it possibly be?! No wonder you've always been so cagey about your past. For all I know, you were, and perhaps still are, shagging my best friend!'

'It wasn't like that. Please, William!'

Struggling to control himself, he looked at her. 'Then tell me, just tell me, what was your relationship with Sacha? And this time, Helena, don't treat me like the cuckold I've obviously been for the past ten bloody years!'

'William! The children! I—'

'I don't give a damn if they hear that their mother is a liar and a cheat! You're not getting out of it this time, *darling*. I want to know everything! All of it! *Now!*'

'*All right!* I'll tell you! Just stop shouting at me, please!'

377

Helena bent her head to her knees and started to sob. 'I'm sorry, William, I'm so sorry, for everything. I really am.'

William knocked back his brandy and poured himself another. 'I don't think "sorry" is quite going to cover this one, but anyway, you'd better get on with your *pathetic* excuses. And of course, I understand now why you've always been so supportive of Jules. I'd thought it was out of kindness, but it was out of *guilt*, wasn't it?!'

She looked up at him. 'Are you listening or are you shouting?'

'I'm listening.'

'Okay, okay.' Helena took a couple of deep breaths. 'I met Sacha in Vienna, a few years before I met you.'

'Jesus Christ!' William swept a hand through his hair. 'The place where *he* told me to go when I was getting over my divorce from Cecile. And like an idiot, I went. He said something like, "I found love there once." It was *you* he was talking about, wasn't it?'

'William, if you want to hear this, please, let me speak! I'll tell you everything, I promise.'

He fell silent. And Helena began . . .

Helena

Was there anywhere more beautiful in the world? thought Helena as she meandered through the elegant Vienna streets on her way to the café. The late afternoon sun, unusually hot for September, was slanting off the grand stone buildings, bathing them in a golden glow that perfectly reflected her mood.

Since arriving here in late summer to take up her role as a principal ballerina with the Vienna State Opera Ballet Company, Helena had already grown to love her adopted city. From her studio apartment in Prinz Eugen Straße, which comprised one enormous room in a gracious eighteenth-century building and boasted huge floor-to-ceiling windows and an intricately corniced ceiling, it was a pleasant twenty-minute walk into the centre of the Austrian capital. She never ceased to revel in the sights she passed, from avenues lined with a delightful architectural mix of classical and art nouveau structures, to the immaculately tended parks complete with old gabled bandstands. The entire city was a perennial feast for the senses.

It had taken a lot to convince Fabio to accept the offer from Gustav Lehmann, the creative director of the Vienna State Opera House. Fabio – a Milanese by birth – had been loath to leave La Scala. But the pair had been enticed with the promise of a new ballet, created especially for them. It was to be entitled *The Artist* and was based on the paintings of Degas, with Fabio in the title role and Helena portraying his muse, 'The Little Dancer'. The ballet was due to be premiered at the start of the spring season, and she and Fabio had already met with the young French choreographer and the rather avant-garde composer. It was to be a modern piece, and the thought of the new challenge sent shivers of excitement running through her.

And now, she admitted to herself happily, there was something else here in the city that sent her spirit soaring . . . she had fallen in love.

She'd met him just a few weeks ago in the public gallery attached to the Academy of Fine Arts, where she had gone to see an exhibition. She'd been frowning at a particularly lurid modern painting entitled *Nightmare in Paris*, unable to make head or tail of it.

'I take it the picture doesn't meet with your approval.'

Helena turned towards the voice to find herself looking into the deep-set, grey-green eyes of a young man standing next to her. With his tousled auburn hair curling over the collar of his faded velvet jacket and a silk cravat spilling carelessly from the open neck of his white shirt, he had immediately reminded her of a young Oscar Wilde.

She pulled her eyes away and concentrated instead on

the slashes and squiggles of bright red, blue and green paint on the canvas in front of her. 'Well, let's just say, I don't get it.'

'My thoughts exactly. Although I shouldn't be saying that about the work of a fellow student. Apparently this piece won a prize in last year's degree exhibition.'

'You're a student here?' she said in surprise, turning to face him once more. His accent was obviously English, what her mother would call 'cut-glass', and she guessed he was probably just a few years older than her.

'Yes. Or at least, I will be; I start a master's degree at the beginning of October. I'm obsessed with Klimt and Schiele, hence choosing Vienna as a place of study. I landed here three days ago in order to find an apartment before term starts, and to brush up my rather rusty German.'

'I've been here for three weeks, but I still don't think my German is getting any better.' She smiled at him.

'You're from England too?' he asked, staring at her so intently that she found herself blushing.

'Yes. But I'm working here at the moment.'

'What do you do for a living, if you don't mind me asking?'

'I'm a dancer with the Vienna State Opera.'

'Ah, that explains it.'

'What?'

'The way you hold yourself. From an artist's point of view, you'd make the perfect subject for a sitting. You may know that Klimt himself had a particular fascination with the beauty of the female form.'

Helena blushed further, not knowing how to reply to such a compliment.

'I don't suppose you'd like to walk with me around the rest of the exhibition, would you?' he continued, changing the subject. 'It always does us artists good to hear the unvarnished views of an impartial observer. And after that, I could show you some of the masterpieces in the permanent collection. More my style, and I'm guessing more yours, too. Oh, I'm Alexander, by the way.' He held out his hand.

'Helena,' she said as she shook it, thinking about whether she'd accept his invitation. She normally refused approaches from men – of which she received many – but there was something about Alexander . . . and she suddenly heard herself saying 'yes'.

Afterwards, they had gone for coffee and spent two hours happily discussing art, ballet, music and literature. She'd learnt that he had graduated in History of Art from Oxford, then, after trying his hand as a painter back in England – and, as he put it, only making enough to buy new canvases – he'd decided to further his qualifications and experience by studying in Vienna.

'If the worst comes to the worst, and the paintings don't begin to sell, a master's in Fine Art should at least get me an interview at Sotheby's,' he'd explained.

She had agreed to meet him for coffee the following day, something which had quickly become a regular habit. He was alarmingly easy to spend time with, with his quirky sense of humour that found the funny side of most things, and his ready laugh. He was also highly intelligent, with a brain that worked at lightning speed, and was so passionate about the arts in general that they often found themselves involved in lively debates over this book or that artwork.

Alexander had regularly begged to paint her, and eventually she had given in.

And that was when it had really all begun . . .

Arriving for her very first sitting at his apartment-cum-studio, which was right at the top of an old house on Elisa-bethstraße, she'd knocked on the scuffed door with equal sensations of trepidation and excitement.

'Come in, come in,' he'd greeted her, ushering her inside.

Helena barely suppressed a smile as she took in the general chaos in the room, which was nestled in the eaves of the building. Every inch of every surface seemed to be covered in pots of brushes, tubes of paint, piles of books and a variety of used glasses and empty wine bottles. Canvases were stacked against the walls, and even against the wooden frame of the double bed in the corner. An easel sat beside the large, open window.

'Before you say it, I know it resembles the set for a production of *La Bohème*,' he said with a grin, noticing her bemused expression as he made a fruitless effort to tidy up. 'But the light in here at sunset is simply wonderful.'

'Well, I think it's the perfect garret for a penniless artist,' Helena teased him.

'That's me,' he agreed as he tipped a pile of clothes off a chair, then fiddled about positioning it and checking the angle of the light. 'Now, sit there.' Helena did so, and Alexander perched himself on the low windowsill with a sketchbook and pencil in hand. He then directed her to adopt different poses. 'Rest your arm on the back of the chair . . . no, try it behind your head . . . put your other hand under your chin . . . try crossing your legs,' and so on, until he was satisfied. Then he began to sketch.

After that, Helena had visited Alexander's apartment every day after morning class. They'd drunk wine and laughed and chatted together as he'd scribbled away, and she'd felt relaxed and carefree in his presence, in a way she'd rarely done before. On the fourth occasion she'd sat for him, he'd suddenly tossed aside the sketchbook with a sigh of frustration.

'Much as I love having you all to myself in here, it's just not working.'

'What's not working?' she asked him, her heart skipping a beat.

'The picture. I just can't seem to get it right.'

'I'm sorry, Alexander. Maybe it's me. I've never done this before and I don't know what else to do.' Helena rose with a sigh. Her body felt stiff from holding the pose, so she absentmindedly began stretching her limbs.

'That's it!' he shouted suddenly. 'You shouldn't be sitting still . . . you're a dancer! You need to move!'

The following day, having been ordered by Alexander to meet him at the Schiller Park in front of his apartment building wearing the simplest dress she had in her wardrobe, he had asked her to dance for him.

'Dance? Here?' Helena looked around at the dog walkers, picnickers and couples strolling arm in arm.

'Yes, here.' Alexander insisted. 'Take your shoes off. I'm going to sketch you.'

'What should I dance?'

'Anything you like.'

'I need music.'

'I'd hum, but I'm tone deaf,' he said, pulling out his sketch pad. 'Surely you can hear the music in your head?'

'I'll try.'

Then Helena, who spent her life *jeté*-ing across vast stages in front of packed audiences, stood in front of him like a shy five-year-old.

'Imagine you're a leaf . . . like the one there that's just blown off that chestnut tree,' Alexander encouraged her. 'You're floating on the breeze, heading in no particular direction . . . just happy to be free. Yes, Helena, that's perfect,' he smiled, as she closed her eyes briefly and her fragile body began to move. He sketched quickly as her arms lifted high above her head, and she started to turn and bend and sway, as light and graceful as the leaf she was imagining.

'Wow!' he whispered as Helena sank to the ground in front of him, oblivious now to the passers-by who had paused to watch her exquisite display. He moved towards her, taking her hands to help her to her feet. 'My God, Helena, you are incredible. Simply incredible.'

His fingers reached out to brush a leaf from her hair, then trailed down her cheek before tipping her chin up towards his face. They gazed at each other, before, very slowly, his lips moved towards hers . . .

After that, it was inevitable that they had found themselves returning to his apartment. They had made love in a glorious *pas de deux* of their own, reaching a passionate crescendo as the sun set over the rooftops of Vienna.

And now here she was, on her way to meet him after class at one of their favourite cafés in Franziskanerplatz, a charming cobbled square just a few minutes' walk from the theatre. She couldn't prevent her heart beating a little faster as she spotted him sitting at a table outside.

'Angel, you made it.' Alexander stood up as she walked towards him, then clasped her gently by her slim shoulders as he drew her towards him and placed a tender kiss on her mouth. As they sat down and a waiter came over to take her order, Helena heard a familiar voice.

'Helena, *cara!*' Fabio called out as he walked across the sunlit square towards them, his floating gait and turned-out feet giving the observer a clue as to his profession. He was flamboyantly dressed as always, today in a yellow linen suit and chocolate-brown suede loafers. His much-lamented thinning hair was covered with a Panama hat set at a rakish angle, and he had a camera slung round his neck. 'I thought it was you.'

'Fabio, how lovely.' Helena rose and kissed him on both cheeks, but as she drew away she frantically signalled to him with her eyes, indicating that this really wasn't a good moment. She had casually mentioned Alexander to Fabio, but didn't feel ready to introduce them yet. Predictably, Fabio wasn't to be deflected.

'So, Helena, are you going to introduce me to your . . . companion?'

'Alexander, this is Fabio, my partner – in dance, that is – Fabio, this is Alexander.'

'Hello, Fabio,' Alexander stood up to shake his hand. 'Won't you join us?' he asked politely.

'Thank you, I will, but only for a short while. I have just bought this camera, so today I am playing – how you say in English – the tourist.'

Helena sighed inwardly as Fabio made himself comfortable and snapped his fingers imperiously to summon the waiter. She supposed the two of them had to meet some time; she'd just have preferred to have decided for herself when that would be.

She studied them as they talked, squirming in embarrassment as Fabio interviewed Alexander like a protective father. Helena was about to protest at his near-interrogation when Fabio, perhaps sensing her irritation, swiftly changed the subject and began to ask Alexander about his work as an artist.

'My course hasn't begun yet, but in the meantime there's so much inspiration here in Vienna,' Alexander ventured, smiling at Helena and laying a hand on her arm.

'That is very true. I, too, wish to have memories of this beautiful city in the sunshine, hence today and the camera. Perhaps I should start with the two of you?' He picked up the camera and angled it at them.

'Fabio, really, do you have to? You know I hate being photographed,' Helena pleaded.

'But you are both such charming subjects, I cannot resist! Come now, smile for me, *cara*. You too, Alexander. I promise it won't hurt.'

Fabio began to snap away, directing Alexander to put his arm around her, and making such outrageously flattering remarks that they were soon both laughing along with him. When he had finished, Fabio stood up, took a last sip of his wine, then tipped his hat to them. 'I wish you both a pleasant afternoon. And I will see you tomorrow, Helena, for our first rehearsal. I hope you will be taking the early night to prepare for it.' With a wink at both of them, he wandered off across the square and out of sight.

*

Fabio broached the subject of Alexander the following day as he and Helena went for lunch after class.

'So, this man, Alexander . . . are you serious about him?' he questioned her.

'I . . . I don't know. It's too early to tell. We enjoy each other's company,' she answered cautiously.

Fabio flicked his wrist dismissively. 'Helena, *cara*, it is written all over your face that you are already in love with him. And while I understand you do not wish to discuss the details with me, I can tell that you have already consummated your passion.'

Helena blushed furiously. 'So what if we have? There's nothing wrong with it, is there?'

Fabio gave a dramatic sigh, wiped his mouth with his napkin and sat back in his chair, surveying her shrewdly. 'Of course not. But Helena, you are sometimes such a *bambina* in the ways of the world that I worry for you. What do you really know about this man?'

'Quite enough, thank you,' said Helena defiantly. 'He's a very talented painter, he makes me laugh, and—'

'But did you not notice,' Fabio interrupted, 'how little detail he gave when I questioned him about his background? He was evasive with me, for sure. I will be blunt: there is something about him that I do not trust. Call it the natural instinct of one man about another. I believe he is a player. And has something to hide. It is there in his eyes. They are . . .' He searched for the right word. 'Shifty.'

'Fabio! For goodness' sake! You met him for half an hour! How can you make such an assumption?'

'Trust me' – Fabio tapped his nose – 'I am never wrong about the men.'

'Anyone would think you were jealous,' she said crossly, rising from her chair and throwing her own napkin onto the table. 'Besides, it's really none of your business. So if you wouldn't mind, I don't want to discuss it any longer.'

'So be it.' Fabio merely gave a sanguine shrug. 'Have it your way, *cara*. But don't say I didn't warn you.'

Helena smarted from Fabio's comments for the next few days, and maintained a cool demeanour with him as rehearsals for the new season began in earnest, but he pointedly didn't bring up the subject again. She had to admit that Alexander didn't divulge much detail when he talked of his life back in England. She knew he lived in a small cottage somewhere in the south of England, and that his wealthy parents had disowned him over his refusal to get a 'proper' job. She did wonder once how he was managing to fund an expensive art course in Vienna, and had asked him the next time she'd seen him. He'd replied that he'd used the last remnants of his trust fund, and that this degree course was 'shit or bust' – as he'd put it.

She tried not to let Fabio's comments cloud her happiness. He was just being overprotective, that was all. And since she could never stay cross with him for long, they soon slipped back into their usual easy relationship.

Helena and Alexander continued to see each other as often as possible. Things were made more complicated by the fact that Helena was very busy with the ballet company, and Alexander's course had finally started, with a full schedule of lectures, seminars and after-class assignments.

Never before had she met anyone with whom she felt

she could truly be herself. And he seemed every bit as smitten as her, leaving little notes for her to find when he'd left her apartment, writing poems and constantly telling her how much he loved her.

As the bond between them grew deeper, Helena couldn't help beginning to tentatively imagine a future with him. Even though Alexander never brought it up and was decidedly vague about his plans once his course was finished, she found herself dreaming that he might perhaps stay in Vienna when it ended the following summer. Or perhaps she could even return to England and the Royal Ballet to be near him, if Fabio would agree.

After all, how could they possibly be parted now?

It was as they lay in bed together in her apartment, while a chill autumn wind rattled the old windows, that he told her he was going back to England the following morning.

'I have a family problem that I need to go and sort out. With any luck, I should only be gone for a couple of weeks.'

'But how will you spare the time from your classes at the Academy?' Helena asked, propping herself up on her elbow and looking down at him, puzzled. 'The academic term's in full swing. Can't it wait until the Christmas recess?'

'Not really, no. There are some . . . things that I need to deal with over there.'

'What "things", Alexander?'

'Nothing for you to worry about. I'll be back before you know it, angel, I promise,' he added as he kissed her.

He refused to be drawn further about what the problem

might be, and Helena had to be satisfied with the fact that he wouldn't be away for long. They made love with particular passion that night, and she dropped off to sleep feeling replete and content.

As it turned out, Helena had very little time to miss Alexander's presence in the days that followed. She was heavily involved in rehearsals for the imminent productions of *L'après-midi d'un faune*, *La Fille mal gardée* and *La Sylphide*, as well as spending two afternoons per week working with the choreographer and composer of the new ballet, *The Artist*.

When the date of Alexander's planned arrival back in Vienna came and went, Helena tried not to panic, although she began to check the noticeboard at the theatre to see if there had been a call for her every time she passed it. Stupidly, he'd forgotten to leave her the number where she could contact him in England, even though he'd said he would.

Eventually, as December approached, she resorted to visiting his department at the Academy of Fine Arts.

'I'm enquiring about a friend of mine who's studying for a master's degree here. I need to know when he's returning to the Academy.'

The secretary gave Helena a beady look over the top of her glasses. 'We don't hand out that kind of information, Fräulein.'

'Please – it's an emergency. He left to deal with a family situation in England and he should be back by now. Surely it wouldn't do any harm if you just checked your files?'

The secretary gave a bored sigh. 'Please tell me his name.'

'It's Alexander Nicholls.'

'I will try. "Nicholls", you said?'

'Yes.'

'Please wait here.' The secretary disappeared for several minutes. When she returned, she shook her head. 'According to the records, we have no student in this department under the name of Nicholls.'

Confused and troubled by what she'd just been told, but frantic with worry to find out what had happened to him – perhaps he'd had an accident, or there'd been a death in the family? – Helena went to his apartment building. There she was told by the doorman that the young man in 14a had moved out nearly a month ago, and that the attic apartment had already been re-let.

She walked away from the building, her finely toned legs shaking as though they were made of jelly. Blindly heading for the park opposite, where she had danced for him as he'd sketched her, she made it to the nearest bench and sank onto it.

The chestnut tree now stood leafless – stark and bare in the bleak November mist.

Helena buried her face in her trembling hands. Like the leaves that had fallen from the tree, Alexander – and their love – seemed to have vanished into thin air.

κγ

Twenty-three

'So' – Helena's entire body drooped from exhaustion – 'in the end, I realised he wasn't ever coming back. And that was that.'

There was a long pause before William spoke. 'Of course, you realise you aren't unusual, don't you? He's always had a short attention span when it comes to pretty women. He's in love with being in love. Don't flatter your-self, Helena. I can assure you that you were only one of many.'

'I'm sure.' She refused to react to the jibe. She knew she deserved it, and far worse besides.

'I'm amazed he never told me about you. He usually gave me chapter and verse on his illicit conquests.' William let out a harsh chuckle. 'If I'd have known you at the time, I could have warned you. But of course, I didn't. And, if I *had* known you . . . well, we wouldn't be here now. The last thing I'd ever have wanted was one of his cast-offs.'

Helena retreated into herself to find the strength not to

run away from William's dreadful words. He was the injured party; he had a right to say whatever he wanted.

'I understand.' She looked down at her hands as she spoke. 'Maybe he didn't tell you because he was ashamed.'

'Sacha, ashamed of bedding a woman?! Hardly. It was what he lived for. Why on earth would he be ashamed?'

'I discovered ... much later, that he'd gone home, because Jules was pregnant with Rupes.'

'I see.' William nodded. 'Well, that must have been a bit of a shock.'

'Yes.' She looked up at him. 'But I didn't know that at the time, *or* that he was married.'

'Really? Isn't that convenient.'

'He didn't tell me, William. He never even gave me a clue, I swear.'

'And it never occurred to you when you met me that your Viennese lover was one and the same as my oldest friend?'

'William, when you first mentioned your best friend "Sacha Chandler" – who granted had been at Oxford with you and suggested that you visit Vienna – how could I have known they were the same person? I knew him back then as "Alexander Nicholls".'

'As I'm sure I've told you before, "Sacha" is his childhood nickname and the full family surname is actually "Chandler-Nicholls". I find it very hard to believe that you wouldn't have known that at the time, seeing as the two of you were so' – he almost spat the next word – '*close.*'

'William, our relationship lasted only a couple of months. We were two strangers who met in a foreign city. Call me naive, but I honestly knew very little about his background. I'm not trying to make excuses, but until I set eyes on him on the day of our wedding, how *could* I have known?'

William glared at her, and Helena knew that nothing she could say would blunt the edges of his shock.

'So, let's move on. Obviously, he left you in the lurch.'

'Yes.'

'And what happened next? Did he contact you once he got home to England?'

'No. I heard nothing at all. I know now that he got a job in the City and Jules gave birth to Rupes a few months later—'

'Hold on a moment . . .' Something was slowly clicking in William's brain. 'Shit!' His expression changed to horror as the reality of the thought took shape. 'There's worse than what you've told me so far, isn't there, Helena? Much worse?'

She was silent. What was there to say?

'Because . . . there's only four months between Alex and Rupes . . . Isn't there, Helena?'

'Yes.'

William looked up to the glorious night sky, studded with glittering stars. It had been there last night, and the night before, and it would be there again tomorrow. Yet, tonight, everything in *his* world had changed irrevocably. And could never be the same again.

Eventually, he stood up. 'Finally, I understand. No wonder you've never told me who Alex's father was. All I can say is God help *him* when he hears all this, Helena. God help your poor son. Jesus!' He paced across the terrace distractedly. 'I'm searching for a way back from here, but at the moment I can't see one.' He shook his head desolately. 'There is no comfort. Anywhere.'

'I know. William, I . . .'

'Sorry' – William held out his hands, as if physically protecting himself from her – 'I really can't. I have to leave, now.'

William disappeared inside, and ten minutes later Helena heard a car engine start up and roar across the gravel and up the hill. She watched the tail lights recede until they faded into the blackness.

ALEX'S DIARY

12th August (continued)

I am sitting on the end of my bed . . .

Waiting.

Waiting for my mother to come in here and wake me up. She will walk in and hold me like she did when I was younger, stroke my hair and tell me I have had a nightmare. That none of it really happened, that I did not hear the terrible words spoken on the terrace just below my bedroom window. That my father who isn't my father did not leave the house in his car, perhaps never to return.

Because of who my real father is.

My brain will burst soon. It will explode into a million tiny bits and make a terrible mess all over the walls. It cannot contain what it knows. It doesn't know how to process the information. It is grinding, churning, going round in circles, but getting nowhere.

It can't cope. And nor can I.

I hit my knees with my fists, hurting myself to make the physical pain worse than the mental, but it doesn't work.

Nothing works.

Nothing can take away the pain I am feeling.

And the worst thing is that the one person who could always make things better has caused it.

So I am alone now. In the dark.

When my brain eventually becomes unblocked, it will start to process the ramifications of what I have just heard. All I know is that I am no longer who I thought I was.

And neither is my mother.

κδ

Twenty-four

Hands shaking as she poured herself a brandy, Helena drained the glass, feeling it burn her stomach with its warmth, but knowing that it could never burn away the horror of what had just happened. Standing up, she walked inside and made her way along the corridor to Alex's bedroom. Summoning every ounce of strength she had left, she knocked on his door.

'Can I come in?'

There was no reply, so she pushed it open.

The room was in darkness, the open shutters letting in the pale glow of moonlight. As her eyes adjusted, she saw a figure sitting on the edge of the bed.

'Can we talk?' she asked quietly.

'Has Dad left?'

'Yes. He has.'

'Will he be back?'

'I . . . don't know.'

She moved across the room and, feeling her way to the bed, sat down before her legs collapsed under her.

'Were you listening?'

There was a long pause before Alex replied. 'Yes.'

'To all of it?'

'Yes.'

'So . . . you know now who your biological father is?'

There was silence from Alex.

'Can you understand why I've never told you? Or anyone else, for that matter?'

'Mum, I can't talk about this . . . I can't.'

'Dad . . . *William* didn't want to hear how, or why. I understand you won't either. But I want to finish the story, explain to you what happened after he . . . Sacha, as you know him, had left me in Vienna. Please listen, Alex, it's so important that you know. And for me to explain why it had quite a lot to do with Alexis, and what happened here, too.'

There was no response, so Helena began anyway.

'I found out I was pregnant with you just after Christmas . . .'

Helena

Helena's breath crystallised in delicate, curling wisps of white in the freezing air as she made her way to morning class from her apartment.

The city was especially beguiling at this time of year; the gorgeous stone buildings adorned with traditional festive decorations and twinkling fairy lights, which were in turn garnished with a lustrous frosting of the fresh snow that had fallen overnight. It was the day before New Year's Eve, and an atmosphere of gaiety and excitement seemed to infuse everything and everyone.

Everyone, that was, except her. Helena wondered whether she would ever feel happy, excited or just . . . *anything* again. It had been almost two months since Alexander had left, and days of desolation and nights spent sobbing herself to sleep had eventually given way to a numbness that seemed to reach the depths of her soul. She'd finally had to accept that, for whatever reason, Alexander wasn't ever coming back to Vienna. Or to her.

Helena paused briefly in front of the State Opera House and looked up at the golden stone arches that, come tonight, would be uplit to spectacular effect. How ironic, she thought, that at the lowest emotional point of her life, her career was reaching new heights. Tonight she was to play the title role at a gala performance of *La Sylphide*, and the new ballet, *The Artist*, was taking shape and would be the biggest production of the forthcoming season. Helena knew that the prestige of creating a role could take both her own and Fabio's career to a new level, but just now she struggled to find the energy to care.

At least, she thought, as she approached the stage door, the discipline and rigour of her professional life had kept her from going completely insane with grief.

Having greeted the doorkeeper, Helena made her way through the maze of corridors to her dressing room, where she shrugged off her fur-collared coat and donned her practice leotard and leg warmers. She added her favourite, somewhat moth-eaten cross-over cardigan to keep out the chill until her slender body had had a chance to warm up.

She scraped her mane of blonde hair back into a bun and laced the satin ribbons of her *pointe* shoes tightly around her ankles before leaving the sanctuary of her dressing room.

Various members of the company were already waiting on the vast stage, chatting in groups or stretching at the barre that had been set up for the purpose. Despite her sombre mood, Helena couldn't help smiling ruefully as she reflected on how the motley assortment of practice outfits – complete with holed tights – and the make-up-free faces of the dancers were so at odds with how they would all appear on the stage that night. She shivered slightly as she turned to gaze for a moment into the darkness of the empty auditorium, which would later be dazzlingly lit to reveal the splendour of the gilded balconies filled to bursting with an expectant audience of over two thousand people.

She greeted her fellow dancers as she took her place at the barre. The *répétiteur* arrived to conduct the class, the lone pianist began to play and the class began with the usual *pliés*. Helena didn't have to think about the exercises; her body had performed them so many thousands of times that it went onto autopilot as it prepared itself for the demanding role of the Sylph in *La Sylphide*. They'd had a full dress rehearsal yesterday and all had gone well, although as it was the first time she'd performed the role, she'd felt nervy and on edge; but from experience, she knew she'd be better in front of an audience when the adrenaline kicked in.

'Good morning, Helena, *cara*,' a voice said behind her, as Fabio took his place at the barre.

'You're late again,' she chastised him, as they all turned to perform the same exercise on the other leg.

'It must have been the alarm clock, it's obviously broken,' he said with a mischievous roll of his dark eyes.

Helena knew this was Fabio-speak for a liaison.

'Well, I'm sure you'll tell me all about it after class.'

That evening, Helena sat in her dressing room, putting the finishing touches to her make-up with a practised hand. It had been a whirlwind of a day, the morning rehearsal followed by a round of media interviews after lunch. She'd had little time to rest, and she felt the electric zing of nervous tension running through her. To distract herself, she picked up the card that sat beside a sumptuous bouquet of white roses – the largest and most lavish of several floral tributes that were dotted around the room – and read it.

'My dearest Helena
Thank you once again for the pleasure of your company at dinner last week and for agreeing to accompany me to the ball tomorrow night. Good luck this evening. I will be out front watching you.
Yours, F x x
Prince Friedrich Von Etzendorf'

She noticed then that tucked in amongst the blooms was a small package encased in silver tissue paper. She unwrapped it to reveal a velvet-covered box, and opened the lid. Inside lay a delicate necklace, comprising a trio of sparkling tear-drop-shaped diamonds suspended on a whisper-thin chain. She sat back in her chair, overwhelmed by the extravagance of the gift. As she looked at her reflection in the mirror, she wasn't sure whether to laugh or cry at the irony of it.

She had first been introduced to Prince Friedrich a month ago, at an after-show drinks reception. Someone had told her that he was descended from one of the oldest and wealthiest families in Austria, and had a particular interest in the arts. Despite the fact that he was handsome and courteous, she hadn't been able to muster much enthusiasm during their conversation. After all, he wasn't Alexander; and the fact that Friedrich *was* – certainly on first impres-sions – just about everything a woman could ask for had somehow depressed her further.

The following day she had received an embossed note from him, inviting her to dine with him. She wanted to refuse immediately, but knew that she desperately needed to move on after Alexander's abrupt disappearance from her life. She told Fabio about the invitation as they waited in the wings together for their entrance.

'Should I go?'

'Helena, this is a prince to rival any fairy-tale ballet story. Of course you must go!'

So, reluctantly, she had accepted the invitation.

And it had been . . . *fine*.

They had seen each other a few times since – he far more eager than she to make it as often as her schedule would allow. Friedrich really did seem too good to be true – handsome, cultured, rich and totally devoted to her.

'What more could any woman ask for? I just do not understand you, Helena.' Fabio had rolled his eyes at her obvious lack of enthusiasm when he asked how the relationship was going.

Nothing, Helena had thought to herself.

It was as if, she mused now as she hung the necklace around her throat and saw how it fitted snugly between her collarbones, she had lost the ability to *feel*.

'You are my very own Grace Kelly,' Friedrich had said to her the last time he'd seen her, as he kissed her fingertips over the dinner table. 'I want to make you my princess.'

Then he had formally requested the pleasure of her company at the Gala New Year's Eve Ball, which was to be held at the iconic Hofburg Palace. 'I wish to show you off to everyone,' he'd said.

Although she hardly felt in a party mood, she had

thought it would be ungracious to refuse, particularly as she knew it was one of the most highly anticipated events in the Viennese social calendar. And at least it meant she would not be sitting alone sobbing as the New Year bells chimed out across the city.

After accepting the invitation to the ball, Helena had realised she had nothing suitable to wear for such an occasion, so she'd explained the situation to Klara, her trusted dresser at the theatre. Klara, in true fairy godmother style, had whisked her off to Wardrobe, where they had found her an exquisite strapless pale-pink ball gown. In which she really did look like a princess.

Helena glanced at it now, hanging sheathed in protective polythene on the rail, ready – after some minor adjustments – for her to take home with her after tonight's performance. As if on cue, Klara herself bustled into the dressing room, carrying the fluttering layers of white tulle, chiffon and sequins that made up Helena's stage costume for this evening.

'Come now, Frau Beaumont, you must get ready, we have little time,' she commanded in her heavily accented English.

She proceeded to style Helena's hair into a high bun, adding small pearl and diamanté clips that would shimmer and sparkle under the lights. Then she sprayed it with enough hairspray to withstand a nuclear attack before helping Helena into the costume, taking great care not to mark it with her heavy stage make-up. Her beady eyes fell on the open velvet box sitting on the dressing table.

'This is a gift?' she said, indicating the box.

'Yes.'

'Who from?'

'A friend.'

'You mean the Prince?'

Helena nodded, embarrassed.

'There is no need to be shy. You are a lovely woman. And I know he takes you to the ball tomorrow night. This necklace will look perfect with your dress.'

'Yes, I suppose it will.'

'And I have been thinking, Frau Beaumont. Tomorrow I will come to your apartment and help you in the preparations,' Klara announced, as though it was a *fait accompli*.

'Really, there's absolutely no need,' protested Helena.

'But how will you fasten the dress without my help? There are many small pearl buttons at the back. And I can also fashion the hairstyle that will make you look your best.'

Helena capitulated, knowing from experience that resistance against Klara was futile. 'Thank you, that's very kind of you.'

There was no time for further conversation as Klara tutted fretfully at the five-minute bell, administering a further misting of hairspray as Helena rose from the chair to inspect herself in the full-length mirror. The exquisite costume, with its delicately beaded bodice and flowing white skirts, epitomised the ethereal qualities of the character she would inhabit in a few minutes' time.

'You are ready,' said Klara, admiring her handiwork too, as 'Beginners' was called over the intercom. 'Good luck,' she added as Helena left the dressing room.

Two hours later, Fabio led Helena forward amid the thunderous applause that signalled the end of what they both knew had been a magical performance. The audience rose to their feet with much stamping and cheering as the two of them took bow after bow and bouquets were flung onto the boards of the stage.

After the curtain fell for the final time, Helena made her way back to her dressing room. The adrenaline was still flowing round her body and despite her current offstage problems, she was still on a high. Almost immediately, there was a knock at the door, heralding the arrival of what she knew would be a steady stream of visitors dropping by to congratulate her.

A handsome face, framed by pale blond hair, appeared round the door.

'I do hope I am not disturbing you,' he said.

'Not at all. Please, Friedrich, come in.'

Helena walked forward to greet her guest, thinking how very distinguished he looked in his white tie and tails, with a scarlet sash bearing his family crest draped across his broad chest. Friedrich took her hand and kissed it.

'Words cannot express how enchanting I found your performance tonight. You are truly the embodiment of a fairy-tale sylph. And I see that you received my flowers,' he added, indicating the roses.

'They're stunning. And the necklace is beautiful too, Friedrich, but really, it's far too generous—'

'Hush, my dear Helena. It is no more than you deserve. Please, I should be most dismayed if I thought it did not please you. And I am very much hoping that you will wear my gift to the ball.'

'Then all I can say is that I will, and thank you.'

'The only thanks I need is to have you on my arm as we walk into the Hofburg Palace tomorrow evening.'

Helena was about to reply when there came another knock at the door.

'So, I will take my leave for now, Helena – and look forward to a wonderful New Year's Eve.' With that, Friedrich bowed deeply and left the room, as a crowd of well-wishers surged inside and swarmed around her.

Eventually, everyone departed the dressing room, leaving Helena alone. The adrenaline that had propelled her through the evening had now left her body and she felt weak and deflated. Once Klara had helped her out of the costume and she'd removed her stage make-up, she changed into her jeans and sweater, shrugged on her coat and snow boots then left the theatre.

The following day, Helena met Fabio for a New Year's Eve lunch at Griechenbeisl.

'*Cara.*' He rose to greet her as the waiter showed her to the table. 'Come, sit, and let us celebrate the success of last night's performance.' He pulled a bottle of champagne from the ice bucket that was already waiting, and poured out two glasses.

'Here's to us! And to the New Year!' he toasted as he chinked his glass against hers. 'I have already read the reviews of *La Sylphide* in the morning papers, and they are superb. They say you are a star rising to the celestial firmament. Now, when we premiere our new ballet, they will know more than ever that we are a force to be reckoned with. We are on our way to the top, Helena, I know it.'

Helena tried to mirror Fabio's obvious euphoria, but was unable to manage more than a weak smile.

'And apart from your triumph on the stage last night, you are to attend the ball at the Hofburg Palace this evening with the dashing Prince. Are you not excited, *cara*? It must be every woman's, and man's' – he chuckled – 'dream to have such a night.'

'Fabio, you must understand that I can't just . . . switch off from what happened.'

'Pffft!' He flapped his hand dismissively. 'You are talking still about that scoundrel, Alexander. Of course I understand how much he hurt you, *cara*, but it is time to forget him and live your life. I thought the Prince pleased you?'

'I . . . he does, I suppose, but . . . I'm not sure if I'm ready.'

'Maybe it is simply because you are exhausted.' He leant forward across the table and examined her face more closely. 'You look pale, Helena, and you have not even taken a sip of your champagne. Are you sure you are not sick?'

'No, no, I'm not . . . it's just that . . . I'm tired, that's all.' She bit her lip as her voice trailed off.

'Then as soon as we have finished lunch, I call a taxi to take you back to your apartment. You must have some rest, so that you are prepared for the ball. I want you to enjoy yourself for a change, Helena.'

'Yes, you're right.' She managed a tight smile to reassure him. 'I'll be fine after a nap.'

Fabio shot her a suspicious glance, but refrained from further comment and changed the subject, quizzing her instead about her gown for the ball, then as usual regaling her with titbits of gossip about other members of the ballet company. When their food arrived, she felt his keen eyes assessing her as she barely touched it.

It was as if, Helena thought, *he already knew.*

Having got through lunch, she went home and did as Fabio had ordered her and lay down on her bed. Try as she might to get some sleep, her brain was whirring and her stomach churning. She found herself trying to calculate yet again if it was really possible, or whether she was simply panicking.

Shortly after her first physical encounter with Alexander, she had been thrust into the maelstrom of the ballet season and, like most ballerinas, had taken the Pill continually without the usual one-week break, in order to prevent the monthly bleeding. This was regarded as an essential practice for performing onstage.

Consequently, she had no clear idea of when she had last bled 'normally'.

But then . . . there was the nausea, the heavy feeling in her stomach, the exhaustion – symptoms that she remembered only too well from last time . . .

Eventually Helena gave up trying to rest, and rose from the bed. She'd procrastinated time and time again, but there was only one way to find out and put her mind at rest.

Realising that the pharmacy on the next street would almost certainly be closing early today, she threw on her coat, grabbed her purse and ran out of the apartment. After she'd bought what she needed she walked back home, her heart sinking as she saw Klara already waiting for her outside the front entrance to her building.

Damn! 'Sorry to keep you waiting in the cold, Klara,' she said. 'I ran out of . . . toothpaste.'

Klara pursed her lips as Helena unlocked the front door. 'We must make a start if you are to be ready in time.'

Back in the apartment, as Klara chattered constantly about the evening ahead, Helena zoned out, merely nodding at what she thought were appropriate junctures, her mind still occupied elsewhere.

I was mad to accept the invitation to the ball. I'm leading Friedrich on . . . What on earth will I do if . . . ?

By the time she was finally ready to Klara's satisfaction, Helena could stand the tension no longer and stood up. Retreating to the bathroom, she locked the door and went to the cabinet, where she had hastily hidden the test away earlier. She drew out the contents of the packet, her heart thumping against her ribs as she stared at it miserably and began to peel off the plastic wrapper.

Then she froze as she heard the door buzzer, followed almost immediately by loud knocking on the bathroom door.

'Frau Beaumont! Your car has arrived! Your prince is waiting for you!' called Klara.

'Coming!' Helena hesitated for a moment, then stuffed the white stick into her jewelled evening bag before she left the bathroom.

Klara was waiting for her outside, holding out a gossamer-fine silk wrap in one hand and a pair of long satin opera gloves in the other. After helping Helena on with the gloves and draping the wrap around her slender bare shoulders, she stood back as she surveyed her charge. The fitted silk bodice of the blush-pink dress was artfully cut to reveal

Helena's flawless décolletage, then cinched around her tiny waist before cascading into voluminous, floating skirts made up of layers of delicate chiffon. Her blonde hair was piled on top of her head, wispy tendrils curling around her face, and the diamond necklace sparkled like tiny shards of ice at her narrow throat.

'You look beautiful.' Klara gave a satisfied sigh. 'Now, *liebling*, you must go and greet your prince.' She shooed Helena out of the front door of the apartment and towards the lift.

'Have a wonderful night!' she called as the doors closed.

Friedrich, looking svelte in full evening dress, was waiting for her in the lobby and let out an audible gasp as Helena emerged from the lift and walked towards him. He took her gloved hands in his and held her at arm's length for a few moments as his eyes swept over her, before drawing her to him and kissing her gently on both cheeks. 'You are radiant, my Helena,' he whispered. 'I will be the envy of every man at the ball.' Then he offered her his arm, and they walked together out to the waiting limousine.

The lightest sprinkling of snow was falling as the imposing curved facade of the Hofburg Palace came into view, aglow with lights. They drove beneath the high ceremonial arch and into a huge lamp-lit inner courtyard, where a red carpet was laid over the cobblestones leading up to the entrance. The car drew to a halt and Helena stepped out, taking Friedrich's proffered hand as he led her inside and up a grand staircase into a sumptuous palace stateroom, where a champagne reception was already in full swing.

Helena accepted a glass from a waiter and took a sip to

413

try and calm her jangling nerves. She was going to need Dutch – and every other nationality's – courage to get her through the evening. She was greeted with deference by an endless stream of other guests, all eager to offer congratulations on her performances at the Opera House and to greet the prince by her side.

Eventually they made their way to their table, where more champagne waited for them and waiters plied them with platters of gorgeously presented canapés. Helena ate nothing, but if the Prince noticed her lack of appetite or her subdued conversation, he gave no indication.

When the announcement came for the guests to enter the main ballroom, Helena couldn't help but gaze in awe at the rows of marbled Corinthian pillars supporting an ornate coffered ceiling, from which hung dozens of crystal chandeliers. An orchestra was playing a Viennese waltz on a raised dais, beneath a huge clock that would count the minutes and seconds leading up to midnight.

Then a hush fell and columns of young women, all dressed in white gowns, filed into the ballroom on the arms of their young men.

'Who are they?' Helena asked Friedrich.

'They are the debutantes, and now they will perform a dance to mark their official entry into Viennese society.'

Wondering if she had slipped into unconsciousness and was actually dreaming a ritual from a bygone age, Helena watched them. She couldn't help but feel a pang in her heart as she saw the innocent, excited faces; young women with their whole lives ahead of them, and not a care in the world.

As she had once been.

She was snapped back to the present as the debutantes departed sedately, to a round of applause. The red cordons that had held back the rest of the guests were swiftly removed so that the dancing could begin. Helena lost track of time as Friedrich swept her into his arms and around the golden parquet floor in waltz after waltz. There were other men wanting to dance with her too, and she did her best to smile and charm them like the princess Friedrich seemed to want her to be.

'You look so ravishing tonight, Helena. You have truly cast a spell on me and every man here,' he murmured as the band at last slowed the tempo, and he took the opportunity to draw her close to him.

Helena felt strangely removed from the proceedings, as though she was watching herself from above. Friedrich bent his blond head to gently caress her neck. 'I hope that you and I will be able to spend a great deal more time together in the new year to come.'

'I'm . . . sure we will,' she heard herself replying.

Interpreting her answer as encouragement, Friedrich pressed his cheek against her hair as they moved in an elegant circle beneath a chandelier. 'Please, Helena . . .' he whispered in her ear, 'say you'll come home with me tonight.'

At his words, Helena came back down to earth with a jolt. She pulled back her head to gaze up at him, his kind eyes shining with obvious adoration.

What am I doing here? she thought in panic. She glanced up at the clock, suddenly feeling horribly sick and very faint, and saw it was barely more than ten minutes to midnight. Friedrich's face immediately became a picture of concern.

'Helena, *liebling*, are you all right?'

'I'm not sure. I . . . feel a little strange. I think I need to sit down.'

Friedrich solicitously escorted her from the floor and settled her back at their table, then left to find her a glass of water. As she sat there, her head continued to spin. Wanting desperately to be alone for a few moments, she rose from the table and headed in the direction of the ladies' powder room.

After splashing her face with cold water, Helena felt a little better. She looked at her reflection in the mirror and her hands reached for her bag so that she could retrieve her lipstick. Still shaky, as she fumbled with the clasp she managed to drop it on the floor, spilling its contents onto the tiles. Bending to pick up the scattered items, she saw the white plastic stick staring up at her like a miniature sword of Damocles.

How can I even contemplate a relationship with another man while this is hanging over me? she berated herself.

She knew Friedrich would be waiting for her, and that this was hardly an appropriate moment, but she also knew that she *had* to find out for sure before she could begin to think clearly.

What the new year would hold for her and her future depended on the object in her hands. Heart hammering, Helena headed for a cubicle.

And three minutes later, she had the answer.

*

Groups of people were milling around the foyer and hardly noticed the young woman running across the marble floor, the skirts of her pale-pink ball gown billowing out behind her.

Almost tripping down the staircase that led to the main entrance, Helena paused for a second to tug off her high-heeled evening shoes, throwing them heedlessly to one side before she fled out into the sparkling, frosty night.

Just as the bells of St Stephen's Cathedral began to toll midnight. And ring in the New Year.

She barely noticed the freezing snow beneath her stock-inged feet as she ran across the courtyard, then under the domed arch and eventually out onto the street. Through the pounding of blood in her ears, she dimly heard a male voice behind her, shouting her name.

She did not turn to look back.

KE

Twenty-five

Helena glanced upwards through Alex's window and saw a full moon shining down, just as it had on the night she'd run from the Hofburg Palace. The mother of the skies – calmly watching over her human children as they tripped and fell beneath her, lighting their way in the darkness as they picked themselves up.

'So . . .' Helena pulled herself back from her memories. 'That's the story. I wish I could make it better for you, Alex, but I can't.'

Finally he spoke. 'No, you can't. But I still don't understand why this has anything to do with Alexis.'

'I . . .' Helena paused in an agony of indecision as to whether she should tell him. It was too much for any son to learn about his mother, let alone at the age of just thirteen.

'Whatever it is, Mum, you can't make it any worse.' Alex read her thoughts. 'So come on then, spit it out.'

'I got pregnant by Alexis when I was staying here at Pandora.'

'But . . . you were only fifteen.' Alex's voice was barely more than a strangled whisper.

'Yes. And I . . . didn't have it. I felt I had no choice. And it was so, so dreadful. I've never forgiven myself to this day for what I did. So, when I found out I was having you, I couldn't, just *couldn't*, do it again. I had to have you, whatever the cost.'

Helena could hear Alex breathing, nothing more.

'With the new ballet looming, it wasn't fair to stay on with the company – after all, I could hardly have portrayed 'The Little Dancer' at six months pregnant when it premiered in March. And in the meantime, it wouldn't have been fair on anyone to continue pretending. I told Fabio to find another partner, and left the company at the end of January. I decided I'd stay on in Vienna. One way and another, going back to England wasn't an option. I had some money saved from what my mother had left me after she died, which I used to get through the pregnancy, and I started working at Café Landtmann, not far from the Opera House, as a waitress. They liked the fact I could speak English as well as basic German, and they were very kind to me. I worked up to the day before you arrived unexpectedly, over a month prematurely.

'But you were fine and healthy, and you were so gorgeous.' Helena felt a catch in her throat as she remembered. 'I called you Alexander, both in remembrance of the little one I'd never had and after your biological father. There didn't seem to be a choice,' she shrugged with a faint smile. 'And of course, Rudolf as a second name, after Nureyev, the famous dancer who died so tragically young, only a few days after I found out I was expecting you.'

There was still silence from Alex. What else could she expect? So she continued.

'After I'd had you, it was a very difficult time. You needed some specialist care as a premature baby, and to top it all I wasn't very well either. I suffered from a rare condition called postpartum eclampsia – I don't want to sound dramatic, but I nearly died, Alex, which meant I struggled for far longer to get back to full health. We were both in the hospital for over two months. After that, returning to dancing simply wasn't an option at the time. It may sound ridiculous to you, but a ballerina has to be as physically fit – if not fitter – than a Premier League football player. I did get better slowly, thank God, and for the first year I was happy just to be with you. And Alex, Fabio was just wonderful with you. He played with you, took you out for walks and was as much of a father as any man could be. As you know, he also gave you Bee, your bunny . . .'

Helena paused before continuing. Unable to see her son's expression in the darkness, it was impossible to gauge what he was thinking.

'And then there was Gretchen, who lived in the apartment above us. When I went back to work at the café, as I needed to earn us some money urgently, she looked after you. You loved her, Alex. She was fat and jolly and used to feed you home-made fruit strudels and pancakes. Do you remember her?'

'No,' came the terse reply.

'Anyway, as I grew stronger, with Fabio's encouragement, I eventually started taking classes, thinking that I might be able to go back to partnering him again. Then Fabio told me he'd been offered a contract at the New York City

Ballet, and begged me to bring you and go with him. He never did like Vienna. But Alex, I knew that I just wasn't anywhere near up to the standard required. The New York City Ballet dancers are amongst the most athletic in the world. I didn't want to arrive as Fabio's partner and not have the physical and mental stamina needed to cope – which would then have set *him* back on his career path, and that wouldn't have been fair.

'So I told him that I didn't want to uproot both of us and go to New York. You can imagine that when he left Vienna, I was distraught. I gave up the idea of ever return-ing to dancing, and continued to work as a waitress. Then we had to leave our lovely apartment, and Gretchen, because I simply couldn't afford it, and we moved to what was little more than a freezing rabbit hutch above the café I worked at. I was at my lowest ebb when, a few months later, I met William.'

Helena paused, trying to find the strength to go on.

'William brought me back to life, Alex, he really did. He was so kind and steady, and such a genuinely good person. And slowly, I fell in love with him. Not in the "first love" way I'd adored Alexis, or in the mad, reckless way I'd felt about Sacha, but something that was deeper and stronger. I'm telling you all this, Alex, because it's the truth and also, it's your story too. I don't expect you to understand or for-give me.'

Helena looked at her son's silhouette, framed against the moonlight.

'When William asked me to go with him back to England, I eventually agreed. I had to take time to make sure I wasn't hanging on to him for the wrong reasons. Not that he was particularly wealthy at the time – Cecile had got the family home in the divorce, so he was living in a poky rented cottage. But we were so happy there, Alex, and I knew it was right. So then he asked me to marry him, and I said yes. We managed to buy Cedar House at an auction and made plans to set about turning it into our home. Honestly, Alex, I've never felt so completely happy and content as I did then. That was, until our wedding day . . .' Helena lapsed into silence.

'What happened?' Alex muttered eventually.

'William had told me about Sacha – this great friend of his from school and Oxford days, who was living out in Singapore, but who would be coming over especially for our wedding with his wife. I was literally walking down the aisle in the registry office when I saw him staring at me in shock. Later, William introduced this man as his best friend, "Sacha" – which I now know is a shortened version of "Alexander". I'm not joking, I nearly fainted during the vows, my heart was racing so fast.'

'Did you speak to him afterwards?'

'No, or at least, not in private. William introduced us, of course, but I'm sure you can imagine how Sacha proceeded to get horribly drunk and had to be carted off to his hotel room by Jules. Not before she'd met you, then told me all about Rupert, their young son, born just four months before you. And of course, I then knew why "Alexander" had never come back to me in Vienna. God, Alex.' Helena put her head in her hands. 'It was dreadful . . . dreadful. I spent most of our lovely honeymoon in Thailand sleepless, trying to decide whether I should just tell William the truth outright, and have done with it. Then it would be up to him to choose whether he wanted to divorce me or not. But I was too scared of losing him. I loved him, Alex, I was so happy, *you* were so happy . . . I just couldn't bring myself to say the words and turn the fairy tale into a nightmare. I comforted myself with the thought that Sacha lived on the other side of the world, that even if they were best friends, our paths were unlikely to cross very often. And for the first few years, that was the way it was. I even managed to forget sometimes, to put it to the back of my mind.'

Helena paused for breath, distractedly running a hand through her hair. 'Of course, I know now in retrospect that I should have told William the moment I saw Sacha. Anything would have been better than living with this awful, awful secret. And waiting for it to be discovered. Then, as you know, Sacha, Jules and the children came back to live in England. We didn't see them very often, thank God. They came to stay for the weekend sometimes, and William saw Sacha by himself in London. Then Jules heard we were coming to Cyprus to stay in the house I'd inherited and, insisting she needed to get away, invited herself and her family. I could hardly say no, but I was absolutely petrified. Something told me disaster was looming. And, my God, I was right.'

Helena shook her head slowly in the darkness. 'And that's all, really, darling. There's nothing more to say. If I've destroyed you, Alex, I can only apologise and tell you that I love you more than anything in the world. I kept the secret to protect you, and William and our family.'

'And *yourself*, Mum,' Alex muttered harshly.

'Yes, you're right: and myself. I know I've only got

myself to blame. The worst thing is that William has been the most wonderful father to you, and now, through my stupidity and selfishness, I've managed to take away the one thing I always wanted you to have. God, how I wish he *was* your real father. I would give anything to turn the clock back. I'm just so sorry I got it all wrong. I know William can never forgive me. It's the most terrible betrayal. But I do love him, Alex. I always have and I always will.'

'Does Sacha, or *Alexander*, or whoever the hell he really is, know? About me being his . . . ?' Alex's voice trailed off.

'Yes. He guessed immediately the first time he saw you at the wedding. For the sake of everyone concerned, there has been an unspoken pact of silence between us.'

'Were you ever going to tell me?'

'I . . . didn't know. I couldn't tell you the truth, but I didn't want to lie to you either. He might have been responsible for your genes, Alex, but he's played no part in your life since.'

'Do you still love him?'

'No. If anything, the opposite. I . . .' Helena stopped herself from saying more – remembering that Alex had just learnt that Sacha was his biological father, and it wasn't right to launch into a negative diatribe about him. 'Part of me wishes I'd never met him, but then, darling, if I hadn't, I wouldn't have you.'

'Okay. Please go away now,' he said.

'Oh, darling.' Helena stifled a sob, then reached out a tentative hand towards him and touched wet fur. Her son's tears had soaked his beloved Bee. 'I'm so very, very sorry. I love you, Alex.'

Then she stood up and left the room.

ALEX'S DIARY

12th August (continued)

I
have
nothing
to
say

KS

Twenty-six

Helena sat on the terrace the next morning, watching the dawn break after a sleepless night. She tried to comfort herself that she'd felt this way before: the agony of loss, of life being changed irrevocably, the road she'd been previously travelling on suddenly blocked. There would be an alternative route – there always was. She'd cope, she'd *survive*, she always had.

But the difference was that this time, it wasn't about *her*.

She could cope with anything, except the thought of her children suffering. Worse still, it was *she* that had inflicted the pain. Her heart contracted yet again as she thought of Alex's devastation, his confusion. Her role as a mother was to bring comfort, to protect and guide him. Instead, she'd broken him.

And William too.

Helena walked down to the hammock, weak with the exhaustion of emotion, and climbed in. As she lay looking at the lightening sky, she clearly understood for the first time why some people saw no alternative to suicide. Perhaps, she thought, it wasn't just about outside events, but to do with the perception of oneself; believing you were a good person, that you'd treated those around you with respect and love, was everything. Now, the thought of living with herself every day for the rest of her life, with those she loved most knowing she *wasn't* and *hadn't*, felt almost untenable.

Helena knew she would find the strength to carry on, but just now, despite the beauty of the warm sun making an appearance on its celestial stage, she felt as cold and bleak as she had that day when she'd sat in the park in Vienna, knowing Alexander had gone for good.

Eventually, she trudged wearily upstairs to her bedroom. The wardrobe door was hanging open; William's side was empty, his travel holdall gone. She shut it miserably, then lay down on the bed and closed her eyes.

'Mummy, Mummy! Where's Daddy? I drewed him a picture of you and Fabio dancing. Look.'

Helena opened her eyes, the memory of what had happened last night hitting her afresh like a punch in the stomach. Tears leapt unannounced into her eyes.

'Mummy! Look at my picture,' Immy insisted, thrusting the drawing in front of her.

Helena sat up on her elbows. 'It's very good, darling. Well done.'

'Can I give it to Daddy? Is he downstairs?'

'No. He's had to go away for a bit. It's to do with his work.'

'On our holiday? Why didn't he say goodbye?'

'He got a telephone call after you'd gone to bed and had to leave urgently very early this morning.' Helena invented the story as she spoke, loathing herself for yet more lies.

'Oh. Will he be back soon?'

'I don't know.'

'Oh. Mummy?'

'Yes?'

'Why are you still wearing your last night dress?'

'I was tired, Immy, that's all.'

'You always make me put my nightie on when I say that.'

'Yes, I do, don't I? Sorry.'

'Are you feeling sick again, Mummy?'

'No, I'm fine.' Helena climbed off the bed. 'Where's Fred?'

'Asleep. Shall I make you breakfast?'

'No, darling, it's okay. I'll come down with you.'

Somehow Helena managed to get through the morning. She took Immy and Fred swimming in the pool, her heart breaking when she glanced at their happy, trusting faces. How would they feel when they understood that the family unit they had once been part of had evaporated overnight? That Daddy was gone, and doubtless would not be coming back? And that it was all her fault . . .

Fabio appeared in the kitchen at half past ten. Helena thought he looked almost as dreadful as she did.

He took her in his arms and held her tenderly. *'Bella, bella*, I am so very sorry. This is all my fault.'

'Don't show me sympathy Fabio, please. I'll cry. And this is not your fault. It's one hundred per cent mine.'

'Helena, your husband, he is a good man. And he loves you very much. He will think, and he will understand and come back. This coincidence that happen to you . . . it is just the cruel hand of fate.'

Helena shook her head. 'No, he won't come back. I've lied to him, deceived him for the whole of our marriage.'

'But Helena, you did not know!'

'Not at the beginning, no, but I should have told him the moment I *did*.'

'Perhaps, but it is easy when we look back to see these things, is it not? Where has he gone?'

'I should think he's flown home to England. I'm sure he wouldn't stay in Cyprus. Knowing William, he'll want to put as much distance between us as he can.'

'Then you must follow him and explain.'

'He doesn't want to hear. I tried last night.'

'It is the shock, *cara*. Give him time, please.'

'How can we have a future together now? He'll never trust me again, and I don't blame him. Trust is everything in a relationship, Fabio. You know that.'

'Yes, but if there is love, there is always a future.'

'Stop, Fabio,' Helena groaned. 'Don't give me hope where there is none. I can't think clearly at the moment. And . . . Jules is living here in Kathikas too at the moment! What is she going to say when she finds out? I'm sure William will tell her. I would if I was him. She thinks I'm her friend! Oh God, what a mess.' She sat down abruptly and buried her face in her hands.

'*Si*, it is,' Fabio agreed. 'But life is a messy thing. You must find a way to sort it out.'

'Should I go and see Jules, do you think? Tell her before William does? It's the least I owe her.'

'No, Helena. For now, she does not need to know. You say yesterday they are divorcing?'

'Yes.'

'So why cause her more pain? If William tells her, then so be it' – he shrugged – 'but let the dust settle a little.'

'It was my fault for wanting to see you so much. I was tempting fate. I should have left the past where it belonged.'

'Yes, but is it not a good thing that Fabio is back to pick up your pieces? And do not forget the pain that bad man causes you. What you went through when he left. It is *him* I blame for all this. I told you back then that I know the minute I see him he is trouble.'

'You did, and I only wish I had listened.'

'But then, Alex would not have been born, and Alexander would not have sent William to help mend his heart. And you would not have had your life with him and your beautiful children. No' – Fabio thumped the table – 'you must never regret anything in your life. The past – good and bad – makes you who you are.'

Helena reached for his hand and squeezed it. 'I'd forgotten how wise you are. Thank you, darling Fabio.'

'And Alex? How is he? Shocked, I think?'

'He's catatonic. I tried to explain it all to him last night, but every word I spoke must have been like an arrow through his heart. To finally discover his father's identity is bad enough, but then to have to acknowledge that his mother is a terrible person, who has lied to everyone . . . I love him so, so much, Fabio, and I've let him down and hurt him . . .' She broke down, and sobbed onto Fabio's shoulder.

'Helena, *cara*,' he soothed her, 'Alex is clever boy. I know this from when he is small and talking to me like an adult when he is only two years old! Perhaps at first, he *will* hate you for hurting him. But he must be allowed to, as anger is part of the healing process. And then his big, kind brain will start to think. He will see the facts and understand. He will know how much you love him, that you are good *mamma*, that you try always to do your best for him.'

'*No!* I'm an awful mother! Can you imagine hearing what he heard last night? I told him about my abortion too because I felt he should know why I was so determined to keep him. How can he ever respect me again?'

'Helena' – Fabio tipped her chin up to look at him – 'he now has to understand you are not just a mother, but a human being. Who is not perfect. This revelation comes to all children and it is hard to accept, especially so young. But he is advanced for his age, so he will cope. Give Alex time, *cara*, I promise he will come round.'

'There are so many ramifications for him to take in, like the fact that he's got a half-brother who happens to be his nemesis.' Helena shuddered at the thought.

'Should I try to talk to him?' Fabio suggested. 'Maybe someone else could help explain. After all, I have known Alex since he was a few hours old.'

'You can try, but I've knocked on his door this morning three times and each time he's told me to go away.'

'*Prego*, let me go up and see if I can speak with him.'

Fabio looked at his watch. 'But I must leave for Paphos to pick up my hire car by two.'

'Do you have to go?' Helena clung to him. 'Couldn't you stay a little longer?'

'Helena, you know the dancer's schedule. I would love to stay, but I cannot. Perhaps you come to Limassol next week to see the performance, and we take dinner together afterwards. Now, I must book the taxi to take me into Paphos.'

'No, I'll take you. I think it's better if I keep busy, and I want to get out of Pandora for a while. Beautiful as it is, this house seems to have brought me nothing but misery ever since we arrived.' Helena watched Fabio move towards the door. 'Please, tell Alex I love him and I'm so, so sorry . . .' Helena's voice cracked and she shrugged helplessly.

'Of course.' Fabio nodded, and left to walk along the corridor to Alex's room. He knocked gently. 'Alex? It is I, Fabio. Can we talk? I wish to speak about what has happened.'

'Leave me alone. I don't want to talk. To anyone,' came the muffled reply.

'I understand this. So, I will stand out here and speak and you can listen if you choose, *si*?'

Silence.

'Okay . . . I have only one thing to say to you, Alex, and it is this: I was there when your mother discovered she had you inside her. Even though I beg her not to have the baby, to realise there is no *papa*, to think of her career and how she is ruining her life, she insists. "No Fabio," she says, "I must have this baby." She cares about nothing else but bringing you into the world. And her world was you when you came. Just Alex, all the time.'

Fabio paused and cleared his throat.

'Now, is this a *mamma* who is bad? No, this is a *mamma* who loves her son so much, she gives up even her great passion for the ballet. She looks after you alone and never complains. Then, when a good man comes into her life, she sees it is the key to make both of you happy. She wants security for you, the best life she can give you, so she takes it. You understand, Alex?'

There was still no reply, so Fabio continued.

'And when fate makes this thing happen and she sees the bad Alexander, who is now "Sacha", at her wedding, she decides to keep a secret. Alex, she made a mistake by doing this, but she did it because she loves you so much. You must see that. I beg you to see it. Yes? She is bravest person I know, but Alex, she is hurting too! And she needs *you* now, like you needed her when you were small. You are big boy, with big brain. You can see what has happened. Help her, Alex, help her. '

Fabio took out his silk handkerchief and blew his nose hard. 'There. That is all I have to say. God willing, this will be resolved and I will see you soon. Goodbye, my friend, goodbye.'

Having bribed the little ones with the promise of a McDonald's on the way back, Helena took them along with Fabio to Paphos to pick up his hire car. It was a relief to be out of the house. Alex was still refusing to come out of his room, but Angelina was at Pandora cleaning for another hour or so, so at least she knew he was physically safe.

433

'Will you try to come to Limassol next week, Helena?' Fabio asked as he gave her one last hug.

'I'll do my best, but under the circumstances, I can't promise anything just now.'

'No, but many things can change in a week,' he said with a sympathetic smile. 'And out of all this, at least we have found our friendship again. Remember I am always there for you, *cara*. Speak to me on the telephone, Helena, as much as you need to. And let me know what happens.'

'Thank you for everything, Fabio. I'd forgotten how much I miss you.'

'*Ciao, cara, ciao*, little ones.'

They waved him off, and even though Immy and Fred were standing on either side of her, Helena remembered then how it felt to be alone.

ALEX'S DIARY

13th August 2006

I have woken up this morning, and I know I have to go. Somewhere, anywhere, away from the pain . . . and *her*.

I lay on my bed last night after Helena – I cannot call her my 'mother' just now – left me, my mind full of images of driving Chevrolets along treeless American highways. Arriving eventually at a one-horse town, only stopping to eat my burger at a diner and checking in to a motel before moving on the next day.

Then I remembered I'm too young to drive. And more importantly, not mature enough to grow a beard, which is an essential feature in all the road-trip movies I've ever watched.

So, where could I run to . . . ?

Spending nights out under the stars in the depths of the Cyprus countryside, or *any* countryside for that matter, does not appeal, due to my phobia of mosquitoes and other creepy crawlies. I loathe camping with a passion, so that idea was definitely off the agenda.

The fact I only have twelve pounds and thirty-two pence left in my bank account, having spent the rest on a blitz in a souvenir shop in Latchi, narrows the options too. I could try selling my treasures, but I doubt I'll get much for my laser pointer, mug and wooden cigar box with *Love from Cyprus* carved into the top of it.

I dozed off for a while again, then woke with an awful sinking feeling in the pit of my stomach as I remembered. I *hate* her at this moment, this woman I've adored since birth. She has fallen off her pedestal and is lying in broken bits on the ground. I imagined stamping on the effigy of her head, and breaking it some more. It made me feel a little better but it did not solve the problem of her betrayal. Which is terrible.

I understand now about the way in which trauma and lack of sleep can calcify the brain; I am not sure I have one left. I am now also starving and very thirsty, but due to the fact I cannot . . . *cannot* open the door to my bedroom and risk bumping into either one of my half-brother(s) or sister, or indeed Helena herself, I am still holed up in my Broom Cupboard. She keeps knocking on my door, and I keep refraining from answering.

I want to punish her.

Then suddenly, it's Fabio knocking on my door.

He talks to me about her, and . . . oh crud, the anger begins to subside. He'll never know, but he had me in *floods* on the other side of the door. And when he leaves, I begin to think more rationally about what she told me last night.

My sense of perspective, which had run away and was lying on a beach in the Bahamas getting a tan, decided to cut short its holiday and return to me.

And the more I thought, the more I realised Fabio was right: that actually, this wasn't her fault. I even managed a wry smile as I remembered the story she'd related about the night when she went to the ball and it struck me that it was like some weird post-modern remake of *Cinderella*. Immy certainly would not have been impressed if the Disney version she loves so much had turned out the same way, with Cinders up the duff and all alone . . .

Admittedly, I am not too keen on the thought of the woman who gave me life playing the up-and-down game with any man, least of all He Who Fathered Me, but she could have killed me. And she didn't.

Because she loves me.

By now I am also desperate to pee, so when I eventually hear the house fall silent and car tyres scraping over the gravel, I creep out and hot-foot it upstairs to the bathroom and after relieving myself, I turn on the tap and fill up all the tooth mugs there are, plus the plastic watering can Fred uses to torture Immy with in the bath. And I'm halfway back to my room with my watery supplies when I hear the patter of tiny feet along the corridor.

'Hello, Alex.'

Damn! I halt abruptly, and half the water splashes into puddles on the tiles.

'You *are* here. Angelina said you were.'

It's Viola. Just what I need. She only ever comes to tell me her problems. And today, to put it mildly, I have some of my own. 'Yes, I am,' I reply.

'Are you all right, Alex?' she asks as she follows me to the door of my room and looks at me, the puddles and the now near-empty containers. 'Are you feeding some plants?'

'No,' I say, as I see her studying Fred's watering can. 'Viola, I'm sorry, but I can't talk right now.'

'That's okay. I just came to tell you that Mummy and me

and Rupes are leaving for England at the end of the week. She wants us to settle in to our new house before the start of term. Oh, and Rupes told me to tell you that he managed to pass his exam, and to say thank you for helping him. He's very happy.'

'Good. How nice. I'm thrilled for him.'

Thrilled for Rupes. My new-found half-brother. I suddenly have an urge to giggle hysterically at the absurdity of it. And of life in general.

'Well then,' I add, as I start to retreat inside. 'Thanks for coming over, Viola.'

'Daddy is here in Cyprus, Alex,' she continues, not to be deterred. 'He brought Rupes back last night and tried to persuade Mum to give it another go.'

'What did she say?'

'No. And then she said he was a drunken bastard and made him leave the house.' Viola bit her lip. 'I'm worried about him. You haven't seen him, have you? I thought he might have come here to Pandora.'

Christ! This episode of my life is now becoming seriously farcical. 'No, Viola. Sorry.'

'Oh.'

I watch as tears spring to her eyes, and then feel bad for being abrupt with her. 'You really love your dad, don't you?' I was desperate to add, *even though he's an out-and-out tosser who has ruined your and your brother's and your mother's and my mother's lives. And actually, Dad's – as in William, and Immy's and Fred's. And for that matter, mine.*

'Of course I do. He didn't mean for his business to go wrong, did he? I'm sure he did his best.'

Oh Viola, if only you knew . . .

But I can't help being touched by her devotion. Especially given she's not even related to him by blood. Which some of us, sadly, are.

'I'm sure he did, yes.' I manage through gritted teeth. None of this is Viola's fault, after all.

'Well, I'll go,' she says. 'I brought *Nicholas Nickleby* back for you. I thought it was the best book I've ever, ever read.'

'Did you? Well, that's good then.'

'Yes, and I'm going to read a Jane Austen next, like you said I should.'

'Fine choice.' I nod.

'Oh, and here's something for you from me, in case I don't see you again. Just to say thank you for being so kind over the summer.'

She hands me an envelope, then reaches up shyly and gives me a kiss on the cheek. 'Bye-bye, Alex.'

'Bye, Viola.'

I watch her disappear along the corridor with her dainty little feet barely touching the floor. She glides, rather like my moth— I mean, Helena does.

Perhaps it's simply stress and exhaustion that prompts more tears to come to my eyes as I look down at the envelope, which has been painstakingly covered in felt-tipped flowers and hearts. I feel moved by Viola's sweetness and, as I negotiate the water vessels back to my room, I only wish it was her I was genetically related to, rather than Rupes.

I sit on the bed, and having taken a few enormous gulps of water, I open the envelope.

Dear Alex, I have written you a poem because I know you like them. It's not very good, I suppose, but it's called

'Friends'. And I hope you are my friend forever. Love and thank you for everything, Viola.

I unfold the poem and read it and to be honest, it isn't great in terms of iambic pentameter or the rhyming couplets, but it is heartfelt and brings tears to my eyes yet again. Talk about waterworks in the past few hours. No wonder I'm thirsty.

I look down at Bee, the bunny rabbit that my new-found Uncle Fabio gave me all those years ago. And at least I now know where my horrific middle name comes from – it's been tough, thinking that I was named after a red-nosed reindeer for the past thirteen years. And then I think about Viola, and her enduring love for the drunken idiot who sired me.

And for the first time since last night, I realise it could have been worse. Taking aside the awful coincidence of the genetic 'Dad' and . . . er, 'Dad' being best buddies, at least my gene pool is of apparently noble lineage, and Sacha has two brain cells to rub together. When they're not alco-hol-soaked, at least. (That is something I realise I must now guard against, as I read only last week that addiction is genetic.)

The other good news is that my biological father is tall. With a decent head of hair and a waistline that is definitely defined. And nice eyes . . .

Oh my God! I stand up and stare at myself in the mirror. And there they are, the clues that have lain there for all of these years; the giveaways, sitting bold as brass in two sockets on either side of my nose. It's just that no one chose to see what was right *under* their nose. Including me.

So I am not the progeny of a grape-stamper or a camp-as-a-row-of-tents ballet dancer. Or an airline pilot, or someone

Chinese . . . I am the son of a well-bred Englishman who has been known to me since I was small.

The best friend of my stepdad.

Dad . . . poor Dad. My heart suddenly goes out to him, too. The thought of his wife being you-know-whatted by anyone, let alone his best friend, must be almost impossible to deal with. It was bad enough when Chloë snogged Airport Guy and Michel.

The question is, can Dad ever forgive Helena?

Can I . . . ?

It strikes me then that me and Dad are both currently sitting in the same leaking boat. I wonder if he's cried the way I have? Somehow I can't imagine it. But if anyone is feeling as bad as I am just now, it's him.

And then I realise — we have finally found a bond. It isn't football, or cricket, or the teapots he likes to collect by the shedload; it's Helena, and the pain she has caused both of us.

My, er, progenitor; his wife.

I attempt to empty Fred's watering can into my mouth as I think, and end up giving myself a refreshing facial shower instead. And I remember hearing her muffled sobs emanating from the terrace after I asked her to go away last night.

I think again about what she told me.

And then ponder how she gave up her glittering career as a famous bendy person in layers of netting, just so she could keep me . . .

And then I cry again. For her.

A few minutes later, I have made a decision. And I begin to put it into action.

κζ

Twenty-seven

Having dropped Fabio off, Helena called Angelina to check on Alex and ascertained that apparently Viola had visited him, and he had come out of his room to talk to her.

A trip to the beach with Immy and Fred filled the rest of the afternoon. At six o'clock, the three of them arrived back at Pandora and Helena went straight to knock on Alex's door.

'It's me, Alex. Would you let me in, please?'

There was no answer.

'Okay, darling, I understand, but you must be hungry. I'll leave you something to eat on a tray outside the door. I'm going to bath the little ones, read them a story and put them to bed. I'll come back after that.'

At eight o'clock, as she sat on the terrace alone, listening to the silence of a house that up until last night had been filled with the sound of happy humanity, she went back inside. The tray she'd left was untouched. She knocked on Alex's door again.

'Alex, darling, please come out. The little ones are in bed and no one else is here. Could we talk? Please?' she begged him.

Nothing.

Helena sat down outside his room, now desperate for some kind of reaction.

'Please, Alex, just say something to let me know you're all right. I understand you hate me and don't want to see me, but I can't bear this, I really can't.'

No response.

'Okay, darling, I'm coming in anyway.' Helena stood up and tried the handle. It turned, but the door wouldn't open.

'Alex, darling, I'll break down the door if I have to. *Please!* Speak to me!' Helena was frantic now, dreadful thoughts starting to run through her mind. Tears of frustration and terror began to course down her cheeks. 'Alex! If you can hear me, for God's sake, open the door!'

With her cries eliciting only further silence, she ran onto the terrace, found her mobile on the table and with shaking hands, dialled Alexis' number.

He answered immediately. 'Helena?'

'Alexis!'

'Helena, what is it?'

'I . . . Oh Alexis, come over here now, please! I need you.'

He arrived ten minutes later. Helena was standing at the back of the house waiting for him.

'What has happened?'

'It's Alex! He won't open his bedroom door. I think . . . Oh God . . .' she choked, 'I think he may have done something . . . Please, come with me now!' Helena grabbed his arm and almost dragged him into the house.

'Where is William?' he asked her, clearly confused.

'Gone, he's gone, but I have to get into Alex's bedroom, right now!' she sobbed as she pulled him along the corridor towards the room.

'Helena, calm down! Of course we will get in.' He tried the handle and, like Helena, found the door didn't budge. He put his full weight against it, but it still wouldn't open. He tried again, but still nothing.

'Alex? Can you hear me? Please answer! *Please!*' Helena banged her fists on the door.

Alexis pulled her out of the way and, using all his strength, ran at it, but it did not give way.

'Okay, I will go outside and try the window.'

'Yes, yes!' Helena said in relief. 'The shutter is open. I saw it earlier.'

'Good. I need something to stand on. The window is set too high for me to see in.' He ran to the terrace and dragged over a chair. 'Can you tell me what has happened, Helena?' he asked as he propped it just below the window and climbed onto it.

'I will tell you in a moment, but please, see if my son is still alive!'

'Okay, okay,' he agreed, 'I am looking inside . . . wait one moment.'

Helena stood below him in an agony of suspense. 'Is he in there, Alexis? Is he . . . Oh God! Oh God,' she murmured to herself.

Then Alexis turned and climbed down from the chair with a sigh. 'Helena, the room is empty.'

κη

Twenty-eight

'His rucksack's gone, and Bee, his rabbit!' Helena said as she swept everything off the bed. Alex had obviously locked the door behind him when he'd left, and she had only just managed to climb through the small window after Alexis had broken a pane of glass to reach the inside catch and open it.

'But why has Alex run away?'

'It's a long story. We need to search the grounds,' she said, running out of the room.

'I don't think Alex would have taken a rucksack to make a stroll round the garden, Helena.'

'I'll check anyway, just in case he's hiding somewhere.'

Helena ran frantically round the grounds and the out-houses, looking in every possible place where Alex might be hidden. Alexis had taken a torch into the dusk to look in the vines beyond the house, and eventually they met back on the terrace.

'Nothing. He has gone, Helena. I am sure of it.'

'I'll try his mobile again.' Helena picked up her own from the table and dialled Alex's number. Again, his voice-mail answered.

'Darling, this is Mum. Please, please, call me just to let me know you're all right. Bye.' Helena paced up and down, trying to calm her mind so she could think.

'If you tell me *why* he has gone,' Alexis persisted, 'then maybe I could help you think too.'

Helena stopped pacing and turned to Alexis. 'He found out who his father was last night. So did William. That's why neither of them are here. They have both . . . left me.'

'I see. Come, Helena, you are exhausted. Please sit down.' He took her by the hand and led her to a chair. 'I will get you a drink.'

'No, I don't want one. But I do want a cigarette.' She reached for the packet lying on the table from the night before, and lit one up.

'So, this man, this . . . father of Alex? He is not . . .' Alexis searched for the appropriate word. 'Not liked by your son or your husband?'

'No. He isn't. You see, Alexis,' she sighed, past caring about what he thought of her, 'it's Sacha, Jules' husband, who I once knew as "Alexander".'

'My name, and Alex's too.' Alexis looked at her, his eyes registering shock. 'No, this would not have been good news. Well, I am sure there is an explanation, but perhaps this is not the time to discuss it.'

'No.' Helena inhaled her cigarette. 'You don't think Alex would do . . . something stupid, do you?'

'No, I don't, Helena. Alex is a sensible boy. Maybe he needs some time alone to think. I would, if I was him.'

'Yes, but he's also a child in a strange country. Where on earth would he go?'

'I cannot say, but wherever he is, Helena, he has planned it.'

'Let me think, let me think . . .' Helena put her fingers to her head. She looked up at Alexis. 'He wouldn't go to Jules, would he? To tell her?'

'I was there earlier and Alex was not, but' – Alexis shrugged – 'I doubt it. They are not close, and he dislikes Rupes. I could call her if you wish.'

'No, you're right. He wouldn't go there, and I can't think of anyone else he knows here, other than you and Angelina. What if he's in trouble? What if he only meant to go for a walk, and . . . ?'

'Helena, please, try to keep calm. Alex took his rucksack. He was prepared to go. The question is, where?'

'I . . . just . . . don't know,' she sighed, stubbing out her cigarette. 'Knowing Alex, he'd look for a place where he felt safe, somewhere familiar.'

'How about his home in England?' Alexis suggested.

'But how would he get there?' She stood up suddenly. 'Oh my God, his passport! Let me check!' She bolted upstairs to her bedroom and pulled open the drawer containing the children's passports and return flight tickets. Alex's passport had gone.

She ran downstairs. 'He's taken it. He could be anywhere, anywhere . . .' She crumpled into the chair and let out a sob.

'Does he have money?'

'He has a bank account with a card he can use to draw

out money, but I've no idea how much he has in it. Not much, knowing Alex. Money burns a hole in his pocket.'

'What about William? Where is he?'

'I don't know,' she cried.

'Then we will find out. You must call him, Helena. He should know Alex is missing.'

'He won't answer his phone if he sees it's me.'

'Then *I* will call.' Alexis took out his mobile. 'Tell me the number.'

He dialled the number she recited, and waited. An electronic voice told him William's mobile was switched off, and to try later. 'What about your house in England? William might be there?'

'If he's gone back to the UK he'll either be there, or at the little apartment we keep in London. Try both,' Helena urged.

Yet again, an answering machine clicked in on both numbers. Alexis left another two messages asking William to call.

'Would you like me to go to the village? Ask if anyone has seen him?'

'Yes, please, Alexis.'

'And you must stay here in case Alex returns. Do you know what time he left?'

'Some time past one o'clock, after Angelina had gone home. I should never have driven Fabio to Paphos, or gone to the beach, but I didn't think he'd run away, I . . .'

'Helena, you must stay calm, for Alex as well as yourself.' He took her hands in his and held them tight. 'We will find him, I promise.'

*

Alexis returned from the village an hour or so later, and Helena searched his face anxiously for news.

'No one has seen him. We will look again tomorrow. For now, there is little we can do.'

'Then surely we must call the police?'

'Helena, it is after midnight. They can do nothing now. Tomorrow we will call.' Alexis looked down at her, and reached out to stroke her cheek. 'My Helena, perhaps the best thing you can do is sleep. You will need all your strength for tomorrow.'

'I couldn't sleep, Alexis. I just couldn't!'

'For me you will try. Come, we will see.' He took her hand, led her into the shadowy drawing room and insisted she lie down on the sofa.

'Will you stay for a while?' she asked. 'Just in case . . .'

'Of course. I am here, as always,' he answered softly.

'Thank you,' she said weakly, as her eyes closed.

Alexis sat quietly as Helena slept. He remembered that evening – maybe fifteen years ago – when he'd seen her dance *The Firebird* with La Scala at the open-air theatre in Limassol. Watching her onstage, he could hardly believe that this extraordinary creature, holding two thousand people enthralled, was once the young girl he'd loved so much.

Of course, Helena had never known he was there. But he'd never forgotten that night. And now, alone with her, as he gazed down at her, he knew that whatever she might have done since, his heart would never stop loving her.

Helena woke with a start to find it was morning. She sat up, reaching straight for her mobile. There was a text message.

449

Heart in her mouth, she opened it.

'*Under the circumstances, want to begin divorce pro-ceedings as soon as possible. Pls advise me of your solicitor. W*'

Helena fell back onto the sofa in despair.

Alexis called the local police as Angelina, her face a picture of anxiety, took the little ones up to her house in the village. Helena was pacing up and down on the terrace, dialling Alex's mobile every few minutes like a mental and physical mantra.

William had not returned Alexis' call either. Helena had tried both their homes in England, but all she got was the answering machine. Then she called Jules and Sadie.

There was simply no sign of him.

Helena watched as Alexis greeted the policeman at his car, and brought him round onto the terrace. 'Helena, this is a good friend of mine, Sergeant Korda. He will do every-thing he can to help find Alex for you.'

'Hello.' Helena stood up, trying to pull herself together, knowing she was in danger of screaming out loud and not being able to stop. 'Please sit down.'

'Thank you,' he nodded. 'I can speak some English, but if Alexis knows details, he can tell me in Greek. It will be faster.'

'Yes. Would you like anything to drink?'

'Water, thank you.'

Helena retrieved a jug and glasses from the kitchen. Taking them outside, she listened as Alexis explained the situation in Greek, but retreated back into the kitchen and spent some time clearing up – anything to take her mind off her anguish.

Eventually, she went outside again. Sergeant Korda was standing, ready to leave. He smiled at Helena.

'Okay, I have the details. We will need a photograph of your son. Do you have one?'

'Yes, in my wallet. I'll get it.' Helena ran to her bedroom to retrieve her handbag. She found her wallet inside and flew back downstairs.

'It's in here somewhere.' She opened it and fumbled through the different compartments. 'There.' She handed the snapshot to Sergeant Korda, tears coming to her eyes at the sight of Alex's beloved apple cheeks and open smile. 'That was taken a year ago. He hasn't changed much since.'

'Thank you. I will give it to our officers.'

'Wait a minute . . .' Helena took another look through her wallet. 'My debit card seems to have disappeared.'

'Debit?' Korda looked at Alexis questioningly.

Alexis translated the meaning. 'Are you sure it's definitely not in there?'

'Yes. Do you think Alex could have taken it?' Helena looked at him. 'He knows my PIN number, because I sometimes ask him to get money out for me if we're in town.'

'This is very good news,' Korda said with a nod. 'If your son has used your card, we can trace the location. Write down the bank details here, please?'

Helena scribbled them onto the sergeant's pad.

'Also, your addresses in England. I will speak to the British police too. We will check all flights from Paphos airport from four o'clock onwards. And as you cannot contact your husband, we will suggest the police go to both your homes to check if Alex is there.'

'Thank you for everything, Sergeant Korda,' Helena

said when she'd written down the details he'd requested and they walked back with him to his patrol car. 'I'm sorry for all this trouble. This isn't my son's fault, it's completely mine.'

As the car pulled away, Alexis put a comforting arm around Helena's shoulder. 'Now, I must go up to my office to check my emails and also take a shower and change. I will be back very fast. Will you be okay here alone for an hour?'

'Yes, of course I will. Thank you for everything, Alexis.'

'You know I am always here for you, Helena. I will see you as soon as I can.'

She watched him stride off towards his car, then walked back to the terrace and sat down. She tried Alex, William, Cedar House and the London apartment yet again. And still there was no answer.

She noticed one of Alex's T-shirts hanging on the line. She got up and pulled it off, breathing in the still-present smell of her son. And closed her eyes and prayed.

A few minutes later, a car pulled up and Jules appeared on the terrace.

'I just swung by to see if there was any news about Alex.'

'No. None.'

'Oh Helena, how awful for you. I'm so sorry. Are you here alone?'

'Yes.'

'Where's William?'

'I don't know.' Helena was far too exhausted to lie.

'What do you mean?'

'He left,' she replied simply. 'I have no idea where he's gone.'

'And Alex has gone missing as well?' Jules eyed her. 'There's something you're not telling me here, Helena. Come on, spit it out.'

'Not now, Jules, please. It's a long story.' Helena couldn't bear to look her in the eye.

'Then I'll have to piece it together myself. You've obviously told them something they didn't know, or they've discovered it by accident. Which is it?'

'Can we leave it there, Jules? I can't cope, I really can't,' Helena begged her.

'No. We can't. Because I've got a feeling I know what it is.'

'No, I don't think you do.'

'Well,' Jules said, slowly, 'if I said it's almost certainly my errant, soon-to-be-ex-husband at the root of all this, I think I'd be right, wouldn't I? Mmm?'

Helena lifted her head and stared at Jules in amazement.

'It's okay, Helena. I've always known about you and Sacha. Oh, and subsequently Alex,' she added.

Helena was too stunned to speak. Eventually, she managed a strangled 'How?'

'Well, it was pretty obvious when he came back from Vienna that something had gone on while he was there. Knowing Sacha as I did, it was almost definitely a woman. For starters, he hadn't been in touch with me more than a couple of times after he left England. To be fair, our relationship had reached crisis point. We'd been married five years by then, and I already knew there'd been at least a

453

couple of affairs. He was miserable, what with his paintings not getting sold, and I was working all the hours God sent at the estate agency. So I decided we both needed some space, and suggested I bankroll him while he took a year out and did a master's degree. At least the qualification might have made him employable at a gallery, or perhaps eventually as a teacher. And besides, you know the old saying, Helena – if you love someone, set them free. So I did.'

'Jules, that was a big sacrifice for you to make.'

'Yes, but I also knew what Sacha was like. He's completely incapable of fending for himself. I had hoped he might realise how much he needed me in Vienna, and come back with his tail between his legs. I'd told him before he left that I wasn't prepared to put up with his womanising any longer. Of course, I wasn't counting on him meeting you. Or on finding myself pregnant with Rupes soon after he left,' Jules continued. 'I can honestly say I hummed and hawed for a few weeks on whether to terminate it, and not even tell Sacha. If I had, he'd have been none the wiser. But as you know so well, Helena, the longer I left it, the more that little thing inside me became real. So, finally, I wrote to Sacha in Vienna and told him he had to fly home, that there was a baby on the way. By the time he did, I knew there was no turning back. I was keeping it.'

'Oh my God . . .' Helena whispered, half to herself.

'For the first few weeks, it was almost as if he couldn't bear the sight of me. He wandered round in a daze, spending most of the time locked in his studio, painting. I really thought he was about to leave me.' She looked at Helena. 'I'm thirsty. Can I get some water?'

'Yes, of course,' Helena whispered. Jules stood up and went inside, while she sat perfectly still, shock rendering her brain too numb to think.

'I've changed my mind. We're both having a glass of wine. It's after midday so we don't need to feel guilty. Here. I'm sure you need one too.' Jules put a glass in front of Helena, took a sip from her own and sat down.

'Thank you.'

'Anyway, one day I went into his studio to ask him something. He wasn't there. He'd taken himself off for one of his long walks – he'd often disappear for hours at a time. And there on his desk were the most fabulous pencil sketches of a dancer. And they were all entitled "Helena".'

Even though she felt sick, Helena took a large gulp of her wine.

'I'm afraid I ripped them all to shreds. Shame, really, as his sketches of you dancing were the best thing he ever produced by a mile. He was never that talented, you know, but love had clearly elevated him. That night I was ready for a showdown. I knew he would have found the sketches in pieces on his studio floor. To my surprise, when he came in, he took me in his arms. He apologised for being so distant, explained he'd something he needed to work through. It was never specified, but we both knew what – and *who* – he was talking about.'

Both women sat in silence for a while, each lost in her own memories of the same man.

'Anyway,' Jules continued, 'over the next few days, we starting talking about the future. Sacha knew he had to take a full-time job, as I'd have to give up work when the baby was born, at least for a while. And his painting wasn't going to feed a family of mice, let alone humans. So he called a few old friends from Oxford and went for some interviews in the City. He was eventually offered a position at a stockbroking company his father had employed for years. Rupes was born, and Sacha settled down at work and was actually doing rather well. As you can imagine, all his natural charm and good looks worked wonders on rich old ladies with money to invest.'

Jules rolled her eyes in distaste and took a slug of wine.

'Then, three years later, just after we'd adopted Viola, Sacha was offered the chance to move to Singapore. I desperately wanted him to take it so that we could really make a fresh start. I loved it there, and so did he. Everything was fine – until we came back a few months later, for your wedding. I recognised you from the sketches immediately, and the look on Sacha's face when he saw you trotting down the aisle was priceless!' Jules gave a grim chuckle. 'Even if I hadn't known, that alone would have been enough to convince me there'd been something between you two.'

'God, Jules, I am so, so sorry,' Helena managed. 'I've never realised you knew.'

'No, well, why should you?' she said abruptly. 'From what I managed to glean at the wedding, I knew I was right. One of the guests told me you were an ex-ballet dancer and then William said during his speech he'd met you in Vienna, because Sacha had suggested he go there to find love . . .' Jules gave a small shudder. 'Then I noticed Alex at the reception afterwards, trailing behind you, like a little lost cherub . . . and I knew instantly. Even though Alex doesn't look much like Sacha, he has his father's eyes.'

'Yes. He does.' Helena looked up at this astonishing

woman, sitting at her table and calmly explaining she knew everything; that she'd always known. 'I really don't know what to say, Jules, other than that I'm so terribly sorry for any pain I've caused you. It's no excuse, but Sacha never did tell me he was married. He said his name was Alexander. In fact, he told me almost nothing at all about the details of his life in England.'

'That hardly surprises me,' Jules sniffed. 'I'm sure he was happy to completely reinvent himself at the time, and conveniently forget that he was married.'

'Did Sacha know it was me who was marrying William, do you think?'

'When we got the invitation, I do remember both of us looking at your name next to William's: *Helena*. But I'm sure he thought, just as I did, it was far too much of a coincidence to be *you*.'

'It was, it *is*. And if he *had* known . . . I've always wondered why he never tried to contact me and warn me.'

'Well, if I'd wanted him – and you – to suffer, watching you both on your wedding day was payment enough. And then, when Sacha set eyes on Alex for the first time that day . . . well.' Jules shook her head and sighed. 'I'm sure it's been hell, especially for you, Helena. After all, I've always known, but William hasn't.'

'And you didn't tell Sacha you thought Alex was his?' Helena was astounded.

'The fact that Alex was almost certainly my husband's offspring was a shock, yes, but what would have been the point of jumping up and down and divorcing him? It was blatantly obvious – given we first met you minutes after you'd just married Sacha's closest friend – that I didn't need to worry about you running off into the sunset together. I saw then how much you and William loved each other.'

'We did, yes, or at least . . .' Helena checked herself. 'I still do love him. I honestly don't know how you've coped with all this, Jules. I know I couldn't have.'

'Of course I'd have preferred you not to have had a raging affair with my husband when I was sitting, lonely, miserable and pregnant by myself in England, but you have to remember that I *did* know. Knowledge is power, and it was my decision to stay with him. Being a single mother didn't appeal, for starters. I left that one to you,' she retorted. 'I wanted a father in situ for my son. And as I've said to you before, I loved him then. He was a flawed, needy man, but you can't choose who you love, can you? And you, more than anyone, should be able to understand. I presume you loved Sacha, too?'

'Once, yes, I did.'

'I always felt rather sorry for you, Helena, watching you having to live a lie. So, tell me – how *did* William find out?'

'I had Fabio, my old dancing partner, staying here. Sacha was with me in a photograph Fabio showed him from Vienna.'

'Whoops. Is he mad? I bet he is.'

'He's divorcing me. I got a text this morning.'

'An understandable gut reaction,' nodded Jules coolly. 'And what about Alex? Horrified at the thought of Sacha being his dad?'

'Yes. That's why he's run away. The police have just been here. The search has moved to England now.'

'Alex'll turn up. And get over the shock, and forgive

you. He adores you. So, what now? With William and me out of the picture, I suppose the two erstwhile lovers can resume their *grande passion*.'

'No, Jules, I—'

'Helena, you're welcome to him, really. I got with the programme, as Rupes would say, a long time ago. This divorce is the best thing I've ever done. In retrospect, I had no idea how miserable that self-absorbed sod made me. If you want him, I'm sure he's yours for the taking. He's always believed you're the love of his life. I see it every time he looks at you. Although I wonder, in reality, whether Sacha knows how to love anyone but himself.'

'I swear to you, Jules, that the last person on earth I would want to be with is Sacha. He lied to me, then vanished into thin air, leaving me high and dry in Vienna. To be blunt, I find it difficult to even be in the same room with him. I just love William, and I want him to come back so very much . . . Sorry,' Helena wiped the tears away harshly. 'I have absolutely no right to cry. You must hate me.'

'I hated the woman in the sketches that day, yes, but how could I hate you, Helena? You're a genuinely nice person who just happens to have an innate ability to make men fall in love with her. But it's hardly brought you happiness, has it? In fact, it seems to me that it's brought nothing but chaos and misery.'

'I . . .' Helena's mobile rang, and she snatched it up instantly. 'Hello? William, have you heard? Alex has gone missing and . . . really? . . . Oh, thank God, thank *God*! Yes, I will. Can I speak to him? Okay, I understand. Just send him my love, then. Bye.' She dropped her mobile onto the table and put her head in her hands. 'Thank God, thank God,' she repeated as tears of relief choked her speech.

'Alex has been found?' asked Jules.

'Yes, he's with William in England. Oh Jules, thank God!'

Jules stood up and moved towards Helena. She put her arms around her shoulders. 'There, there,' she soothed. 'Told you he'd be all right, didn't I? He's a survivor, just like his dad. Talking of Sacha – I kicked him out of the house last night. He arrived uninvited from England with Rupes – drunk as a skunk, as usual, and begging me to take him back. It really was quite satisfying to tell him to bugger off. He probably slept under a grapevine last night. God, he smelt awful, Helena.' Jules wrinkled her nose. 'He needs serious help, but luckily, I'm no longer the one to persuade him to get it.'

'No.' Helena only half listened, inwardly hugging herself with the relief of knowing Alex was safe and well in England with William.

'So, we're leaving in a couple of days. I've found a sweet little cottage to rent near Rupes' new school. Not quite what we've been used to, granted, but I've already contacted the local estate agents and I've got a couple of job interviews lined up. Do me good to get back to work, and there's a nice local primary school for Viola too.'

'I thought you loved it here?'

'I do, but let's face it, Helena, I'd simply be running away. And I've got the children to think about.'

'Yes, you do,' Helena agreed. 'I . . . will you tell them that Alex is actually Sacha's son?'

'No. I think they've got enough on their plates just now. And besides, it's Sacha's job to give them the bad news, not mine, though I'm sure he won't. He's too much of a coward. So . . .' Jules sighed. 'It's time to say goodbye. Thanks for your support over the summer, Helena. And maybe now the air is cleared, we can think about being proper friends. Don't be a stranger in England, will you?'

'No, of course not. Though God knows where I'll be living.'

'Oh, I wouldn't worry about that,' Jules said airily as she stood up. 'Unlike Sacha, William loves you far too much to let you go. See you soon – *ciao*.'

ALEX'S DIARY

14th August 2006

Well.

It's been an adventure, that's for sure. In the past twenty-four hours I have transmogrified from an unknown, chubby thirteen-year-old boy with no distinguishing features, into a thieving, renegade runaway. Who is on the missing list across Europe.

I wonder if Interpol were contacted. I do hope so, as it would look rather good in my future biography.

Once I'd decided I'd found a way to kill two birds with one stone, I moved fast. I knew where Mum kept my passport, and also her English debit card and a wad of Cypriot pounds. I called the taxi company she uses and got a very nice man who spoke some English to take me to Paphos airport. On the way there, I made a big show of saying there was an emergency in England – God bless her, I used my already-dead granny's ailing health – and by the time we got to the airport, even I had begun to believe she only had hours left to live. And so had he.

When we arrived, I handed him a big tip and asked him if

he could help me buy a ticket on the next flight to England at the Cyprus Airways desk, as I spoke no Greek. And told him that my dad, who was meeting me there, had just texted me to say he was delayed and I was to go ahead and buy the ticket. I'd already checked out that children over twelve can fly alone on some airlines, but others insisted on them being accompanied by an adult.

Then fate took a hand. I'd befriended a sweet old lady standing in front of me at the queue for check in. I'd loaded her suitcase onto the weighing machine then helped her as she fumbled with bird-like, shaking hands in the plastic wallet for her passport and ticket. And I handed them with my own passport and ticket to the check-in lady. Subsequently, we were allocated seats together and during the long wait in departures, the two of us became firm friends. Using the same technique I'd employed at check-in, as we boarded, I handed over both our passports, making it obvious to the lady checking them that I was caring for my companion. Whom she hopefully believed was an elderly relative of mine. Grannies – dead, dying or alive – seemed to have come in very handy in my plan to escape back to England.

Thankfully, once we got onto the plane, my 'borrowed granny' fell asleep next to me immediately. Which gave me the time I needed to think as I made the journey back home. Thoughts that had never entered my head before.

In my fervent lifelong quest to discover my real gene pool, I hadn't seen what was right under my nose.

So, I am back in England.

I am here for me. And her.

I am about to embark on the most important conversation of my life so far.

I must save the day.
Because I love my mother.
And
My father.

κθ

Twenty-nine

William switched on the kettle to make some tea, and stared out of the kitchen window across the garden. Immy's and Fred's swings and climbing frame stood in a corner, and Fred's beloved water shooter – almost as big as he was – lay where he'd last dropped it on the grass.

Cedar House, on the outskirts of the beautiful village of Beaulieu in Hampshire, had been bought as a dilapidated wreck just before they'd married. Slowly, he and Helena had brought it back to life. Since it was just after his divorce, and before his architecture practice really took off, they'd had to scrimp and save to transform what had been a rather austere and dark Edwardian red-brick house into something special. Fortunately, the building wasn't listed, so there had been free rein to make the material changes William wanted. He'd designed the huge, airy kitchen extension so that that it fed seamlessly through the floor-to-ceiling glass windows onto the terrace and garden. He'd also opened up the dark, poky rooms by knocking through

465

interior walls, allowing the light to pour in. Once the structural work was finished, Helena had done a wonderful job with the decor. She had a natural flair for blending colours and fabrics and for choosing furniture that suited the space, which she had added to over the years on antique hunts and various overseas holidays. They had succeeded in turning mere bricks and mortar into an eclectic and welcoming home.

William shivered. He had always felt so proud of what they had achieved here; but the house felt desolate today.

He went to the fridge – its door covered in magnets holding Immy's and Fred's paintings – and pulled out the milk he'd bought from the petrol station on his way home. He supposed that, just as when his first marriage had collapsed, he would lose the house in the divorce – either to Helena, or by selling it to another, happier family. The thought made another fissure in his already battered heart.

'Tea, Alex!' he shouted up the stairs.

'Coming, Dad,' Alex shouted back.

William walked across the kitchen, opened the French doors, and made his way onto the sun-dappled terrace. He sat down on the wrought-iron bench, which nestled within a hundred-year-old wisteria and was flanked by a bed of sweet-smelling roses. Whilst their mistress was away, they had gorged on light and sun. Now they were fat, bloated and in urgent need of pruning.

'Thanks, Dad.' Alex brought his tea out and sat down next to him.

'Feels weird to be home, doesn't it?'

'Yes,' Alex agreed. 'It's because of the quiet. I didn't realise until today how noisy we all are.'

'You must be tired after your epic journey.'

'Not really. It was sort of . . . exciting.'

'Well, please don't repeat it. I've never driven so fast in my life. I only arrived here ten minutes before you did.'

'You were at your London place when the police arrived?' Alex asked.

'Yes. When they turned up on my doorstep, I must admit, I imagined the worst. They told me you were on the evening flight to Gatwick last night, and the plane had landed just before midnight. But they didn't know where you'd gone since.'

'Sorry.'

'It's okay. I thought you'd probably head for here.'

'Well, if I'd known you were in London, I'd have come straight there. I had to spend the night at Waterloo station, because I missed the last train to Beaulieu by hours. It was quite scary, actually,' Alex commented. 'Lots of drunken hobos and me.'

'I'm sure.'

They sipped their tea companionably.

'How's Mum?' Alex asked.

'Better now she knows you're safe, but she was obviously beside herself.'

'Yeah . . . it was a pretty rotten thing to do, but I had my reasons,' Alex said.

'How was she when *I* left?' William asked carefully.

'Awful. She came to my bedroom to explain. Told me all about what happened when I was born. You know she nearly died after she had me?'

'No, I didn't, but there's obviously a lot of stuff I didn't hang about to hear.'

'Do you think Mum's a bad person?'

'No, not really.'

'A "liar and a cheat"?'

William looked at Alex. 'You were listening.'

'Yes. Sorry.'

'Of course I don't really think that. I was just . . . very angry, that's all. I still am.'

'I was angry, too. Like, mega. I'm calmer now though,' Alex nodded.

'How come?'

'Because I think I understand.'

'Understand that your mother has lied to you, *and* me, for years?'

'Well, to be fair, she didn't exactly lie to me, she just . . . didn't tell me.'

'No, I suppose not.'

'I was thinking on the plane over what I'd have done in her shoes,' mused Alex.

'And?'

'I think I'd have lied, too. What would you have done?'

William shrugged. 'I honestly don't know.'

'But that's the thing, isn't it? Like, no one knows what they'll do in a situation until they're . . .' – he shrugged – 'in it.'

'I suppose so.' William sighed. 'It makes no odds anyway, I'm afraid. I'm sorry to have to tell you this, Alex, but I've told your mother I'm starting divorce proceedings.'

'That's okay. I understand.'

'Do you?'

'Yeah, seems a pity, though. You love Mum, and she loves you big time, especially now she doesn't have to lie to you anymore. And as for Immy and Fred – well, it's not going to be great for them, either. But I can see that if I was you, I'd probably feel the same.' Alex kicked at the moss peering out between the paving stones with his trainer. 'I mean, it's kind of a male-pride type thing, isn't it?'

'Well, a bit, I suppose,' William admitted.

'If you think about it, like, all this stuff happened before you two even met. Mum hasn't gone off with anyone else or done anything really bad during your marriage, has she?'

'Not that I know of. She may well have seen . . . *him* since. And may still be in love with him, for all I know.' William was astounded that he was having this kind of conversation with a thirteen-year-old boy.

'If she'd wanted to be with him, don't you think she'd have left you a long time ago? No' – Alex shook his head – 'she doesn't love him, she loves *you*.'

'The fact remains, she lied to me for the whole of our marriage, Alex.'

'S'pose. But we both know why she did it. Dad?' He looked at William. 'Do you love her?'

'You know I do.'

'Then why are you divorcing her?'

'Alex, I know you're mature for your age, but there really are some things you just can't understand.'

'Well, I get that you have the option of divorcing my mother. I don't. I'm stuck with her forever. So tell me how it's worse for you than it is for me? I also have to deal with the fact that Sacha is my genetic father.'

'I know you do.'

'*And* that he left Mum in the lurch when she was pregnant. Also, I was thinking earlier . . .'

'Go on?'

'Well, Mum said that he told her his name was Alexander Nicholls.'

'Apparently, but to be fair, that is his real name in a way.'

'But everyone knows him as Sacha Chandler. Like, forever. So why would he do that?'

'I don't know, Alex, really. Perhaps he was trying to create his artistic alter ego.'

'Well, I reckon he was deliberately covering his tracks with Mum. After all, he was already married to Jules at the time. To be fair, how was Mum to know he was the same person as your oldest friend? Until she, er, *did*?'

'I hear what you're saying, Alex, but once she knew, she should have told me. The point is, she didn't trust me. And to be honest, she never has.'

'Maybe not, but I dunno,' Alex sighed. 'Perhaps she just finds it hard to trust people in general. She seemed to have a pretty crap childhood. With a mum who didn't really want her, from the sounds of things. She had to fend for herself.'

'Yes. From what little she's said, it didn't sound good.'

They both lapsed into silence.

'You know the worst thing of all?' Alex said eventually, looking up at William. 'Rupes is my half-brother! Now, that really is a sticking point for me. I'm gutted that we share the same bloodline. But we do.'

'Genes are funny things, Alex.'

'Yeah, but as I can't divorce my mother and walk away, I have to accept it. *And* the fact that Sacha is my genetic dad. And for all that you're mad that your best friend had an affair with Mum, it *was* before you met her. The fact he is . . . or was, your best friend, must mean there's *some* good in him. And just because you have the same taste in women, it doesn't suddenly morph Sacha into a different person, does it? He's still exactly the same as he always was. And Mum, too. The only difference is, you – and I – know the secret now.'

William slowly turned towards him and shook his head. 'How did you get to be so wise?'

'It's in my genes. On the other hand, maybe it's not.' Alex shrugged and gave a short chuckle.

'Will you want to see him now?'

'You mean, as my "father"? Bond with him, and all that stuff?'

'Yes.'

'Who knows? I'll have to think about it. Just now, I loathe him for what he did, but maybe when I get over that, I'll feel differently. But,' Alex sighed, 'that's irrelevant anyway. It always has been, but I've only just realised it.'

'What do you mean?'

'Like . . . do you remember when I fell off that climbing frame, literally head first, and you had to rush me to hospital?' Alex pointed to the bottom of the garden.

'Of course I do. Mum was pregnant with Immy. I thought she might go into labour at the sight of the blood pouring out of you.'

'And when you taught me to ride a bike? You walked me down to the tennis courts along the road and took the stabilisers off. Then you ran round and round with me, holding me and puffing and panting and then you let me go and I wobbled off by myself.'

471

'I remember,' replied William.

'And that time when I didn't get into the Colts A rugby team and I was so, like, upset. And you told me how you hadn't been picked for your school cricket team and felt the same, but the next year, you had got in?'

'Yes,' nodded William.

'Dad?'

'Yes?'

'You see, the thing is this . . .' Alex snaked a hand into William's and squeezed it. '*You're* my dad.'

λ

Thirty

Jules left soon after she'd heard the news that Alex was okay, and Helena decided she would save the dissection of *that* conversation for another day. The fact that her life was in shreds paled into insignificance compared with the news that her son was safe.

Having called everyone to tell them Alex was fine, Helena went upstairs to take a shower. She came out refreshed and went downstairs to telephone Angelina, to tell her she could bring Immy and Fred back as soon as was convenient. She desperately needed to hear the sound of their voices. The relentless silence in the house kept reminding her of what she had lost, and of the dark future she now had to face.

While she was waiting, she walked to her hammock and lay in it, too tired to even think. She knew she needed rest to clear her addled mind. She closed her eyes and dozed, comforted by the gentle rocking motion. Then she heard a car draw up and opened one eye, thinking it must be

Angelina with the children. She was halfway up the steps to the terrace when Sacha appeared round the corner.

'Hello, Helena.'

'What do you want?' Helena walked past him and into the house.

'Wine will do, or whisky if you have any,' he quipped, as he followed her through to the kitchen. ''S'pose it's been fun and frolics this end, since the shit hit the proverbial? I went to the house just now to say goodbye to the kids, and Jules told me William knows.'

'You could put it that way. Or you could say it's been the worst twenty-four hours of my life. Alex ran away, and I only heard he was safe an hour ago.'

'I hear he's in England with William.'

'Yes.' Helena handed him a glass of wine.

'Thanks.' He drank it thirstily, then handed it back to her for an immediate refill.

'So what are you doing here?' she asked wearily.

'Isn't it obvious? I came to see you,' Sacha replied. He walked towards her as she put the wine bottle back in the fridge, then wrapped his arms around her waist. 'Where are the little ones?'

'Back any minute with Angelina.' Helena tried to wriggle out of his grasp. 'Sacha! Let me go.'

'Helena, don't fight me.' His lips nuzzled her neck. 'We've waited years for this moment, haven't we, lovely?'

'No! Stop it!' She wrenched herself away. 'What on earth are you talking about?'

'Helena, you must know how I've felt about you all these years. I've had to watch you with William, wishing every moment you were mine. Remember Vienna? It was the most beautiful few weeks of my life. Now there's nothing to stop us being together. We're free, angel.' He advanced towards her, but she edged away.

'All I remember is a man who promised to return to me, and never did.'

'Is that why you're angry? Still, after all these years? Surely you understood why I couldn't? Jules was pregnant. I could hardly leave her, could I? But I've never stopped thinking about you; not for one moment.'

'And I've never stopped thinking that you forgot to mention you were married.'

'I'm sure I must have done. You just didn't want to hear it.'

'No! Don't you *dare* give me that shit! You didn't tell me. Nor did I hear a word from you after you'd left.'

'Surely I wrote to you to explain?'

'Oh for God's sake, Sacha.' Helena slammed the fridge door. 'You're pathetic, you really are.'

'You don't love William, do you, Helena? He just happened to be there to rescue you when you needed him.'

'I'm not interested in your opinion.'

'Is he divorcing you? I'd take a bet that he is. Good old Will, straight as a die. God knows why he ever had me as his best friend. We couldn't be more different,' he slurred.

'Shut up, Sacha! I will always love him, whether we're together or not.'

'And Alex? What of him? He's my son, after all. I've stayed away until now, for obvious reasons, but I might want to get to know him a little better.'

'I . . .' Helena did her best to control her fury. 'I would very much appreciate it if you would refrain from contacting

Alex. If he wishes to get to know *you*, then that's his decision.'

'He's my son. I can do what I wish.'

Helena's hand itched to punch his selfish, bloated face, but she realised antagonising him would get her nowhere.

'Okay. Then I beg you to leave him alone until he's at least had time to come to terms with all this. I beg you for our family's sake too. If not for me, do it for your oldest friend, who is feeling so betrayed.'

'So you're still protecting him.' Sacha gave a slow handclap. 'Well done, Helena. You always did like to be seen as perfect, didn't you? I'll have to tell Jules the truth, of course.'

'Go ahead. She already knows,' Helena said lightly.

Sacha's face registered shock. 'How?'

'She knew it immediately, at the wedding. She thinks Alex has your eyes.'

'Shit! I had no idea.' Sacha sat down abruptly. 'She never said a word.'

'No. Actually, your wife is pretty amazing. She loved you enough to turn a blind eye to our betrayal, and apparently, others besides. Astounding, really.'

'Well. That makes me feel like a *complete* bastard. I suppose you'd agree?'

Helena refused to rise to his bait. 'What I think is that I'm a different person now to who I was in Vienna. The problem is, you're still exactly the same.'

Sacha put a hand through his greasy auburn curls. 'Are you telling me that even if you are single, you wouldn't think about us trying again?'

Helena did her best not to giggle hysterically. 'No, is the

short answer to that. I've told you: I love William. I always have, and that's all there is to it. And even if I didn't, I'd still feel the same. I'm sorry.'

'Come on, angel, you're just still angry about me not coming back for you.'

'You can think what you want, Sacha, but there is no future for you and I. Ever. Okay?'

'I hear you,' he said with a nod. 'It's too soon, that's all. I should have waited a few days before coming to see you. You're in shock from what's happened.' He stood up. 'I won't give up on you, lovely, I really won't.'

'Do what you want, Sacha. But I promise you, you're wasting your time. You have a son and daughter, not to mention a wife, whose lives you've recently ruined. Perhaps it's time to grow up and start taking responsibility for them. *And* yourself.'

'Okay, Helena, but I bet you'll change your mind when you feel the cool breeze of loneliness. Can't see *you* lasting long without a man. Not your style, is it?'

Helena ignored his vitriol. 'I think it's time you left.'

'Fine. I'm going.' He stood up and lurched towards the door. Then he turned back, the expression on his face suddenly contrite. 'Forgive me, angel, please.'

'I did. A long time ago.'

'I love you, you know. I really do.'

'Bye, Sacha. Have a nice life.'

She watched him wobble to his rental car and climb in. 'I don't think you should be driving!' she called to him from the back door, but she knew it had fallen on deaf ears as the car door slammed and Sacha drove at full pelt up the hill.

Helena felt a sudden wave of relief.

Whatever the future might bring, at last the past had been put to rest.

ALEX'S DIARY

14th August (continued)

I've left Dad to it.

After we'd had our little chat, he went very quiet. Then he said he needed to mow the lawn. I watched him from my bedroom window. He was aboard his precious ride-on for hours, going round and round the garden in circles, shearing it into submission. It's the first time I've ever felt sorry for blades of grass. Then he came inside. He's downstairs some-where, but I feel I mustn't disturb him. It's getting dark now, and our house is silent. I'm not used to it and I don't like it.

I wish he'd hurry up and decide what he's going to do: 'To Divorce or not to Divorce. That is the question.'

Then I can go downstairs and get a Pot Noodle, as that's all there is in the kitchen cupboard. I checked earlier – and I am now starving!!

So, I ponder to pass the time, what is it about men and emotion? The dreadful truth is, I fear most of my sex would prefer to end up dead than admit they're scared shitless. Then I think of the trenches in the First World War, and all that live cannon fodder. Those men seemed to go over the top like they were embarking on a nice morning stroll in the country:

'I'm off, Sah!'

'Yes, Jones, have a good one. Put a word in to Big G for me when you see him, won't you?'

'I will, Sah. Goodbye, Sah!'

And off Jones would go, to be peppered with bullet holes or to survive minus a limb or two, with a mind as shot as his body.

God, it makes me want to cry just thinking about those poor sods. Walking to their inevitable deaths. Almost one hundred years on, I shudder at the thought, because I know if it was me, I'd be wetting myself and blubbering like a blubbery thing. They'd probably have to drug me to get me over and then lay me out, comatose, to be used as target practice.

Which brings me back to my current main thought topic:

What do women want of us?

There's Chloë, the Love of My Life (so far), initially mooning over brain-dead Rupes; loving his swagger, his full-bodied Neanderthal-ness, never doubting he could kill a woolly mammoth with one blow, swing it over his shoulder and bring it home to their exquisitely furnished cave.

Then (having had a quick fumble with Airport Guy) she turns in an instant to 'Michelle'. Even though he's a nice guy, the way he did show-off wheelies on the gravel when he arrived on his moped tells me that, despite his girly name, he would be regarded as 'buff', 'butch' . . . where all I have in the 'B' category is, er, Bee – for Bunny.

I am a touchy-feely man. And my goodness, I want to touch and feel Chloë. But not just physically . . . emotionally, too.

Does the fact I empathise make me unattractive?

Yet . . . All my information sources on the subject – notably, an article I read yesterday on the plane home entitled 'The Five Main Reasons for Divorce', courtesy of the *Daily Mail*, lead me to believe that women want a man who 'gets' them emotionally.

Like Sadie does with Mum. I.e., they want their man to be their best friend.

But how can us men be *both*? Embody the quintessential qualities of male and female at the same time??

It seems to me, women actually don't know what they want. Which means we men can never bloody well get it right.

And Dad is most certainly all male . . .

Well, I sigh, I just hope Mum knows what *she* wants.

I hope I got my point across to Dad, too. After all that time on the mower, he must be thinking about it: thinking about Mum and me, and Immy and Fred and now, I hope, Chloë too.

Our family.

It may be a little unorthodox, but that doesn't make it bad, or wrong.

We are the best family I know. I was reminiscing on the plane home how much fun we all have. How much we laugh. And how much I love him – my dad. It took a 'real' one to make me realise how I will miss the so-called pretend version, if he suddenly isn't around anymore.

Which he might not be.

If he decides on the Big D.

He's treated me like his own son all along. He doesn't pick me out for special treatment either way. The fact he finds it frustrating when I have one of my moods is not because I'm not his blood, but simply because I am his son and can be irritating. And he gets irritated, just as any blood parent *naturally* would.

He – William – isn't perfect. He has his faults. Like all of us imperfect humans. Including my mum.

However, she – and he – are more good than bad. And perhaps that is all one can hope for, because I've realised we're all somewhere on a spectrum, with black at one end and white at the other. Most of us seem to hang about somewhere in the middle, veering one way and the other within a narrow margin.

And as long as none of us get too close to either extreme – then I think we are basically okay. And me, and Mum and Dad, and even Sacha and the dreaded Rupes (for now) are in the central milieu somewhere.

I mentally piece back together the broken bits of my mother's statue, but leave her pedestal behind. She will stand from now on her own two feet. On the ground: neither saint nor sinner.

Just a human being, like my dad.

And *if*, and it's a big *if*, he decides he can swallow his pride and take my mother back, I'm going to ask whether he will adopt me. We will do the legal thing and as a mark of my respect and love, I will change my name to his and finally be a fully surnamed-up member of our family.

'Alexander R. Cooke'. And God, I wish he would hurry up and do my new surname – cook, I mean. I haven't eaten since yesterday on the plane.

So, there was me searching my whole life for something I

thought I wanted . . . and now I've got it, I don't want it at all. Not one little bit.

I just want back what we had.

Hang on! Dad is knocking on my door. My heart is in my mouth. Actually, it's not. I would eat it if it really was.

'Come in.'

Dad puts his head round the door. 'You hungry?' he asks.

'You bet,' I reply.

'Fancy an Indian?'

'Yeah, sure.'

'I was thinking we should have something English whilst we can,' he quips back.

'Why is that?'

He looks away for a moment, then smiles at me. 'We're going back to the Land of Feta Cheese and Fish-Poo Sauce tomorrow morning. I've just booked our flights.'

λα

Thirty-one

Helena awoke to another beautiful day, astonished at how well she'd slept – and, ironically, how peaceful she felt.

She got out of bed, put on her leotard and ballet shoes, and went downstairs to the terrace. She began the *pliés* and her body automatically took over, which disengaged her brain and allowed her to think.

The house . . . Pandora . . . the instinct she'd had about coming back here had been right. The box *had* been opened; its dusty contents had been disgorged from the dark corners and flown free, causing chaos and pain. Yet, just as in the myth, there was still one thing that remained: hope.

There were no more secrets, nothing to hide and no shadows to haunt her. Whatever would come – and she acknowledged how dreadful a world without William was likely to be – at least it was honest. From now on, she would stand or fall by the truth.

*

Alexis arrived at ten o'clock, just as Helena, Immy and Fred were having a late breakfast on the terrace.

''Lo 'Lexis,' said Fred. 'Did you bring me a prezzie?'

'Fred!' chided Immy. 'He asks everyone that when they arrive, and it's very rude.'

Alexis kissed Helena warmly on both cheeks. 'How are you?'

'Much better. Thank you for all your help, and I apologise for losing the plot the other night.'

'Whatever a "plot" is, I understand why you lose it. When your child is in pain or danger, it is the worst thing. I know,' he agreed.

'Coffee, Alexis?' asked Immy importantly, holding up the pot.

'I would like one, Immy, yes.'

'I'll get you a clean cup from the kitchen,' she said, climbing down from her chair.

'Me come too.' Fred followed her inside.

'Your children, they are delightful, Helena, really.'

'For a change, I agree. They've been particularly angelic in the past twenty-four hours.'

'Maybe they know their mother needed them to be.'

'I did. You're right.'

'So, when is Alex coming back?'

'I don't know. I texted him last night to ask him whether he wanted me to fly home. I haven't received a reply yet. I'm sure he's still very angry with me. But at least I know he's safe.'

'So, you might be leaving here very soon?'

'If Alex needs me in England, then of course, I will go.'

'Helena, if you are leaving, then there is something I should show you.'

She looked at his serious expression. 'Alexis, what is it?'

'I have come here to tell you so many times but . . .' he shrugged, 'the moment has never seemed right. Is Angelina here?'

'Yes, she's upstairs making the beds.'

'Would she watch the children? There is somewhere I need to take you. Don't worry, it is not far away.'

'Alexis, please, not bad news. I really couldn't cope,' she groaned.

'No.' He laid a calming hand on her shoulder. 'This is not bad news. It is just something you must know. Trust me.'

'All right. I'll speak to Angelina and we'll go.'

'Where on earth are you taking me?' she asked a few minutes later, as Alexis led her down towards the swimming pool.

'You will see.' He walked across the pool terrace, and at the far end, unhooked and pulled back a panel of the wooden fence which separated the grounds from the olive grove that surrounded Pandora.

'Goodness, I'd never noticed this gate was here before,' she remarked.

'No, you were not meant to. It was a secret.'

'Who put it there?' Helena asked, as she followed Alexis through the trees.

'Patience, Helena, please.'

They walked on for a while, steering their way under the branches of the tightly packed grove, until they entered a small clearing. They stood side by side, looking at the mountains surrounding them, the olive trees tumbling down the valley beneath them and the thin, shimmering line of sea in the distance.

'Is this what you wanted to show me, Alexis?'

'This is the spot, yes.' He turned slightly to his right and pointed. 'But *that* is what I brought you to see.'

Helena followed the direction of his finger, and walked over to it.

'Oh, how beautiful. It's a statue of Aphrodite, isn't it?' she asked as she stood in front of it.

'No. Not quite.'

She looked up at him. 'Then who is it, and what's it doing here?'

'Look at the bottom of the statue, Helena. Look at the name.'

She bent down. 'I can hardly read it, it's so badly worn.'

'You can, if you try.'

Helena cleared away the leaves that had collected around the small plinth and rubbed a finger across the inscription.

'There's an "*I*" and an "*E*" . . . and an "*N*" . . . and a "*V*" is the first letter, I . . .' She looked up at Alexis in confusion. 'It spells *Vivienne*.'

'Yes.'

'But Vivienne was my mother's name.'

'That is right, yes.'

'What does it mean? Is this meant to be her? Fashioned as Aphrodite?' Helena traced her hand across the alabaster face.

'Yes.'

'But Alexis, why? And why here?'

'Angus had it sculpted after she died,' he replied. 'This, so my grandmother Christina told me, was your mother's favourite spot.'

'But . . .' Helena put a hand to her brow. 'I know she came to Cyprus regularly, and loved it, but I . . .' She looked up at Alexis, and suddenly understood. 'Are you telling me Angus was in love with my mother? Is that right?'

'Yes, Helena. Vivienne was a guest at Pandora many times. She was known both here at the house and in the village.'

'Really? So . . . *that* must be why so many locals have said I reminded them of someone. I know I'm thought to look like her.'

'You do. My grandmother could not believe the resemblance when she came to Pandora that night.'

'I saw her here in the old photographs we dug out of the box room. So' – Helena's mind was racing now –'all those letters Alex found, were they written to her? Was she the mystery woman?'

'Yes, she was.'

'But how do you know all this?'

'Helena, Christina worked here for almost thirty years. She saw everything. And those letters – they were returned to Angus by your father.'

'So he knew?'

'For certain, if he sent back the letters.'

'Well,' Helena breathed, trying to make sense of what Alexis had told her, 'to be honest, my parents never seemed very close when I was growing up. My father seemed to spend more and more time in Kenya. I rarely saw him.'

'Perhaps it was an arrangement that suited them both. Every marriage is different, after all,' added Alexis.

'Maybe, but why didn't Angus and my mother ever get together? It's obvious from the letters he wrote that he adored her.'

'Who knows, Helena? We both know there are many reasons why those who love each other spend their lives apart,' he commented quietly.

Helena looked down at the dead leaves fallen from the olive trees. She took one between her fingers, felt its roughness.

'Angus left me everything.'

'He did, yes.'

'I was his goddaughter.'

'You were. And . . .'

'What, Alexis?'

'Christina always wondered if you were more than that.'

'What are you trying to say?'

'I think you know, Helena.'

'I do, yes,' she whispered.

'Those letters were returned soon after your birth. My grandmother remembers it vividly. She found Angus sobbing at his writing desk. Your mother never came here again.'

'But I did. And . . .' Helena searched her memory. 'It was only a few months after my father had died.'

'Perhaps by sending you here, you became the way in which your mother could show her love.'

'Why didn't she come with me herself?'

'Helena, I do not know. Perhaps she felt it was better

not to reignite the flame. Maybe the life here did not suit her, as it would not have suited you.'

'Maybe . . . but now, I can never ask her. Or find out who really was my father.'

'Does it matter? Angus loved you like you *were* his daughter. He gave you the gift of Pandora. I hope this shows you that everyone has secrets, Helena. That no one is as you think they are.'

'Yes, you're right. Do you have any?' she asked him with a wry smile.

'I have none from you. But from my wife, yes. She did not know why I could not love her enough. I still feel guilt for that. Come, we should go back.' Alexis offered Helena the crook of his arm.

'Thank you for showing me that,' she said, as they made their way up to the house.

'Well, we can both say that is what you call putting a woman on a pedestal!' he chuckled.

'And that, Alexis,' Helena sighed, 'is a very dangerous thing to do.'

After Alexis had left, Helena walked into the kitchen and found Immy and Fred at the kitchen table. She sat down, feeling suddenly drained from yet more revelations.

'You're back! I've made something with honey that are really sticky with Sesame Street nuts on them!' said Immy.

'I help make them too, Immy,' added Fred.

'Mummy, you look funny. Are you funny?' Immy climbed onto Helena's knee and hugged her.

'Mummee, you look funnee!' copied Fred, enjoying the rhyme and giggling. He tried to climb on too, and Helena pulled him up onto the bit of knee that Immy wasn't inhabiting.

She hugged them both tightly to her.

'We love you, Mummy,' said Immy, kissing her face. 'Don't we, Fred?'

'Yeah, we do,' he added.

'And I love you too.' She returned their kisses onto sticky cheeks. 'How do you fancy going to the beach, chaps?' she asked.

'Yes, pleeease,' they chorused.

They arrived back as the sun was starting to set. Helena fed the little ones, then gave them a bath and put on the DVD of *Cinderella* for them in the drawing room.

Taking a glass of wine upstairs onto the balcony, she saw dusk was falling already, even though it was just past seven o'clock.

Summer was coming to an end.

Could she live here, she pondered, knowing she was no longer welcome at Cedar House?

The answer was no. As she – and maybe her mother before her – had known all those years ago, her life was meant to be lived elsewhere.

Where, with whom and how, she didn't yet know . . .

Loneliness suffused her then, and she physically ached for her husband and her son.

Wandering inside and shutting the balcony doors behind her, she took a shower, then sat at the dressing table brushing her hair.

Putting down her hairbrush, she traced her fingers along

the swirls of inlaid mother-of-pearl on the lid of the jewellery box Alexis had retrieved from the rubbish dump.

'Pandora's Box,' she murmured.

And then she saw it.

Subtly entwined in the decoration on the lid of the box were her own and her parents' initials.

Tears sprang spontaneously to Helena's eyes.

Eventually, she came downstairs to check on the children. They were absorbed in *Cinderella*, so she left them and stepped out onto the terrace. She jumped in fear as she saw two figures emerging from the deepening shadows, climbing up the steps from the swimming pool.

'Hello, Mum. Dad and I thought we'd have a quick dip to cool off from the journey.'

'Alex!'

'Yep. That's me. You can't hug me, I'm wet.'

'I don't care.'

'Okay.' He walked into her outstretched arms, and she held him tight.

'How are you?'

'Good, very good.' He looked at her, his vivid green eyes telling her he was. 'Love you, Mum,' he whispered.

'I love you too, Alex.'

'Where are the little ones?'

'Watching a DVD in the drawing room.'

'I promised Chloë I'd give Disney a go, so I will. See you in a bit.'

As he squelched inside, she didn't shout at him not to drip all over the fragile damask sofa. Because it didn't matter a damn if he did.

'Hello, Helena.'

She was so choked, she couldn't speak.

William stood in front of her, also soaking wet from the pool.

'How are you?' he asked her.

'Fine.'

'Really? Then why are you crying?'

'Because if you've just come here to chaperone Alex back and you're about to leave again, I . . . can't bear to see you.'

'No. Well, could I at least stay the night? See Immy and Fred?'

'Yes,' she agreed desolately, 'of course.'

'And perhaps tomorrow as well? And the day after that?'

'I . . .' She looked at him, still not sure what he meant.

'Helena, you have . . . *we* have, one hell of an amazing son. He . . . Alex, showed me the way back. To you.'

'Did he?'

'Yes. And . . .' William's voice broke, 'I don't ever want to go away again. I love you.'

'And I love you, darling. Believe me, I do.'

They stood ten yards apart, both of them longing for there to be no distance between them.

'But, Helena, you have to promise me: no more secrets. Please, just tell me now if there's anything else I should know.'

'Actually,' she said slowly, 'something happened here earlier.'

'Did it?' The muscles in William's face tensed.

'Yes, it did.' She nodded. 'And it's a *big* secret. Perhaps the biggest of them all. And . . .'

'Oh God! What?'

She smiled then, her blue eyes lighting up as she walked slowly towards him.

'I just can't wait to tell you all about it.'

ALEX'S DIARY

25th August 2006

We're on our way home tomorrow.

I mean, *our* family.

We're leaving Pandora and her Box behind.

Mum told me all about it – the box, I mean. And took me to see the statue of naked Granny in the olive groves.

Even though it's morally reprehensible, everyone involved is dead. Except my mother, who seems to be fine about it, so it can be beautiful instead.

We have something in common now, my mother and me. I like that.

And besides, I got two for the price of one:

'Find out who your Daddy is and get Grandpa for free!!'

I'm glad Angus and I are probably related. He was a real man, doing butch things, like going over the top and commanding armies. But at the same time, he cried like a girl, and he knew how to love.

I have someone else to aspire to, as well as my father.

The Cash's name tape people, plus the solicitor, have been duly alerted. 'Beaumont-Cooke' is where it's at. I decided to honour both of my parents. Under the circumstances, it only seemed fair, or Mum might have felt left out.

Dad and I will become officially 'wed' in a few months' time, but for the moment, I shall trade illegally on my surname when I start school.

I reflect on whether I am sad to be going home.

And I conclude I am not.

I have not had a holiday so much as an emotional, mental and physical assault course. In fact, our whole family has had a serious, sweaty workout, which hopefully has equipped us all to move on and face the future.

I also had a heart-to-heart yesterday with my parents about the impending school situation. It turns out that my mum is dreading me going away, and that Dad is just genuinely proud that I won the scholarship and thinks it's a fantastic opportunity.

They both thought that I really wanted to go. I explained I thought they wanted me to go. So, the upshot is, I *will* go. At least for a term or two. And if I hate it, I can leave and come home.

And now that I understand they are not going to hold a celebration in my empty bedroom for all their friends and relatives on the night me and my trunk have been removed to my *new* Broom Cupboard, I feel far more relaxed about the whole thing. I understand they just want the best for me.

I have also grown up in the past few weeks. *Literally.*

When Mum took some final measurements for the horrendous school uniform she's ordering me, I was almost five foot five.

So, I muse, what have I learnt, on this holiday?

That there are all kinds of love, and it arrives in different shapes and forms.

It can be earned, but not paid for.

It can be given, but never bought.

And once it's truly there, it holds fast.

This love thing.

Alex

'Pandora', Cyprus

19th July 2016

I turn to the next page and see the rest of the diary is empty. I could have died the following day, for all the future readers of this diary might know.

I glance at my watch and see that it is midnight, local time. Picking up the diary, I walk back inside Pandora, closing the shutters behind me. This simple act alone reminds me of how much has changed since I was last here. I am now the adult, who takes responsibility and is trusted with it.

Walking along the corridor, I hesitate at the bottom of the stairs, then walk past them and along the corridor to my Broom Cupboard. Opening the door, I switch on the light and the electric fan, which groans with the effort of turning after so many years standing idle.

There are no sheets on the camp bed – *or* gusseted tights – to protect me from anything that might bite me in the night.

But since I was last here, I've travelled to South America

and stayed for four long nights in a tent in the Amazon. I've encountered spiders the size of dinner plates, flying cockroaches that would provide a decent supper for two. Mosquitoes are now a mere irritation.

Removing my clothes, I turn off the light and lie down. And feel Pandora's atmosphere closing in around me. Faces from the past appear like a beauty parade behind my closed eyelids. They remind me that all the protagonists who played a part in that dramatic summer ten years ago are due to arrive back here in less than forty-eight hours' time.

Except for one . . .

I sleep then, deeply and peacefully, and for a change, I have no dreams that I wake up remembering. I fumble for my phone to check the time and see it is ten o'clock. I stand up, inch around the bed, and walk upstairs to take a shower in bitingly cold water. Having dressed, I make a cup of coffee and stand at the back door sipping it, blinking myopically in the harsh morning sunlight.

I decide then that I should go upstairs and air the bedrooms, relieve them of their odour of uninhabited house. It's not that any of us have deliberately stayed away for ten years. It's just . . . the way things worked out.

Opening the shutters as I walk from one room to the next, I am glad to see that the beds are already neatly made up with fresh white sheets, towels laid at the bottom of each. Angelina seems to have done a sterling job of taking care of Pandora over the years, and I emerge onto the terrace thinking about what I should do next. I hear the sound of tyres on the gravel and turn to see a white van approaching the house. I watch as two familiar figures emerge from it and walk towards me.

'Alex! My God! Can it really be you?'

An Alexis who seems to have shrunk in stature approaches me. When he clasps me to him in a man hug, I realise I am looking him in the eye.

'Yes, it's me, really,' I assure him.

'How are you? It has been far too long. But I understand the reasons,' he sighs. 'And of course' – he beckons forward the woman standing shyly behind him – 'you remember Angelina?'

'Of course I do. In my opinion, her baking skills are unmatched to this day.' I smile.

'Hello, Alex,' she says, kissing me on both cheeks. 'Why, you are very handsome man now. You remind me of Brad Pitt!'

'Do I?' I reply, and decide I like her even more than I remembered.

'Yes. So, I have many foods in the van and I must start preparing in the kitchen for tomorrow.'

'Perhaps you can help me unload the wine and glasses, Alex?'

We all go to the van, and as we carry the food and then the boxes of wine and glasses into the storeroom at the back of the house, I study Alexis. The years, I think, have been kind to him, and the silvery highlights that now pepper his dark hair give him a certain gravitas.

'Let us go into the kitchen and drink some water,' Alexis suggests, as we dump the last of many cases and the sweat pours off us both.

Angelina is already at the fridge, storing cheeses and salamis. I watch in surprise as Alexis walks towards her, puts his hands on her shoulders and kisses her on the top of her head as he reaches inside for the bottle of water.

'Here.' He passes me a glass of water.

'Thanks.'

'Alex, you look confused. What is it?'

'I . . . are you two . . . together?'

'Yes,' he smiled. 'When Pandora no longer needed Angelina's help after your family had left, I employed her as our family's housekeeper. And one thing led to another. We married six years ago and I became a father two years ago, on the very day of my fiftieth birthday!' Alexis grins. 'I have another son.'

'And I live in a houseful of man!' Angelina chuckles happily. 'And now, I would ask that you both leave my kitchen so that I can start preparing the feast.'

'And I must go back to the office.' Alexis checks his watch. 'Come up and see the winery when you have time. We have doubled in size, and Dimitrios works with me making and selling the wine.'

'And Michel?' I ask tentatively.

'He runs the internet sales side of the company. So, we are a true family business. You will see my sons later today, as we have much more to do at Pandora yet. Call me if there's anything else you need, Alex, and I look forward to hearing later of *your* life over the past ten years.'

I watch him blow a kiss to his wife, whose dark eyes follow him lovingly out of the kitchen.

'Is there anything I can do, Angelina?' I ask politely.

'Nothing, Alex. Why don't you go for swim in the pool?'

It's obvious that she wants me out of her hair, and I

oblige. I take a swim, remembering as I dive into the deep end the horror of rescuing my poor, drowning bunny. More and more I feel Alice-like here – the pool, too, seems to have shrunk as I reach the other end in five strokes instead of ten.

After padding back up to my Broom Cupboard and changing into a dry pair of shorts and a T-shirt, I take hold of the collected works of Keats. As I do so, various pieces of paper fly out of the pages. I look at them with a fond half-smile, but one sheet in particular actually brings tears to my eyes. I read it, and my heart immediately starts to bump against my chest.

Will she come . . . ?

I just don't know.

What is it, I wonder, about Pandora, that seems to unlock the emotions? Its walls seem to contain an intensity of energy within them that removes your outer protective skin and burrows deep inside you, revealing the source of your pain. Like a surgeon's knife slices through effortlessly to one's diseased innards.

Dearie me, I think, *if it's started already, I'm going to be a snivelling wreck by tomorrow night.*

I replace the poems in the book and put them back on the shelf. Then I take down the diary again. As it seems there's nothing else to do, I grab a pen and sunglasses from my rucksack, plus a cold beer from the kitchen. And I go outside to sit at the table on the terrace.

I open the diary to the clean page beyond the last entry. Simply because – me being me – I don't like unfinished business. And if I *was* me in fifty or sixty years' time, my frustration at its abrupt ending would be beyond measure.

Of course, I cannot compete with Pepys and his dedicated nine years of daily detail, and all I will be able to manage is a 'memoir' – a potted version of my life over the past ten years. But at least it will be something. Which, as everyone knows, is better than nothing.

Or is it?

We shall see . . .

ALEX'S MEMOIR

September 2006 – June 2016

School

The one where one eats one's Frosties in white tie and tails. I don't care how PC everyone believes boarding schools to be these days – my first term was far closer to Tom Brown than Gordon Brown, i.e. HORRENDOUS.

Nowadays, bullying at such establishments is no longer thought of as 'toughening young men up' – things have moved on since the old days, when the masters would virtually cheer the bullies on from the sidelines. Instead, it has become invisible and insidious.

The bullies have become like renegade torturers trained by the SAS. The kind who challenge you to a 'friendly' pillow fight, then whilst you're using your fluffy down version, they are bashing your brains to mulch with a cotton sackful of box files. Or sending you hate mail by text from a pay-as-you-go mobile that can't be traced. Or 'fraping' you on Facebook and changing your status to 'In a relationship with a transvestite'.

Luckily, having learnt my lesson about the ribbing I'd got over Bee the Bunny in Cyprus – it's about the only thing I can ever say I'm grateful to Rupes for – Bee arrived prepared in a cotton cradle, which I surreptitiously attached to the under-side of my wooden-framed bed with drawing pins. This meant that during the night, even though there was a mattress sep-arating us, I could at least reach out my arm underneath the bed and feel the security of his non-furry fur, and whisper to him through the slats beneath me.

I admit that, during the first dreadful weeks, I nearly ran away again. However, I wasn't going to give Rupes the pleas-ure of gloating over my departure, and besides, the teaching *was* incredible.

And it got better, as these things usually do, as I grew in mind and body. By the time I arrived in the sixth form, I was equipped with a stellar set of GCSEs. Fifty years ago I'd have had a 'fag' as well, i.e. a terrified first-former given to me to do my bidding: shining my shoes, laying my fire and toasting my crumpets upon it. The practice was abolished in the sev-enties, and a jolly good thing too, although some of my peer group continued to act as though it hadn't been, seeing it as a rite of passage.

'Fag': I discovered recently that its original meaning was from the . . .

I pause in my musings and ponder whether anyone who is reading this diary in fifty or a hundred years' time is really going to be interested in the provenance of the word 'fag'. The chances are that we'll all be speaking Mandarin as the world's main language by then, judging by the number of Chinese pupils at my school.

Anyway, the upshot of five years of school was that I won a place at Oxford University, reading philosophy.

Family

Mum, Dad, Immy and Fred continued their own lives along-side mine. Fred managed to kill my goldfish within two weeks of me leaving home. When I asked if he'd given it a decent burial, he told me he'd chucked it down the toilet, as he thought it should be buried in water.

Mum seemed far more relaxed and content than I'd ever seen her before. Too content, obviously, as the minute Fred began school, she announced her intention to establish a school of her own.

Suffice to say that the Beaumont School of Dance grew apace into what could be regarded as a multinational company. Apart, that is, from the actual cash such a venture is meant to generate. Mum, being Mum, seemed to teach most of her pupils for free. It was rare to come home for the school holidays and not find a sobbing person in a leotard sitting at the kitchen table, taking advantage of her listening ear as they poured out their life's problems.

That is, until the words that everybody dreads more than any other arrived at that same kitchen table. And Mum found herself with new problems of her own.

I pause again at this point, because I still feel unable to put into words the horror of the moment she and Dad told me. I stand up and get another beer from the fridge to drown the memory, and decide I will fill in the blanks on all that later on.

Family continued

Apart from Mum's problem, which obviously turned all of our worlds upside down, Immy and Fred seem to have done little more than grow quietly upwards. Maybe they didn't have much choice, given the circumstances.

It was Dad who shouldered a lot of the pressure when Mum couldn't. He's now a dab hand with the tumble dryer, and can make a decent Pot Noodle of his own in a pan from scratch. He's a seriously good bloke, my dad. And the best thing I ever did was to legally adopt him and his surname.

As far as Genetic Dad is concerned, he turned up one day near Christmas at Cedar House about a year after the apocalyptic summer and demanded to see me, his 'son'. Mum came upstairs to my bedroom, with that look of concern I know so well written all over her face. She explained that Sacha was downstairs. She said I didn't have to see him. I told her not to worry, and that I would.

When I arrived downstairs, he was at the kitchen table, knocking back whatever alcoholic beverage my father had just handed him. He looked dreadful. His hands shook, his bones stood up under his papery skin . . . And despite my determination to hate him, as usual, I felt sorry for him.

He wanted to know whether I wanted a 'relationship' with him.

Of all the people in the world, this poor, sad man was not top of my personal relationship list. So, with much effort, I told him no. In fact, I told him no so many times, I felt I was repeating a mantra. Until Dad realised I'd had enough and bundled Sacha out of the kitchen to drive him to the station.

I didn't see or hear from him again, until . . .

I shall move on.

The rest of the Pandora Posse

Sadie had her baby, a sweet little girl who she named

Peaches – so typically Sadie – although I suppose it could easily have been Melon, or Gooseberry . . . and she made *me* a godfather!

Now, that was a really nice thing to do, even though every time I see Peaches, I struggle to say her name out loud, especially if we're in public. And it really is one of those monikers that you can't possibly shorten. I tried 'Pee' once, which really doesn't work, so I now try to avoid calling her anything at all. She's a friendly child who has placidly accepted a succession of 'uncles', as Sadie has continued to swap boyfriends the way I used to swap football cards. In that regard, it makes my own childhood look like a walk in the park.

Andreas the Carpenter has never known about his daughter. This may be why, in retrospect, Sadie made me a godparent. Perhaps she thinks that when the time comes for Peaches to discover her mother's behaviour was less than unimpeachable, she can send her to me for counselling.

As for the rest of the Chandler clan: Jules moved to her cottage near Oundle with Rupes and Viola, and put down roots there like a particularly ferocious specimen of ivy. According to her annual round-robin Christmas letter – posted like clockwork on the first of December to arrive (second class) on the fourth, just when every other mortal is making their list of People They Must Send Cards To – she quickly established herself as head of every parent–teacher association and fundraising committee going. I imagine that if there was a fête, bring-and-buy or bazaar, there she'd be, chivvying time and money out of the other parents.

Basically, she went to school with Rupes (who ended up captaining the First XV rugby team, so he was happy). And in between, she managed to keep the family body and soul together by working as an estate agent.

I have to hand it to Jules: even if she is one of the most irritating human beings I know, she gets stuff done. In fact, she'd make the most wonderful sergeant major.

As for little Viola, her name was always in the Christmas letter Jules sent, so I presumed she was still alive. Although I didn't actually set eyes on her until . . .

At this point, I must apologise to the reader of this memoir for all the 'untils'. There are a lot of things to tell and it's going to be quite difficult to write some of them, so please bear with me.

And, last but not least, there's Chloë. One way and another, I've seen rather a lot of her in the past ten years. It turned out that our schools did have 'dances' together, which turned out to be less *Strictly* and more a sweaty grapple on a makeshift dance floor in the school hall.

As she was still in love with Michel at that point, she'd search me out, asking me to 'protect' her from the attention of other boys, and we'd sit in the corner together sipping our bottles of pop as she poured out her heart and told me how much she was missing him.

She also spent an awful lot of time with all of us at Cedar House. She truly became part of the family – much-needed, as it happened, especially for the little ones.

I calmly bided my time, hoping her Michel fixation would dissipate. It did not. And nor did my fixation with her. I was close enough to her, certainly; she called me her best friend.

But, as every male best friend to a female knows, trying to alter the relationship status from that to the 'something else' I dreamt of every night, seemed to slip further away from my grasp.

When she finished school, she took a gap year and then went off to London to study fashion.

It was when she graduated that the spell Michel had held over her was finally broken. She sobbed onto my shoulder, telling me she still loved him, but that the 'long-distance' relationship had finally taken its toll and it was over between them.

And, around the same time, everything changed for me too.

λβ

Thirty-two

I put down my pen and stretch, feeling sleepy from the sun and beer, plus the exhaustion of recalling the events of the past ten years. I look through what I've written, wondering if I've missed anyone out, and realise that I have. It's me. Or at least, the rest of me, up to date. But I'm too hot and tired and sad to continue.

And besides, a car and the white van have just pulled up on the gravel. I see the van disgorge two men who I recognise immediately as Alexis' sons. And out of the car comes Alexis himself, with a toddler who takes his hand as they walk towards me. Dimitrios and Michel have opened the back of the van and are lifting more boxes out of it.

The little boy – the image of Angelina, I see as he draws closer – looks at me shyly.

'Say hello, Gustus,' his father encourages.

Gustus will not play ball, and hides behind Alexis' long legs.

'We thought that we could put up some lights on the

terrace and hang lanterns from the olive trees in the grove,'
continues Alexis.

'Good idea,' I agree.

'This must be a celebration, yes?' Alexis eyes me.

'Yes,' I say firmly. 'It absolutely must.'

We spend the next couple of hours getting hot and sweaty
again, as the four of us string lines of bulbs from the balconies upstairs and attach them to the pergola. We talk of
nothing much – just man-banter, revolving mainly around
football.

On my travels abroad I have noticed that the mere fact
I am English makes me – to all foreigners, at least – an
acknowledged expert on the Premier League; in particular,
Manchester United, which is the team all the Lisle men
support.

Given I am more of a rugby man myself and I don't
have a personal *entrée* into the bedroom of Wayne and
Coleen Rooney, I struggle to give them the information
they seek. I take furtive glances at Michel, who, if anything,
is even better-looking than last time I saw him. I want to
ask him if he has a girlfriend, a fiancée or even a wife, but
nothing so intimate is mentioned.

Angelina arrives on the terrace with a big jug of home-
made lemonade, and little Gustus. He immediately climbs
onto his father's knee as we sit down in the chairs and
drink thirstily.

'It is odd, is it not, Alex?' Alexis chuckles. 'I had hoped
so much to be a grandfather. Now I am the papa of a little
one and my two sons are still to have children of their
own.'

'Papa, I am only in my early thirties and Kassie is twenty-nine,' reprimanded Dimitrios gently. 'There is plenty of time left. And besides, you work us too hard to have time for children,' he added with a smile.

'You are not married, Michel?' I ask him.

'No,' he answers firmly.

'I think my son is a confirmed bachelor,' Alexis sighs. 'There seems to be no woman who can catch him in her net. And you, Alex? Have you found the love of your life since we last met?'

'Yes,' I reply after a pause. 'I have.'

'Papa.' Gustus opens his mouth and points his finger in it, saying something in Greek.

'So, Gustus is hungry for his supper. We must go home,' translates Alexis. He calls for Angelina, who appears and issues me with instructions that basically run along the lines of not touching anything in the kitchen or the pantry until she is back early tomorrow morning. As if I might eat the whole lot single-handedly in the night.

'Alex, do you wish to come up with us to our house for supper?' Alexis asks me.

'That's very kind of you, but tomorrow will be a very long day and I think I'll stay here and have an early night.'

Alexis picks up a wriggling Gustus in his strong, tanned arms. 'Then we will say good night.'

I watch the family pile into their vehicles and drive off. Dusk is beginning to fall, the sun setting once more over Pandora – just as it has here for the past ten years, its beauty unappreciated by human eyes. I walk into the kitchen and see it is awash with trays and dishes covered with foil, the pantry equally crammed with mysterious desserts of all shapes and sizes. I dole out the moussaka that Angelina has grudgingly told me I can take a slab of for my supper.

I sit and eat my solitary meal on the terrace, and hope that Alexis hasn't thought me rude for refusing his invitation. I just need a night alone to gather my thoughts and my strength for tomorrow.

Then I pull the diary back towards me, thinking that actually, writing it all down might just help.

ALEX'S MEMOIR

'Me' Continued

I spent half of my gap year saving up the money to go travelling by pulling pints of beer in the local pub, and the second half conquering my phobias of possibly every single thing I could imagine.

And developing some more – e.g. foreign travel.

Then I began my philosophy degree at Oxford, in Dad and Genetic Dad's old college. Three years later, when Dad came to see me graduate, there were genuine tears of pride in his eyes as we did the man-hug thing afterwards.

I read in my ten-year-old diary only last night that I couldn't imagine him crying – well, sadly he has cried rather a lot since then.

I continued for another year at Oxford doing an MA (more of *that* year later). And then – just as I had given up on just about everything, and was about to settle for the academic life and turn myself into a 'Dr' and eventually a professor of philosophy – I had an email forwarded on to me, from my own professor.

It was sent from a government department in Millbank,

which I knew was a street slap-bang next door to the Houses of Parliament. In essence, the email was offering me an interview for a job in a government policy think-tank.

I admit that after I'd read it I lay on my narrow bed in my shabby Oxford lodgings and had a laughing fit of humongous proportions. Apparently the year-old government wanted, and I quote, 'to include the brightest young minds on subsequent policy decisions taken for the future of Britain'.

On the agenda was the EU referendum, what to do about Scotland, the NHS, immigration . . .

In other words, THE LOT.

Well!

To be honest, I went along for a laugh, just to say I had, so I could put it on Facebook and Twitter and impress my friends. Especially certain female friends, who just might be looking, even if I didn't know they were.

After all, it was what we'd both dreamt of . . .

I sat there in the swish offices – the very nerve-centre of British government – and looked around excitedly for the red button that would start World War III. Then I craned my neck to the right to see if it was possible to signal directly across from here to the MI6 building just over the Thames.

They asked me lots of questions, which may have been trick ones, as they were incredibly easy to answer. Admittedly, I found it harder than normal to concentrate, as I kept imagining Daniel Craig bursting in to tell me I was giving away highly confidential information to a set of Russian spies. And the shoot-out that would follow as he saved my sad backside.

Sadly, Mark and Andrew – 'Call me Andy' – were a couple of rather dull middle-aged civil servants, who plodded through my hastily-put-together CV, then asked me to give my views on how I thought the 'yoof' of today felt about the Tories being back in power. And what I would do to change their (apparently negative) opinion.

I didn't use many of the fine Kantian quotes I could have trotted out. Instead, I spouted the pocket philosophy I'd understood instinctively as a child, feeling that Mark and 'Andy' might appreciate a man of the people more than a boffin full of psychobabble.

Afterwards, I walked away chuckling at the ridiculousness of it. Having always been a Liberal Democrat voter, then swerving to the left with the rest of the Philosophy Department, here I was being asked to bat for the other side.

Having taken a Snapchat video outside on Millbank proclaiming where I was and what I was doing (probably immediately putting myself out of the running, given how one must surely behave with discretion if one wishes to work for the government; but who cared?), I then walked away past the Palace of Westminster towards the tube station, knowing there wasn't a hope in hell of me being offered the job. If there is one area in which I can't be swayed, it's in my fundamental beliefs:

Equality, Egalitarianism and Economy . . .

Interestingly, I do remember thinking as I walked down the steps to the tube that the last 'E' was the one thing that fitted with the current government manifesto. Fact: If you work hard, you should be rewarded. Fact: The capitalist nations of the world become the richest. Fact: They can then feed, educate and care for the most vulnerable amongst us.

Or they should do, anyway. In Utopia, and in my dreams.

There was no one who knew more philosophical theorems

than me – the incredibly irritating (and endlessly fascinating) thing was that there was always another viewpoint or opinion; one contradicting the other. Sadly, I'd also realised during my four long years of theorising about humanity and the world that knowing as much on paper as a person my age probably could about how people ticked hadn't helped me one iota in my personal life. Which was at that point – to put it mildly – a car crash.

I also wasn't convinced that in practice, it helped anyone else either. In rereading this diary I realise that, despite having called myself a right pain in the backside at thirteen, I haven't changed very much at all. I've simply learnt how to frame my childhood thoughts and feelings in an academic manner.

A week later, a letter arrived on the doormat and told me I'd been offered the job.

And again, I lay on my narrow bed and laughed hysterically. I then read the letter again more carefully, and resorted to language I do not approve of when I looked at the salary they were offering me.

Well. Er . . . blow . . . ME!

And then I cried. Loudly and indulgently and messily, wiping snot from my nose for a good ten minutes.

Pathetic really, but understandable under the circumstances.

Because there was someone I was desperate to share the moment with. But who wasn't with me, and would probably never be again.

I'm sitting here now, a few weeks on, thinking about the fact I will probably have to wear a suit – or at least a smart jacket and chinos – when I begin my new job in under a month's time. It's not in the City, but it's still an office job.

I hope I can use my voice for good when I'm there – I want to, at least. But my study of humans tells me that politicians – and all people for that matter – believe they will do good, and then get corrupted by power. I've actually no idea if you can get corrupted in a think-tank, but I also think anything is possible. Only last week, I received another envelope – this one thick, cream vellum, inviting me to No. 10 Downing Street for a 'cup of tea' with the man himself. Like, the Prime Minister! Apparently, he wants to get to know all his new young think-tankers personally.

He wants to know *me*.

λγ

Thirty-three

I am still chuckling as I put the pen down and wend my way inside the house, closing shutters and switching off light bulbs, which seem to have spawned considerably in number since this afternoon. Finally satisfied that I won't blow up with the house tonight due to the overloading of Pandora's already ancient electrics, I shut myself in my Broom Cupboard, then switch on the fan and sit on the bed. Then I reach down into my rucksack for the remnants of Bee.

'Can you believe I'm going to meet the Prime Minister of Great-Britain-slash-the-United-Kingdom? Or in fact, dear rabbit of mine, Not-so-Great Britain and the Disunited Kingdom, given the Scotland situation,' I add soberly. 'Still, it's pretty bloody impressive at the age of twenty-three.'

Then I stick him under my armpit.

Tonight I need his comfort to face tomorrow.

I am just dozing off when I hear my mobile. I've become used to the missed heartbeat, the sense of dread I feel every time it rings.

'Hello?' I bark.

'Alex, it's me.'

'Oh, hi, Immy. How is everything at home?' I ask nervously, as I always do these days.

'Fine. I mean, Fred and I are here by ourselves at the moment, but Dad knows the arrangements for tomorrow.'

'Are you okay?'

'Yes, I'm okay. Is it all cool at Pandora?'

'I wouldn't say it's cool, as it's bloody boiling. But yes, everything's organised.'

'Cool,' she repeats, and I take heart that at least one word in the English language – however naff – has managed to stand the test of time with fifteen-year-old girls.

'Is the taxi going to be waiting for us when we arrive?' she asks.

'It should be, yes. At least, I've booked it,' I say. 'Has Fred packed?'

'Sort of. You know what he's like – he'll probably forget to bring any clean underwear, but I'm fed up of reminding him. Anyway,' Immy let out a small sigh, 'we'll see you tomorrow.'

'You will. And Immy?'

'Yes.'

'It's going to be a great night.'

'I hope so, Alex, I really do. Night.'

'Night.'

I lie back then, with my head resting on my hands, thinking that this has been so hard for both of them. I've done my best, and so has Chloë, and Dad, but we can never make up for the difficult years. Chloë and I even took them to counselling – we'd all been told that whatever was happening with Mum, we couldn't feel guilty about living our own lives and worrying about our own problems. However irrelevant they might seem in comparison.

I think it helped *me* far more than it helped them, to be honest. I'm always a sucker for that kind of thing.

So now I turn my mind to my own personal relationship issues. And as I do, every muscle in my body tenses as I wince in pain at the thought of *her* not appearing tomorrow night. I've made sure she got the invitation, of course, but I haven't heard a word from her since.

And who could blame her if she didn't come?

Christ! Why is life so bloody complicated?

Yes, we were related on a technicality, and yes, it was complex, but we *loved* each other, for God's sake!

Well. Here I was, in the same bloody house, in the same bed where it had all begun. And surely, despite everything, it had to continue?

Just because . . .

It *did*.

Again, I sleep the sleep of the dead (perhaps not an expression I should currently be using, one way or another) and wake to another glorious morning at Pandora.

At least, I think, as I shower and then find Angelina in the kitchen already hard at work and indicating the cafetière she's prepared for me, I don't need to look up at the skies and ponder whether there'll be rain later.

The rain that seems to be the personification of the Vindictive English God of Outside Events. Every 'happy' photograph I've seen of English people, taken at weddings, fêtes, concerts and the like, does not necessarily mean they are smiling at the camera because they have just married their one true love, or won 'guess the name of the guinea pig'. They are smiling in relief because the entire event hasn't been a total washout.

Maybe I'll get married in Cyprus, which would at least rule out one question mark which always hangs over such a day . . .

Meanwhile, out on the terrace, all is in full swing. Dimitrios and Michel are setting up trestle tables on which to place the beer, wine and glasses. Under the pergola, the long iron table has been covered in a freshly laundered tablecloth ready for Angelina's feast to be laid out.

'Good morning, Alex.' Alexis appears out of nowhere and slaps me hard on the back. 'What time are the first guests arriving?'

'Mid-afternoon, I think. Let's hope everyone makes it.'

'Yes. Let's hope they do.'

From that point on I'm kept busy, and in between I find I am checking my mobile, Facebook, Twitter – would she seriously have tweeted me?! – for news of her impending arrival. I know switching on data roaming will later bankrupt me, and I don't care. But there are no messages. Not even an automated voicemail to tell me I'm owed compensation from an accident I've never had.

I take a quick swim to cool down from the effort it takes to make a party. Checking my watch as I get out, I realise there's less than an hour to go before the first guests arrive. I then recall that my pink shirt – indeed a girly colour and reminiscent of Rupes, but a colour I have surmised makes most women find you irresistible – is screwed up in a ball at the bottom of my rucksack. I search desperately around the house for an iron and ironing board, pieces of equipment I have battled with for years.

Eventually I find a rusting, creaky version in the pantry and, thank God, Angelina sees the screwed-up bit of rag in my hand and takes pity on me, so I leave the shirt in her capable hands.

Then I start to pace around the house like some kind of weird patrolman. Everything is ready. I *know* it's ready. But, like checking my mobile, the pacing has become a nervous twitch. The pounding of my feet gives me something to concentrate on, because I can't bear to concentrate on who may or may not be here tonight.

In this very house. Within a few hours.

I am beside myself – another ridiculous turn of phrase, I think randomly – and decide that I will continue to write the final chapter of my memoir to take my mind off the situation. Even though I will not know the denouement until later tonight.

The first taxi pulls up and, just (or almost) like ten years ago, Jules and Sadie emerge onto the drive. Then Rupes, and little Peaches, Sadie's daughter. My heart catches suddenly as I walk towards them, but I paste a smile onto my face. Three of the passengers look almost exactly the same as they did: Jules hot and cross, Sadie inappropriately dressed, and Rupes as bullish and florid as ever.

At least this time I'm prepared for his handshake, and even pull my stomach in and flex my shoulder muscles to steel myself against having my arm torn off.

'My God, that journey hasn't got any better!' Jules puffs and pants. 'And doubtless the house is in a worse state than

it was before. It's ten years older and bound to have deteri-
orated.'

'We're *all* ten years older, Jules,' I say, hoping she gets
the inference.

Sadie rolls her eyes at me and then gives me a hug.
'Ignore her,' she whispers into my ear. 'She hasn't changed a
bit. Say hello to your godfather, Peaches darling,' she says
to the child standing by her side.

I sweep Peaches into my arms and hug her. 'Hello, sweetheart, how are you?'

She giggles with pleasure. 'I'm fine, Uncle Alex. How are
you?'

'I'm very well, thanks, Peaches.'

As I lie to her, Sadie taps me on the shoulder and indicates another person whom Jules is helping out of the taxi.

'I'm warning you, Alex, if you think Jules is a pain in
the bum, just wait until you meet her new boyfriend,' she
mutters under her breath.

I watch as a man with a scarily similar complexion to
Rupes, but minus the hair and bedecked in a pair of bright
red chinos and checked shirt, dislodges himself from the
front seat of the car.

'My God! He looks old enough to be her father!' I
whisper to Sadie, as he clings onto Jules' arm and attempts
to walk across the gravel towards us.

'He probably is, but apparently he owns half of Rutland
and has an entire stable of thoroughbreds. Jules is a tenant
on his country estate and they met when he came to check
out her, er, frozen pipes,' Sadie smirks.

Jules introduces him to me as Bertie, while he looks up
in horror at the accommodation.

'You told me I should expect the worst, but I'm sure we'll make the best of it,' he says, with possibly one thousand plums in his mouth. 'C'mon Jules, old girl, show me up to our suite!' With that, he slaps her on the bottom and she giggles girlishly. Sadie and I, and even little Peaches, make quiet sick noises.

'Isn't he awful?'

I realise I have completely forgotten Rupes, and turn to find him standing behind us, hands in his pockets. None of us comment; we just turn as red as he is naturally.

'I did tell Mum she should ask if he could come. And she said she'd always slept in a double bed here anyway, so she was sure it would be fine. Anyway, how are you, Alex? Hear you're doing rather well at the moment?'

'I'm okay, thanks, Rupes. And I hear that you're training to be a teacher?'

'Yes.' He laughs loudly and raises his eyebrows at me. 'How ironic can you get, given the last time we were here at Pandora? Hardly Classics, as you know, but since I had to give up professional rugby because of my knee injury, I started coaching and I've really been enjoying it. So I thought, why not? Sadly there's no family money to fall back on, as you know.'

'Well, Rupes, I think you'll make a perfect sports teacher,' I say with feeling. Personally, mine were all trained by the Triads.

'Thanks.'

'Fancy a beer?'

'Why not?' he agrees.

'Sorry to interrupt, Alex, but are we in the same room I was in last time?' Sadie asks.

'Yes. Angelina's put in a camp bed for you, Peaches, just like the one I sleep on in my Broom Cupboard.'

'You sleep in a cupboard?' she asks me, fascinated.

'Not really. It's what you might call an affectionate term, because the room's so small,' I explain to her as we all traipse into the house.

'You stay down here with Rupes, I know where we're going,' says Sadie as she heads towards the stairs.

'Meester Rupes!' Angelina appears in the corridor and I thank my lucky stars, as the last thing I wanted was a DMC with my half-brother, who doesn't even know he *is*. 'How are you?'

'Good, thanks, Angelina,' he says as he kisses her on both cheeks.

'Come into my kitchen, Rupes. I have made you the cakes you like so much last time you was 'ere.'

I follow them into the kitchen, and whilst Angelina fires a barrage of questions at him, I furnish him with a beer. As I listen to him answer politely, I decide that Rupes has definitely calmed down since I last saw him. He'd been crying then, but that had probably been for himself, which happens a lot on such occasions.

I check my watch. It is nearing six o'clock. Just over an hour to official lift-off, when the main protagonists in tonight's drama will make their appearance.

'Rupes, if it's okay, I'm going to go upstairs and take a shower,' I say.

'Of course,' he nods. 'Where am I sleeping?'

'On the sofa in the drawing room, I'm afraid. We're full to the brim tonight.'

I walk away before I can ask him the question that is burning on my tongue. Chances are he won't know the answer anyway, and he may give me the wrong information, which would just make things ten times worse.

So I will hold my peace. I smile wanly to myself, remembering how I once believed it was spelt 'piece' and all that entailed, then walk upstairs to take a shower.

Stepping out, dripping wet, I read a text from Immy that has obviously only just decided to slide through the Cyprus wires.

'*Plane delayed. Now landing at six thirty.*'

Damn! This means they won't be here until at least half past seven, when the party has already begun. What if they're even later?

Downstairs, Jules and Bertie are sitting at one of the small café tables laid out along the terrace. I see they've already helped themselves to wine, and I hear him complaining loudly about the quality of it. I'm just restraining myself from punching him when thankfully, Sadie appears through the French windows.

'Hello, sweetie. Everything ready to go?'

'I think so, yes. We're just missing a number of important guests.'

'I'm sure they'll be here. I think it's a lovely thing you've done to organise this, I really do.'

Sadie gives me a spontaneous hug, and I know she is feeling emotional too. 'By the way' – she lowers her voice as Peaches brushes past them, heading for the bowl of crisps she's just spied on the table – 'you don't think that, er, Andreas will be here tonight, do you?'

'I really don't know. Maybe you should ask Alexis. He's the one who's been in charge of the Cypriot guest list.'

'Right, I will.' She looks across at Peaches stuffing her face with crisps. 'He won't suspect anything, will he?'

I glance at Peaches – a little blonde replica of her father. 'I doubt it,' I lie.

Rupes ambles onto the terrace, and we all turn and stare as we see a car bumping along the gravel towards the house.

'It's Alexis and his family,' I say. 'Right, Rupes, I think it's time to get the bottles of white wine out of the fridge, don't you?'

By seven thirty the terrace is brimming with people I barely remember, but who all seem to know me. Just as I am starting to worry about death by hugging, I feel a light tap on my shoulder.

'Alex! It is I! I am here!'

'Fabio! You made it!' It is my turn to hug him. He's been a tower of strength to all of us over the past few years, especially to my father.

'See? I have brought Dan with me. Now you can meet him for the first time.'

A tall, dark-eyed man who looks – spookily – only a few years older than myself, steps forward and kisses me on both cheeks. 'It's a pleasure to meet you, sir,' he says in a pronounced American accent.

'Please, call me Alex. And it's a pleasure to have you here.'

'It's a pleasure to be here, Alex.'

'So,' Fabio's eyes dart across the terrace, before I answer

Dan with the word 'pleasure' again. 'Where are the rest of you?'

'The plane was delayed, so they're late. I'm hoping they'll turn up before everyone goes home.' I indicate the terrace tensely, and the small band limbering up in the corner of it.

'They will be here, Alex,' Fabio comforted me. 'And now, both of us ought to try the wine your mother's friend makes that I enjoyed so much the last time I was here.'

I take them across to the table, and while I make further small talk about Dan's permanent struggle to learn Italian and wonder if I should get the details of his cosmetic surgeon, I feel my heart drumming in my chest.

Where the hell are they?

I decide to walk across and grab myself a calming beer, but I'm constantly waylaid by guests, and questions from Angelina as to what time should she serve the hot food, and should the band start playing now?

'*Hot, cold, or frozen bloody solid! Who cares?!*' I only just refrain from snapping at her, such is my agitation. Because it really doesn't matter just now.

I have just reached the table with the booze when an arm is put on my shoulder.

'Alex, they've arrived.'

'Thank God,' I say in relief, as I turn and follow Alexis through the crowd. 'How many of them are there?'

'I'm sorry, I didn't notice.'

We both hurry around the house and up to the driveway, now packed with cars. I see shadowy figures emerging from the car in the distance, and count just . . . four. And my heart sinks as I know that this was the last flight in from England tonight.

Immy is the first to reach me. She looks as tense and strained as I feel.

'Sorry, Alex, but there was nothing I could do. I had to sit there at Gatwick, like, pretending it didn't matter if the plane was late. Fred was no help whatsoever. As usual.' She rolls her eyes as a gangly youth – my little brother – wanders towards us.

'Hi, Fred, good flight?'

'Boring,' he says with a shrug.

Currently, this seems to be the only word in his thirteen-year-old vocabulary.

'So, I will go and tell the guests you're here,' Alexis says to Immy. 'You will bring them round, Alex.'

'Yes,' I say, as I look towards the two figures walking slowly towards me, an expression of total surprise on their faces.

'Hi, Mum, hi, Dad,' I say, as I guiltily search behind them for any further figures remaining in the car.

'What on earth is going on, Alex?' asks William as my mother hugs me.

'Well . . . you'll have to wait and see. How are you, Mum?' I look at her, searching her face for clues.

'I'm very well indeed, Alex,' she says as she smiles at me. And it isn't the painful 'I'm not really, actually, but I am pretending for you that I am' type of smile that I've become used to in the past three years. It's one I actually believe.

'Your mum got the final all-clear yesterday,' William says. And again, I see tears brewing in his eyes. 'It's finally over.'

'Oh my God, Mum! That's wonderful news! Wonderful!'

'Did you just say you've got the all-clear?' says Immy from next to me. Even Fred looks as if he's paying attention.

'We didn't want to tell you until we were all together. But I'm going to be fine.'

'For certain, Mum?' Immy clarified, having been given false hope before.

'For certain.'

'Forever?' asks Fred, his bottom lip wobbling like it did when he was little. I move towards him protectively and place a hand on his shoulder, sensing his vulnerability.

'Well, that may be pushing it, but tonight I feel it could be, yes, darling,' Mum says as she kisses him.

Then we all have what is commonly termed a group hug, and have to wipe away the tears to make ourselves presentable.

'Right,' I say, clearing my throat, 'we'd better make a move. A pity Chloë couldn't have joined us. She didn't make it, then?' I say.

'She said she'd try, but you know how demanding her boss can be,' Mum says as I marshal them along the drive towards the house.

'At least she gets free designer clothes, which is more than I get doing my babysitting,' remarks Immy.

'Do you want a free baby, then, Im?'

'Oh, shut up, Fred! You're such a douche.'

'Alex, what exactly *is* going on here tonight?' my mother asks me.

'You'll just have to wait and see.'

'You might have told me, Immy – I'm hardly dressed for

an occasion.' Mum indicates her jeans, flip-flops and white cheesecloth blouse.

'Alex put me on pain of death not to. We've been planning it, like, forever.'

And I realise we can all use expressions like that again now, without flinching.

'I'm so happy, Mum, really,' I whisper to her. 'It's the best news I've ever had.'

'You've been amazing, Alex. Thank you.'

Then we have another, private hug – just her and me. And I try to feel that whatever *didn't* happen tonight, shouldn't really matter in the grand scheme of things.

'So,' I say as I pull myself together and we reach the edge of the terrace, from which a noisy hush is emanating. 'Mum and Dad, this is a present from all of your kids. Happy twentieth wedding anniversary!'

Then I lead them onto the terrace, where everyone shouts the same in Greek and begins to cheer and clap. Champagne corks pop, and I watch my parents being smothered in hugs and kisses, and my mother's delighted face when she sees Fabio and Sadie.

There is no question that I organised this for her. In the bleak years after her diagnosis, when we had no idea if the treatment would work or not, I thought about it many times. Here at Pandora there are so many memories for her, and although some of them are less than happy ones, at least they were forged in the days before hospital beds and pain.

Right now, I can't take in the fact that it is really over. That she is going to *live*.

So tonight, I will do my best to put aside the other

dreadful pain in my heart; the one that is not life or death, yet feels like it. And celebrate – literally – my mother's life.

The evening wears on and the stars shine down on the tiny pinprick of celebrating humanity. The sound of the bouzouki takes me back to that night ten years before, and I hope there will be no similar revelations to spoil the moment when Alexis once again calls for silence and proposes a toast. I drink more beer than I should, to celebrate the joy of my mother's recovery and to drown my private sorrows in equal measure.

'Thank you, darling Alex, for organising the most amazing and beautiful surprise I've ever had.'

My mother has sought me out, and reaches up on tiptoe to put her arms around my shoulders and kiss me.

'That's okay, Mum.'

'Tonight could not have been more perfect,' she says with a smile.

'Are you sure you're absolutely one hundred per cent well, Mum? You wouldn't lie to me, would you?' I ask her again, still struggling to believe it.

'Well, *I* might, as you know,' she smiles. 'But Dad definitely wouldn't. Seriously, Alex, I feel wonderful, I really do. Finally, I can get on with my life again. I'm so sorry I haven't been there for you the way I wanted to be in the past three years. But it seems you've done absolutely fine without me. I'm so proud of you, darling, I really am.'

'Thanks, Mum.'

'Oh, Alex,' Mum turns and points, 'look who's just arrived! Let's go and say hello.'

As I turn around too, and stare in wonder and amazement at the familiar, beloved face smiling at both of us, my heart does one of those dreadful flippy things that contains elements of excitement and fear.

But most of all, *love.*

'Chloë! Oh my God. How did you get here?' Mum asks as we both reach her.

'Don't ask, Helena. We came from Paris.' Chloë grins, hugging her. 'Happy anniversary. Hi, Alex,' she says, kissing me on both cheeks. 'I promised I wouldn't let you down, didn't I?'

'You did, yes,' I reply, not really concentrating on what she says, because standing just behind her is the subject of all my dreams and nightmares in the past year. 'Excuse me.'

'Of course.' Chloë gives me a knowing wink of encouragement.

I walk a few paces to where she is standing alone, half hidden in the shadow of the house.

'Hello,' she says shyly, and then averts her beautiful blue eyes in embarrassment.

'I didn't think . . . I didn't . . .' I swallow hard, feeling tears rise to my eyes and urgently instructing Sergeant Major Brain to send them into retreat immediately.

'I know.' She shrugs. 'It's been' – she looks everywhere but at me – 'difficult.'

'I understand.'

'But Chloë was the one who helped. Talked me out of the place I was in. She's been great, Alex, and I think that maybe we both have a lot to thank her for.'

'Do we?'

'Yes. She's the one who persuaded me to come with her

tonight. And . . . I'm glad I have.' She reaches her slim, pale hand to me, and I raise mine to clasp it. 'I've missed you, Alex. Really, really badly.'

'I've missed you too. Worse than "really, really badly", to be honest. Actually, I'd go as far as gut-wretchingly, or perhaps heart-breakingly, life-threateningly . . .'

'Well.' She giggles. '*You* would. But it's really okay, isn't it? For you and I to be together?'

'Well, it's not exactly the norm, but at least our kids won't end up with six toes if we are. It's just the semantics which were . . .' I swallow hard. 'Complicated. And I'm so sorry I didn't tell you sooner.'

'So am I. But I understand why now.'

I *had* to ask the question before we went any further down this bumpy, hazardous road. 'Are you here because you're prepared to give us another go?' Instinctively, my other hand, the one that isn't holding hers, reaches out to brush a lock of her glorious Titian hair back from her face.

'Well, I'm hoping it'll be rather better than just a *go*.'

'Is that a yes, in Viola language?'

'Yes, but you do understand why I had to take some time to work stuff through? I was . . .' She gulps. 'Broken.'

'I know. And of course I understand.' I edge closer to her, then wrap my arms around her and hug her to me. She melts into me. I kiss her then, and she kisses me back, and I feel an immediate need to do things with her that are entirely inappropriate at my mother and father's twentieth wedding anniversary party.

'Ladies and gentlemen,' booms Alexis' voice from the terrace.

'Come on.' I pull her by the arm. 'We should be there

for the speeches. And by the way,' I add, as I lead her through a sea of people gathering round to listen, 'my mother is completely well. She's got the all-clear.'

'Oh Alex! That's wonderful news!'

'Yes.' I look at her. 'There's been a lot of wonderful news today.'

ALEX'S MEMOIR

Viola

It all began just over a year ago, when my mum called me.

'Alex, sorry to disturb you in the middle of your finals, but there's a letter for you here from Sacha.'

'Is there?'

'Yes, he's in a hospital in London. Dad got a call from Viola a few days ago saying Sacha wanted to see him. It's not good news, I'm afraid. He's had a huge heart attack, apparently, and of course, his liver's shot to pieces . . .'

I remember my mother's voice trailing off, and me thinking how I might not have either blood parent alive by this time next year.

'What does he want?'

'He asked Dad if you would go and see him soon. And I think the accent is on the "soon". Alex, really, it's up to you. I know you've had your fill of hospitals in the past two years.'

'Give me the address of the hospital, and I'll think about it. Okay?'

She did, and I asked her to forward the letter to me. When it arrived two days later, even though I knew what it was likely to contain and had sworn to myself not to let it get to me, of course it did. Sacha wanted to say goodbye.

So, on the Sunday before my finals were due to begin, when everyone else in Oxford was holed up feverishly revising/recovering from a hangover/contemplating suicide, I boarded a train to London and took the underground from Paddington to Waterloo, then walked from there to St Thomas' Hospital.

Hospitals are depressing any day of the week, but somehow on Sundays I've always found them worse. The dull hush was unbroken by the usual bustle of the Monday to Friday routine, and the rank smell of boiled beef and damp cabbage – the sad facsimile of a roast lunch – permeated the air.

I can't say Sacha looked much worse than the last time I'd seen him six years earlier – just even older. Yet he was only the same age as Dad; fifty-five – a virtual teenager in this day and age.

He was in the ICU department, plugged in to all sorts of drips and monitors that beeped and clanked. He wore an enormous oxygen mask with a big pump in the centre of it that made him look bizarrely like an elephant. The kind nurse explained that he wore the mask because his lungs had filled with water after the heart attack, and his heart wasn't up to pumping enough oxygen through them to expel it.

He was asleep when I got there, so I sat quietly by him, taking in for what I knew might be the last time the exponent of the physical seed that had produced me.

As I did so, I saw a young woman – or should I say, an angel of perfection – walking along the ward towards me. Tall and willowy, with unblemished alabaster skin and a heart-shaped face containing pink rosebud lips and startling blue eyes. Her long Titian-coloured hair fell to beyond her shoulders and immediately reminded me of a figure from a Rossetti painting. For a second I genuinely wondered if she was a famous model whose face – and body – I'd seen staring down at me from Adshel boards all over the place.

But as she came closer, I realised it was Viola Chandler. Sweet little Viola; she of the rabbity teeth and freckles, and a penchant for bursting into tears all over me.

'Bloody hell!' I muttered under my breath as she stopped at the end of the bed and stared at me quizzically.

'Alex?'

'Yes,' I managed, having spent the past nine years training my mouth to form actual words when approached by a beautiful woman. 'It's me.'

'Oh my God!'

And then, this exquisite creature walked towards me and threw her arms around me.

'It's so wonderful to see you!' she said as she buried her head in my shoulder – admittedly not the way beautiful women normally greeted me. 'Why are you here? I mean,' she corrected herself, 'it's very nice of you and all that, but . . . ?'

As I looked at the confusion in her eyes, I realised there was every chance that neither Jules nor the elephant man in the bed beside me had actually told her of my genetic link to her father. And here, now, was not the moment if they hadn't. Particularly as, when she pulled away from my chest, my shirt was damp from her tears. And close up, as I looked at her lovely face, I saw the dark circles beneath her eyes and the misery beaming like lasers from her pupils.

Perhaps, I thought, I'd mention it casually to her over coffee later. Or something.

We talked in whispers about how serious the situation was – but she said that she hadn't given up hope.

'Miracles do occur, don't they, Alex?'

And as she looked at me in desperation, just as she had all those years ago – a look that held an irrational belief that somehow, I'd be able to make everything better, know all the answers – I nodded.

'Where there's life, there's always hope, Viola.'

She told me that Sacha had been slipping in and out of consciousness for the past forty-eight hours. That she'd called her mother – who had refused to come – and Rupes, who'd said he might.

'But I doubt he will,' she sighed. 'He's never forgiven Daddy for what he did that night in Cyprus. Embarrassing Mum like that at the party, and then leaving us virtually destitute.' We left Sacha's bedside and headed downstairs to have a coffee in the cafeteria. 'But surely, whatever's happened in the past, a son should come to see a father on his . . . death-bed.'

'Yes.' I gulped at her remark, realising then that she definitely *didn't* know.

'Thank you so much for coming to see him, Alex. Your dad came last week too, but apart from that . . .' She shrugged. 'No one else. Not much to show for a life, is it?'

She then told me how she'd been here at the hospital for the past two weeks, sleeping in the relatives' room, not wanting to leave Sacha alone.

'It means I won't be taking my first-year exams at uni next week, but they've said that under the circumstances, they'll be prepared to give me a predicted grade, based on the assessed stuff I've done so far.'

'Where are you?'

'I'm at UCL, not far from here. I'm doing English Literature and French. Luckily, a lot of it is essay-based, so I shouldn't come out of this year too badly. You know, Alex, it was you giving me *Jane Eyre* that began it,' she said softly. And for the first time, a ghost of a smile appeared on her lips. 'I've always meant to write to you and tell you thank you, but . . .' She sighed. 'Life goes on, doesn't it?'

I nodded in agreement.

'Even our families have lost touch over the years. I suppose it's because Dad left, and it was always the friendship between him and your dad that linked us all. And maybe Mum just wanted to make a fresh start after the divorce.'

That, and other things I could think of.

'How is your mum?' I asked politely.

'Oh, the same as ever.'

For a while she chatted on randomly about the past nine years, and I listened to her. And looked. I felt my heart begin to do that terrible hammering thing it had done with Chloë all those years before.

'I did hear about your mum. I'm so sorry, Alex. How is she?'

'Oh, you know, good days and bad. The first treatment didn't work and it came back elsewhere, but they seem pretty hopeful they've got it nuked this time,' I replied, trying my best to sound light-hearted.

'God, Alex.' Viola bit her lip. 'We are a pair, aren't we?'

Oh Viola, I do hope . . . I do so hope that we could be.

I nodded sagely, and then she said we'd better go back upstairs to ICU and check on her dad.

We sat by Sacha, me willing him not to wake up, see me and do some great 'Oh my God! It's my long-lost son come to see me and say goodbye' thing. Viola's obvious exhaustion and fragile emotional state made it essential that he didn't. So, after an interminable hour and a half as he lay inertly between us, I eventually stood up.

'I'm so sorry, Viola, but I'm going to have to leave now. It's finals week in Oxford for me, you see, and . . .'

'Alex, you don't need to explain. I'll walk you to the door.'

'Okay.'

I then bent over the man who was technically my father and kissed him on the forehead, trying to think all the thoughts I needed to at a seminal moment like this, because I knew instinctively that it was goodbye.

None came, because my head was so full of *her*.

With one last glance back at him, I followed Viola out of the ward.

'I just can't tell you how grateful I am that you came,' she said again as we stood on the busy street outside the hospital. She lit a roll-up, her hands shaking slightly as she did so. 'It's just like you to do something like this, Alex. I've never forgotten how kind you were to me that summer, when everything was so difficult.'

'Really, Viola, London's not that far from Oxford,' I replied, feeling like an absolute jerk that she thought I'd visited Sacha simply because I was a nice person.

'I'll tell him you came if he wakes up. He always was very fond of you. I remember telling him you'd got into Oxford – you know how your dad, being my godfather, always sends

me a cheque and a card at Christmas with all the news – and
Dad looked so proud! I literally thought he might burst into
tears. Anyway, you'd better go and get your train.'

'Yes. I'd better.'

'I . . . would it be okay if I took your mobile number? So
that I can text you and let you know . . .' Her voice trailed off
as she dug around for her phone, head down to hide the
tears I knew were brimming in her gorgeous eyes.

'Of course.'

We did the exchange, and I said we'd keep in touch.

'Oh Alex, I . . .'

Then I did the only thing I could, and pulled her into my
arms. And held her there. And hoped – irrationally – it could
be forever.

'Bye, Alex,' she said eventually.

And I walked away, knowing I was lost.

I called Dad as soon as I arrived home in Oxford, told him I'd
seen Viola at the hospital and how Sacha hadn't properly
regained consciousness for the past couple of days. And then
I asked him whether Sacha had ever told either of his children
about me being his son.

'I doubt it, Alex,' he said. 'Rupes loathes him anyway, and
as you know, Viola adores him. I wouldn't have thought Sacha
wanted to destroy his relationship further with either of
them, particularly Viola. She's been pretty much all he's had
over the past few years.'

'What about Jules? Do you think she'd have said anything?' I asked, for the first time in my life hoping that she
would have opened her big trap and spilled the beans.
Because it would mean I wouldn't have to.

'I'll have to ask Mum about that. She was the one who had the conversation with her after the shit hit the fan in Cyprus. Again, I doubt it. Jules may be difficult, but given they had just lost their home, their money and their father, I don't think she'd have wanted to bring an illegitimate half-brother into the mix. God, sorry, Alex,' he apologised immediately, realising how blunt he'd sounded.

'That's okay, Dad.' I knew he always said it like it was.

'Anyway, I'll ask Mum. And best of luck with your exams this week.'

He did ask my mother, who duly called me and said that Jules had told her she wouldn't tell Rupes and Viola.

'If I remember, she said, "It's his job to give them the bad news, not mine, but I'm sure he won't as he's too much of a coward." Or something like that,' she added.

'Do you think I should tell Viola, Mum?'

'Not at the moment, no. From the sound of things, she's got enough to cope with. There's no rush, is there?'

'No. Thanks, Mum. Speak soon.'

That night I decided I would go to London as soon as my finals were over and tell Viola the truth. After all, the situation was hardly my fault.

But then, as shitty fate would have it, at five a.m. on the day of my last exam, I felt my phone vibrate next to me. It was a missed call from Viola, and the voicemail message brought the news I'd been expecting. I rang her back immediately, and listened to her sobs. I asked her who was with her, and she said there was no one.

'Rupes says he's too busy. And I have to do all these awful things, like get death certificates, find an undertaker and . . .' There was an odd sound on the line, and I knew she was wiping her hand across her nose. 'Stuff.'

'Listen, my last exam finishes at midday. I'll get on a train to London and come and help you.'

'No, Alex! You should be celebrating tonight! Please, don't worry . . .'

'I'll text you when I'm on the train and meet you outside the hospital. Just hang on till then, sweetheart. Okay?'

So instead of spending a solid twelve hours haunting the bars and clubs of Oxford with the rest of the third-year undergraduates, I found myself up in London going through the grim legalities of the death of my father with his heart-broken daughter.

Who wasn't really his daughter. And who didn't know that I, actually, *was* his son . . .

And she was so bloody grateful, and alarmingly gorgeous in her grief. She looked at me that day as if I was her saviour, her one touchstone, and kept thanking me over and over again, until I wanted to vomit from the deceit of it all.

Although it wasn't really deceit, because whether or not Sacha was my father, I would have been there for her. All I wanted to do was protect her, an instinct I still remembered vividly from our time together at Pandora. And given the state she was in, there was no way in the world I could follow my better instincts and tell her the truth. Because I thought it might break her.

So, I didn't.

That evening, we repaired to a grotty pub somewhere in Waterloo and I sank three pints to Viola's two glasses of white wine. She laid her head in the crook of my arm, exhausted, and I tried to concentrate on lists of things to be done the following day.

'Why are you being so kind?' she asked me suddenly, turning her precious pink and white (now puffy and pale) face up to me.

'I just . . . wanted to.' I shrug, for once lost for words. 'Another drink?' I said as I stood up.

'Thanks.'

I came back to the table, having already slugged back a third of the new pint, comforting myself that I'd have been doing far worse damage to my liver tonight in Oxford. Sitting down, she took hold of my left arm and manoeuvred it around her right shoulder, so she was once again cuddled into me.

'We're sort of like family, aren't we, Alex?'

I almost choked on my beer.

'I mean, your father is my godfather, and Dad and he knew each other from when they were kids. And we spent lots of time at each other's houses when we were younger, didn't we? Alex, can I ask you something?'

Oh Christ. 'Yup.'

'That summer at Pandora . . . were you in love with Chloë?'

I looked down at her with a frown. 'How do you know?'

She giggled then. 'Because I was jealous!'

'Jealous?'

'Wasn't it obvious? I had a massive crush on you.' She waggled her finger at me and I realised she was tipsy, having probably eaten nothing for days.

'To be honest, Viola, I didn't realise.'

'Not even after I'd spent approximately two hours and twenty minutes colouring in that envelope with the hearts and flowers? Not to mention how long it took me to write that poem I gave you.'

'I remember it.' God, *I was glad I did*. 'It was called "Friends".'

'Yes. But surely you read between the lines?'

'No.' I looked down at her. 'You were only ten years old at the time.'

'As a matter of fact, I was nearly eleven, only two years and four months younger than you,' she answered primly.

'You were still a little girl!'

'Just as Chloë probably thought you were a little boy.'

'Yes,' I sighed. 'She probably did.'

'It's quite funny really, isn't it?'

'Is it?'

'Sort of, yes. You dreaming of Chloë, me dreaming of you?'

'I suppose it is,' I said, wanting to reassure her that that bit of my plot needed to be swiftly and completely edited out, because it was no longer valid.

She then sat up straight and looked at me. 'Are you still in love with her?'

'No.'

It was the easiest reply I'd ever given.

'Right.'

Then she looked at me as though I should elucidate further. I couldn't, without telling her that she herself was the one who'd finally broken the spell, just a few days ago. Which was, at that moment, the most inappropriate thing I could say, given the reason we were sitting there in the first place. Any sniff in the future of me having taken advantage of the current situation – once she finally knew the truth about my sudden reappearance in her life – would mean me and my poor heart were dead ducks.

'There's nothing more to say.'

I was relieved when she settled back into the crook of my arm. 'Good. I mean, it's a bit weird, having a crush on your stepsister, isn't it?'

'I don't know, Viola,' I said, trying to keep the wobble out of my voice – and boy, did I need to give her a convincing answer. 'I mean, I wasn't related by blood to Chloë or anything, was I? And let's face it, in the olden days, most small communities intermarried. Not to mention generations of royal families. Cousins would often marry cousins – it was the thing to do. As I'm sure you know from all the Jane Austen novels you must have read since I last saw you,' I added, just for good measure.

'Yes, I suppose so. Actually, I've seen quite a lot of Chloë recently,' she said, out of the blue.

'Have you?'

'I'm sure you know she's been interning in London at *Vogue*, and she sweetly texted me and invited me for lunch when I first arrived at uni. I think it was your dad that asked her to.'

'Oh,' I said.

'Yeah, and honestly Alex, I understand why you've always had a thing for her. She really is drop-dead gorgeous. And so sweet, as well. Do you know, she actually asked me if I'd like to come in to *Vogue* and meet the fashion editor? She said I'd make a fantastic model. I mean, I knew she was just being kind, 'cos who would ever think I was beautiful?' Viola chuckled at the very thought.

Me, Viola, and in fact, every man – and woman – who passes you in the street.

But I understood why Viola thought Chloë was only being kind. Talk about an ugly duckling turning into a swan.

'She's off to Paris in the autumn,' Viola continued. 'She's been offered a job as a junior designer in a fashion house there. It's a new one with an unpronounceable name. Jean-Paul someone, I think . . .' Her voice trailed off suddenly, and she swallowed hard. 'Oh dear, I just remembered.'

'What is it?'

'Sorry . . . I mean, I forgot for a bit, and that was lovely. But Daddy died this morning, didn't he? Oh dear, oh dear . . .'

Then she burrowed her face back into my armpit, onto which I hoped I'd sprayed enough deodorant to overcome the rank smell engendered by Final Exam, plus Her, plus Genetic Dad dying today.

'Can I get you something to eat?' I asked, trying to say something practical, like Real Dad would do.

'No, thank you,' came the whisper from my armpit.

'Viola,' I continued in the same 'Dad' vein. 'I really think you should get some sleep. You must be exhausted.'

At this, she emerged from my armpit and looked at me, and I watched her try to gather herself together. 'Yes, I should,' she replied staunchly. 'And you must be getting back to Oxford.'

'I don't have to go back to Oxford, it's all over there now until September. I'm going to stay at Mum and Dad's apartment tonight. I called them on the train to ask if I could.' I looked down to check my watch. 'I should make a move, actually, as the crazy old woman who holds the keys and lives in the basement goes to sleep at ten o'clock and I won't be able to get in.'

'Of course,' she said. 'We'd better go.'

I watched her drain her wine, her cheeks losing the blush of alcohol as she stood up, and the frown creases on her forehead reappearing. We walked out of the pub in silence.

'Well then, thanks again, Alex. You've just been amazing.' She pecked me on the cheek. 'Good night.'

'Viola!' I said as she pulled away from me. 'Where are you going?'

'Home,' she said forlornly.

'Who's there for you?'

This time she shrugged without words.

'Look, do you want to come home with me . . . I mean, surely you need some company tonight?'

'It's so sweet of you, Alex, but really, I think you've done enough.'

Viola, I will never, ever have done enough for you. In fact, I haven't even begun 'doing' yet . . .

I held out my hand then, and grabbed her and pulled her back. 'Don't be silly. There is no way on earth I'm leaving you alone tonight.'

And then it was me who took her into my arms, and as her lips puckered up towards my face, it was also me who pretended not to notice. And me who clumsily put my own mouth to her delicate little ear as I hugged her.

When we arrived at the apartment in Bloomsbury, which, as it happened, was only a few streets along from Viola's halls of residence, I managed to gain access by enticing the little old lady to come to the door of her basement flat. She handed me the key through the narrow opening that the series of chains on the inside of her door provided; her bony arm reminded me of the twig Hansel stuck out to fool the witch, in the fairy tale.

I showed Viola the bathroom, which she said she needed. I was in the bedroom taking a jumper out of my holdall – the apartment was chilly – when Viola walked in behind me and fell onto the bed.

'Sorry, Alex, but oh my God . . . I am soooo tired.'

'I know.' I watched her as she closed her eyes. 'Are you sure you shouldn't have something to eat?' I asked her as I looked at her fabulous self, lying there like a nymph on the bed – hair splayed across the pillow, long legs elegantly and photogenically placed, even though she'd literally thrown herself onto it.

There was no reply. She'd gone to sleep.

So I went and made myself a strange supper of baked beans and a can of tuna I'd found in the cupboard, and ate it in the sitting room, watching the BBC news (*why?*). As I ate I tried to put my brain into rational order and plunder my own psyche for a reaction to Sacha dying. But Viola had scrambled my rationale, and every time I thought about Genetic Dad lying in a freezer drawer in a morgue, and how I felt about it, instead I saw her, and my mind went off at another tangent altogether.

Besides, beyond the fact that I felt sadness for a life brought to an end far too soon, the terrible truth was, using Sondheim's famous lyric . . . that I felt nothing.

Then I heard Viola whimpering through the thin stud wall, and went to her.

'What is it?' I asked, immediately chiding myself for the ridiculousness of the question.

She didn't answer. I groped in the dark for a square of free mattress on the edge of the bed so I didn't sit on bits of her.

'I had a dream . . . that he was alive . . .'

'Oh Viola.'

'I know he isn't.' I felt her arm swipe across her eyes and cheeks, wiping away the tears, and wished then that I could feel the same pain for our father as she did, but I couldn't. And that made me feel even worse.

'I'm so sorry, sweetheart,' I said softly, 'but he isn't.' And at that moment I cursed Jules and Rupes. No matter what Our Father Who Art in Heaven had done or not done, he was hardly Saddam or Stalin or Mao. Or even a seriously bad human being. He was just flawed and selfish and weak, and rather pathetic. And surely a mother and a brother – adoptive or not – should be here to support the one family member who had loved Sacha enough to be devastated by his departure? 'It's only me, I'm afraid.'

'Oh Alex, don't say that.' The hand that had been wiping away her tears reached for mine, and I extended it into the near-darkness. It was taken, and squeezed. Very, very tightly. 'I didn't mean it like that. I know Daddy's dead. I meant that you don't need to be sorry that it's only you. Of all the people on Earth, I can't think of anyone I'd like more to be here with me now. It's like some kind of surreal dream. Really.'

She squeezed my hand even tighter as a sort of extra emphasis on the last word.

'Alex?'

'Yes, Viola?'

'Would you . . . Would you come and give me a hug?'

Christ!

''Course I would.' So I stood up and made my way round to the other side of the bed, groped again for a spare bit of mattress, then lay down next to her. She snuggled into me as if we were two pieces of a jigsaw puzzle, separated for years in different boxes, then finally put together. My arm moved to her tiny waist and my knees did a bendy thing and fitted in perfectly behind hers.

'Thank you,' she said eventually, just as I was thinking she'd probably gone to sleep.

'For what?'

'For being here. For being you.'

'That's okay.' Then I *really* thought she'd gone to sleep, as there was silence for an awfully long time. And believe me, I was counting the seconds.

'Alex?' she murmured drowsily.

'Yes?'

'I love you. It sounds corny, but I always have. And I think I always will.'

The worst thing was, even though every brain cell and sinew in me was desperate to reciprocate the words, I felt I couldn't. Because I was again thinking about how she might feel when she found out the truth.

That night was one of the most torturous of my life. And it wasn't because I had just lost my father – rather that I had just found my future. All night I lay there, wide awake, as Viola slept fitfully in my arms. Every time she stirred, I'd raise the hand that was around her waist to her silken hair. And as she whimpered, I'd stroke it and she'd go back to sleep.

'I love you,' I mouthed into her ear. 'I love you.'

To be fair, I defy any man to lie for an entire six hours with one of the most gorgeous females on the planet in their arms without feeling illicit carnal desire – even leaving aside the complexity of the 'illicitness' of my relationship with Viola.

Viola . . . I must have been hallucinating at some point, as I suddenly saw an instrument floating across my vision, made of shiny, nut-brown wood and complete with strings.

Violin, cello . . . trumpet! Perhaps I did doze on and off that night, but it wasn't very deeply, as I remember thinking at one point that maybe we could call our first-born 'Harp'. But then I remembered that we'd only have to add an 'er' to end up with the same name as a child spawned by a famous footballer and his equally famous wife.

Drum? Or how about Bassoon?

At some point, I must have really fallen asleep, because the next thing I knew, there was a strong smell of coffee being floated under my nose.

'Alex?' My Titian muse was upright above me, her hair wet from the shower. She proffered a mug. 'Wake up.'

'I am! I mean, I will.'

'Here, I made you some coffee.' She put it down on the table beside me, then walked to the other side of the bed and sat on it cross-legged, a pad and pen in her lap. 'Okay: so what was it you said we had to do today?'

Sacha's funeral was held in the chapel of Magdalen, his and Dad's old college. And now, of course, mine. I admit to having pulled a few strings when Viola mentioned how lovely it would be to hold it there. Given that Sacha's life was hardly going to stand out against the achievements of his fellow alumni, I had a word. (There had to be some advantages to doing philosophy for the past three years; it had included a heap of incredibly dull theology lectures given by the college chaplain.)

Between us we managed to get at least thirty people to attend – the Pandora posse, plus a number of oldies that Dad had managed to convince to come and swell the numbers, promising (I'm sure) a serious piss-up in the college bar afterwards. Whoever and however, they duly arrived.

Just as I was walking towards my parents, Viola took my hand and insisted that I come and sit in the front pew with her. Rupes sat on my other side, and Jules on Viola's.

'Alex has been wonderful,' she told them both.

So in the end, there I was on the front pew, mourning my father next to my half-brother – who wept like a bloody baby – and Viola, my, er . . . well, what the hell *was* she to me?

I spent most of the service pondering this conundrum. And in the end – though I decided I should double-check on the internet to confirm it – I deduced that she was actually nothing at all. Which meant, I thought in relief, that it was possible for her to be *everything* to me in the future. And that made me feel much better.

Whatever Mum felt about me being plonked in the centre of a Chandler sandwich at Sacha/Alexander's funeral like the proverbial cuckoo in the nest, she didn't say. She sat with William, Chloë, Immy and Fred just behind us.

I kept in the background at the wake, feeling Jules' eyes upon me, whether real or imagined. Although at one point she did thank me for being so kind to Viola.

Having recovered from his tears, all Rupes could ask me was whether I thought there'd be a will. I assured him that there wasn't. Viola and I had already checked that out, and Sacha hadn't even made one (thank God).

Our father had nothing left to leave anyone.

My mother came up to me just before they left. 'Viola says you've been wonderful.'

'Not really, Mum.'

'You haven't told her yet, have you?'

I shook my head.

'Alex.' She took my hands in her desperately bony ones, and I thought how fragile she looked. 'Please, learn from my mistakes. As soon as you can is best . . .'

Then she kissed and hugged me with all the strength she possessed, which at the time wasn't very much, and said goodbye.

That night, I'd managed to secure two rooms in college – one for me and one for Viola. It was obvious she'd drunk far too much, and alcohol and emotion had mixed together to form a lethal combination of false euphoria and despair.

She babbled on about how she hated – yes, *hated* – her mum. Apparently, Jules had once had too much to drink, and said it was Sacha who'd wanted to adopt her.

'From now on, she can go fuck herself,' Viola announced. 'I never want to see her, or that idiot of a brother, ever again!'

I knew she didn't really mean it – she was just distraught and exhausted – but I understood her sentiment. And then she fell onto the bed in *my* room, not hers. And again, sobbed pitifully and asked me to hold her.

And my resolve to tell her the truth disappeared.

Not tonight, I thought, *tomorrow* . . .

And the truth was, tomorrow never came. It. Just. Didn't. And then there was a night a couple of weeks later, when I'd suggested to her that it might do her good to get away, and why didn't she come with me to a rather grand house party I'd been invited to in Italy by a friend of mine from Oxford. There, truth be told, my resolve left me completely. The host simply assumed that we were a couple. And there, in our beautiful Florentine bedroom, we made love for the first time.

After that everything was so incredibly perfect that I just couldn't bear – like my mother before me – to impart the terrible news. And so it went on, and on . . . and with it going on, my guilt built up until I became someone who looked like Alex from the outside, but in fact personified a small, ugly lying troll of deceit.

Those few months – ostensibly – were the best of my life. I was working in London for the summer, having secured myself an internship at the British Library in King's Cross, documenting and filing the hard copies and digital details of philosophical works. Mum and Dad had lent me their little apartment in Bloomsbury for the duration.

During the day I handled works of literary art and by night, Viola, who was the most perfect physical work of art I could ever imagine.

Having refused to go home to her mother's cottage for the summer, as she wasn't speaking to either Jules or Rupes, Viola found herself a job at a supermarket round the corner. Then she asked tentatively if she could move in with me, as she had nowhere to live. And I readily agreed.

Some mornings, as I cycled – yes, cycled – off down the Euston Road to work, I felt like something out of a novel. My world was perfect.

Except for the fact I was living a lie.

Every day I sat in a basement surrounded by books full of wise words, knowing that every last one of them, from Sophocles to the modern self-help versions, would tell me I must 'fess up. And every evening, I'd prepare myself on the wacky race back home to her, swearing to myself that tonight would be the night.

And then I'd arrive and there she would be, having made something yummy for supper with all the almost-out-of-date food bargains she'd brought home from the supermarket. And looking so lovely and so fragile that I just . . . *couldn't*.

Eventually an autumn chill entered the air, and Viola moved into the rabbit hutch she'd be living in for her next year at uni, and I began packing to return to Oxford to do my MA.

Both of us were as miserable as hell at the thought of our love-nest being disrupted and torn apart by a mere thing called life. By that time, we'd named all our babies and arranged our wedding, which wasn't really so stupid anymore, given the fact that we were now both in our twenties: it was perfectly possible that it *would* happen. We were attached by some kind of invisible glue, and yet neither of us had really said much to anyone about the new and wonderful world we had discovered with each other. Just in case they spoilt it.

Even though it was under an hour from London to Oxford, and we'd already arranged a schedule which involved one of us travelling to the other on alternating weekends, I remember the last night together being as painful as if I was sailing for the Indies and wouldn't be back for three years – if ever. We had forgotten what it was like to exist without each other.

The Michaelmas term passed in a blur of missing her, and my normally invincible concentration flew out of the window as I sat in a dreamy daze during lectures and tutorials. Comfortingly, Viola was just as bad, and when Christmas arrived, I asked Mum and Dad if she could come home with me. She was adamant she didn't want to spend the holiday with Jules and Rupes.

'I always went to Daddy's flat to keep him company, you see,' Viola explained. 'I was all he had.'

My mum, who thankfully seemed to be recovering well from her final treatment, pounced on me when we arrived and told me again I *must* say something. And again, I promised I would, but then . . . it was Christmas, after all. And Viola, ensconced in the bosom of our loving and welcoming family, looked as happy and relaxed as I'd seen her since Sacha died.

So I didn't.

In the New Year, we went back to our term-time routine, me having already decided that I would do my best to get a job in London when I finished my MA. I didn't particularly care if I had to sweep the streets, as long as I could hold Viola to me every night when I arrived home, dusty and smelly.

Easter came, and Viola had to go off to some French literature exchange thing for a month. We spent the night before she left in the Bloomsbury flat. She asked to borrow my holdall, and while she packed I went out to buy a bottle of wine and an Indian takeaway as a treat.

When I arrived back, I called out to her as I walked along the corridor and went into the sitting room. And there she was, sitting on the floor cross-legged, holding the letter Sacha had written to me just before he died.

My heart sank right down through my body and lay in a pulsating, terrified mass at my feet.

'I . . . how did you find it?' I asked.

'It was in the front pocket of your holdall.' Her face was tear-stained and grey. 'It's all been a lie, hasn't it?'

'No, Viola, of course it hasn't been a lie!'

'Well, it has as far as I'm concerned,' she whispered, almost to herself. 'There I was thinking you cared enough about my father to come to the hospital that day . . . Jesus! The number of people I've told how marvellous you were . . . when you were there for *you*! Not me!'

'You're right,' I agreed. 'That first day I came because I felt I should. But the minute I saw you walking towards me across the ward, everything changed.'

'Please, Alex, can you just stop lying!'

'Viola, I understand this is a shock, but these last few months, all we've shared . . . how can that be a lie? How can it?'

'Because you're not who I thought you were. "Caring, sharing Alex", who all the time was pretending to be there for me . . . And you know the worst thing of all?'

I could think of many 'worst' things, but I refrained from saying any of them.

'No.'

'I'm actually envious of you. Because *you* were his real flesh and blood, and I wasn't.'

'Viola, seriously, he meant nothing to me—'

'Oh, thanks!'

'I didn't mean it like that! But really, I was totally horrified when I originally found out I was his son. I mean,' I checked myself, 'in shock.'

'Like I am now.'

'Yes.' I held onto that lifeline, and walked towards her. 'Of course you are. It's a dreadful thing to have discovered and Viola, I'm so, so sorry. You have no idea how many times I've tried to tell you, but you were so distraught, I couldn't bring myself to say the words. And then you . . . we were happy. So happy that I didn't want to spoil it. Can you understand?'

She rubbed her nose in the painfully cute way she always did, and shook her head viciously. 'At the moment, I can't understand anything. Except for the fact that I'm in some sort of weird relationship with a . . . relative!'

'Viola, there's not a shred of common blood between us. As you well know.'

'And my father . . . how could he have done this?! Christ, I worshipped him, Alex. You know I did. No wonder my poor mother hates him.' She looked up at me then. 'Does she know?'

'Yes.'

'Since when?'

'It all came out in those last few days at Pandora. Apparently, she'd always known.'

'Jesus Christ! It's like my whole life is a lie!'

'Really, Viola, I understand it might feel like that, but—'

'And what about your mother?' She rounded on me. 'What the hell was the sainted Helena, as my mother always called her, doing shagging my dad?'

'Look, it's a long story. Why don't I open the wine, and —'

'No!' She looked at me with what I can only describe as complete derision. 'Even *you* can't make this one better,

565

Alex. And the worst thing is, I trusted you above everyone, but you've lied to me along with the rest of them. And, like, about the most important thing in my life! I thought you *loved* me, Alex. How could you have been with me for all these months and *known*?'

'I . . . oh God, Viola, I'm so, so sorry. Please,' I begged her, 'try to understand why.'

'I have to go. I can't cope with any more of this. I need to get my head together, try to think.'

I watched her as she stood up and reached for the holdall, which I noticed with horror was already packed.

'Please, Viola – I beg you! At least let's talk about it.'

She walked straight past me, out of the sitting room and towards the front door.

'I . . . *can't*.' I watched as her lovely eyes filled with further tears. 'It's not just you that's been living a lie, it's me. I just don't know who I am anymore.'

'Will you be coming back?' I asked her. 'I love you, Viola, so much! You have to believe me.'

'I don't know, Alex. Bye.'

And with that, she opened the door and walked out, crashing it shut behind her.

In retrospect, the only thing that night that stopped me from drinking myself into oblivion, with perhaps a few bottles of pills thrown in for good measure, was the fact my mum called me out of the blue to say hello. Perhaps she had simply sensed something.

As usual, she had instinctively been the first person I'd thought of calling in the terrible silence after Viola had left.

But as any child with a sick parent will know, one doesn't feel one should burden them with minuscule problems like one's entire world collapsing. After all, my mother was living each day with the possibility of hers ending completely.

As it was, I sobbed – and then sobbed some more – down the line to her. And then two hours later, there she was, like an angel of mercy on the doorstep. We talked a lot that night, as she cradled her big son in her arms, about the parallels between her situation with William and mine with Viola. Of course, she took full responsibility for causing it in the first place, which in truth, she did. But at least if there were any remaining shreds of doubt as to why she had never confessed to William after she'd seen Sacha at the wedding, they were banished completely. Because I now understood completely why she hadn't:

It was called *fear*.

'Would you like me to speak to her?' she suggested.

'No, Mum, I have to fight my own battles.'

'Even if your current battle originated from what I did?'

'I don't know,' I sighed. 'All I know is that I love her, and I can't bear to even begin to contemplate a life without her.'

'Give her time, Alex. She's got some serious stuff to work out, and remember that she's still grieving for her father. It's a good thing she's going away to France. It'll give her some headspace. She's seeing Chloë in Paris, apparently.'

'God, Mum,' I shook my head, 'how can I deal with this?'

'Because you have to. One of my nurses once told me that people are only given in life what they can cope with,' she mused.

'Unless they can't, and commit suicide,' I said morosely,

as I lay with my head on her knee and she stroked my hair as if I was still a child.

'Well, I think she's right. Take me, for example. Yes, there's been pain and misery, but I know it's made me a better person. And probably everyone in the family, too. Even though it's been hardest on Immy and Fred, in the long run, it will almost certainly have made them more independent and stronger. And of course, your father's been wonderful.'

I looked at Mum and saw the love shining bright in her eyes, which then made me think of my own *lost* love, and got me depressed all over again.

'I often think of life as a train journey,' Mum said suddenly.

'In what way?'

'Well, there we are, chugging along towards the future, and then there are those occasional moments where the train pulls into a pretty station. And we're allowed to get off and order a cup of tea. Or in your case, Alex, a pint of beer,' she chuckled softly. 'And we sit there drinking it for a while, looking at the lovely view and feeling still and peaceful and content. I think those are the moments most human beings would describe as "happiness". But then of course, you have to get back on the train and continue your journey. But you'll never forget those moments of pure happiness, Alex. And they're what give us all the strength to face the future: the belief that they'll come again. Which they will, of course.'

Wow, I remember thinking, *perhaps it wasn't just my father from whom I inherited my philosophical meanderings. For an amateur, that really was pretty good.*

'Well, I've just sunk about one thousand "pints of beer" with Viola over the past few months. And I'd really like to sink a hundred thousand more,' I mumble miserably.

'You see?' My mother smiled down at me. 'You already have hope that you will.'

λδ

Thirty-four

As I stand here alone on the terrace – Viola has gone upstairs with Chloë to freshen up – I am struggling to believe that life has given me a second chance, that she is back. I want to run to the nearest church, go down on my knees and give thanks to whichever deity has granted it to me. And swear I will learn from my mistakes.

It's all we humans can do.

I also understand that my own personal traumas – and those of the rest of the Pandora posse – are minor compared to the suffering happening elsewhere in the world. None of us have experienced war or famine or genocide.

My ten years' worth of diary is merely a snapshot of small lives lived in a vast universe. But they are *our* lives, and our problems are big to us. And if they weren't, then I doubt humanity would still be around, because, as my mother so wisely said to me (and I'm sure Pandora would agree) we have been granted the innate gift of hope.

I watch the crowd begin to dance as the band moves

into party mode. I see Jules on the floor with Bertie, and Alexis with Angelina. I then notice a familiar figure staring intently at little Peaches, who is dancing with her mother.

Andreas – or Adonis, as Mum and Sadie used to call him – her father.

I gulp, wondering if I am having some weird, karmic out-of-body experience and revisiting that moment when Sacha first set eyes on *me* at Mum and Dad's wedding all those years ago. Perhaps I will talk to Sadie later. Try and give her the benefit of my experience on the subject. The 'subject' which has been the cause of the deepest pain for most of those (who are not Cypriot) gathered here tonight.

The spectre at the feast – the one who is *not* here – is, of course, my father. Sacha – Alexander, or what you will.

Just a man, born to a woman . . .

I walk to the edge of the terrace, lean over the balustrade and look up to the stars. And wonder if he *is* looking down on all of us as he sinks a bottle of whisky, laughing at the mayhem he's caused beneath him.

And for the first time, I actually feel a stirring of emotion. An empathy with him. After all, I have recently got my own life horribly wrong: I made a simple, human error, and almost lost what is most precious to me.

I know I will strive all my life to be a better man, but equally, I know I may not always succeed. I can only *try* to be the best I can be.

'Alex! Come and join us!' Mum and Dad and Immy and Fred are now holding hands in a small circle.

'Night, Dad,' I whisper to the glorious night sky.

I walk up to the terrace to take my mother's hand on one side, and Immy's on the other. We jig round in a circle to some strange bouzouki version of what I believe was originally a song called 'Pompeii'. Or at least, that's what Fred tells me, since these days, he's the one who's up on that kind of thing.

Then I see Chloë arrive on the terrace.

As Mum beckons for her to join us, I see another pair of eyes upon her. Michel is transfixed, as if he has been turned to stone by Medusa in the Greek myth.

I watch, fascinated, as Chloë glides towards us, then stops as if she can feel the heat of his stare through her back. Then she turns, slowly, and looks at him. And they both smile. She gives him an almost invisible nod, then reaches for her father's hand and joins our family circle, as the band begins to play again.

I see Viola – who has changed into a white, one-shouldered number that makes her look very similar to the statue of naked Granny/Aphrodite – appear behind her. Jules comes up to her and Viola surveys her mother, then goes slowly towards her and kisses her on both cheeks.

It is not a hug, but it is a start. An olive branch held out.

It is the beginning of understanding.

And forgiveness.

Viola turns towards us, pulling Jules with her, who in turn pulls Rupes in to join the circle. And soon Alexis follows with Angelina, then Fabio and Sadie and Peaches and eventually, all the others around us, until we are one long human chain, holding hands under the stars and celebrating life.

The music ends and everyone roars their applause. Then they begin to shout for Alexis and Helena to recreate their performance of *Zorba* from ten years ago.

'Hello,' I say to Viola as she walks over to me. 'You look beautiful.'

'Thank you.'

She continues talking softly into my ear, but I'm distracted by the expression on my father's face as my mother walks towards Alexis and takes his hand. Then she blows a kiss to Dad and mouths 'I love you' as she is led into the centre of the circle. And Dad smiles too, nods, and blows a kiss back.

I turn to Viola. 'Sorry, what did you say?'

'I said,' she chuckles, 'that I love you, Alex. I always have, and I think I always will.' She shrugs. 'It just . . . *is*.'

I look at her as the haunting music begins to play, and I realise she wants me to say something in return.

Immy's hand grasps my shoulder and chivvies me and Viola into completing the circle of arms and bending bodies.

'Concentrate, Alex!' she reprimands me.

'Sorry, Immy, I can't.'

And with that, I pull Viola away. We leave the terrace, and the human circle is quickly closed behind us. Like thieves in the night we run down towards 'Old', its branches supporting lanterns that sway very slightly in the gentle breeze, to be together and alone. I take her face in my hands and the moonlight shines down on it.

'I love you, too. And I always have and I think I always will.'

And then I kiss her, and feel her respond with equal fervour. And as I hear the music rising to a crescendo above us, I know for certain that our dance of life is only just beginning.

It. Just. *Is*.

Acknowledgements

I began writing this book ten years ago after a family holiday in Cyprus. We were staying in a beautiful old villa just outside Kathikas, where *The Olive Tree* is set. At the time, our five children were of similar age to the children in the book and we had family friends visiting, too. Even though much of the plot and the characters are of course fictional, there is no doubt that this is the closest I've come to drawing from my own life experience of being a mother, a stepmother, a wife and a trained dancer . . .

I put the manuscript away and then found it again last year when I was clearing out my desk drawer. Of course, my children are ten years older now and it was fascinating to read the descriptions I'd written when they were young. In a way, it was *my* journal of their childhood, so I decided I should finish it. And yes, it was a departure, with no 'sweeping' historical backdrop or one-hundred-year time-span – just time spent in the same house, with a small cast of characters. I learned so much during the writing of it.

So of course, the first and biggest thank you goes to my amazing family: Olivia, Harry, Isabella, Leonora, Kit and of course, Stephen, my husband, for inspiring me in the first place.

Thanks also go to my wonderful band of international publishers who gave me the confidence I needed to finish the book and actually send it to them when I had: Jez Trevathan and Catherine Richards at Pan Macmillan, Claudia Negele and Georg Reuchlein at Goldmann Verlag, Knut Gørvell and Jorid Mathiassen at Cappelen Damm and Donatella Minuto and Annalisa Lottini at Giunti.

To those at 'Team Lulu': Olivia Riley, Susan Moss, Ella Micheler and Jacquelyn Heslop. My sister, Georgia Edmonds, and my mother, Janet.

And to all my wonderful readers around the world: thank you.

OUT NOW

The Seven Sisters

A MAJOR NEW SERIES FROM LUCINDA RILEY

Maia's Story

Maia D'Aplièse and her five sisters gather together at their childhood home, 'Atlantis' – a fabulous, secluded castle situated on the shores of Lake Geneva – having been told that their beloved father, the elusive billionaire they call Pa Salt, has died. Maia and her sisters were all adopted by him as babies and, discovering he has already been buried at sea, each of them is handed a tantalising clue to their true heritage – a clue that takes Maia across the world to a crumbling mansion in Rio de Janeiro in Brazil. Once there, she begins to put together the pieces of where her story began . . .

Eighty years earlier, in the Belle Epoque of Rio, 1927, Izabela Bonifacio's father has aspirations for his daughter to marry into aristocracy. Meanwhile, architect Heitor da Silva Costa is working on a statue, to be called Christ the Redeemer, and will soon travel to Paris to find the right sculptor to complete his vision. Izabela – passionate and longing to see the world – convinces her father to allow her to accompany him and his family to Europe before she is married. There, at Paul Landowski's studio and in the heady, vibrant cafés of Montparnasse, she meets ambitious young sculptor Laurent Brouilly, and knows at once that her life will never be the same again.

In this sweeping, epic tale of love and loss – the first in a unique series of seven books, based on the legends of the Seven Sisters star constellation – Lucinda Riley showcases her storytelling talent like never before.

Turn the page to read the spellbinding opening chapters now.

1

I will always remember exactly where I was and what I was doing when I heard that my father had died.

I was sitting in the pretty garden of my old schoolfriend's townhouse in London, a copy of *The Penelopiad* open but unread in my lap, enjoying the June sun while Jenny collected her little boy from nursery.

I felt calm and appreciated what a good idea it had been to get away. I was studying the burgeoning clematis, encouraged by its sunny midwife to give birth to a riot of colour, when my mobile phone rang. I glanced at the screen and saw it was Marina.

'Hello, Ma, how are you?' I said, hoping she could hear the warmth in my voice too.

'Maia, I . . .'

Marina paused, and in that instant I knew something was dreadfully wrong. 'What is it?'

'Maia, there's no easy way to tell you this, but your father had a heart attack here at home yesterday afternoon, and in the early hours of this morning, he . . . passed away.'

I remained silent, as a million different and ridiculous thoughts raced through my mind. The first one being that

Marina, for some unknown reason, had decided to play some form of tasteless joke on me.

'You're the first of the sisters I've told, Maia, as you're the eldest. And I wanted to ask you whether you would prefer to tell the rest of your sisters yourself, or leave it to me.'

'I . . .'

Still no words would form coherently on my lips, as I began to realise that Marina, dear, beloved Marina, the woman who had been the closest thing to a mother I'd ever known, would never tell me this if it *wasn't* true. So it had to be. And at that moment, my entire world shifted on its axis.

'Maia, please, tell me you're all right. This really is the most dreadful call I've ever had to make, but what else could I do? God only knows how the other girls are going to take it.'

It was then that I heard the suffering in *her* voice and understood she'd needed to tell me as much for her own sake as mine. So I switched into my normal comfort zone, which was to comfort others.

'Of course I'll tell my sisters if you'd prefer, Ma, although I'm not positive where they all are. Isn't Ally away training for a regatta?'

And as we continued to discuss where each of my younger sisters was, as though we needed to get them together for a birthday party rather than to mourn the death of our father, the entire conversation took on a sense of the surreal.

'When should we plan on having the funeral, do you think? What with Electra being in Los Angeles and Ally somewhere on the high seas, surely we can't think about it until next week at the earliest?' I said.

'Well . . .' I heard the hesitation in Marina's voice. 'Perhaps the best thing is for you and I to discuss it when you arrive back home. There really is no rush now, Maia, so if you'd prefer to continue the last couple of days of your holiday in London, that would be fine. There's nothing more to be done for him here . . .' Her voice trailed off miserably.

'Ma, of *course* I'll be on the next flight to Geneva I can get! I'll call the airline immediately, and then I'll do my best to get in touch with everyone.'

'I'm so terribly sorry, *chérie*,' Marina said sadly. 'I know how you adored him.'

'Yes,' I said, the strange calm that I had felt while we discussed arrangements suddenly deserting me like the stillness before a violent thunderstorm. 'I'll call you later, when I know what time I'll be arriving.'

'Please take care of yourself, Maia. You've had a terrible shock.'

I pressed the button to end the call, and before the storm clouds in my heart opened up and drowned me, I went upstairs to my bedroom to retrieve my flight documents and contact the airline. As I waited in the calling queue, I glanced at the bed where I'd woken up this morning to Simply Another Day. And I thanked God that human beings don't have the power to see into the future.

The officious woman who eventually answered wasn't helpful and I knew, as she spoke of full flights, financial penalties and credit card details, that my emotional dam was ready to burst. Finally, once I'd grudgingly been granted a seat on the four o'clock flight to Geneva, which would mean throwing everything into my holdall immediately and taking a taxi to Heathrow, I sat down on the bed and stared for so long at the sprigged wallpaper that the pattern began to dance in front of my eyes.

'He's gone,' I whispered, 'gone forever. I'll never see him again.'

Expecting the spoken words to provoke a raging torrent of tears, I was surprised that nothing actually happened. Instead, I sat there numbly, my head still full of practicalities. The thought of telling my sisters – all five of them – was horrendous, and I searched through my emotional filing system for the one I would call first. Inevitably, it was Tiggy, the second youngest of the six of us girls and the sibling to whom I'd always felt closest.

With trembling fingers, I scrolled down to find her number and dialled it. When her voicemail answered, I didn't know what to say, other than a few garbled words asking her to call me back urgently. She was currently somewhere in the Scottish Highlands working at a centre for orphaned and sick wild deer.

As for the other sisters . . . I knew their reactions would vary, outwardly at least, from indifference to a dramatic out-pouring of emotion.

Given that I wasn't currently sure quite which way *I* would go on the scale of grief when I did speak to any of them, I decided to take the coward's way out and texted them all, asking them to call me as soon as they could. Then I hurriedly packed my holdall and walked down the narrow stairs to the kitchen to write a note for Jenny explaining why I'd had to leave in such a hurry.

Deciding to take my chances hailing a black cab on the London streets, I left the house, walking briskly around the leafy Chelsea crescent just as any normal person would do on any normal day. I believe I actually said hello to someone walking a dog when I passed him in the street and managed a smile.

No one would know what had just happened to me, I thought, as I managed to find a taxi on the busy King's Road and climbed inside, directing the driver to Heathrow.

No one would know.

Five hours later, just as the sun was making its leisurely descent over Lake Geneva, I arrived at our private pontoon on the shore, from where I would make the last leg of my journey home.

Christian was already waiting for me in our sleek Riva motor launch. And from the look on his face, I could see he'd heard the news.

'How are you, Mademoiselle Maia?' he asked, sympathy in his blue eyes as he helped me aboard.

'I'm . . . glad I'm here,' I answered neutrally as I walked to the back of the boat and sat down on the cushioned cream leather bench that curved around the stern. Usually, I would sit with Christian in the passenger seat at the front as we sped across the calm waters on the twenty-minute journey home. But today, I felt a need for privacy. As Christian started the powerful engine, the sun glinted off the windows of the fabulous houses that lined Lake Geneva's shores. I'd often felt when I made this journey that it was the entrance to an ethereal world disconnected from reality.

The world of Pa Salt.

I noticed the first vague evidence of tears pricking at my

eyes as I thought of my father's pet name, which I'd coined when I was young. He'd always loved sailing and often when he returned to me at our lakeside home, he had smelt of fresh air and of the sea. Somehow, the name had stuck, and as my younger siblings had joined me, they'd called him that too.

As the launch picked up speed, the warm wind streaming through my hair, I thought of the hundreds of previous journeys I'd made to Atlantis, Pa Salt's fairy-tale castle. Inaccessible by land, due to its position on a private promontory with a crescent of mountainous terrain rising up steeply behind it, the only method of reaching it was by boat. The nearest neighbours were miles away along the lake, so Atlantis was our own private kingdom, set apart from the rest of the world. Everything it contained was magical . . . as if Pa Salt and we – his daughters – had lived there under an enchantment.

Each one of us had been chosen by Pa Salt as a baby, adopted from the four corners of the globe and brought home to live under his protection. And each one of us, as Pa always liked to say, was special, different . . . we were *his* girls. He'd named us all after The Seven Sisters, his favourite star cluster. Maia being the first and eldest.

When I was young, he'd take me up to his glass-domed observatory perched on top of the house, lift me up with his big, strong hands and have me look through his telescope at the night sky.

'There it is,' he'd say as he aligned the lens. 'Look, Maia, that's the beautiful shining star you're named after.'

And I *would* see. As he explained the legends that were the source of my own and my sisters' names, I'd hardly listen, but simply enjoy his arms tight around me, fully aware of this rare, special moment when I had him all to myself.

I'd realised eventually that Marina, who I'd presumed as I grew up was my mother – I'd even shortened her name to 'Ma' – was a glorified nursemaid, employed by Pa to take care of me because he was away such a lot. But of course, Marina was so much more than that to all of us girls. She was the one who had wiped our tears, berated us for sloppy table manners and steered us calmly through the difficult transition from childhood to womanhood.

She had always been there, and I could not have loved Ma any more if she had given birth to me.

During the first three years of my childhood, Marina and I had lived alone together in our magical castle on the shores of Lake Geneva as Pa Salt travelled the seven seas to conduct his business. And then, one by one, my sisters began to arrive.

Usually, Pa would bring me a present when he returned home. I'd hear the motor launch arriving, run across the sweeping lawns and through the trees to the jetty to greet him. Like any child, I'd want to see what he had hidden inside his magical pockets to delight me. On one particular occasion, however, after he'd presented me with an exquisitely carved wooden reindeer, which he assured me came from St Nicholas's workshop at the North Pole itself, a uniformed woman had stepped out from behind him, and in her arms was a bundle wrapped in a shawl. And the bundle was moving.

'This time, Maia, I've brought you back the most special gift. You have a new sister.' He'd smiled at me as he lifted me into his arms. 'Now you'll no longer be lonely when I have to go away.'

After that, life had changed. The maternity nurse that Pa had brought with him disappeared after a few weeks and Marina took over the care of my baby sister. I couldn't understand how the red, squalling thing which often smelt and diverted attention from me could possibly be a gift. Until one morning, when Alcyone – named after the second star of The Seven Sisters – smiled at me from her high chair over breakfast.

'She knows who I am,' I said in wonder to Marina, who was feeding her.

'Of course she does, Maia, dear. You're her big sister, the one she'll look up to. It'll be up to you to teach her lots of things that you know and she doesn't.'

And as she grew, she became my shadow, following me everywhere, which pleased and irritated me in equal measure.

'Maia, wait me!' she'd demand loudly as she tottered along behind me.

Even though Ally – as I'd nicknamed her – had originally been an unwanted addition to my dreamlike existence at Atlantis, I could not have asked for a sweeter, more loveable companion. She rarely, if ever, cried and there were none of the temper-tantrums associated with toddlers of her age. With her tumbling red-gold curls and her big blue eyes, Ally had a natural charm that drew people to her, including our father. On the occasions Pa Salt was home from one of his long trips abroad, I'd watch how his eyes lit up when he saw her, in a way I was sure they didn't for me. And whereas I was shy and reticent with strangers, Ally had an openness and a readiness to trust that endeared her to everyone.

She was also one of those children who seemed to excel at everything – particularly music, and any sport to do with water. I remember Pa teaching her to swim in our vast pool and, whereas I had struggled to stay afloat and hated being underwater, my little sister took to it like a mermaid. And while I couldn't find my sea legs even on the *Titan*, Pa's huge and beautiful ocean-going yacht, when we were at home Ally would beg him to take her out in the small Laser he kept moored on our private lakeside jetty. I'd crouch in the cramped stern of the boat while Pa and Ally took control as we sped across the glassy waters. Their joint passion for sailing bonded them in a way I felt I could never replicate.

Although Ally had studied music at the Conservatoire de Musique de Genève and was a highly talented flautist who could have pursued a career with a professional orchestra, since leaving music school she had chosen the life of a full-time sailor. She now competed regularly in regattas, and had represented Switzerland on a number of occasions.

When Ally was almost three, Pa arrived home with our next sibling, whom he named Asterope, after the third of The Seven Sisters.

'But we will call her Star,' Pa had said, smiling at Marina, Ally and me as we studied the newest addition to the family lying in the bassinet.

By now I was attending lessons every morning with a private tutor, so my newest sister's arrival affected me less than Ally's had. Then, only six months later, another baby joined us, a twelve-week-old girl named Celaeno, whose name Ally immediately shortened to CeCe.

There was only three months' age difference between Star and CeCe, and from as far back as I can remember, the two of them forged a close bond. They were akin to twins, talking in their own private baby language, some of which the two of them still used to communicate to this day. They inhabited their own private world, to the exclusion of us other sisters. And even now in their twenties, nothing had changed. CeCe, the younger of the two, was always the boss, her stocky body and nut-brown skin in direct contrast to the pale, whippet-thin Star.

The following year, another baby arrived – Taygete, whom I nicknamed 'Tiggy' because her short dark hair sprouted out at strange angles on her tiny head and reminded me of the hedgehog in Beatrix Potter's famous story.

I was by now seven years old, and I'd bonded with Tiggy from the first moment I set eyes on her. She was the most delicate of us all, suffering one childhood illness after another, but even as an infant, she was stoic and undemanding. When yet another baby girl, named Electra, was brought home by Pa a few months later, an exhausted Marina would often ask me if I would mind sitting with Tiggy, who continually had a fever or croup. Eventually diagnosed as asthmatic, she rarely left the nursery to be wheeled outside in the pram, in case the cold air and heavy fog of a Geneva winter affected her chest.

Electra was the youngest of my siblings and her name suited her perfectly. By now, I was used to little babies and their demands, but my youngest sister was without doubt the most challenging of them all. Everything about her *was* electric; her innate ability to switch in an instant from dark to light and vice versa meant that our previously calm home rang daily with high-pitched screams. Her temper-tantrums resonated through my childhood consciousness and as she grew older, her fiery personality did not mellow.

Privately, Ally, Tiggy and I had our own nickname for her; she was known among the three of us as 'Tricky'. We all walked on eggshells around her, wishing to do nothing to set off a lightning change of mood. I can honestly say there were moments when I loathed her for the disruption she brought to Atlantis.

And yet, when Electra knew one of us was in trouble, she was the first to offer help and support. Just as she was capable of huge selfishness, her generosity on other occasions was equally pronounced.

After Electra, the entire household was expecting the arrival of the Seventh Sister. After all, we'd been named after Pa Salt's favourite star cluster and we wouldn't be complete without her. We even knew her name – Merope – and wondered who she would be. But a year went past, and then another, and another, and no more babies arrived home with our father.

I remember vividly standing with him once in his observatory. I was fourteen years old and just on the brink of womanhood. We were waiting for an eclipse, which he'd told me was a seminal moment for humankind and usually brought change with it.

'Pa,' I said, 'will you ever bring home our seventh sister?'

At this, his strong, protective bulk had seemed to freeze for a few seconds. He'd looked suddenly as though he carried the weight of the world on his shoulders. Although he didn't turn around, for he was still concentrating on training the telescope on the coming eclipse, I knew instinctively that what I'd said had distressed him.

'No, Maia, I won't. Because I have never found her.'

As the familiar thick hedge of spruce trees, which shielded our waterside home from prying eyes, came into view, I saw Marina standing on the jetty and the dreadful truth of losing Pa finally began to sink in.

And I realised that the man who had created the kingdom in which we had all been his princesses was no longer present to hold the enchantment in place.

2

Marina put her comforting arms gently around my shoulders as I stepped up onto the jetty from the launch. Wordlessly, we turned to walk together through the trees and across the wide, sloping lawns that led up to the house. In June, our home was at the height of its beauty. The ornate gardens were bursting into bloom, enticing their occupants to explore the hidden pathways and secret grottos.

The house itself, built in the late eighteenth century in the Louis XV style, was a vision of elegant grandeur. Four storeys high, its sturdy pale pink walls were punctuated by tall multi-paned windows, and topped by a steeply sloping red roof with turrets at each corner. Exquisitely furnished inside with every modern luxury, its thick carpets and plump sofas cocooned and comforted all who lived there. We girls had slept up on the top floor, which had superb, uninterrupted views of the lake over the treetops. Marina also occupied a suite of rooms upstairs with us.

I glanced at her now and thought how exhausted she looked. Her kind brown eyes were smudged with shadows of fatigue, and her normally smiling mouth looked pinched and tense. I supposed she must be in her mid-sixties, but she didn't seem it. Tall, with strong aquiline features, she was an elegant, handsome woman, always immaculately attired, her effortless chic reflecting her French ancestry. When I was young, she used to wear her silky dark hair loose, but now she coiled it into a chignon at the nape of her neck.

A thousand questions were pushing for precedence in my mind, but only one demanded to be asked immediately.

'Why didn't you let me know as soon as Pa had the heart attack?' I asked as we entered the house and walked into the high-ceilinged drawing room that overlooked a sweeping stone terrace, lined with urns full of vivid red and gold nasturtiums.

'Maia, believe me, I begged him to let me tell you, to tell all you girls, but he became so distressed when I mentioned it that I had to do as he wished.'

And I understood that if Pa had told her not to contact us, she could have done little else. He was the king and Marina was at best his most trusted courtier, at worst his servant who must do exactly as he bade her.

'Where is he now?' I asked her. 'Still upstairs in his bed-room? Should I go and see him?'

'No, *chérie*, he isn't upstairs. Would you like some tea before I tell you more?' she asked.

'To be quite honest, I think I could do with a strong gin and tonic,' I admitted as I sat down heavily on one of the huge sofas.

'I'll ask Claudia to make it. And I think that, on this occa-sion, I may join you myself.'

I watched as Marina left the room to find Claudia, our housekeeper, who had been at Atlantis as long as Marina. She was German, her outward dourness hiding a heart of gold. Like all of us, she'd adored her master. I wondered suddenly what would become of her and Marina. And, in fact, what would happen to Atlantis itself now that Pa had gone.

The words still seemed incongruous in this context. Pa was always 'gone' – off somewhere, doing something, although none of his staff or family had any specific idea of what he actually did to make his living. I'd asked him once, when my friend Jenny had come to stay with us during the school holidays and been noticeably awed by the opulence of the way we lived.

'Your father must be fabulously wealthy,' she'd whispered as we stepped off Pa's private jet which had just landed at La Môle airport near St Tropez. The chauffeur was waiting on the tarmac to take us down to the harbour, where we'd board our magnificent ten-berth yacht, the *Titan*, and sail off for our annual Mediterranean cruise to whichever destination Pa Salt fancied taking us.

Like any child, rich or poor, given that I had grown up knowing no different, the way we lived had never really struck me as unusual. All of us girls had taken lessons with tutors at home when we were younger, and it was only when I went to boarding school at the age of thirteen that I began to realise how removed our life was from most other people's.

When I asked Pa once what exactly it was he did to provide our family with every luxury imaginable, he looked at me in that secretive way he had and smiled. 'I am a magician of sorts.'

Which, as he'd intended, told me nothing.

As I grew older, I began to realise that Pa Salt was the master illusionist and nothing was as it first seemed.

When Marina came back into the drawing room carrying

two gin and tonics on a tray, it occurred to me that, after thirty-three years, I had no real idea who my father had been in the world outside Atlantis. And I wondered whether I would finally begin to find out now.

'There we go,' Marina said, setting the glass in front of me. 'Here's to your father,' she said as she raised hers. 'May God rest his soul.'

'Yes, here's to Pa Salt. May he rest in peace.'

Marina took a hefty gulp before replacing the glass on the table and taking my hands in hers. 'Maia, before we discuss anything else, I feel I must tell you one thing.'

'What?' I asked, looking at her weary brow, furrowed with anxiety.

'You asked me earlier if your father was still here in the house. The answer is that he has already been laid to rest. It was his wish that the burial happen immediately and that none of you girls be present.'

I stared at her as if she'd taken leave of her senses. 'But Ma, you told me only a few hours ago that he died in the early hours of this morning! How is it possible that a burial could have been arranged so soon? And *why*?'

'Maia, your father was adamant that as soon as he passed away, his body was to be flown on his jet to his yacht. Once on board, he was to be placed in a lead coffin, which had apparently sat in the hold of the *Titan* for many years in preparation for such an event. From there he was to be sailed out to sea. Naturally, given his love for the water, he wanted to be laid to rest in the ocean. And he did not wish to cause his daughters the distress of . . . watching the event.'

'Oh God,' I said, Marina's words sending shudders of horror through me. 'But surely he knew that we'd all want to say goodbye properly? How could he do this? What will I tell the others? I . . .'

'*Chérie*, you and I have lived in this house the longest and we both know that where your father was concerned, ours was never to question why. I can only believe,' she said quietly, 'that he wished to be laid to rest as he lived: privately.'

'And in control,' I added, anger flaring suddenly inside me. 'It's almost as though he couldn't even trust the people who loved him to do the right thing for him.'

'Whatever his reasoning,' said Marina, 'I only hope that in time you can all remember him as the loving father he was. The one thing I do know is that you girls were his world.'

'But which of us knew him?' I asked, frustration bringing tears to my eyes. 'Did a doctor come to confirm his death? You must have a death certificate? Can I see it?'

'The doctor asked me for his personal details, such as his place and year of birth. I said I was only an employee and I wasn't sure of those kinds of things. I put him in touch with Georg Hoffman, the lawyer who handles all your father's affairs.'

'But *why* was he so private, Ma? I was thinking today on the plane that I don't ever remember him bringing friends here to Atlantis. Occasionally, when we were on the yacht, a business associate would come aboard for a meeting and they'd disappear downstairs into his study, but he never actually socialised.'

'He wanted to keep his family life separate from business, so that when he was at home his full attention could be on his daughters.'

'The daughters he adopted and brought here from all over the world. Why, Ma, why?'

Marina looked back at me silently, her wise, calm eyes giving me no clues as to whether or not she knew the answer.

'I mean, when you're a child,' I continued, 'you grow up accepting your life. But we both know it's terribly unusual – if not downright strange – for a single, middle-aged man to adopt six baby girls and bring them here to Switzerland to grow up under the same roof.'

'Your father *was* an unusual man,' Marina agreed. 'But surely, giving needy orphans the chance of a better life under his protection couldn't be seen as a bad thing?' she equivocated. 'Many wealthy people adopt children if they have none of their own.'

'But usually, they're married,' I said bluntly. 'Ma, do you know if Pa ever had a girlfriend? Someone he loved? I knew him for thirty-three years and never once did I see him with a woman.'

'*Chérie*, I understand that your father has gone, and suddenly you realise that many questions you've wanted to ask him can now never be answered, but I really can't help you. And besides, this isn't the moment,' Marina added gently. 'For now, we must celebrate what he was to each and every one of us and remember him as the kind and loving human being we all knew within the walls of Atlantis. Try to remember that your father was well over eighty. He'd lived a long and fulfilling life.'

'But he was out sailing the Laser on the lake only three weeks ago, scrambling around the boat like a man half his age,' I said, remembering. 'It's hard to reconcile that image with someone who was dying.'

'Yes, and thank God he didn't follow many others of his age and suffer a slow and lingering death. It's wonderful that you and the other girls will remember him as fit, happy and healthy,' Marina encouraged. 'It was certainly what he would have wanted.'

'He didn't suffer at the end, did he?' I asked her tentatively, knowing in my heart that even if he had, Marina would never tell me.

'No. He knew what was coming, Maia, and I believe that he'd made his peace with God. Really, I think he was happy to pass on.'

'How on earth do I tell the others that their father has gone?' I entreated her. 'And that they don't even have a body to bury? They'll feel like I do, that he's simply disappeared into thin air.'

'Your father thought of that before he died, and Georg Hoffman, his lawyer, contacted me earlier today. I promise you that each and every one of you will get a chance to say goodbye to him.'

'Even in death, Pa has everything under control,' I said with a despairing sigh. 'I've left messages for all my sisters, by the way, but as yet, no one has called me back.'

'Well, Georg Hoffman is on standby to come here as soon as you've all arrived. And please, Maia, don't ask me what he'll have to say, for I haven't a clue. Now, I had Claudia prepare some soup for you. I doubt you've eaten anything since this morning. Would you prefer to take it to the Pavilion, or do you want to stay here in the house tonight?'

'I'll have some soup here, and then I'll go home if you don't mind. I think I need to be alone.'

'Of course.' Marina reached towards me and gave me a hug. 'I understand what a terrible shock this is for you. And I'm sorry that yet again you're bearing the burden of responsibility for the rest of the girls, but it was you he asked me to tell first. I don't know whether you find any comfort in that. Now, shall I go and ask Claudia to warm the soup? I think we could both do with a little comfort food.'

After we'd eaten, I told Marina to go to bed and kissed her goodnight, for I could see that she too was exhausted. Before I left the house, I climbed the many stairs to the top floor and peered into each of my sisters' rooms. All remained as they had been when their occupants left home to take flight on their chosen paths, and each room still displayed their very different personalities. Whenever they returned, like doves to their waterside nest, none of them seemed to have the vaguest interest in changing them. Including me.

Opening the door to my old room, I went to the shelf where I still kept my most treasured childhood possessions. I took down an old china doll which Pa had given to me when I was very young. As always, he'd woven a magical story of how the doll had once belonged to a young Russian countess, but she had been lonely in her snowy palace in Moscow when her mistress had grown up and forgotten her. He told me her name was Leonora and that she needed a new pair of arms to love her.

Putting the doll back on the shelf, I reached for the box that contained a gift Pa had given me on my sixteenth birth- day; I opened it and drew out the necklace inside.

'It's a moonstone, Maia,' he'd told me as I'd stared at the unusual opalescent stone, which shone with a blueish hue and was encircled with tiny diamonds. 'It's older than I am, and comes with a very interesting story.' I remembered he'd hesi- tated then, as if he was weighing something up in his mind. 'Maybe one day I'll tell you what it is,' he'd continued. 'The necklace is probably a little grown up for you now. But one day, I think it will suit you very well.'

Pa had been right in his assessment. At the time, my body was festooned – like all my schoolfriends' – with cheap silver bangles and large crosses hanging from leather strings around my neck. I'd never worn the moonstone and it had sat here, forgotten on the shelf, ever since.

But I would wear it now.

Going to the mirror, I fastened the tiny clasp of the delicate gold chain around my neck and studied it. Perhaps it was my imagination, but the stone seemed to glow luminously against my skin. My fingers went instinctively to touch it as I walked to the window and looked out over the twinkling lights of Lake Geneva.

'Rest in peace, darling Pa Salt,' I whispered.

And before further memories began to engulf me, I walked swiftly away from my childhood room, out of the house and along the narrow path that took me to my current adult home, some two hundred metres away.

The front door to the Pavilion was left permanently unlocked; given the high-tech security which operated on the perimeter of our land, there was little chance of someone stealing away with my few possessions.

Walking inside, I saw that Claudia had already been in to switch on the lamps in my sitting room. I sat down heavily on the sofa, despair engulfing me.

I was the sister who had never left.